LI-EMBA

THE COMMUNITY DESTROYER

LI-EMBA

THE COMMUNITY DESTROYER

MARTIN MOLUWA MATUTE

ARPress
45 Dan Road Suite 5
Canton MA 02021
Hotline:	1(888) 821-0229
Fax:	1(508) 545-7580

Ordering Information:
Quantity sales. Special discounts are available on quantity purchases by corporations, associations, and others. For details, contact the publisher at the address above.

Printed in the United States of America.

ISBN-13:	Softcover	979-8-89356-214-9
	eBook	979-8-89356-215-6
	Hardback	979-8-89356-240-8

Library of Congress Control Number: 2024908128

TABLE OF CONTENTS

DEDICATION

Professor Paul Musonge, Emeritus Professor of Chemical Engineering

ACKNOWLEDGMENT

Nyango Nalova l'Eko and Etonde, Musonge, Efosi, Livena, Ngowo, Moluwa, Mbella, Ndiva, and Limunga

CHAPTER 1

Li-emba and Nyo-ngo

Humanly speaking, I am a so-called "no-nothing!" But I feel privileged to hail from a place whose people are blessed with extraordinary gifts of perspicacity or a keen vision in being able to discern that which is seen and that which is not seen and, in addition, of prophecy in being able to predict the future in no uncertain terms. Discernment is usually manifested in one of two ways: either they discern by themselves or by proxy through their *Mot'a Nga-Nga* or *Mot'a Yowo* who does the discerning for them.

So, I may not necessarily consider myself a smart aleck or a know-it-all; still, I know things that lots of my other mates in school and Sunday school do not know. Take this example of one thing I know: I can tell the difference between a Mot'a Nyo-ngo and a Mot'a Li-emba. The commonality between these two types of *wu-nya-na* (men) is their mystical powers; the difference is their sociological or economic status. Another thing I know is that these wu-nya-na powers cannot be possessed or claimed by *walana* (women). Any *molana* tagged as a *Molan'a Nyo-ngo* or *Molan'a Li-emba* is nothing but a misnomer because such mystical powers are only associated with *wat'o wa wu-nya-na* (males).

The *Wat'o wa Nga-Nga* or *Wat'o wa Yowo* only came out to our clan on Fridays and Saturdays. They only started their mystical works at night and then continued until the following morning. Depending on the severity of the job at hand, they worked Friday night through Sunday morning or merely Friday night through Saturday morning for the relatively simpler or "overnight" job. Sometimes these Wat'o wa Yowo or Wat'o wa Nga-Nga knew in advance if it was going to be a difficult job or not. At other times, they had anticipated a 'simple" job, only to realize that it was not that simple. This is when they had to spend an extra day after intense negotiation with my family as to what would constitute acceptable additional compensation. Many a time, they had threatened to leave the work undone if their terms or demands were not met.

So, it was unheard of that a Mot'a Yowo or a Nga-Nga was a molana. If Nga-Nga could not be walana, then Wat'o wa Nyo-ngo and Wat'o wa Li-emba could not be Walana either. Therefore, Yowo, Nga-Nga, Nyo-ngo and Li-emba were all the exclusive preserves and attributes of wu-nya-na. This is a debate I tried hard to sell and win, sometimes with some support and other times with laughter only. However, I know that if you are an E-wa-ng'a Moto (rich man) and you lived in the village and you were dark-skinned, then that qualified you for a Mot'a Nyo-ngo; conversely, Wat'o wa Li-emba were poor people, but not all poor people had Li-emba because just about all of us in the village were poor. You had to be especially knowledgeable to discern a Li-emba poor person.

A Mot'a Nyo-ngo is rich and kills people mystically through sudden deaths. In the absence of death, a Mot'a Nyo-ngo could turn his victim into an *E-fu-le-fu* (an empty, worthless man) or rather an *E-lay-ngeh* (someone who has lost his or her senses and acts accordingly or someone insane). These are biological humans who are like empty shells, not the people they once were (kind of like zombies but without the obvious phenotypic attributes) because their true selves—that is, their very souls—have been sold to nyo-ngo. So, the Mot'a Nyo-ngo gave away "a life" (that is, someone's life) in return for riches, and the lives given were of close relatives; it could not be a distant relative or someone the Mot'a Nyo-ngo did not know. Thus, the Mot'a Nyo-ngo was an E-wa-ng'a Moto (a rich man).

In contrast, the Mot'a Li-emba did not kill his victims; rather, he just put them in a miserable state for a long time. For example, it could be prolonged illness, not getting a job, not getting married, not doing well academically, sabotaging a business, causing the victim to be irresponsible, turning the individual into a thief or a miscreant, and so on. Evidently, the Mot'a Li-emba got little or nothing for it because he remained poor without evidence of progress of any sort. Thus, the Mot'a Li-emba was a Mo-li-szr'a Moto (a poor man).

A Mot'a Yowo or Mot'a Nga-Nga went by other names amongst us. "Jazz-man" was the most common one among us *wana* (children); he was otherwise generally referred to in the community as a Juju Doctor. These spiritual men were specially gifted in knowing all those who had Li-emba and Nyo-ngo. They were capable of removing the spiritual "jazz" (or medicine) that Wat'o wa Li-emba and Wat'o wa Nyo-ngo put in you, your house, or property to harm you in one way or another. When they removed the implant in you or from any of your property, they would also stop the jazz from being reimplanted and replanted, and the affected would also be given *ngweh* (medicines) to drink and certain acts to perform, including chants and recitations that will remove the spell and or sickness brought about by the planted jazz.

The removal required some elaborate mystic ceremony in darkness, during which walana and wana (children) were totally excluded, and the name of the Lord God or any person of the Holy Trinity was not to be mentioned at any time. The mention of God rendered useless the yowo-man's power. When I learnt of this as a lad, I tried to make sense of it. The impression I had—and which was the general and accepted conclusion and understanding of children—was that the name of God will 'spoil" the yowo being made. If this was true, was the name of God superior, therefore, to the yowo they were performing? Or was it just that the mention of this name was in itself a spoiler? I was in no position to advance my thoughts. I would not have been able to articulate my thoughts correctly. I was not smart enough, and I was just another village ignorant lad amongst older and wiser folks.

We lived on the west side of our village. Topographically, our portion of the village was geographically separated into the lower third plateau and upper third, but it was all one steep hill as one climbed.

The upper hilliest third bordered the forest which, in turn, bordered the Vako; that is, Mount Fako. The whole village was a hill, being situated at the foot of Mount Fako or Vako as properly called by my people. It is this Vako that was described by the first Wakala (Portuguese exploiters) who saw it as the "Chariot of God." They had arrived at a time when E-va-szra-Moto, the deity of the Vako, had brought about its periodic eruption.

Mola Mo-li-szra was poor, had Li-emba, and had his house and family in the plateau third. Mola E-wa-ngeh lived in the upper hilliest third, had Nyo-ngo and was rich. Evidence that he was rich included his home being electrified; he had a phone line and a car, and he worked with the government in a managerial position. Our portion of the village was dominated by my extended family or, more correctly, my clan. The aliens were the Li-emba and Nyo-ngo families, and I was never able to learn how they came to settle in our village. However, as we grew up as kids, our instructions were clear: "stay away from the Mot'a Li-emba and Mot'a Nyo-ngo" and, by extension, their families. Therefore, deciding to greet or not to greet the Wa-mba-ki (older folks) in these families whenever we came face-to-face in the village narrow footpaths became an internal turmoil.

Playing and /or interacting with their wana (children) was non-existent or, at best, very minimal, even when the parents of both families seemed absent. As a consequence, my village friends and playmates were, in effect, my blood family. For the siblings and cousins that one could play with by virtue of age, I was somewhere in the middle, and I also came from the poorest of families material-wise, or so I thought. As wana, we seldom ventured out of our own portion of the village; if we did, it was transient—only in passing—when we ran errands for the family.

The Wa-kpwes or Vakpwes (Bakweris) used the combined terminology *Yowo* to refer to both Nyo-ngo and Li-emba, otherwise known in English-speaking West Africa as Juju or witchcraft, in French-speaking West and Central Africa as "sorcellerie." In the western hemisphere, what is called Voodoo is, at best, third-rate yowo because "yowo nodi cross wata." When yowo traverses (crosses) water or the ocean, it is neutralized; therefore, it could not be claimed that you were bewitched from a village in Africa while a resident overseas. Such claims were considered outlandish in the yowo world.

The Nga-nga were the masters of yowo. They determined who had li-emba or nyo-ngo and were responsible for treating the affected by removing the evil spirit planted in the humans, their domestic animals, or buried somewhere in their yards. They also prevented future occurrences and put in place spiritual strategies meant for harming any li-emba or nyo-ngo practitioner who dared return to do harm. This prevention was normally exhibited by charm-like bundles tied and hung in strategic places in affected homes or some bundle buried in the yard, around the house, and especially at the entrance or gate. In rare cases, the Nga-nga's mission was to kill outright the yowo practitioner. The Nga-nga normally dressed in flawless and seamless gowns that covered the feet, they wore no shoes, and their gowns were black or red, depending on the severity of the job. I could not tell which one was more powerful. The color regardless, the gowns had bells attached to the waist area that served as a belt, and smaller ones interspersed at the hems, sleeve ends, and around the neck area. The bells in the neck area were interspersed with the skulls of small animals, particularly rodents and birds being the favorites. In areas not occupied by bells hung small, dry, hollow calabashes containing small rocks, teeth of large herbivores, skulls of small carnivores, and the multicolored feathers of wild *we-nor-ni* (birds). This was a sign of power, knowledge, restoration, and masculinity, and certainly an attractant to us young lads in the village.

CHAPTER 2

E-wa-ng'a Moto

E-wa-ng'a Moto lived in the upper hilliest third of our village. When I was old enough to understand, I was told that there was a *mba'a-mba* (*Dendroaspis polylepis*; black mamba) lurking around in the village that was his, some kind of zoomorphism. Our property bordered his to his southwest; to his west was one of my Mola's (maternal uncle's) residence. My Mola had many peculiarities: he had no family of his own—that is, no wife or kids—he was barely able to keep a job when he got one, and it was a boisterous and carefree life for him whenever he got paid and then back to earth with a bump shortly after. He was handsome with fair skin, like his parents, he dressed smartly with a permanent moustache, he was short of stature, and so on. Because of the permanence of his moustache, we called him Ji-fu-man or just simply Majifu.

Majifu looked like a bodybuilder that operated a gym, and his large blood vessels seemed even more superficial than was known for other men of his age in our vicinity. He had a protruding chest with the hypertrophied nature of his skeletal muscles very overt in his arms and forearms. Among the adults in our clan and village, Ji-fu-man was a playboy, limited only by cash flow. Mola Ji-fu, we also called him sometimes, was the bouncer of our clan and a well-known hot-headed no-sense-Moto who seems to have made himself a point man for the family to harass and terrorize Mola E-wa-ng'a Moto at the slightest provocation that he often orchestrated, and especially when he was intoxicated with Palm wine or *Nkwa-tcha* (corn beer) or *A-fvoh-fvoh* (locally brewed gin estimated at 90 percent alcohol by volume [ABV], making it 180 proof [United States equivalent]) as the case may be or sometimes a combination of any.

Verbal abuses and threats of physicality to the hearing of E-wa-ng'a Moto's molana, wana, wards, and the entire household were commonplace. This happened for the most part at night when we, as wana, were already in bed but had to be woken by the loud, high-pitched voice of Ji-fu-man in the still night, dominated by voices of insects and croaking amphibians. I will assume E-wa-ngeh's children all heard these insults, although I wish they did not have to. But if I was awoken and alert by first my Mola's songs and then the insults, it should have been more so with E-wa-ng'a Moto's kids who were physically closer to the source of the annoyance. My uncle Mola Majifu (a.k.a. Pami-man or Palmirite) had to pass through our yard to get to his; we got to hear him before he got to his house whenever he could manage to return home at night, all boozed up.

A rich Mola of mine who lived far away from our village had a large *ngo-wa* (piggery) commercial project next to our property. This project was mostly surrounded by bush and, as time went on, occasionally, a ngo-wa (*Sus scrofa domesticus*, pig) was found dead in the morning. As I was to learn later on, my family concluded that these ngo-wa were being killed by venom from the mba'a-mba, that is, the mba'a-mba stung these ngo-wa. I was confused and amazed in equal measure one evening when I noticed that there was an abnormal or unusual activity in the homes of some extended family members. Eventually, I saw a "jazzman" or Mot'a Nga-Nga (a.k.a. Mot'a Yowo) and what I learned later to be two apprentices of the jazzman. What was a Mot'a Yowo doing in our mba-mbeh wa molana's (grandmother's) house? My mba-mbeh lived south of us less than 100 meters apart, and we used to play in her yard, making it easy to spot or notice abnormal activity.

I made an effort to stay up late before going to bed, very curious to know what the jazzman was up to. His garish attire made him look scary for a kid and also ridiculous. Details of his garb aside, when I woke up the next morning, and based on what I saw and heard, a red *wuwa ya mo-meh* (*Gallus gallus domesticus*; rooster or cock), black *wuwa ya mua-li* (hen), and white *ngo-wa* (*Sus scrofa domesticus* or pig; are domesticated, large, even-toed ungulates closely associated with and commonly related to the sociology of the Mot'a Mokpwe or the Bakweris) had been butchered, and their blood used as part of the mysterious concoction that the jazzman's team used to chase in the physical and spiritual realm, the mba'a-mba spirit that terrorized and killed my Mola's (uncle's) ngo-wa.

In addition, I also learned that lots of misfortunes, especially ill-health suffered by certain members of my extended family, were also attributable to this mba'a-mba (black mamba). Further, the jazzman followed the mba'a-mba spiritually across the three topographical regions of our portion of the village in a to and fro manner. Proof of the physicality of the mba'a-mba was the two grave-like pits dug near my mba-mbeh wa molana's house and near the piggery premises—spots I was told the mba'a-mba hid itself in when the pursuit became too hot. But the Nga-Nga, being a superior force, was determined to capture and destroy once and for all this evil menace and force.

I neither saw a physically dead mba'a-mba nor did I learn of a spiritually dead mba'a-mba. I guess time would tell. However, evidence of the existence of a spiritual mba'a-mba was presented in the form of a dead male *njol-lo* (an *Agama agama* rainbow-colored lizard), ngo-wa hair, a mammalian *li-szro-nga* (tooth), a *mbo-ti yi-nda'a* (piece of black cloth), *li-wa-nya la njor-ngoh* (piece of a broken clayey pot), and some others I could not decipher—all placed on the floor on freshly cut green *weh-ya-li weh meh-kor* (plantain leaves) surrounded by two blood-dripping headless *wuwa* (black and white chickens) and the *mo'o-vho na weh-tay-ni* (that is, the head and offals) of the butchered ngo-wa.

As I grew bigger and before I went to secondary school, two or three other Nga-Nga were hired by my family to continue the physical and spiritual chase of this mba'a-mba. The ill health of my family members originally affected by this spirit snake got worse; indeed, newer family members got added on to the mba'a-mba's list. Millions of francs CFA (Communauté Financière Africaine, the French African currency, a.k.a. the African Strangler) were spent by my family; their health got worse, and the early morning tu-ndey intensified (a *tu-nda*, singular, and *tu-ndey*, plural, is some kind of a revelation giving instructions that must be followed by an early morning action if one was the no-nonsense type).

So, you had a troubled sleep, and in your dream or vision, you saw a Mot'a Li-emba or Mot'a Nyo-ngo, which could be a molana or mu-nya-na. But for the most part, you could not tell if it was a molana or mu-nya-na because they came to you in disguised form. The E-li-ngeh (a spirit you encounter) may wu-szra-na (go out with) another person's image as a disguise. For example, a son who had li-emba may wear the Iyaka's (mother's) image as a disguise, so when you see "him," it looked as if it was the "Iyaka"—this will be called or termed wu-szra-na, translated as a form of "homomorphism."

In other cases, instead of the E-li-ngeh assuming the whole image of another, this E-li-ngeh, intent on disguising itself, will just wear some clothing or outfits that can easily be associated with someone in the immediate environment, within or without the family. In very rare occasions would the E-li-ngeh visit its victims in the dream or vision without disguises. We did not know what transpired between the E-li-ngeh and the visited, but we knew who the visited was by her "Tu-nda." Note I say "her," because I do not remember any mu-nya-na who ever came out in our village to "Teh-Tu-nda" (shout out a tu-nda). The Tu-nda or Tu-ndey was or were simple. In the very early hours of the morning, when the whole village was still asleep, a molana dressed up warmly and, with a lantern, would walk from her home to some distance away from the home she was targeting. While at the appropriate spot and distance, she would start narrating in singing form, for example:

"Those people who live in houses built on hills leave me alone, leave me alone, stop visiting me and despite your disguise, I know who you are and stop going out with your mother; 'should you continue to visit me, we will cut ourselves with cutlasses (machetes) in broad day light and I will show you who truly I am."

People who did the Tu-ndey did not do a good job of disguising who they were targeting or were just poor at it. After every Tu-nda, we knew who the target was. Combined targets were also known to exist; that is, two Wa-i-emba joining forces to get one victim or one family.

Tu-ndey that crisscrossed the village were of another rare type. The dreamer wanted the whole village to know that she was a victim, and the visionary also wanted the village to know *wa-i-emba* (witches and wizards) around the village had combined their forces against her or her *li-tu-mba* (family). It was also common knowledge that any part of the village that they visited or passed through—or better still in the vicinity where they stood and emptied themselves of the torments received from wa-i-emba—the signal was that there was one of them, in this area, sometimes known and sometimes not so clearly known.

One main characteristic of Tu-ndey is that they must be accomplished in a *Teh* (shouting) form. If not shouted, it could not be considered a Tu-nda. Tu-ndey. "shouters" had the right to disturb the early morning peace of the village whenever they wanted because they were victims of the village. Daylight Tu-ndey were rare but not impossible. When a molana engaged in a daylight tu-nda, that meant she was ready to physically attack the human E-li-ngeh that visited her in her dreams. Such fistfights had been only between walana. It was also common practice for two walana to join forces and do a joint tu-nda as joint victims. Such walana, having a common adversary, are usually best friends or it could be a mother and child or mother and daughter-in-law.

Two years later, I returned home for holidays from secondary school when the day came at last for the Mba'a-mba to be physically caught by the Wat'o wa Yowo. We had always been told that it was just a matter of time and now the day had come. My immediate family reared *wuwa* (chickens) on a semi-commercial basis, but mostly for home consumption. Our house was surrounded or enclosed up to about 85 percent with domestic crops such as *meh-kor na mbo-oh* (plantains and bananas), *nda'a na makawo* (cocoyam and the mother cocoyam), and the rest by plain *wa-nga* (bush). We had woken up a couple of times to find out that some mother hens that were incubating their eggs were dead and some of the eggs missing. This was blamed on the mba'a-mba, and it was very scary to imagine a snake, whether real or spiritual, coming into our house at night while we were sleeping.

The *Dendroaspis polylepis* (black mamba) is considered to be the longest venomous of all snakes found around Africa. It is also considered to be one of the deadliest. It features a very powerful venom and that has many people running scared from it. They are fast-moving snakes and are known to be aggressive and strike at a moment's notice. Despite the suggestion of its name, black mambas are actually brownish in color, ranging from olive to greyish tones with paler bellies. They are named for the coloration of the inside of their mouths, which is a deep, inky black. However, the mba'a-mbas in the village were all blackish or dark gray in coloration and were described as shiny, for that matter.

Similar to *Agkistrodon piscivorus* (cotton mouths), when threatened, a mba'a-mba will open its mouth to show the black lining as a warning signal. Mba'a-mbas have coffin-shaped heads and are lithe, athletic snakes. The mba'a-mba is the longest venomous snake in Africa and the second-longest venomous snake in the world, following *Ophiophagus hannah* (the king cobra). Size-wise, the adult mba'a-mbas seen and killed in our village of Wonya-Libiyeah approximated to about five meters in length and an estimated weight of about four kilograms, for they made good "bush meat" for bush "meaters" that considered them a delicacy and a rare catch or kill. The killing, catching, and eating of a mba'a-mba was associated with some special powers, and an extracted fang was tenaciously guarded, for if it fell into the wrong hands, it could be used in various nefarious ways, physically and spiritually.

This fateful night, the mba'a-mba came to our house and headed for the wuwa corner. The wuwa house, as we called it, was a room attached to the main house and accessible from the inside next to the kitchen. We were awoken by the alarm noises of the mo-m'a wuwa (rooster or cock), the noise of an incubating mother hen, and the fluttery wings of a mother hen in a life and death combat.

Alarmed, fearful, and with a bush or oil lamp that could barely penetrate the pitch darkness that characterizes the tropics at night, my *iyaka* (mother), cautiously and trembling, approached the wuwa house. She immediately spotted the mba'a-mba glittering in the dark and a dead incubating mother hen in its enfolds, and in terror, my mother sounded the village alarm for mortal danger. My *ta'a-the* (father) was an evangelist, and on this eventful night, he was out on an evangelical mission to the Duala Mbedis, making it an evangelical mission from the Mo-kpwe-di Mbedis to the Duala Mbedis. Even in the darkness of the night, the mba'a-mba shone with brilliance coupled with an enormous size. The venomous and lethal nature of the mba'a-mba was legendary in our village, and therefore, an immediate and instant source of mortal danger.

"*Eeh je-eeh* (Come, people, come)."

"*Na way-li-eeh* (I am dead)."

"Mba'a-mb' E-nay (This is an encounter with a black mamba)."

This must have been before midnight, and the men in our portion of the village who were home came out with all the war gear they had. These included *va-ow* (machetes), *may-tor-ni* (mortar pestles), *may-ko-mba* (guns), *weh-yey* (sticks), and any other readily available combat weapon as dictated by the rush of adrenaline. I have never seen or known the village to be in such an alert state, ready for combat or hostility within a very short summons period.

When the Wakpwes fought the great war with the German occupiers, long before my coming into being, as wana of the village and as a litumba that had played a prominent leadership role in this struggle against the Germans, we learned through oral history the mobilization of the Mokpwe Mbe-szra (youth) fighters as they faced off the Mokala (white man or an albino) invaders.

Ji-mbi i-ku-mbi
(The drum beats)
E-szray-wa e-to-ngi
(The horn is sounded)
E-to-ngi di mao-ngoh
(It signals danger)
Wana wa njuma eszra-weya
(Fighters do you not hear)
E-vo-nd'a nju ma e-mu-ka
(It is the time for battle)
I-ta-nay-ya o mafany
(We meet at our rallying point)

We sang this song in the village as often as possible, and it was a very familiar tune in upper Mokpwe Land that engaged the Germans in battle. While it was now sung at social events, it was a reminder for those who knew their history of the bravery of the Mokpweli against a European and World power. Before the Europeans and the World had to face and confront the Germans, the Wakpwes at the foot of the Vako in faraway West/Central Africa had been there.

What was unfolding in our village and our house and yard as the center was and seems like a reenactment of the history of the Wakpwes. It seemed like a dream, reliving the past. I pinched myself several times to ensure that I was awake.

The sleeping village came alive with anxiety as concerned armed men congregated in our yard, talking in hush-hush tones and strategizing as to how to corner and kill the reptile. Besides the humans, dogs were barking, cats were crying, and more roosters made their presence known. Those who congregated in our compound included Mola E-wa-ng'a Moto a.k.a. Mola Mba'a-mba, a grand maternal uncle, Mola I-nor-ni, who owned a *mo-ko-mba* (hunting gun) that had been used to kill many *weh-nor-ni* and *ka-weh* (birds and antelopes). The gun used powdered bullets, and we jokingly called the gun *Cha-fvu*, which meant unreliable. Oftentimes, the gun will not fire when required because of a faulty cartridge or some other malfunction, but what was more than sure was the possibility of a fault.

My frantic, brave, singing, and cursing iyaka had started the deadly assault on this deadly reptile creature before the wu-nya-na arrived. When they did take over from her, the job was finally finished by my Mola I-nor-ni with his cha-fvu gun. They did acknowledge however that mo-ko-mba or no mo-ko-mba (gun or no gun), my fearless and brave iyaka had mortally wounded the reptile with her *ja-mbi* (cutlass) such that it had to die of the multiple deep cuts inflicted on it. The danger was that in such a wounded state, the reptile could strike back hard as it fought to the death.

Before it was shot dead, my iyaka was practically shielded by wu-nya-na and seated somewhere in the periphery of our property. When the deadly reptile charged in its wounded state, armed wu-nya-na surged backwards or simply fled, leaving those more equipped to face the mortally dangerous *gbwa-wa* (snake). When it lifted its head up ready to extend and strike its nearest *Mot'a weh-na-ma* (human being) opponent, the extended fangs were pulled out, and what seem like slimy thick fluid (venom) could be seen dripping out of its mouth as it made some strange and frightening sounds that sent cold chills down my spine. The mba'a-mba continued to extend its head, striking from one direction to another with the hope it would get at least one of its assailants, but the men kept a reasonable distance away from this source of death and striking back from vantage positions.

With the gunshot, the gbwa-wa was now bleeding profusely in addition to the previous mortal wounds inflicted by my fearless iyaka and the other wounds subsequently inflicted by the other mba'a-mba assailants. Slowly the mba'a-mba began to lose its ability to raise itself for a possible distant strike, and eventually, not even its head could be raised as the life was sucked out of it.

The dead, extraordinarily large, shining black snake was taken outside, and after hush-hush consultations, it was agreed that it should be burned immediately. Mola E-wa-ng'a Moto sent large quantities of kerosene from his house, and my family added some assorted green leaves in addition to certain weird chanting that accompanied the burning. The burning of the mba'a-mba was headed by Mola Majifu who seemed just too eager to start a confrontation or a fight with Mola Ewang'a Moto should he had dare to suggest otherwise or be in the way in form or sort.

In the wake of this very fearful event, my siblings were whisked out of the house when the village arrived, but somehow, they missed me and were not level-headed enough to do a quick head count. We were indeed terrified and very afraid, all huddled in one corner of the house, mesmerized, while my *ndoh-meh wa mu-nya-na wa mo-mba-ki* (older brother) kept telling me to hang in there like a *Mot'a mu-nya-na* (strongman).

When they came to get us out, he was the first to run to safety, and being forgotten, I climbed on a table that was next to a window, opened the window, and then sat on the windowpane, one leg out, the other leg in. This gave me a vantage position to see what was happening but also got me all set to take flight should the gbwa-wa come charging.

Throughout this action-packed event that lasted about one hour, a very deliberate effort was made to keep all gbwa'a (*Canis lupus familiaris*; dogs) away. It was known that the gbwa'a will attack the gbwa-wa and most probably kill it but only for the gbwa'a to die later of the snake's poison. So, the restrained dogs, frustrated, could only bark as loud as they could. In our community, gbwa'a are used for hunting and security; they are only used as pets when they are puppies. The mba'a-mba affront was a hunting matter as well as a security matter, so being excluded from doing their work or being part of the action, they were met with very loud barking and a challenge to their handlers.

The ashes of the burnt reptile were scooped up by Mola Majifu, and after conferring with my other uncles, he disappeared into the night, most probably to bury it somewhere later and somewhere that was not known, especially to Ewang'a Moto. We all knew that this mba'a-mba belonged to Ewang'a Moto, and therefore, we referred to him sometimes as Mola Mba'a-mba. This creature was a source of terror and fear for all of us in this portion of our village. Adults knew it existed, and it had been sighted several times basking in the sun, crossing the road or the footpath, and it was credited specifically by my family clan as being responsible for the death of many of the pigs that were reared by my Mola Ma-ku-mba. Considering that the gbwa-wa will not eat a dead ngo-wa but will feed on eggs, our residence was a logical and convenient destination. This horror creature had visited our house several times, but there was going to be a last day as accurately predicted by the wato wa yowo.

In the early days following this traumatic event, it was common conversation among my family members that E-wa-ng'a Moto will soon die because the snake's death should herald his own. Contributing to kill the snake effectively meant killing himself. Family members praised themselves for deciding to burn the snake immediately, that way not giving him the opportunity to transfer his force or spirit in it to another snake or animal.

Lo and behold, E-wa-ng'a Moto died shortly after. We were woken by cries from the hilly rich house of his molana, wailing and weeping as she mourned the passing of her *mu-nya-na* (husband). While I felt sorry for him that he died, I was terrified that now that he had transited into the spirit world, I may not be safe from his *molimo* (ghost). While my family was rejoicing and beating their chests for what good soothsayers they were, his family maintained that he died of a kidney disease. I remember this exchange with my older brother.

"Dat witchman don die (The wizard is dead)," he said.

"*Na e kinie kill-e* (He died of a kidney problem)," I said.

"*Waiti you sabi* (What do you know)?" my older brother asked. Coming from an older brother, that meant you should shut up.

One sign of E-wa-ng'a Moto's impending demise came shortly after the mba'a-mba was burnt. His house was northbound, but when it came to departure time, he found himself amongst those who were headed south. Then halfway to the lower quarters, E-wa-ng'a Moto realized that he was going the wrong way.

"Nay-mi yeah (I am confused)," he said loudly as he made a U-turn.

His being confused was evidence used against him by the villagers, evidence of the turmoil inside him. He had to look for a new animal really quick to transfer into, but if this process was already blocked as the villagers intended to, then what would become of the freed spirit. It is such free and roaming spirits that end up harming or terminating the lives of their owners if they are not rehoused immediately. This was a very precarious moment of his life, enough for him to be confused. Normally, snakes simply *szro-mba* (sting) the mother hen, kill it, and then swallows their eggs quietly; better still, unguarded eggs were preferable.

That this particular outing for food hunting did not end well for Mola E-wa-ng'a Moto's mba'a-mba was enough to signal his own death. What I did not understand was, what stopped E-wa-nga Moteh from rearing his own wuwa to be used as food for his mba'a-mba? For then, there will be no fear or chance of it being attacked, for he will know how to control the situation in his own family and property. Evidently, the poisonous and venomous reptile could only feed and depend on food sources outside its owner's jurisdiction.

Not all black mambas are black, but the mba'a-mbas in my village are huge and shiny black. Their black hue is such that they shine even in the thick blackness of a tropical night. Mola E-wa-ng'a Moto was a tall, very dark-skinned, bald, and handsome man with no social life to speak of. He was a man devoid of friends and family, and it was rumored that he had been excommunicated and exiled from his village of origin because he was known to be a Mot'a Nyo-ngo, but we never knew his village of origin. The only visitors to his home were from his molana's village. Mola E-wa-ngeh was of more than average height for wu-nya-na of our village, and his skin tone was approximated to real black as opposed to the chocolate brown of most of us. His was easily the darkest in the village, and his blackness shone with the sun and moon. It was this blackness we saw in the mba'a-mba, further buttressing the point that the venomous reptile was his.

Before Mola E-wa-ng'a Moto died, I remember one New Year's Day when my big man mola visiting our village from Yaounde had an exchange with him. My very rich and influential mola visited the piggery project owned by his *ndoh-meh wa mu-nya-na mo-sz-ra-li* (younger brother) mola Ma-ku-mba, which was near our *ndawo* (house) and on his way back to the lower third, Mola E-wa-ng'a Moto called after him in reverence from his hilly vantage point.

"Lawyer Blokeh, Lawyer Blokeh," also known as Molaleh by our *mba-mbeh wa molana* (grandmother).

When my Mola Blokeh stopped, he spoke loudly so that Blokeh could hear, and being on the hill, anyone around could hear him.

Mola E-wa-ng'a Moto declared he wanted a peaceful coexistence this New Year with all his neighbors and hoped that everyone would turn a new page.

Mola Blokeh listened intently and then asked, "Way-nga wa-szra di li-li-ya la gbwa-mu (So you just want a peaceful co-existence for all?)" He then added, "No-weh-yi koi-koi (I hear you loud and clear)."

And then Mola E-wa-ng'a Moto said, "Eeh, Nor-meh-neh (Yes, that is it, it is all I ask for)."

I heard the whole exchange from our house and was able to see Mola Blokeh resume his downward trip while Mola E-wa-ngeh watched him disappear from sight. I do not know how Mola E-wa-ngeh felt, but I was disappointed with Blokeh's response or lack thereof. This was a man clearly reaching out, and he barely had anything to say to him despite this overture of peace made public and for the records. Blokeh was the de facto leader of our clan, a lawyer by training, an administrator, an influential government employee, and with lots of dictatorial tendencies toward the larger family he led and assisted. He did not live in the village and therefore was not poisoned or biased by the village intrigues or politics.

E-wa-ngeh knew that Mola Blokeh, a.k.a. Mo-la-leh, could broker some kind of peace between his family and our clan if he tried. I do not know whether Mola Mo-la-leh ever had this conversation with any of his siblings or with his parents (that is, my grandparents) who all inhabited the village. That nothing happened was proof to me that he did nothing. Where was the legal practitioner side of Mola Blokeh? And why did he not use his high social status and power? Did he know something I did not know with Mola E-wa-ngeh or our clan?

E-wa-ngeh was a soft-spoken man who had worked in Kumba, a.k.a. K-Town, before being transferred to Gbwea (Buea). In contrast with prevailing attitudes, he stayed home while the rest of his household went to church. He did find common ground that got him interacting somewhat with the community in one particular area: football. As a Gbwea man or a Mo-kpwe-li, he was a passionate supporter of Prisons Buea Football Club. With his hilly vantage position, he did not have to go and pay to enter the stadium to watch a football match. He simply sat on his verandah or balcony and watched the game downhill in full view.

He shared his views during games to the hearing of all. While he was not necessarily addressing our portion of the village, his loudness and enthusiasm as he exchanged thoughts and opinions with members of his house could not escape the ears of those of us who were downhill and interested in the topic. Oftentimes, he was conflicted between supporting the K-Town team, Power Works Department (PWD) Kumba when they came to town for a match, and the home team Prisons Buea Social Club. Eventually, his son, King Kuleh, played for Prisons Buea, which made his home a continuous spot for football (soccer) analysis. However, this socializing through football was with visitors of his son; it did not include his neighbors, and thus, they remained isolated, feared, and disliked, if not hated.

Mola Majifu had threatened several times to cross over the fence to his property and physically manhandle him. This never happened, partly because as time passed, the *wana wa wunyana* (male children) in that household became adults, and Jifuman was certainly no match for them, physically and otherwise; they became a deterrent to my relief. I was always afraid that one day, my Mola Majifu may actually physically harm Mola E-wa-ngeh. I found it very shameful, embarrassing, and hurting to see adults engage in "physicalities" or other forms of hostilities—verbal or otherwise—with each other, and especially hearing or being in the presence of wana. It was the height of disrespect for each other and certainly a very poor example for the wana; that is, if they cared.

Mola E-wa-ng'a Moto came to our village before I was born, and by the time I was a *mua-na* (child) with some sense, he had divorced his molana with whom he had four grown adult wana (children), and in some cases, grand wana who were my age group. But he did not send his divorced molana away entirely; he built her a house in another nearby property he purchased there in the village, which was northwest of my immediate family's home.

Mola Ewangeh's divorced wife's home was less than one hundred meters away from Ewangeh's main mansion. I do not know what caused their divorce, but it seemed to have been on very amicable terms because the divorced wife still visited the Ewangeh mansion with ease and sat in the balcony (veranda) for hours, chatting about nothing in particular in the presence of the new wife and Mola Ewangeh. I do not remember that these were frequent chats that actually involved the new molana (new wife) and Mola Ewangeh, but occasionally, the new molana and Ewangeh responded to her. I wondered for a very long time why the divorced molana thought it a good idea to frequently visit the Ewangeh mansion and stay there for hours, chatting about nothing. The divorcee molana lived in her own newly built house with her two older wana (a male and a female), while the two younger *wana wa wunyana* (male children) lived with their ta'a-teh, Mola Ewang'a Moto, and their new stepmother in the hilly mansion.

This was very strange for a Mokpwe molana. *Wakpwe wa Walana* (Mokpwe women) normally left with all of their children after a divorce onto the next marriage and next house; there was no leaving anything behind. In this case, there was a "leaving behind" of the youngest of the wana—strange and strange—but perhaps the proximity of the properties played a crucial role in this decision, and also, the younger wana preferred a life in "Hilly Mansion" as opposed to the less ostentatious life in the "valley house."

The new wife bore no wana for Mola E-wa-ngeh but came with two wards, a *mua-na wa munyana* (male teen) and *mua-na wa molana* (female teen), and it was her family that visited and seemed to bring life to Mola E-wa-ngeh's environs. Walana village gossip described Mola E-wa-ngeh's new and younger wife as a *Yo-mba ya Molana* (a childless or barren woman); She was, however, very pretty, fair-skinned, and had ladylike characteristics and mannerisms written all over her. She did not associate with any other women in our village, though there was the time and again chitchat between her and my iyaka, probably because of the proximity of their homes.

The village gossip wondered if she had wana in a previous marriage or if there was a previous marriage in the first place. She kept to herself, just like her husband, and occasionally complained loud about the *wana wa wunyana* (male children in the house) finishing all the food or milk or sugar or something that was related to gastronomy. Mola E-wa-ngeh's wana in the lower house made frequent trips to the to the upper house and demanded for and expected food and other necessities from time to time. Because it was a hilly home, their conversations seemed all to take place in the veranda, and seeming to all have high-pitched voices, all residents of the valley houses could not help but overhear their conversations, especially folks like me who had a knack for stories.

Sometimes it was conversations from the hilly mansion that woke me up from bed in the morning, if the wuwa failed to. The Hilly Mansion was abuzz with life and activities when there were some exciting news items either at the village level or the Gbwea Town level. It was even more so when E-wa-ngeh's muana eventually started playing for the Prisons Buea Social Football Club as a junior player.

Visited by his own friends and sometimes football (soccer) teammates, the hilly house provided younger folks like me who had a keen ear for stories and analysis from older and better-informed persons a reason to sometimes slow down and just be and just listen to these stories. I also thus benefitted from the hilly mansion.

Time passed, but nothing changed; E-wa-ngeh remained isolated. I could not make up my mind about him, although from what I had seen, he must have wanted true peace and a normal life with his neighbors who essentially were our clan members. Mola E-wa-ngeh knew that Mola Blokeh—a.k.a. Mo-la-leh (he was thus called Mo-la-leh by his iyaka, my *mba-mbeh wa molana* [grandmother])—could make inroads into my family. E-wa-ngeh also knew that Blokeh for sure knew of the tensions and uneasiness that existed between Blokeh's clan and E-wa-ngeh and Mo-li-szreh families. Their being ostracized, isolated, attacked, and referred to as Wa-i-emba in many forms, including the morning tu-ndeys, and more, all made life impossible for them.

Mola E-wa-ng'a Moto was a relatively rich man. While the rest of us in the village—meaning every other household—had to do subsistence farming in order to collect firewood and to harvest cocoyams and plantains and other crops, E-wa-ngeh bought all of these from the market. Thus, he and his molana and their wana did not experience the normal or even hard life of villagers. I only knew him, though, in his second marriage, for which there was no issue. His divorced wife lived less than one 100 meters away downhill away from his hilly *nda-wo* (house), a property E-wa-ngeh had prepared for her and her wana after the divorce. She frequently visited the up ndawo.

The first and divorced molana's name was Nya-ngo Ma-ngoh-ngi ma Lio-va. She lived in her lower quarters or house with her two oldest wana, while the two younger wana lived up the hilly ndawo with their ta-teh and step iyaka. E-wa-ngeh must have been a very good manager of walana, for there was never a day that there was a clash between the divorced molana and the second and current molana.

I always wondered why Nya-ngo Ma-ngoh-ngi ma Lio-va always thought it wise to be visiting the upper house. E-wa-ngeh's second marriage bore him no issues by design or by nature. It seemed it was more by nature because his new molana Nyango Bi-t'a Molombeh was far from being a spring chicken, and while I did not know if she was in a previous marriage before Mola E-wa-ngeh, there was no one known to be her wana. She, however, came with two wards that we knew as her nephew and niece. She was a peace-loving molana who kept to herself. That she was a *yo-mba ya molana* (childless woman) also meant that she could not afford to be arrogant or pompous, for she certainly knew that all other walana in the village referred to her as "yo-mba yoma;" that is, a childless thing. To be a yo-mba was a high caliber insult in the village among the walana. A yo-mba ya molana meant that you were a "mu-nya-na," and therefore, if walana were speaking, you could not speak. For if you dared to speak arrogantly or with authority, especially if it were a contentious issue, you were sure to be asked, "Waveh njeh (Who are you)?" This is a very loaded question among the Wa-kpwe-li. It can lead to fights, enmities, insults, and all other sorts of negatives such as aggression that bred strife in societies, especially in small village communities.

Our village bordered an elementary school, Presbyterian School Buea Town, a.k.a. PSBT. There was this one time when E-wa-ngeh bought a truckload of firewood, and it was dropped about the school premises. School wana were eager to assist for a token payment. All they had to do was to obtain permission from the headmaster. It soon became a regular event. E-wa-ngeh had school wana carry his wood and related items from the school area and up to his house on many occasions. But of course, the wana in our families (clan), including myself, were self-excluded because we knew something about Mola E-wa-ng'a Moto that others did not know. A younger cousin of mine knew eventually and variously as Nga-nga, Ngo'e-lo-ngoh, Onana, Okala, and others made it their point of duty to educate the other wana in the school not to assist E-wa-ngeh for pay because he had Nyo-ngo.

The next time Mola E-wa-ng'a Moto needed such assistance from the pupils for token pay as usual, he was surprised that no pupil volunteered. He did learn eventually that it was my cousin's fault, and he marched down to their house to complain to his parents. My cousin's parents paid him lip service while he was there, and when he turned his back, they laughed at him. Our people normally have utmost respect for *wa-mba-ki* (elders, also parents) and growing up as a *mua-na* (child), you knew that even without it being said. It was abnormal for a *mo-mba-ki* (an elder or a parent) to actively encourage a mua-na to be rude or disrespectful to wa-mba-ki.

E-wa-ng'a Moto never got the peace he so wanted, and unlike Mo-li-szr'a Moto who had family that came visiting him from time to time, he still remained isolated and excluded in his own village. It was also clear that E-wa-ngeh did not have parental roots in our village, but I do not know how he came to settle there with a big yard. Unlike E-wa-ngeh, Mo-li-szreh did not make any efforts to integrate in our village, and it also surprised me that there was absolutely no socialization between E-wa-ng'a Moto and Mo-li-szr'a Moto and their families.

I interacted to a very limited extent with kids from both families, and occasionally, there were brief exchange visits to our respective playgrounds. Mola E-wa-ngeh might have been a senior technician with the post and telecommunication department who seemed to have spent most of his life working in Kumba or K-Town. This might have facilitated his having the first phone line in our village. He returned to Gbwea (Buea) where he worked for some more years and then retired. His return to Gbwea, his working in Gbwea, his living in our village, and particularly his living next to my family clan and his retirement all seemed like hell for him; that is, if his life was summed up by my mua-na observation and analysis. Many years later, I often wondered if Mola Dan'a Mo'o-li's—a.k.a. E-wa-ng'a Moto— life was the "miserable" life I saw. Perhaps there was a bright side that a mua-na like myself could not comprehend.

Several years after E-wa-ng'a Moto's death, all those problems attributed to him by my family still lingered on: bad dreams, ill health, wana not doing well at school, wana not getting married, wana not getting jobs, pigs, goats and chickens dying, and many more wato wa yowo had been brought in to fight the spiritual battle. I must add that years after his death when things were no better but rather getting worse in my extended families, at least two other persons were accused of Nyo-ngo and Li-emba in the village by my family members.

My clan went on a hunt for new recruits, or better still, new punching bags were needed. When I asked my iyaka the significance of all these Nga-Nga or Wat'o wa Yowo and they're not delivering, she said, "O-weh-li di mua-na (You are but a child)." This also meant shut up.

CHAPTER 3

Mo-li-rz'a Moto

By virtue of our clan background and emboldened by our clan's attitude toward Mo-li-szr'a Moto and his family, we, the wana (children), gave him a nickname. The derivation of this name remained our exclusive. He was a bricklayer (stone builder) and a soft-spoken man who did not seem to have friends or other relatives apart from his nuclear family comprising of his molana (wife) and wana (children). They lived in the plateau portion of our village and were practically and geographically the nearest neighbors to my immediate family's landed property. Using the mathematical symbol of the "less than" sign (<), my immediate family lived at the intersection while Mo-li-szr'a Moto lived at the end of the lower stroke and E-wa-ng'a Moto at the end of the upper stroke. I was, therefore, strategically placed to observe and analyze them…or so I thought.

Mo-li-szr'a Moto was a poor man. I found out that he was brought into the village as a *mbe-szra* (lad) by a *ndo-meh wa molana* (sister) who came into the village by marriage. This ndo-meh wa molana of his was married to one of my *ti-mba li-mba-mbeh wa mu-nya-na* (great grand uncle) who died before I was born. Mo-li-szra's ndo-meh was therefore a very old molana that we scarcely saw. I might have seen her occasionally, but she was known to be mysterious, and she had a reputation of being a "master" witch by my clan. She therefore scared the living daylights out of me and others. She was dark-complexed, an ashy dull black, bent over, shriveled, used a walking stick, and wore black or dark-colored clothes, which only intensified her mystery. Whenever we passed by her roadside house, we ran through the stretch or walked hurriedly without looking toward her door for fear that our eyes could lock together with grave Li-emba consequences on our part.

When this ndo-meh died, the village was very quiet, and we, the children, did not venture out to play in the yard for a couple of days. She had a bent over house in front of which were two graves simply filled with soil and stones. We never knew who was buried in them. Mo-li-szr'a Moto therefore became even more mysterious after the ndo-meh's death because she had apparently transferred her Li-emba or Yowo to him. Some in the village even rumored that they witnessed the transfer ceremony. Age was a qualifier for Li-emba, making the very elderly in our community prime candidates, especially those who had gone through a tortuous road of poverty in their younger days and possibly throughout their lives. Given that walana were more likely to live to ripe old ages in our community than men, yowo seemed an exclusive of the *walana wa-mba-ki* (older women).

Compared to E-wa-ng'a Moto, Mo-li-szreh married a loud, showy molana, a choir mistress (conductor) in one of the local churches. On one occasion, they had a church function, and Iya Mo-li-szreh took on the responsibility of cooking the E-kwa-kok'a Szreh-szreh, commonly called Kwa-ko-ko and Mba'a-ga soup (ground cocoyams and palm nut soup) and precisely as *ti-mba na mbu-szra* (which literally means when you "go," you will "come back"). She cooked the food with "broke mar-ret" fish [a.k.a. *kwa-ko-lo*, which is the African catfish] and loaded all of it into a Gbwea pan (a big bowl commonly used in Buea to put large quantities of cooked food). Somehow, she managed to convince her husband, Mola Mo-li-szreh, to carry the food on his head and trek from our village to the church, which was perhaps a little above three miles away.

Mola Mo-li-szr'a Moto was a slim, dark-skinned, handsome man with a thick black moustache and who smoked the pipe. Dressed in cream white khaki shorts, a short-sleeved, white, hanging shirt, black heavy-soled shoes of the German type, and thick wool socks pulled to just below the knees and a short, broad, spade-like red tie (and yes, this tie was short because it stopped above the end of his sternum; we called such short ties spades). Mola Mo-li-szreh delicately placed the Gbwea pan of steaming deliciously smelling e-kwa-koko on his head, atop his fez cap. This was an unusual task for a mu-nya-na in our society, and we thought he was either a softy husband that had been sissified or just that he had been charmed by his wife and therefore under her spell or total control. We called such men "Woman-man," meaning a weakling. In short, the wife had some sort of hold on him, and we the boys did not like that; we thought she was "unmanning" him and adding to his already existing social problem.

I was visiting my *ndo-mehs* (cousins) who were situated in the first third or lower portion of our village. It was during the third term holiday (June–August), and it was raining heavily, so we all wana congregated in my Mola's (maternal uncle) verandah (or porch), looking at the road directly ahead of us. The first third portion of our village is a steep hill. When it rains in my village, the ground becomes muddy and slippery; call it black slippery snow. It had almost stopped raining when Mo-li-szreh came with his Gbwea pan of steaming e-kwa-koko delicately balanced on his head and his pipe oozing with thick black tobacco smoke. As he started descending the steep hill, he was aware of the hostile children's eyes that were fixated on him. He therefore made very deliberate efforts to remain calm; each step was calculated and precise. A misstep was not an option.

The whole image of Mola Mo-li-szreh coming down the steep hill with the giant pan of e-kwa-koko was very hilarious and comical. When one of my *ndo-mehs* (cousins) first spotted him, a hushed silence fell over all of us. And then we started pinching one another and nodded our heads in his direction. Still, we did not dare laugh out loud because we were afraid of consequences we knew all too well: Li-embah! Yes, he will "la'a us li-emba" (bewitch anyone who dared to laugh), even if he did not look at us directly because he had mystical powers.

However, two of my Mola's hunting and guard dogs, which were with us, came to our rescue. When they saw the comic bright figure coming down the hill and perhaps sensed that we may be terrified or scared, they started growling and then barked out loud in unison. My two older ndo-mehs ja wu-nya-na tried to restrain them with trembling hands, but the *gbwa ja mo-vao* (hunting dogs) broke loose with ease, jumped over the verandah walls, and headed straight toward the comical figure. At the sound of the loud barking and the approaching gbwa ja mo-vao, Mola Mo-li-szreh naturally panicked and called out to us in what I thought was a cry for help:

"Eh weh-leh ee gbwa janu (Call your dogs back)! Eh le-mbeh ee gbwa janu (Hold your dogs back)! Na Szra-Szra Mo-fvu-ngu (I do not want trouble)! Mameh nay gbwe-yi (What have I done to you)?"

My older cousins rushed out in an attempt to stop the gbwas, putting aside all fear. This was to no avail.

What happened next will become part of the village folklore. It all happened so fast. One moment, Mola Mo-li-szreh was uttering his pleas, attempting to hold steady the pan on his head whilst negotiating the slippery road and contemplating the approaching dogs. The next moment, Mola Mo-li-szreh suddenly lost his balance and then slid for about fifteen meters down the hill at the end of which he was face up, lying flat on his back in the mud, his moustache and creamy outfit all coated with *mba'a-ga* soup (palm kernel soup), e-kwa-koko, and dark brown mud.

As we ran forward to see clearly, for he was further down the hill out of clear view, I could see him trying to lick his oily moustache as one of the dogs was licking the thick soup on his hair and face, and the other was helping itself to the food that had spilled over. As we formed a semicircle around him like some sort of crown, some ten meters away, he did not utter a word. When he lifted and turned his head toward our direction, we all fled, also falling on the mud in our own paths. We were not sure what our fate was with him, especially me, for I had to pass by his house before reaching our house, except I used some other bush road or shortcut ("cut short" as we called it). But I was afraid of bush roads for good reason. Mola Mo-li-szreh's wife threw a fit; our parents got an earful from her. My cousins attributed it all to me. That was the norm.

Mo-li-szr'a Moto was a builder. House building was not something frequent in our village, especially when it involved bricks or blocks. This was the exclusive preserve of the rich, and there were not many of them in my whole town, much less in my village. However, there seems to have been many building opportunities in neighboring Mongo and Duala Mbedi land because Mola Ma-ji-fu was of a similar trade, and he too, from time to time, went off to those territories to build houses. Third term holidays were usually very long, boring, with lots of rain, bushy environments, sickness—especially malaria—or sickness due to li-emba. We spent most of our time playing football (soccer) among ourselves, a team from the eastern parts of the village, and neighboring villages or quarters.

This third term holiday, I learned from my iyaka that Mola Mo-li-szreh had answered a call as a bricklayer or builder around the Duala Mbedi land; hence, his absence from the village. Mo-li-szreh did not return by the time school resumed for the new academic year in September. In fact, he only showed up again around Christmas time. This was approximately a six-month absence. He looked slimmer, and his thick black moustache was now even more prominent with grey shoots. His demeanor was quieter than what I knew of him. He looked sad, and I pitied him.

I continued to observe Mola Mo-li-szreh as the days passed. When he was cutting grass in his yard, I could not stop wondering what he was thinking, surrounded by hostile neighbors. I also began to think that his molana was pregnant, and this became more evident by the day, especially when our paths crossed on one occasion, and I observed her vomiting by the side of the road. I greeted her and later asked my iyaka why she was vomiting. Contrary to the husband, his wife was a "showy" type, a loud talker, very opinionated and, dare I say, bold. She was the choir conductor of one of the choirs in the local church attended by both of our families. For fear of tongue lashing, she was greeted when met at close quarters but at the same time avoided. She was not said to have li-emba.

Eventually, I learned about her pregnancy based on conversations of some adult walana in the neighborhood. I overheard them say the pregnancy was not due to Mola Mo-li-szreh, her mu-nya-na; she was seeded in his absence. It so happened that the seeding was done by the only 'mbou-nda (friend) that Mola Mo-li-szreh seemed to have had in the entire village!

The "supplanter or seeder" was one of those weirdoes we had in the village. A tall, very dark figure who cut his grass at night using a lantern, he would cut his grass even in the rain, no matter how heavy; he cut his grass so low that it seemed he was instead digging the grass out or perhaps tilling the soil for planting. Oftentimes, by the time he did half of his yard, the starting point was ready to be cut again because it took him days or weeks. When he did finish cutting one round of yard upkeep, it took him months to return to the same chores, making his yard, for the most part unkempt. He also wore rumpled clothes all the time and wore the same outfit sometimes for weeks. His name became a byword for untidiness. He was, however, a very smart man and used big words although he did not go to Sasse College (St. Joseph's College, Sasse, the first and most prestigious secondary school in Anglophone, Cameroon). B a' a-b a (barber), as we called him, was a court clerk, and when he had retired, he served as some sort of a "lawyer" to the uneducated (from a Western point of view), economically disadvantaged persons who needed legal representation; that is, he would write their story (case) at their narration and present it to the judge and also stood in lieu of his clients to answer questions or present their case as and when necessary.

Mola Mo-li-szreh did not show his disappointment outwardly, or so I thought. But a careful observation of his mannerisms revealed a very withdrawn man whose step even faltered during his walks around the village. He was tormented inside. Hostile neighbors and now a tormentor under his own roof. The *e-li-mo* (devil) in the house, no less!

In our entire village, members of my clan celebrated Christmas and New Year in a "civilized" manner, or at least we thought so and prided ourselves in it. We were a small group of *ndo-meh ja wu-nya-na* (male cousins), and I was about the youngest. The head of our group was our college cousin. He was more handsome, richer, and more knowledgeable than the rest of us. He came back home for the holidays with ideas from a technical college that was a mixture of boys and girls and Anglophones and Francophones. The name of the College was VOCAST (Vocational College of Arts, Science and Technology) Muyuka, a vocational technical institution.

He was our local champion, and he also treated us well, and for various reasons, we called him Mo-m'a Yoma, Mo-m'a Gbwa, Mot'a Gbwa, or just plain Mo-meh; he was a wild "dog killer." He introduced us to the use of mba-nga knockouts (loud fireworks). These fireworks exploded with great glare and deafening noise. It was the louder the better, especially when it exploded in midair. And, of course, it could burn flesh and clothes and maybe even start a fire. This made it all the more fun. Lighting these large cigar-like knockouts (fireworks) and throwing them at individuals, crowds, or open homes seemed great fun for Christmas, especially for the thrower and the cheerers.

Small groups in the village went from home to home, singing Christmas carols at night and day or night dancing. We thought this was begging for money and, therefore, beneath our level (pride aside, if truth be told, we fell short of anything resembling harmonious singing, we lacked the skills to make the drums, and importantly, we were also lacking in the requisite dancing skills. In short, did we have what it took to be a choral or dance group? No!). Then night caroling groups became our targets. In midair, we would explode a mba-nga knockout over their heads to their horror, screams, and cursing.

One of my uncles, Mola Mi-szro-li, was a "big" man (or an important person) in a local church. When one of their bigger choirs came caroling, he gave them drinks, chin-chin, groundnuts, and money. We listened to them sing and concluded they did not do a great job. They sang carols in English, but we thought we heard more of Bakweri in their singing. There was also absolutely no harmony between the men, older women, and younger women who all seemed to have had different parts. It would have been better if they sang entirely in Bakweri, just pure Mokpwe songs. But then if they sang purely Mokpwe songs, then it would not have been caroling. Did I mention that the men in the choir seemed already intoxicated with palm wine or some other form of alcohol before they reached my Mola's residence? You could smell the *afor-for* (locally and illegally brewed gin) and *kwacha* (corn beer) in addition to the palm wine, in combination or singularly, depending on the efficacy of your olfactory epithelium and nerves.

As they departed, descending the steep hill that had previously dealt a serious blow to Mola Mo-li-szr'a Moto, and in the tropical darkness, there were three loud successive explosions in the rear, front, and overhead. This Godfearing caroling choral group of approximately thirty-five to forty persons, in a panic, were scattered in all directions, cursing and calling the e-li-mo throwers devil-possessed and all other sorts of names.

"Devil pikin dem (Children of the devil)!" some said.

"Witch pikin dem (Possessed children)!" others said.

"Va-i-mba or Wa-i-mba (Witches or wizards)!" even more added in the Mokpwe language.

"Wana wa woweh (Bad children)!" some threw in.

It was dark; one could not tell who did what. We heard screams of pain, especially from the *walana wa-mba-ki* (elderly women) who ordinarily cannot walk fast but, on this occasion, decided that they had to run for their dear lives. They could run after all. Their leader decided that they were going to pray for these anonymous mba-nga knockout throwers to rescue them from the grip of the devil.

I was neither financially loaded enough to contribute to the purchase of these fireworks nor was I old enough to plan the "throwing or attack" strategies, but I was considered smart enough to follow instructions. Therefore, I was the main "thrower," but only as instructed. When I missed the target, I was reprimanded and reminded how much it cost to buy one of these precious terrorizing fireworks, and there had to be a repeat throw except in the case of a shortage in supply.

After Christmas and before New Year, a big target was planned. This man had an unfinished stone house. He was the architect and builder of his own house, but he was not rich enough to finish what would have been considered a "state-of-the-art" house in the village. If he finished this house, his name would also change from Li-emba to Nyo-ngo. There were some things in the semblance of doors and some thin cloth that acted as windows. The house was not protected and very accessible.

I knew the situation of this house, but I never imagined it to be a target. I was only told it was a target a couple of minutes before launch time, and I was the main launcher. I felt uneasy about this project but kept such thoughts to myself. I acted as if I was cool with the idea for fear of being labeled weak or feeble-minded like a mo-gwe-gweh a wor-lor-kor or an e-fu-le-fu as worthless people are called elsewhere in East Africa. Worse still was the moniker "she-she" for weaklings.

She-she is a terminology we youngsters used in Gbwea (Buea), derived from Chinese action films on which we were hooked. The she-shes were the weak, almost comic characters we were sure would be given a whooping by the "real" men. Sometimes the strong guys just needed to look their way, and the she-shes fled for their lives, falling atop each other and sometimes forming a pile of *homo sapiens* if not caught in the most ridiculous manner. As pre-teenagers, we loved these comic characters who made us laugh our lungs out, but we did not want to be associated with them in the open if we were to keep our "strongman" tag.

And so, I could not say no to the launching instructions, despite my misgivings and wrongdoings, proximity to our own house, consequences, and the "excitement" that would follow the reaction of this to-be-attacked family. From behind the bushes, I hurled the first missile through an open window, and then out of nowhere, two more followed in quick succession (I did not know who the other launchers were). Mo-li-szr'a Moto was eating his supper of *E-kwa-kok'a Szreh-Szreh* (commonly known as *ti-mba na mbu-szra*), when suddenly, the dark and quiet night air was pierced by explosions, flares, and smoke.

"Ah-ga-na (What is happening)?" he cried out, frightened out of his wits. In this state of blind panic, he knocked over his food bowl, the contents of which discolored his moustache and his clothes.

Then Mo-li-szr'a Moto's wana and molana started screaming bloody murder:

"Ie-way-li eh, Ie-way-li (We are dead, we are dead)!"

"Wama ju-mua na may-ko-mba (We are being shot with guns)!"

"Eh mboa a-jay eh (Everybody come)!"

"Li-tu-mba l'ami li-way-li (My family is dead)!" Mola Mo-li-szreh's molana summed it up.

As Mo-li-szr'a Moto came out of his house, uncharacteristically making shrieking noises, asking the village why his family was being attacked by guns, one of my molas, Mola Ma-ji-fu—a president of a palm wine club, a bricklayer like Mo-li-szreh, and an antagonist of Mola E-wa-ng'a Moto—was returning home, well-soaked with palm wine and passing by Moliszr'a Moto's roadside house to go up to his own house. While Mo-li-szreh was not addressing anyone in particular, Mola Ma-ji-fu decided to retort in mockery, "Ou-gbwaa (You smelly man)! Which guns are you referring to? These small knockout things that children throw all over the place is what you call a gun?"

Then Mola Mo-li-szreh asked him, "Mbo-ma eh, Mbo-ma eh! Owa di ou-mui eeh? Owa di ou-mui eeh? (Drunkard, drunkard! Are you the one who shot at us? Are you the one who shot at us)?"

Mola Ma-ji-fu, the palm wine "drunkard" resorted to other forms of insults including *Li-emba* (wizard), *Mo-li-szra* (poor man), and *Mo-gwe-gweh* (weakling).

Enough was enough! Mo-li-szreh approached the "palm winer" menacingly, showing his aggressive nature for the first time, having been pushed to the wall for so long. As he narrowed the distance between them, Mola Ma-ji-fu said, "O-jay-li-teh li-no-ko-mbe-neh nua-nana (If you come close to me, I will beat you up)."

And Mo-li-szreh echoed in mockery and daring exclamation, "Ah-na-na hoh. O-na-na-ney (I dare you then to beat me up)."

Things were escalating too quickly, and this turn of events was not anticipated. We were now expecting and witnessing a possible chance of a fight between two adults, never before seen in our own portion of the village. Crouching in the bushes, almost breathless and daring not to reveal my position or existence, I was very conflicted. Mola Majifu was in no position to fight. He was visibly drunk while Mola Moliszr'a Moto, usually so composed but now at his wits end, could go for the jugular and damn the consequences. He was a fallen man, so what else could go wrong?

Fortunately, the fight never took place. Mo-li-szreh's molana pleaded with the mu-nya-na to let go and return into the house. My *ta-teh* (father) too had appeared in the scene from the opposite direction, approached Mola Ji-fu-man, and urged him to go home for the sake of peace.

I breathed a sigh of relief. Phew! That was very, very close! And who knows how it would have ended? My role in the night's events was weighing heavily on me. Mola Majifu was a strongman, very muscular and very aggressive; he was like a man driven by extra doses of adrenaline. But that is when he was normal. In his drinkard (one who does not get drunk, regardless of the amount of alcoholic beverages consumed) state, his cerebellum was not in control of skeletal muscles and fine movements required for punching and dodging or avoiding punches.

Mola Moliszra, on the other hand, sober, with a strong builder's build and with accumulated anger, was in an implosive state. I did not think Mola Majifu was a match for him; at least, not this evening or night.

While everyone in the village knew the families from which fireworks "pranks" came from, even if they did not know the specific wana who did it because it was always done in the dark, no one came out to reprimand the obvious culprits. We had grown up learning that Mo-li-szreh and E-wa-ngeh deserved anything that came their way. Still, that was my last launching of mba-nga knockouts! Aside from the fear and traumatization, the Mo-li-szreh family was not "hurt" by the triple knockout explosions. Years later, I can still hear the cries of the wana, some older and some younger than me. Though the local authorities had banned the use of such fireworks partly because of abuse by folks like us, the Igbo traders from Nigeria still managed to sell them to folks like us; they managed to convince the same authorities to turn a blind eye during the day while officially maintaining the ban. The Igbo traders just had to bribe the police, and it was business as usual.

We bought these fireworks in broad daylight in the market; one did not have to be the FBI or KGB or even MI5 or Mossad to know where to buy them in the local market. The Igbo traders knew exactly how to deal with police, first by learning the French language, even if it meant, in its most rudimentary and broken form. Though none of us in our clan was ever arrested or beaten by the police for possession or throwing a dangerous firework, elsewhere some other kids were indeed arrested. Kids like us were just acting to have fun; we did not plan to make life unbearable for other families.

Mola Mo-li-szreh eventually sold his house and relocated to another village. I do not remember that I ever saw him again. In fact, I learned that he died not too long thereafter. Mola Ndiv'a Tor-neh, commonly known as Mola Moliszreh, was also called Ndi-Tor, by us, the male cousins in crime. He sold his house, which was in a prime property location (next to ours) to a local crookish Mokpwe businessman who was just too happy to pay peanuts for Mola Ndiv'a Tor-neh's house. Technically, Mola Ndiv'a Tor-neh did not own the piece of land on which his house was built, for he had no local standing; that is, he had no inheritance right in our village. He was brought into the village by a *ndo-meh wa molana mo-mba-ki* (older sister) as part of a marriage package; that was common among my people, for you married her family, and they were sure to come with a *ndo-meh* (sibling) or wards in the absence of ndo-mehs.

This did not grant Mola Ndiv'a Tor-neh land r property rights. In fact, after the death of his ndo-meh wa molana who brought him into the village, some extended clan members who were anxious to inherit this piece of property were already asking him to leave in plain hostility. Therefore, when he sold his property for 150,000 francs cfa (cfa differentiates the African franc and the French franc), the buyer was willing to pay "that much" with the hope that he was also paying for the piece of land on which the unfinished house was built. The crooked businessman was told pointedly when he wanted to start a house project on the land that he had no right to the land and was given a short notice to uproot his "house" and vacate the landed property. The case lingered in court for a while, and I think he eventually gave up his claim for the land. He did not also uproot the house he purchased.

By my estimations and observations, Mola Ndiv'a Tor-neh had several problems and troubles. His mbou-nda and his molana, a mua-na he did not seed but had to raise as his own, my immediate family accusing him of li-emba, his being socially isolated in the village, his employment being erratic and ephemeral, his not having a family that he interacted with or who ever visited him, the pressure for him to leave his home because he had no rights to the land, and possibly many others, his life did not seem an enviable one and yet you did not see a bitter man, he seemed a model *mu-nya-na* (husband) and model *szrango* (father), a Christian man that was god-fearing.

Several years later, I employed that son of his he had in absentia in a private business that I owned. Note that while my family branded him as a Mot'a Li-emba, I do not recall any particular troubles in the extended families attributed to him. Once in a while, though, the woes of the piggery business owned by Mola Ma-ku-mba were timidly attributed to him. It was all some genetic, lame, loose associations of attributions that the accusers did not seem to be convinced of themselves but had to blame someone. All in all, with the exit of Mo-li-szreh from our village, the Li-emba problems still persisted in my clan, taking different dimensions.

With Mola E-wa-ngeh dead and Mola Mo-li-szreh leaving and dying later, my clan's nyo-ngo and li-emba problems continued to intensify to the point of becoming an "eyesore" several years down the line. My clan, the Li-bi-yeah clan (the "knowledgers"), now started looking inward for their witches and wizards. Their common enemies were gone, but the hatred in them was just beginning to brew, and there needed to be outlets at all costs, no matter the results. This took a toll on our finances and also bred very deep divisions that it seemed were never to be healed. Li-bi-yeah family members were heard saying of each other, "Na'a-teh no'o kwelli (Until death)" or "Na'a-teh no'o weh-li-mo (Until in the land of the spirits or ancestors)."

This essentially meant there was no chance or consideration for reconciliation, ever. They swore to each other. They were the elders, the choristers, the conductors, and other functionaries in their respective church denominations, and they were a clan of families.

"Ma-meh nde-nga-teh? Ma-meh nde-nga-teh (Why? Why?)?"

In all of these, the Nga-ngas and Wato wa Yowo were the beneficiaries. They made millions of francs out of the Li-bi-yeah family while using them against one another. The Nga-nga's modus operandi is simple and straightforward. They get information from neighbors or other family members to make their case. For example, if two adult siblings had a quarrel and exchanged heated words, this could end in words being said like, "Nou-mue-leh (I will show you)" or "Whe-neh (You will see)."

If the recipient of these words eventually had a headache or some other form of misfortune for himself or herself or any member of their immediate family or if he or she saw the one who said those words in a dream, the "sayer" of the words would automatically be declared the culprit and having li-emba or nyo-ngo and, therefore, responsible for these ills. The Mot'a Yowo would now come in to fix the li-emba or nyo-ngo problem, all based on information gotten from family, other family members, or neighbors. The gullibility of those involved was palpable.

Nga-ngas and Wat'o wa Yowo received manifold payments: cash, food, drinks, and the animals they killed. The cash they received was in the hundreds and thousands of francs (cfa), the amount depending on the severity of the job—one night, two nights, or the rare three nights and also the difficulty associated with tracking down the *e-li-ngeh ya wo-weh* (evil ghost), but it could also be measured via what they termed the strength of the li-emba or nyo-ngo person.

For food, these folks chose the choicest and most delicious of the Mokpwe dishes and in large quantities so, for example, it could be ti-mba na mbu-szra with expensive, large smoked fish from Vo'o (Limbe) or Ti-ko-wa (Tiko). Special trips had to be made to go and buy the smoked fish from Ti-ko-wa or Vo'o, a distance of approximately fifty kilometers one way. The drinks of choice were mainly beer and whisky. The beer usually came in crates and included 33 Export, Amstel, Nga-ngi or Beaufort, and the Guinness stout. Johnny Walker whisky was a favorite "hot drink," while those who preferred liqueurs or cordials typically plumped for Chapman's Schnapps.

With authority, greed, shamelessness, and arrogance, they made for and commanded their choices. The brands and the quantities were specific and had to be provided as specified; otherwise, the yowo process would not proceed to a smooth and swift conclusion. Animals required for their job usually included *mbo-li* (Capra hircus; the West African Dwarf goat), *ngo-wa* (*Sus scrofa domesticus*; pigs), and *mo-meh ja wu-wa* (male *Gallus gallus domesticus*; roosters or cocks). Occasionally, it was the *mor-leh-ngu* (*Ovis aries*; the Cameroon Dwarf sheep). I suspected the reason the mor-leh-ngu did not regularly feature in their list of materials required is because the typical Mokpwe does not eat mutton for various reasons.

These animals were beheaded, and their dripping blood used as part of the yowo process. The only part of these *weh-embeh* (animals) that was used for their work was the blood; the rest of the animals, dead or alive, became spoils for the nga-nga team to take home. Again, depending on the demands of the yowo or nga-nga team as to the size of each *e-mbeh* (animal), the color, and the number required for the work, the cost was in the hundreds or thousands. Occasionally, their demands included a puppy, and given that the Wakpwes (Bakweris) do not eat dogs, the headless remains of the beheaded dog were buried in the yard before the yowo team departed. Practically, there was to be no yowo process if their demands were not met.

All of the li-emba and nyo-ngo problems that affected the Li-bi-yeah clan boiled down to the li-emba or nyo-ngo person having buried some *yowo* (evil) in our yard, and the only way to get rid of the buried yowo was logically to dig it up. This was only done at night and during the weekends. It also happened that the buried yowo was mobile, so in their night pursuit, the buried yowo, in an attempt to escape its captor, and therefore destruction by the Wat'o wa Yowo, was able to run below the ground and change its location when digging started at a particular site where it was known to was located. These buried yowo had limited escape and relocation routes confined to the Li-bi-yeah family properties. Thus, the nga-nga will start digging on the first night from one Li-bi-yeah clan property, a digging that continued all night and only for the nga-nga to realize when they got to the end of the digging that the planted yowo had moved. By this time, it was daybreak, so it had to be re-spotted, and a fresh digging would start the next night in a different location.

The nga-ngas did not dwell indoors in any of the main houses of the Li-bi-yeah clan when they came for work, and it was often. Their favorite lodgings were those of our *Mba-mbeh ya molana* (grandmother) and our uncle, Mola Mi-szro-li. During the day, the nga-nga or Wat'o wa Yowo lived outdoors during their stay. They normally took over an animal house where the likes of dogs, goats, and chickens were kept or, on rare occasions, erected their own tent-like dwelling next to these animal shelters.

We spied on them sometimes just to see what they were doing. Initially, we were quite afraid of them, but due to the frequency of their visits, our fear of them somewhat dwindled. Some of them were friendly, especially when one had to run some small errands for them, such as going to the market to buy *szri-ka* (cigarettes), *ta'a-ko* (snuff), or sometimes *ma-weh-lu* (kola nuts; which could be the regular kola nut, *Cola acuminate*, or the bitter kola, *Garcinia kola*). Our exploits spying on them revealed a merrily feasting bunch, by and large, "lazying" about whilst waiting for the deep of the night to start their work. In one of our spy exploits, we got clumsy and revealed our presence! Soon enough, we got some serious reprimand from our parents for supposedly attempting to spoil the nga-nga work that was about to take place. The reprimand also implied that we could be harmed by these Wat'o wa Yowo.

But just how powerful were these Wat'o wa Yowo? What harm could they cause? We lived in the village amidst lots of vegetation of wild plants or crop plants around the homes. Because the nga-ngas chose to dwell in habitations that were removed from the main house, it meant they lived very close to nature with its attendant consequences. Different groups of nga-nga came over the years, although occasionally, there was a repeat nga-nga visit. They all came and did the same thing; that is, remove the yowo planted, prevent its replanting or reburial, and put in place charm-like bundles that were meant to kill or do serious harm to any li-emba or nyo-ngo person who dared transform into a spirit and come around to do harm, physically or in dreams. In other words, the household was protected from further attacks.

On this one occasion, the yowo group was having a feast, as usual, while waiting for the deep of the night to start working when a *veh-yi* (*Bitis gabonica*; West African gaboon viper) came their way. The large reptile easily found its way into their makeshift home and stationed itself in the bar area of their command post. When the chief Moto yowo reached for his umpteenth bottle of beer from the crates lined out for them, he pulled out a beer bottle intimately attached to a veh-yi. Being already tipsy from the amount of alcohol in his system, and as he related later, he thought this was an unusual weight for a bottle of beer, but his vision was not clear enough for him to tell differently. Wat'o wa Yowo were strong men and had no need for bottle openers. They used their teeth to open the very tightly sealed beer covers. The chief nga-nga thus raised the bottle to his face to use his teeth as an opener. It was then that an assistant nga-nga seated opposite to him saw the reptilian attachment on the master Mot'a Yowo's bottle.

"Veh-yi e-nay (This is a viper)!" he shouted.

What a sight! The master Mot'a Yowo dropped his composite beer bottle in the blink of an eye, and the group of four inside their tent-like command post all struggled to let themselves out of the purpose-made tiny exit. The flimsy structure collapsed on them all, including some of the sacrificial wu-wa kept inside their tent. Humans falling on each other, a *gbwa-wa* (snake) wanting out, and the fluttering wings of wu-wa in a confined space—the word *chaos* did not begin to describe the drama aptly enough!

"E-veh-yi ya jo szro-mba (We are being stung by a viper)!" the chief nga-nga declared.

"Iyaka Koko na way-li (Mother, I am dead)!" lamented the young apprentice.

"Li-emba li-ni (This is witchcraft)!" another member of the team declared and announced.

With this commotion, both *wato* (*homo sapiens*; humans) and *gbwa'a (Canis lupus domesticus,* dogs) headed to the nga-nga quarters, with the *gbwa'a ja mo-vao* (hunting dogs) barking as loud as possible. We kids were mesmerized and hushed down from talking. By the time the living creatures in the nga-nga tent were all untangled from the fallen house, there was no gbwa-wa to be seen. If this gbwa-wa alarm was sounded by a *mua-na* (child), the mua-na would have been reprimanded for just imagining things. The Wat'o wa Yowo insisted that the veh-yi attack was from the li-emba person that they came to fight; it was a calculated attempt to scare them off and was proof of someone's guilt.

The *wa-mba-ki* (adults) in the Li-bi-yeah clan seemed to be hanging on every word from the Wat'o wa Yowo and bought their explanations wholeheartedly. Indeed, it was further justification why it was worth bringing the yowo crew. We, the wana, thought otherwise, though. This was an affront to the invincibility of these nga-ngas and that they would flee in panic in the presence of a gbwa-wa could not be more deflating and humiliating. "Who were they?" we asked. This was a recipe for them to ask for monetary compensation after their difficult work and to increase the number of days they needed to work. "Who were they? And we were the Li-bi-yeah Clan?" Western education wise, our clan was very educated and yes more educated than the hired Yoworites, so why was the clan allowing itself to be made a fool off by wat'o of lesser knowledge and lesser understanding?

CHAPTER 4

Wu-wa ya E-li-mo

My immediate family was not at the top of the economic ladder in our clan. In addition to subsistence farming, we reared *wu-wa* (*Gallus gallus domesticus*; chickens) and *ngo-wa* (*Sus scrofa domesticus*; pigs) as a mini-commercial venture. I was the main animal caretaker and took delight in feeding and caring for those animals, including the dogs we had.

I had returned from school one day and found that a *mor-sz-roh-szreh mo wu-wa* (young Gallus gallus domesticus) had been mortally injured by a predator that intended to use it for a meal. It had a broken leg and a broken wing, added to which large chunks of tissue were missing randomly including an eye. This *i-nor-ni* (bird) lay at the edge of the bush, almost lifeless, barely breathing. I could tell it was clinging onto life because of the slight movement around the chest area. I was amazed that the small bird could fight for its life and manage to escape to "safety" by leaving the bush to a clearing near to the house where it could be saved. This wu-wa was smart, for it knew where to go to.

My parents and siblings could not agree on which predator was responsible. Maybe an *e-szru* (*Vulpes zerda*, the Fennec fox) or a *nju-weh* (Lycaon pictus manguensis; bush dog—a subspecies of the African wild dog native to West Africa) because the domestic hunting dogs were discounted. We had once hunted down a fox near our home with our *gbwa'a ja mo-vao* (hunting and guard dogs). It was not a big animal, though it was the most significant catch thus far for our hunting group. I was thus not "afraid" of an e-szru.

I had never seen a nju-weh, and the thought that there could be one in close proximity to our home was sending cold chills down my spine. We had heard not-so-good stories about nju-weh, their strength and cunning, and if the small chicken had outsmarted a nju-weh, then it meant this was no ordinary chicken. I was instructed to put it out of its misery and then throw it back into the bush for the predator to feed on or just let it expire where it was, or better still, throw it back alive into the bush for the predator to finish its hunting. I was not in agreement with any of the options as I thought they were all very cruel.

I decided that I was going to try and nurse it back to good health as much as possible. My siblings all laughed at me. It was not the first time they thought of me as living in some strange world of my own.

"Eh-geh wu-wa szre-keh e-ma-wa (That wuwa is practically dead). Ma-meh o ta-neh li-gbwea (What do you think you can do)," my parents said repeatedly.

"Na ke-ka (I will try)," I said.

We only spoke the Mo-kpwe language to our parents and other wa-mba-ki within the clan families and also wa-mba-ki without the families that were of Mo-kpkwe-li derivation (using another language to communicate with wa-mba-ki was not an option and was considered rude and disrespectful); but amongst us wana, English and French were permitted. What was not permitted was Pidgin English. We, however, spoke it when our parents were not around or when they could not hear us.

In our village, time and again, we saw wato with a broken lower or upper limb, and so it was fairly common to see gbwa with broken fore and hind limbs. There was no surgery, per se, to repair the broken bones. We saw external tow sticks or pieces of plank wood lateral to the broken bones and sandwiched by the broken part of the body. The sticks were tied together with bandages or just plain robes. Before the bandaging, extracts of certain herbs were topically applied to the affected areas, and then using special plant leaves, the broken area was covered, then the bandage was used to cover the entire broken region.

"E-mo-weh-meh (Leave him alone)," my ta-teh declared, and his word was law. He made his declaration after looking at me intently for a few seconds, looks that seemed to be saying, "Are you sure? Is this what you want?"

I carefully lifted the *mor-szroh-szreh mo wu-wa* and placed it onto a board that served as its stretcher. I got some sticks and cut them into appropriate sizes and then rushed to look for *weh-wu-lay weh vako*, literally meaning mountain grass. We used weh-wu-lay weh vako a lot in our village as wana playing around and sure to incur wounds now and again. We normally squeezed the leaves by rubbing them hard in both palms, and the thick, dark green extract that it contained was filtered out through the spaces between our fingers. The filtrate collected was then applied topically onto the affected area. It was painful, but it sure did have a healing effect, starting with the stoppage of bleeding via coagulation.

I quickly applied the grass extract onto the injured areas of the wu-wa and then tied the broken bones accordingly with the extract of the *e-wo-lay* (grass) and also use the leaves to cover the wounds before applying the bandage (actually being ropes that held the plant extract, sticks, and leaves together and in place). I did this very quickly while praying silently that the wu-wa would not die. The whole assemblage was like a cast.

When I was done with the "surgery," I mumbled some incantations over the wu-wa. Incantations were necessary as the rule of all the nga-ngas that I had seen. You do not understand what is said because it is speaking in "tongues." So, I did my incantations incoherently but loud enough so that I could be heard clearly. I knew someone was watching me—*ndo-m'ami wa mu-nya-na wa mo-szra-li* (my kid brother)—a man with several names. He was known variously as Tanko or Tandril, but also Ndiv'a Molimo, and sometimes Mai-ye Sunseye, and other times just simply Chef (for he was and is a legend and story of his own). I had always wanted to prove to him that I was a Mot'a Yowo, but all in vain because each time, he caught my trick. This wu-wa episode was going to yield a validation for me or no confidence at all.

I took the wu-wa to the chicken house, lit a fire, and laid it close by, and I also put some mo-lay-li and ma-li-va (food and water) next to its head. It was still breathing, but very slightly; nothing had changed with its health condition. I, however, remained optimistic.

After twenty-four hours, I lifted the wu-wa and put its beak next to the mo-lay-li. It was soft food, semi-fvu-fvu of ma-kao (the mother plant that produces the cocoyams, as called in pidgin English—mami koko; fvu-fvu is pounded ma-kao in this case). To my delight, it made an attempt to peck at the mo-lay-li, so I quickly reduced the size of the particulate matter and then tried again. The wu-wa ate a little. I did not share this with anyone.

After three days, I did another fresh extract, this time a mixture of two plants. The e-wu-l'a vako and a reddish plant we called ma-ngoh-ngi. These extracts were mixed, and this time, I added a little bit of salt and pepper. When I applied the mixture onto the parts of the wu-wa, it emitted a sound of pain, and Ndiv'a Molimo, a.k.a. Tanko, said, "Nobi Ibi tell you say e go hurt (Did not I tell you that it was going to be painful)?"

Ndiv'a Molimo had started having some confidence in me and become an able assistant in this project. That the wu-wa could feel the pain and expressed thus overtly meant the injured areas were regaining their vascularization and innervation; these were further steps in addition to the stoppage of bleeding achieved on the very first day when the plant extracts were applied to the injured parts and brought about immediate coagulation. It had worked before on human skin; there was proof of its efficacy.

Somehow we had also learned as kids that the "hotter" or more painful a treatment regimen was, the more it revealed its efficacy, and in the case when applied onto human bodies, resisting to overtly show that you were hurting, not expressing painful internal feelings was expected of us, the *wat'o wa wu-nya-na* (males); it made you a man or rather made a man of you. Suffering in silence were mannerisms and characteristics associated with the strong.

We continued to care for this wu-wa, and after four weeks, it ventured out of the fowl house unaided, making baby steps, the first steps after a near-death experience. To show their pride in me and to encourage me, my parents declared that *mor-szroh-szreh mo wu-wa* that I nursed back to life was mine, and I was free to do with it whatever I willed. My status in the family and our clan just became a little bit elevated as some sort of a nga-nga and a lad chicken owner. The saved i-nor-ni was named Wu-wa ya E-li-mo. In Mo-kpwe culture, there are three spirit or ghost types recognized—the E-ko-ngi, the E-ku-mu-ti, and the E-li-mo or Mo-li-mo. For the wu-wa to have "returned" to life when it had been declared dead meant there was something spiritual in this i-nor-ni or something mysterious.

Mola Ma-ku-mba, a *ndo-meh ya mu-nya-na mo-szra-li* (kid brother) of my iyaka, had a pig farm within our Li-bi-yeah clan property that bordered our primary school. Its fence was right on the border of our village, next to the church grounds that now occupied thousands of land acreages obtained from the Wa-kpwes via the German exploiters and then the English using Machiavellian tactics and terror. We called his pig farm, ndaw'a ngo-wa or "swine house." A hot-headed intellectual, he had tried for many years and spent quite a fortune in the tens of millions of francs (f cfa) to reclaim some of the land that was usurped by the religious mission but all in vain.

This religious mission started as the Basel Mission and now the Presbyterian Church in Cameroon (PCC), the headquarters always having been situated in Gbwea or Buea. When the German Occupiers and Economic Exploiters came, they asked my people, the Wa-kpwes, to give them a piece of land to build a church and later to build a school. My people, hungry for Christianity and western type education opportunities for themselves, quickly obliged. The Germans were shown a piece of land, but there was no surveyor map or demarcations, and neither was there any written document between the Wa-kpwes and the Germans. The good faith of the Wa-kpwes in which verbal agreements and gentleman agreements was the norm became instead a gold mine situation to be exploited by the Germans and their Cameroonian successors thereafter. They eventually made documentation and determined where the boundaries were, and these documents had only one copy, the copy they made and kept which was to be used later on by their Cameroonian successors as "proof" of boundaries and "proof" of the gift made to the religious mission by my people.

The brunt of this illegal and exploitative scam/scheme was borne by my family clan, for we were the ones pushed eastward from the west, and we could not expand our territory eastward, for that would have meant encroaching on other family and clan lands, and that would have made us occupiers. My family or clan, led by Mola Ma-ku-mba, fought this illegal expansion in vain. The Wa-kpwes knew where the true boundary was. It was a ravine that still exists to this date and is very unmistakable. This was certainty because my people preserved facts, records, dates, and history via an impeccable system of oral traditions. My family clan was abandoned in this "fight" by the larger Mo-kpwe community for many reasons—political, personal, socio-cultural, etc.

The Basel Mission, and when it transformed to the PCC was, for all intents and purposes, the "government" or an arm of the government. My family could not win. My Mola Ma-ku-mba was a French-trained and then an American-trained engineer, an educated radical; he paid a heavy price for that later on in his life. He was a man frustrated beyond measure, an almost wasted brain.

Mola Ma-ku-mba had a modern pigsty modelled after American standards as he had studied in the Democratic Republic of the Congo and then in Colorado in the United States after he left Saint Joseph's College, Sasse, Gbwea. It was built with blocks and appropriately partitioned so that the pigs were grouped together according to age or reproductive functions. The floors were cemented, the building was electrified, and it was equipped with pipe-borne running fresh water. The ngowa were fed on specially formulated diets purchased ready-made, for the most part, from Douala or Gola (the common name for the "main streeters") or made from scratch by his piggery workers based on formulation proportions communicated to them by the brilliant Mola Ma-ku-mba. An engineer by profession, he was part of the team who were the backbone and foundation behind Power Cam of West Cameroon and then Southern Cameroon.

A remarkable omission in his modern pig farm was the lack of appropriate waste disposal. Initially, it was not a problem; the wastewater generated from the farm was simply channeled into the nearby forest. But as time went on, that part of the bush became saturated and inundated with this liquid waste, bringing about surface land pollution and, of course, the below ground pollution we could not see. It was a matter of time before the surface flow of waste, having saturated its initial forest path, freely flowed downhill, crossed the main street that led to Buea Town, and started soaking up property on its way that belonged to or was part of the Buea Town Football Stadium.

There were complaints by the general public and from a prominent family that lived on the other side of the fence as a good neighbor and friend to the religious mission. The pig farm was located on the middle third plateau of our portion of the village after having ascended a steep hill. The wastewater, therefore, flowed down the hill passively and effortlessly. Besides the polluted water flow on land surface, there was also the issue of air pollution. Certain evenings were unbearable because of the thick stench in the air. Folks who were between 300 to 500 meters away complained about the polluted air and the smell. I never heard any adult member of our family complain about the pollution; when we the wana did, it was hush-hush amongst ourselves.

Following the huge public outcry about the pollution, Mola Ma-ku-mba had a storage tank built that was a confluent of all of the pipes that contained water waste from the ngo-wa farm. The waste was mainly their feces, urine, leftover food, and dirty water when the ngo-wa were washed. Though this holding reservoir was a large one, it started overflowing eventually. The situation was, however, better than it was before, a partial and temporary solution.

When the waste from the swine house was channeled into the open reservoir, the heavier particles sank and settled onto the bottom as expected while the liquid layer floated and eventually overflowed. Less than two years after the reservoir was constructed, the solid waste accumulation had almost filled the tank. This waste was thick and mud-like, and during the dry months, it was dry and formed a cake-like matte appearance. This thick top layer could be walked upon by small, light animals. And yes, it was attractive to small animals because it seemed to contain a rich fauna of invertebrate animals and sometimes algae; that is, it teemed with zooplankton and phytoplankton, making a luxuriant and an attractive aquatic ecosystem. Birds, squirrels, lizards, rats, and other small animals visited this semi-solid surface layer created by the waste to hunt for food.

This surface layer of the waste reservoir was also a trap. Wu-wa ya E-li-mo was still a very young wu-wa who was yet to attain reproductive maturity (it was thus called a *mor-szroh-szreh mo wu-wa* in the Mo-kpwe language), and by virtue of the near-death incident of Wu-w'E-li-mo (wu-wa ya E-li-mo) had gone through, Wu-w'E-li-mo walked with a limb and one wing drooping lower than the other. Wu-w'E-li-mo was a special need wu-wa that could not compete in the wild for food like the other wu-wa in its midst. We therefore always ensured that it was fed extra, outside the normal feeding provided to the other fowls.

Returning from school one afternoon, just after 2:00 p.m., I had to go past the reservoir pit. Because of the strong smell that exuded from it, when passing by, we usually ran and covered our noses. Sometimes as we ran past, we even avoided looking at the tank. On this day, I thought I saw something at the corner of my eye as I ran past, but my preoccupation was to get to our abode. When I reached home, it seemed to have registered in my brain that there was some kind of bubbling movement at the surface of tank. Though I would have loved to dismiss the thought, it persisted. So, I made a U-turn just after I got home to see what was happening. And then I saw it: the beak of a chicken with the nares barely above the pit!

In my mind, I debated rescuing the wu-wa or what i-nor-ni it might have been: on the one hand, it seemed there was no use. Surely it was going to die. On the other hand, I thought I had nothing to lose if I gave it a try. I hurriedly searched for some stick that was forked at one end and started to attempt to hook and then pull the bird out of the pond. It seemed I was making good progress until the stick broke. In a panic, I left the pond and looked for a similar shaped stick which I cut off from the fence that surrounded the pig farm. I immediately returned and continued my attempts. It might have taken me a total of ten to fifteen minutes, and to my amazement, I was able to pull the chicken to the banks of the pond and then realized that it was my own wu-wa ya E-li-mo.

The smell of the waste pond now meant nothing to me. I grabbed it with both hands and rushed it to a running tap and washed it clean of the feces and other waste mixture. Then I took it home, made a wood fire, and put it close to it. After about ten minutes by the fire, it started moving parts of its body gradually, and from there on, it was a matter of time before it walked away from the warmth or heat of the fire. Once it left the fireside, I got some food and threw it on the ground as we normally fed them, and wu-wa ya E-li-mo fed hungrily. None of my family members were at home when all of this took place. When I narrated my story later on as to how I had saved wu-wa ya E-li-mo a second time, I do not think anyone believed me; it seemed like a made-up story. It was a matter of time before my narration of the event was being used in the village either as a lie or further proof of mysticism.

About two months after the pond rescue of Wu-wa ya E-li-mo, he was found dead on the other side of the fence that bordered our house; that is, within the property of another extended family member with whom we shared our immediate southern border. I vaguely remember someone bringing the dead bird to my attention. I knew it was Wu-wa ya E-li-mo because it had a robe tied to its right leg as some sort of identification because phenotypically, it could pass for any other chicken in the village as they were all range chickens with similarity of feather colors and size. And of course, Wu-wa ya E-li-mo also had unmistaken anatomical features associated with a broken leg and wing. My dead i-nor-ni was left for me to deal with. It was painful, but boys do not cry as my mother had a habit of reminding me.

For days, I could not quite understand and kept on wondering how Wu-w'E-li-mo died; there were wounds on its body and no missing parts. It could have been beaten by a *gbwa-wa* (snake) or just simply *li-embah* (witchcraft), considering that our house was practically sandwiched by *wae-i-emba* (wizards and witches). I did not bury it but simply flung it deep into the bushes for it to decompose there. My many dreams about the bird soon came to an end, but the word was that it had finally died because of the earlier lie I told about saving it from death, and therefore, the blame was mine. For the most part, I was known to hardly talk, so I just ignored them and wondered how they could be so insensitive. It was also a reiteration that I was a "natin" man, a "no-nothin."

We fed our chickens twice a day: In the morning, before they were let to roam the village within their ecological ranges; and in the evening when they assembled in the front house, readying to retire for the day. If we were not home by sleeping time for the birds, we met them clutching on the entrance of the house or to the side of the house, especially the young roosters or cocks to avoid harassment from the older cocks. However, once the door was opened, they all hurried from their respective temporary resting sites and found their way into their specific resting places.

One week after Wu-w'E-li-mo had "died" and I had flung it to its final rest, I thought I saw it when I was feeding the chickens in the evening but quickly dismissed the idea, for we had tens of chickens and many of them phenotypically similar if not identical. The phenotypical similarities amongst the numerous fowls in village households were due to few dominant roosters mating with just about all of the females of reproductive ages; it was some kind of reproductive monopoly common in natural zoological communities. But it was not an idea, and neither was it an illusion.

Was I daydreaming? Surely not because I was seeing it right there! I pinched myself and could feel the pain, and then I froze. But to be cocksure, I called my ndo-meh wa mu-nya-na wa mo-sza-li, that is, Ndiv'a Mo-li-mo, also known as Tanko, who happened to be around, and then pointed Wu-w'E-li-mo out to him without uttering a word. At first, he did not get it and simply said, "We sabi say na ya fowl (Yes, we know that it is your fowl)."

Then I said, "You remember say ibi die (Do you remember that it died)?"

At that, he shot a quick look and then he fled away from me saying, "Na szra-szra risk (I do not want any risk)!"

Tanko was known as a brave young man whom I admired, even though I was older than him. If he fled in fear, then it was serious business, and besides, he was called Ndiv'a Mo-li-mo, implying one with spiritual powers.

A Mo-li-mo or an E-li-mo is a type of ghost or spirit in the Mo-kpwe language. At one stage, Tanko was the oldest mua-na at home, and by oldest mua-na, I mean about nine or ten years of age. The other mua-na in the house was his direct follower seven or eight years of age.

At this point in time, I was in St. Joseph's College, Sasse, a Catholic boarding secondary school for males. Our iyaka had gone to farm as she had done all of her life and did not return when she was expected. Tanko and Li-mu-ngeh (also known as Auntie "I" and Mbo-mboh) returned from school and had to wait for three hours normally or four hours max to welcome their iyaka back from the farm. This meant she was expected at 5:00 p.m. or 6:00 p.m. at the latest.

In the tropics, it gets pretty dark 6:00 p.m., especially toward the end of the year. Tanko and Li-mu-ngeh had waited until about 6:30 p.m., and their iyaka was nowhere to be found; they had been expecting her in vain, hoping she would appear any moment from now. After 6:30 p.m., when it was fully dark, Tanko decided he and his *ndo-meh wa molana wa mo-szra-li* (kid sister) were to head to the farm and look for their iyaka. Our crop farms were situated in the depths of the forest, and at night, in the depths of a tropical forest was real darkness that would more than merit the name Black Forest. Instead of alerting other members of the family, and more particularly the older males, Tanko took a kerosene lantern, lit it, and urged the sister to follow him to the bush (farm) to look for their iyaka.

Li-mu-ngeh obliged, though no one knows how he managed to convince her. They set out across the village, heading northeasterly and, within ten minutes, had traversed the village clearings and now started the entry into the dark night forest. Aside the pitch darkness, the forest at night was an assorted mixture of sounds and voices from invertebrates and vertebrates, plants, plant branches and leaves, whispering plants, and the whisperings of the *wa-li-mo* (ghosts or spirits) that were known to be surely there, not forgetting the lurking wa-i-emba evil spirits. Tanko and Li-mu-ngeh met their iyaka some twenty minutes into the forest. They called out to her in the dark as they penetrated the forest, and when eventually she responded to their call, she urged them to stay where they were, for she was on her way to meeting them.

Tanko refused and told her they would instead come to her because she needed the lighting source they had. Tanko's story narrated several times in the village and in the family made him respected and feared. It was during the planting season, and their iyaka lost track of time, which was naturally tracking the position of the sun as it settled west, moving from behind the Vako. As her own atonement, Tanko's iyaka never returned late from the farm again, 4:00 to 5:00 p.m. becoming her limit. The bravery and fearlessness exhibited by Tanko earned him the name Ndiv'a Mo-li-mo or Ndiv'Elimo. It is noted that in this narration, the role of Li-mu-ngeh has never been emphasized; she is the silent heroine of the event.

Now I was really afraid because I knew for certain I was not daydreaming. My ta-teh (father) always said, "Mu-nya-na aszra-vhe mo-gwe-gweh (A man cannot be weakling). Mu-nya-na aszro-ka wo-ngoh."

So, I kept a brave face, despite my pounding heart, and attended to Wu-w'E-li-mo and ultimately fixed it a sleeping place. I was worried all evening, not knowing what had happened and how it could be explained. When my *iyakeh* (mother) and later my *ndo-meh wa mu-nya-na mo-mba-ki* (older brother, Dee Lawrence) came home, and the story was narrated to them, they simply dismissed it. Either it did not die in the first place, or it was not the one we thought died. But they could not explain the identical nature of the dead one and now this one and the absence since the dead one was discovered. My *ta-teh* (father), on the other hand, simply surmised that, "Oma e-wo-l'a Lowah (It could be the work of God)."

I continued to tend to Wu-w'E-li-mo with suspicion, but as time passed, my concerns started subsiding, though Wu-w'E-li-mo still remained a mystery. I could touch it and associate with it as I would normally do before the inexplicable as time went by. Many of my *wo-nya-nyango wa litumba* (cousins) and other village mates came to our house at one time or another to see Wu-w'E-li-mo during feeding times. Their take on the matter differed wildly. For some, it was a lie because they did not know when Wu-w'E-li-mo died; others asked if Wu-w'E-li-mo really died, and yet for a few, the "Wu-w'E-li-mo" they saw belonged to someone else and it was just a matter of time before this stray fowl would be claimed by a villager from another part of the village and so on. Some elders in the clan and village pointedly asked me if what they were hearing was true or if I was just making it up. Some asked mockingly or jokingly while others asked too seriously for my liking. I did not understand those who tended to be very serious.

I did not take anything from them and did not see how this affected them.

News about Wu-w'E-li-mo spread, and the village had one more item to add to my file or resume. Most questions and interrogations directed at me concerning this issue remained unanswered. If you were a *Moto mo-mba-ki* (an older person), you would be respected by me stopping and pretending to listen to you, and when I saw that your lips had stopped moving, I proceeded to go my way. Naturally, I was not talkative, so nodding or shaking my head usually sufficed. I wonder if they knew I simply tuned them off while they rambled and babbled.

Kah-jah was renamed Wu-wa ya E-li-mo; for short, Wu-w'Elimo, meaning ghost fowl, was what we all thought of this i-nor-ni. It was appropriate that its original name be changed. Kah-jah went on to be very productive because dozens and dozens of eggs and tens of wu-wa were produced by Wu-w'E-li-mo. Kah-jah's unusual anatomy and phenotype did not help; it was part of its mystique. Kah-jah are red soldier ants with very painful bites. As wana, urged by our older *ndomeh ja wunyana* (older male siblings) and to prove that you were a "strongman," one subjected himself to the pleasurable torture of these kah-jahs. You were encouraged to put your *li-ta-nga* (foot) or *liya* (hand) partially immersed into the colony of these *szri-ya-wu* (soldier ants), or in some other occasions and situations, you placed these body parts of yours on their pathway as they commuted in transportation to and from their colony.

The szri-ya-wu attacked with voracity, inflicting maximum pain, while their recipients of this assault kept a straight face with gnashing teeth, conscious of the fact that any admission of pain or any form of distress was being watched very carefully by those who will decide whether you were to be considered a munyana or not. The longer you endured the torture, the more munyana you were. Sometimes we returned home with swollen features the next day and signs of bites as miniature teeth. When the wambaki learned of this, they scolded the older wana for being inhumane, but not even they, the wambaki, thought their scolding was of any consequence. It was going to continue, and someday, those now being tortured would be the torturers. It was bullying in St. Joseph's College, Sasse, Buea.

The bullied became the bully with a first taste in Form 2 (Grade 8), and then the grand finale in Form 4 (Grade 10) after the "handing over." Kah-jah was an inorni of endurance, an endurance that soon transformed into "mysticism," thus Kah-jah transformed from endurance, a test of character to a ghost or mystic inorni, a "Wuw'a ya Elimo."

CHAPTER 5

Nyango Likao

"Bwan-ghai."

"Moi-ghai."

That was me being called from behind, but I did not turn around immediately. Judging from the tone of the voice, it was a *mua-na mbe-szra* (a male youth) calling after me, probably about my age. Of course, this was certainly a *ndo-meh ya mu-nya-na weh-va-ru ya szrango* (a paternal male cousin), but I could not tell which one because they were *mai-szreh me-a-ke-neh* (identical twins). I needed to gaze upon the caller physically, and even then, I could not be sure who was who, except when they were seen together in which case I could look for a small scar just under the right eye of the "older" one. Their names were Yoka-duma, also known as Mo'o-mba and Naga-eboko, also known as Nge-kay. I had enough time to ponder because the mai-szreh was behind me some distance away and on the small, windy, and near bushy village road path. It was early in the morning, and the music of the chirping crickets and singing birds gave me an excuse to pretend not to hear.

These mai-szreh were folks I wanted to avoid at all times. By virtue of their birth, there was some mystique attached to them. Whenever our paths crossed, they did most of the talking with me just listening as in a trance, waiting for them to finish. You were wise not to anger them and pretend that they were your friends. Not answering meant that I did not hear him, and after the sharp bend ahead of me, I planned to run fast out of sight by the time he got to the next clearing.

Another reason why I did not have the time to stop and start a chitchat with my mai-szreh ma ndo-meh was because I was on an errand for which I could not afford to be late. I was also aware that these identical twins had been known to cause headaches and other forms of ill health to children who had dared not toe the line in accordance with their wishes. For example, you learned to let them win if you were competing with them; you neither want to commit fouls against them during a football game (soccer) nor would you want to win against their side; you also avoided arguing with them, even if you knew they were wrong.

When I was born in our village of Wo-nya-Mo-ngo, my father gave me a name which could be Bwan-ghai or Moi-ghai, depending on the context or on how you used it in the sentence. For all intents and purposes, these names were to be used interchangeably, but some family members stuck to one form only almost certainly with blatant disregard for the Mo-kpwe grammar or more accurately their lack of knowledge of it. As I grew older, I found myself telling folks my name was Bwan-ghai Moi-ghai when asked or the other way around. Sometimes I only gave one of the names with good reason. One had to have had some deep knowledge of the Mo-kpwe culture and language to know that these names were at once the same but different and to understand their significance, which at face value just seems to be alphabetical.

In our Mo-kpwe culture, names carry meanings both in the physical and spiritual realms, but for the most part, name-givers and owners are ignoramuses. Thus, my people will bear names like *Wolowa* (toilet), *Mai-jah ma Nju-weh* (fox blood), *Njoh-leh* (lizard), *Makao* (the mother cocoyam), *Njoh-ku* (elephant), *Ndi-ma* (blindness), and so on. Suffice it to say, my name means a "hot-headed mystic."

I had a *nya-nga'a litumba weh-va-ru yama iyakeh* (maternal aunty) by the name Nyang'a Likao. I do not know how this nickname came about or who started it. I learned it from my *ndo-m'a molana wa mombaki* (older sister) who, on a day she was in a very good mood, explained the genesis and justification of the name. Because her account had an artistic and phenotypic basis, my internal official position to this name was neutral. I was the errand boy for Nyang'a Likao, fetching her water, cleaning the yard, going to the market for her, and so on. I had many siblings and cousins, but none would subject himself or herself to her services. She was a *nyo-mba molana* (childless) and without a mu-nya-na or husband.

I never was able to find out how we were exactly related or even who her parents or siblings were. It was not customary for parents to give details of extended family members. It sufficed to know that they were your "auntie" or "uncle." It was also considered rude if you insisted on knowing exactly how you were related. You were simply told that was your brother or sister, that was your uncle or auntie. It is also fair to add and say that we as wana were not really interested in such details, and as such, our parents left alone and spared us the details and "agony" that we considered boring. As wana, we also found it really different to comprehend any blood-relatedness that transcended first cousins. Second cousins were known without difficulty only because of or by virtue of proximity; that is, if we knew we were second cousins, it was those who lived in close proximity to us.

We grew up to know Nyang'a Likao as a *Nyango ya litumba* (a family mother) since in our culture, we do not have "aunties." She hardly expressed any gratitude for my services, and any sort of compensation remained wishful thinking on my part. If I did some heavy-duty service like cleaning the whole yard that could take days, then I got "paid" a ridiculously small amount that made my siblings and other cousins laugh at me. My services were taken for granted, and there were days when I longed for her even to offer me some food because I was so hungry, but she never did. When I did some heavy work for her, which was very obvious to all in the village (she had a roadside house) who passed by, for those days, I went hungry for most of the time. My iyaka would not give me food for most of the day, "justifiably" saying that I should have eaten where I had been working. I continued working, though, convinced that it was the right thing to do. Everyone thought of me as some kind of a fool or maybe blamed her for perhaps exploiting me.

On the day I heard my name being called, Nyang'a Likao had sent me on an errand, and I had to return fast, so I hardly had any time to stop and start a long chat with the mai-szreh brother.

With my age and schooling, I left the village eventually and only returned during vacations, for I was in a boarding school. I had come home on one such vacation and arrived at the village at night when most folks were already sleeping. I passed Nyango Likao's house and went to ours. The following morning, I was woken up by noises from her house, and when I looked out, I saw that there were walana moving in and out of her house. So I asked what could be happening and was told that Nyango Likao lost her *ndo-m'a mu-nya-na* (brother), and the walana were assembling to prepare for the Szra-Szra (the third day after death ceremony of my people, the day the departed spirit was finally cut off from the land of the living and sent once and for all to the land of the dead to become an ancestor).

I eventually went to her house full of women and greeted her. She did not respond, and I repeated my greeting, thinking that she did not hear me. Another molana who was in her parlor did respond to me, trying to pepper down the embarrassment somehow. With a swollen head, I left her house.

Ma-meh na-gwe-yi (What have I done)? I thought to myself.

My vacation lasted about three weeks. I did not make any more attempts to visit her, but whenever I passed by her house and she was in front, I threw a greeting her way, which she did well to ignore while obviously murmuring some things to herself. So, after a couple of greetings, I stopped pretending that I was desperate to greet her. Soon I stopped greeting her, even if we met in our village path roads or she was in front of her house as I passed. I had also noticed that my siblings and iyaka were not associating with her. I tried to find out more, but no one offered me an explanation. My last night at home before my return, my iyaka told me the reason.

Nyango Likao had consulted with a Mot'a Yowo that revealed to her the secret behind her childlessness. The root cause was my *mba-mbeh wa molana weh-va-ru ya nyango* (maternal grandmother). My *mba-mbeh wa molana weh-va-ru ya nyango* removed me from her womb and transferred me to her daughter's womb, meaning my iyaka! Proof that I was originally her mua-na or was to have been her mua-na did abound. My working so tirelessly for her without compensation and my being closer to her than all of the other family kids that surrounded her and were "equally" related to her; that is, I was closer to her than all of her other "nieces" and "nephews," a closeness that could only be interpreted as one who was her child. That meant my mba-mbeh, ya molana's *li-emba* (witch), and my iyakeh had stolen from her, preventing me from being even closer to her than I was. This information had spread all over the village while I was away; I therefore returned to a village that looked at me differently. I was a mystical being!

As I returned to my schooling out of town, I kept on wondering what the villagers thought of me and sometimes also wondered if I had any special powers. Thus, my grandmother, my mother, and myself became her enemies, and by extension, enemies of her sympathizers. Several years later, I learned that her claim might have included some more of my other siblings. I did not know what to think about her except to simply keep my distance. In our culture, a *mo-mba-ki* (an elder or older adult) is always right, vis-à-vis a mua-na. While I thought of Nyango Likao's accusations as being clownish, probably borne out of frustration, I did not see or know the very deep rift it had caused the larger family. While my mother summarized it as jealousy, my grandmother was irate and would not even talk about it.

For the adults who "really knew" Nyango Likao, her story of childlessness and barrenness evolved over the years with an additional twist at each stage.

Nyango Likao's late teen years, and up to her thirties, were spent out of the village in faraway Nigeria. When she returned to the village a grown-up woman, she came back an expert of some sort in the Yuruba and Hausa languages, two of three dominant languages in Nigeria. There are a sizable number of Hausas in Buea, and all we seemed to know about their men was that they were not known nor seen to be engaged in any productive economic activities, and therefore, we all were wondering how they managed to survive with their families. They were popular, however, as Wat'o wa Nga-Nga and were considered reliable and effective as compared to the local Mo-kpwe and Grassland

Nga-nga. These Hausa Wat'o wa Yowo were popularly known as Malams and sometimes as "Ma-ghi-da Kai."

Generally, Malams did not get involved in issues of li-emba and nyo-ngo; they concentrated on health issues and aspects of a detective nature; for example, when something disappeared suddenly and mysteriously or was stolen, the way to go was to the Malams to "find out." The Malams were so trusted that the second largest Christian Church in Gbwea (Buea) had to patronize their services at a time when the church was determined to find out how large sums of money disappeared from their vault, a vault that could only be accessed by the three "big men" of the church. While this was considered scandalous by the Christian community and used as capital by political opponents and the government, they seemed to oppose by virtue of their partisan affiliation; the big man trio was adamant. The public never knew the outcome of the "finding out."

Issues of barrenness were another good business for the Malams until increasing their deliverance rate approached the zero limit. Love charms still remain a very popular aspect of their trade and business. In cases where it has not worked, it has been blamed on the client not following the rules associated with the application. A young woman had been known to attack a Malam in his house for a charm failure. The man she wanted to marry ended up marrying her sister instead. The Malam therefore had to refund the money she paid him for non-deliverance.

However, while Malams might have been popular with love charms, the word around was that you must think twice before engaging their services. There was a young molana in town who had taken leave of her senses or had become a Mo-kwa-nyi (gone crazy) because of a charm she wrongly applied. Deaths have also been reported due to misapplied charms acquired from Malams.

A Malam duo arrived in our village from somewhere and rented a two-bedroom apartment from my mba-mbeh wa molana weh-va-ru ya nyango that was attached to my mbambeh's residence. These two Malams had Hausa women visit them now and again from somewhere, and it was not clear what their relationships were. But they were always inside their apartment and had absolutely no interaction whatsoever with anyone in the larger house, the yard, and the village. One main reason for this was that they spoke none of the languages that were understood by those surrounding them. They were "Aucun Anglais Aucun Français (No English, No French)." And then add "Aucun Bakweri Aucun Pidgin (No Bakweri, No Pidgin English)."

It was clearly evident that the property they rented in our village was purely for commercial purposes, and I must add that their clientele pool was not necessarily from our village; in other words, our village was not the target market, but how other clients knew they were now in our yard remained a mystery, at least to us wana of this yard. They may just have been carry-over clients from their previous business premise.

Naturally, we were afraid of these Malams for what they could do to us if we angered them, given that they were wato wa yowo and from entirely a different culture. Aside from their mysterious way of life alien to us village kids, their phenotype and manner of dressing was equally alien. They were tall and lanky, very black, and on either side of their faces and on their jaws were four deep engraved longitudinal lines that stretched from above the ear right down to the chin level. Their teeth were huge and red-brownish by virtue of their continual chewing of *ngoro* (*Cola acuminata*); that is, kola-nuts, like *nya-kas* (Bos taurus africanus; cows) chewing the cud. They dressed in what seemed like seamless gowns or tunics from head to toe, and it would seem they had minimally three atop each other in layers, thus making them a tunic. However, unlike the Wa-kpwe nga-nga we were used to, the cloaks were white, a semblance of white or light blue. Occasionally, their tunics were black accompanied by a turban.

The faces of the Malams were heavily laden with hair. There was facial hair in abundance, eyelashes, eyebrows, moustache, and beards so long that it could have easily touched the nju-ngu or navel. Their manner of talking to each other when they were seen briefly out of their apartment occasionally did not seem to help. All we heard as kids was *kai, kai, kai, kai* in rapid successions and very loud. They were truly aliens.

Our Libiyeah clan landed property bordered our primary school, and it was a matter of time before our class and schoolmates came to know that the center of yowo in our village was hosted by our family.

They even suggested that folks who associated with us should better watch out. Sometimes this worked to our advantage, and at other times, it was certainly a liability that came with isolation.

In less than no time, there was a close association between Nyango Likao and the Malams. She visited them frequently, and we heard them chat excitedly. She became their connection to the rest of the family, the village, and the larger public or clients who eventually were streaming into our village and yard to consult with the Malams. Nyango Likao became an official interpreter for these Wat'o wa Yowo and perhaps therefore part of the business or just a paid facilitator. The Malams, in my understanding, just abruptly stopped being tenants of my mba-mbeh wa molana, just as they mysteriously became tenants of hers, and I am sure they had left for a while before we really knew they had left. I did not like our family being a hub for Wat'o wa Nga-Nga, especially mysterious Malams, and we wana did not feel very comfortable visiting with our mba-mbeh since their arrival. Their departure for whatever reason was therefore a welcome development.

When the Malams left and Nyango Likao tried for several years to conceive but all to no avail, she went to Wat'o wa Yowo to find out. Verdict after verdict was the same as she sought third and even fourth opinions. The reason for not being able to have a child was because of her association and working with the Malams. The Malams had "taken" all of her children from her womb, and she would never be able to bear a child as a molana. The wana removed from her womb by the Malams are now being used by these Malam Nga-ngas to enhance their mystic powers and therefore remain in business. It was an irreversible situation.

Nyango Likao cried bitterly for many days, saying she was just helping, and now see how she had been repaid. What gave Nyango Likao some sort of special status in the village had now become a negative and a liability. The local Nga-nga she consulted went ahead to precisely state that the Malams left just after they did the transfer of her to-be-born wana from her womb to service in their mystical world.

Nyango Likao brooded over this for a while and then decided that there must have been more to this than she knew, and she found it hard to believe that the Malams would want to repay her this way for her meritorious services to their business. She thus started looking for other possible ways of explaining her predicament. As we grew up as children, Mola Professor was our pride. He was a historian of repute at the University of Yaounde, then the only University in Cameroon. A St. Joseph's College, Sasse, graduate and a Mo-kpwe and a member of our extended family (third or fourth cousin), he was perhaps an inadvertent role model to wana in the family who eventually became college or university professors.

An author of many books and academic articles, he was also an expert of Guinea Equitoriale (Equatorial Guinea) history. Nyango Likao was his cousin, and he did not buy this Malam business story resulting in barrenness, and because he was a sympathetic ear, he decided to do something about it. He arranged with a fellow Soban who practiced as an obstetrician and gynecologist to carry out a thorough examination of his ndo-m'a molana.

The examination was simple and straightforward as the fellow Soban physician declared after his examination, due to a previous medical condition, an anatomical destruction occurred to part of Nyango Likao's reproductive system, which prevented a pregnancy. His verdict, therefore, was that a pregnancy was impossible in her lifetime. Nyango Likao was again very distressed, and she was tired of being called a Yomba Molana by just about any woman she had a quarrel with; and quarrel she had, more than enough of her own share. Her quarrelsome repute heralded her, only comparable to that of Nyango Mo-fvu-ngeh.

Nyango Likao stayed in this state of biological impossibility of a conception for a couple of years until she resumed the "finding out" business with newer nga-nga from Ekona Leh-lu (a Mo-kpwe village reputed for the effectiveness and thoroughness of their nga-nga and a land far removed from our own village of Wo-nya-Lyo-nga), and that is when my Mba-mbeh wa molana and my Iyaka came into the theatrics and became middle stage and principal characters. The Ekona Leh-lu trip was actually some kind of a local complementation of information she already obtained from I-je-bo-de, supposedly the yowo or juju capital of Nigeria and Oku known as the yowo capital of the grasslands in the northwest. Thus, the transplant intelligence that Nyango Likao (and eventually Nyango Mo-fvu-ngeh) had from Wat'o wa Yowo far removed from Buea, and these nga-nga did not know each other and, therefore, could not be under the spell of those wa-i-emba they were determined to catch and kill. These nga-nga were also of superior power. Therefore, there was solid proof of the yowo intelligence they had.

Nyango Likao had at one time confided in me when I was slaving at her yard that she had gone to "find out" and was told that all of her problems were caused by someone right under her own roof. As camarade Bwaszra would say, "Le serpent sous mon propre toit."

I did not understand what she meant, neither did I understand where she was going with this from the blues narrative to a mua-na like me. She was the only adult in our family who dared speak to us in another language other than Mo-kpwe. She normally spoke to us in Pidgin, even if she started the conversation by calling out in Mo-kpwe, "Moighai a-weh-li a'ga (Is Moi-ghai there)?"

Nyango Likao was a small business molana with a rare gift for bakery and the making of E-kwa-ko-ko. Ekwakoko is essentially ground *nda-a* (*Xanthosoma sagittifolium;* cocoyams), and it is the traditional dish of the Bakweris or Wa-kpwes. One form of Ekwakoko variously known as E-kwa-kok'a weh-ku, in the Kwa-koko bible, "Endeley bread," or by the younger folks as "Kwa-koko burger" was ground nda-a enriched with fish, crayfish, vegetables, and palm oil, salt, pepper, and other such ingredients tied with leaves from Musa species (plantain or banana) plants, and then cooked by boiling. When cooked, it could be unwrapped and eaten directly, just as one will peel and eat a ripe banana.

This is delicious food to get if prepared by an expert. In Buea, walana make these type of Ekwakako and sell by the roadside, mostly in the evening, and it is a sure hunger quencher with its deliciousness. It is a food you could buy or pick by the roadside as you passed by on foot and you can also be on your bicycle, bike, or sit in your car and make your order. It is the most portable drive-through *wak* (food) in Buea, a balanced diet wrapped in leaves in compact portable format. This is food that was borne of necessity when the Wa-kpwes fought the occupying Germans in Vakoland.

The making of cakes and meat rolls and kwakoko burger were Nyang'a Likao's specialty, and she seemed to have had no rivalry in Buea or at least our village. Her meat rolls and kwakoko were supplied to government offices in Buea during lunch hours, and therefore, she was fairly well-known as "Mami Meat Roll" or "Mami Kwakoko," the name preference being what the caller cherished most. She was also a supplier of her bakery products and kwakoko to many a social occasion in town.

Her woes were also countable, and this became very apparent when her business was going down the hill with age and her physical health. She lived alone all of her life that I knew her. She was the only one in the entire clan who lived such a solitary life. While all other family homes had extended family members living with them—and sometimes even non-Bakwerians living with them as was the case with my immediate family—she was a loner. Her business, church, and local partisan politics consumed her life. When she took leave of those activities or mellowed down her involvement for one reason or another, then she could now fully concentrate on the witches and wizards that were all now, all of sudden, out to get her.

Our homes were close, about thirty to fifty meters apart, so calling out was okay. I suspect the reason she would call in Mo-kpwe instead of Pidgin was because there was always a chance that it was my iyaka who would pick up the call and transmit to me, or in the alternative, inform her of my absence or unavailability.

"You see all dis ma problem dem, like dis ma sick, na Mola Majifu di witch me (My sickness and all other problems are due to Mola Majifu bewitching me)," she would say. And then she would continue to add some more information and details based on revelations by Wat'o wa Yowo. She did not directly say anything to me about her barrenness, although in hindsight or as a Monday morning quarterback, I suspect that was a major point she was trying to raise or, more correctly, the information she was conveying. Of course, all of us wana were wondering why she did not have any children like the rest of the adults in our community. Such conversations when I was toiling for her meant nothing to me; I just wanted to finish the work and go.

So naturally, I did not reply. I must add that unlike what I had said before that all wa-mba-kis within and without our clan that were Wa-kpwes addressed us wana in the Mo-kpwe language—that is, we communicated in the Mo-kpwe language—that was with the exception of Nyang'a Likao. She addressed us in Pidgin more often than not, and therefore, we communicated in Pidgin. Initially, I thought that she was not versed with the Mokpwe language, especially given that she had spent long years outside the village; but then she spoke Mokpwe with her peers, with our parents. Why not us the wana, when every effort was being made by the wambaki to ensure that we were grounded in this aspect of our heritage and especially growing in the village?

A couple of times, I heard her being reprimanded gently by Mola Miszroli who was older than her, "E-wo-wa-ney di e-bo-szra Mokpwe (Let's to talk to them only in the Mokpwe language)." He had said this very firmly but also gently because he was addressing a mombaki in the presence of wana.

"Na-geh wa-weh-li o mboa, e-wo-ko-leh di e-mbo-szra Mokpwe (Now that they are still in the village, let us teach them the Mokpwe language)."

Names were eventually whittled down to three persons in the clan who were responsible for Nyango Likao's problems and woes— My Mba-mbeh, my Iyaka, and Mola Majifu. While she had a "good reason" why my Iyaka and Mba-mbeh were her enemies, she never gave any good reason for Ma-ji-fu being a wizard. She had timidly attributed her ill-health to the Ji-fu-man, and that was all I knew. Over a period of time, I reluctantly attended to her needs, all the while wondering what was going on in her mind. She never mentioned to me directly that I was her "son," but I am sure she knew the information was transmitted to me in its entirety. Only our grandmother really knew how we were related to her, but how related we were; she was family from Wojongo wo Mbeng'a Mboa (down country of the Bakweris). This just further isolated her, alienating those who were close to her. Majifu had gone on an insult spree on her and was fined by the Walana wa Mboa (the village women council) for titikoli crimes.

In our custom and traditions, a mu-nya-na never insults a molana, no matter what. Majifu was not one for conventions; he unleashed his venom on her and threatened physical assault but was stopped by other family members. Our clan paid the Walana wa Mboa council and withdrew the case to be settled as an in-house affair. Even in this family meeting, Majifu was defiant and unapologetic.

A permanent, irreparable enmity and hatred ensued, and until their respective deaths, there was almost no communication and interaction between Nyango Likao and the trio in the Libiyeah clan she had accused of witchcraft, specifically as it pertained to her childlessness, her remaining a spinster, her business not flourishing at a certain point and then turned downhill thereafter, her ill-health that set in when she was advanced in age, and anything thinkable under the sun that came her way and that she considered a negative toward her.

This brought about expected divisions in the clan. She made it very difficult to help her openly, and her very free mouth was also not helpful at all. She was an expert in using her mouth to "wash" others with her words and it was the source of negative propaganda toward individuals and families. Because she was ignored or just plainly pitied, she interpreted it as having an upper hand. Clan members remained mostly respectful to her, but outsiders were not so tolerant. She thus got a dose of her own medicine time and again from non-family members. Her *bad mot* (bad mouth) was legendary.

"Na true say yubi Nyango Likao i-pikin weh ya mbamba mofam for i-belleh (Is it true that you are Nyango Likao's child that your grandmother removed from her womb)?" they would ask me.

This was a question I was asked over and over in the village, at school, and outside the village. I was mute about this and never responded because I did not know what to say. More often than not, the saying that "silence is golden" proved true.

The mai-szreh, Yoka-duma, caught up with me eventually.

"I say eh Moighai, nobi you I di cal'am (Moighai, is it not you I am calling after)?" he said.

"My man, I di hiyop, no tam (I am in a hurry with no time to wait for you)," I replied. I knew this was not a good answer for reasons already listed, but like I already said also, Nyang'a Likao was anxiously waiting for my return from this errand, and she had emphasized and stressed that I had to return immediately from the errand.

"Make you come back now now, no go start play for road," she had said ("Return from your errand immediately," she had emphasized, "do not go start playing along the way.")

With my disrespectful and rude reply to Yoka-duma who was still behind me one or two steps behind, I raised my head and looked forward, and coming in the opposite direction was Naga-eboko. Where one of these mai-szreh was, the other was sure to follow as they were almost inseparable phenotypically, so also were they inseparable in lots of other aspects of their lives.

"I say eh Moighai, na for me tok so (Is it me you talk to like that)?" Yoka-duma asked in an irritated and threatening tone.

While Naga-eboko said nothing, he was looking at me very intently, and his eyes conveyed the message clearly, "You are trapped."

I could not retreat, neither could I progress. My inner person was telling me that I was finished. Physically, these maiszreh were bigger than me, older by at least two years, and evidently more muscular and more powerful. Do not forget that they were mai-szreh (identical twins) also with attributes of mysticism.

"Wona tink say I di fear wona (Do you think I am afraid of you folks)?" I managed to have said to them with a quivering voice, pretending to be bold or courageous, trembling inside me, with a heart rate equal to the bass drum of the Sasse Band and clearly with body fluids that were in a hyperthermic state. Very surprisingly, I seemingly remained calm phenotypically, though I think my knee joints were warbling, even if not externally visible.

"Because dem mof you from one belleh and dem put you for anoda belleh no mean say you get power (That you were transferred from one uterus to another does not make you powerful or invincible)," Naga-eboko said.

"Na wati I do wona (What have I done to you folks)?" I asked them. "Wona jus leave me make I go (Just let me go)," I seem to have pleaded.

They were closing in on me from both directions, and I was already imagining blows landing on face, bleeding gums, kicks in the rear and belly regions, etc. Then as I exchanged the first blows with Naga-eboko, while Yoka-duma strapped me with both hands around my waist with the intent of wrestling me to the ground, a village Mola came by, appearing from the rear direction of me. "Ya nji-anu na mono moloko-szro (Get away from here with your foolishness)!" he roared in a commanding voice.

The village path was small, blocking any other trekker if there was a fight going on, for the fighters must be cleared before any passage was possible or as a mombaki of the village. He could not see mbe-szra fighting and just pretended nothing was happening, for discipline in the village was the collective responsibility of all wam-baki. While I may not have known him well, the mai-szreh did.

"Moighai di a-szra e-ka-yeh (It is Moighai that is seeking for trouble)," Yoka-duma said.

The punching stopped after only the first blows were exchanged, and the *homo sapien's* upper limbs belt around my waist was eased and released, restoring my circulation from a vice-like grip. I was like an animal freed from a trap, not believing my luck.

"E-szra-wie e-ma Moighai a-weh-li di mua-nyo-ngoh wa-nyu (Do not you know that Moighai is your brother)?" The Mola asked them in an admonishing tone.

"Mola Litute, mor-di a-szreh kayeh (He looked for the trouble)," the mai-szreh said in unison. By referring to him as Mola Litute, by calling him by his name, this meant they knew him and he knew them, and therefore, I was the odd one out.

He was my savior. While they talked, I ran like a caged animal released from its captivity. Running like a *kaweh* (Taurotragus derbianus gigas; a hunting species antelope; deer-like mammal that used to abound on the slopes and forests of the Vako) and panting like a *gbwa mo-vao* (hunting Canis lupus familiaris; hunting dog) and a heart pounding like the bass drum of a brass band, I eventually stopped running after about one hundred meters away from the battle scene. I was at last able to catch my breath.

The bleeding gums were secondary, and so was the swollen lower lip the next day. Naga-eboko could not hide his partially closed swollen eye that turned black twenty-four hours later. Word eventually came back to me that they were waiting for me and that next time, there would be no savior for me. This round one made me a miniature hero, having stood and taken on the Naga-eboko and Yoka-duma duo, feared identical twins in our community, and in a way, this was demystifying them. Would I be ready for a second round, and would I survive? Some attributed my victory over the mai-szreh to my own apparent mysticism that surrounded me. It was more like demystification for confirmed mystification.

CHAPTER 6

Nyango Mo-fvu-ngeh

In our village and as probably expected, playmates revolve around similarity in age and not necessarily siblings. My growing up environment was my family and extended family and the small portion of the village that our clan occupied. We did not normally venture outside our borders to go play; instead, other kids came to us.

Mola Miszroli was my Iyaka's *ndomeh wa munyana wa mo-sz-ra-li* (a younger brother of my mother's) and both of our homes—at least in terms of kids playing together—had the most interactions. For the most part, each kid in each family had a counterpart in the other family, i.e. were roughly of the same age. My Mola married a woman from another village (Wo-nya-Mo-fvu-ngu), and in principle, my Mola's molana and my iyaka were *monyas* (sisters-in-law) and *mbounda* (friends) and interacted accordingly. Mola Miszroli was born without one of his upper limbs, and he lost an opposite ear from a gunshot during a hunting expedition for which he was mistaken for a *nyama wanga* (game animal).

Despite the agricultural and other economic opportunities that abound in our land, my people do not seem commercially savvy. The importance of education could therefore not be overemphasized. Schooling was therefore a very important theme in our families and my cousins, and we all went to the same elementary school. We were thus schoolmates and classmates, at least initially. Eventually, as schooling progressed and became harder, my Iyaka's kids apparently were doing better than my Mola's kids.

Mola Miszroli's wife's name was Mofvungeh, which literally meant trouble. Considering that materially, my Mola's family was better to do than ours, it seemed unacceptable and inconceivable that my Iyaka's kids should be doing better at school. While this was socially not acceptable, the root cause needed to be exposed, regardless of the cost.

Mola Miszroli and his molana, Nyango Mo-fvu-ngeh, attended different churches. Mola Miszroli was an elder in his church while Nyango Mofvungeh was the third assistant leader of their Walana group (women's group) in their church. One Sunday, after Mitayli (church service), Mola Miszroli and Nyango Mofvungeh headed to a Mot'a Nga-nga, determined to "find out" what was happening, i.e. seeking an explanation as to why their wana were not doing well at school as compared to economically disadvantaged folks like my siblings and myself. To be sure, the Miszrolis consulted with several Wat'o wa Yowo. The verdicts from the Nga-ngas were consistent and unanimous as they returned to them year after year and/or brought them to the village to fight this injustice and correct the ill.

The reason the Miszroli wana were not doing well at school was because their Libiyeh (intelligence) was "removed" from their brains and transferred onto my Iyaka's kids. Mola Miszroli's iyaka, who is my Iyaka's iyaka and who is also my grand-iyaka was responsible for this transplant of brain knowledge and intelligence from my cousins to us. Therefore, any academic success that my family "enjoyed" was ill-gotten. This had to be fought spiritually and physically by the Miszrolis until the situation was reversed, for nature must take its course.

For several years that followed, the Miszrolis brought in Wat'o wa Yowo for night spiritual work to reverse this brain knowledge transplant or transfer. The decapitated heads of animals were buried in our yards and that of my *mbambeh* (grandmother), and some nights you could tell there was Nga-nga activity in our yard and as confirmed later by my mbambeh and evidence of yowo-related activities in her yard also. Their nga-nga activities included chanting in gibberish (because it was like speaking in tongues in the "Do Me, I Do You" Church in Gbwea), a language that was not Mokpwe; it was said to be a language that belonged to the Bayangis and/or similar folks in the Cross River State of the Federation of Nigeria, the Efiks.

It soured family relationships as the Wat'o wa Yowo got richer with their now annual trips or perhaps as "one can afford" basis, and nothing changed except that the bitter became more bitter and poorer and angrier. After years of trying in vain to reverse the brain knowledge and intelligence transfer, the Miszrolis changed gears. They suffered from several forms of ill-health that were attributed to li-emba. The same Wat'o wa Yowo who had failed to reverse the brain drai, presented themselves as ready and reliable spiritualists capable of taking care of business. Thus, the Miszroli compound was a constant hub for Nga-nga business as often as they could be afforded.

Their ill-health was attributed to my grand-iyaka and iyaka, and all the harm the nga-nga had promised to inflict on my grand-iyaka and iyaka did not materialize while their ill-health state persisted and even got worse. Even their trips to "Bam'da" or "Bameda" in the northwest part of the country, where it was believed they had very powerful Wat'o wa Yowo, yielded no fruits, except to make them poorer, angrier, crankier, and full of bitterness. The "Lightning and Thunder" they paid for to descend like a tornado touchdown and kill their enemies wherever they were, all the way from Bam'da, seemed a huge disappointment, a waste of time, and a toll on the scarce funds. Their success, however, was the social stain they inflicted.

The li-emba and nyongo accusations, you will remember, started with Mola Moliszr'a Moto and Mola Ewang'a Moto. Their leaving the village and/or dying subsequently did not change anything, and as said before, if for anything, all of these problems seemed aggravated with their exit. Then it was the turn of my grand-Iyaka and my Iyaka with such powers as to effect knowledge transplant and also to transplant babies from one uterus to another.

Earlier on, I explained what Teh-Tundey means. You saw a li-emba or nyongo person in your dream or you were told of a li-emba or nyongo person in your life, responsible for all your woes by a hired yowo man. When you identified this le-imba person directly or indirectly, then you went on the attack to make the person and the entire village know that you knew him/her as was revealed, and you were exposing him/her so that the whole village knew the story. Tundeys are done very early in the mornings to the hearing of all and with very little disguise as to who was being addressed.

A tundey could be sung or just simply recited. It requests the li-emba person or persons as the case may be to back off, "remove," or "reverse" the problem they have caused and given a deadline. No compliance meant physical and spiritual attacks of any sort to payback and then extract a pound of flesh. Bewitched persons normally went for the jugular by hiring Wat'o wa Yowo to kill their target revealed.

A tundey we heard more than once was a duo between my mbambeh and Nyango Mofvungeh. They directed their attacks at the people with hilly homes, i.e. those with homes in the upper third of our village. There were only three such homes belonging to Mola Ewangeh, Mola Majifu, and Mola Wotany. Mola Wotany was my *Timba-limba-mbeh wa munyana* (that is, granduncle); a younger brother to my mbambeh and Mola Majifu was therefore his nephew. Mola Wotany married a second wife from another village, and before this molana could move in to settle in our village and as part of our clan, it was an all-open secret that she was a nyongo molana because it was commonplace talk amongst our parents. So, when the duo (my mbambeh and Mofvungeh) Teh-tundey specifically targeted the wat'o with dwellings on the hill, they could not be more specific in referring to my grand Mola Wotany's new molana and Mola Ewangeh. Even a dummy like myself could figure that out.

My mbambeh and Mofvungeh were immediate neighbors with adjacent yards and homes almost touching each other. One early evening, after they had an early morning tundey targeting the hilly dwelling wa-i-emba, Mola Wotany came down from his hilly residence and stationed himself in his *ndomeh wa molana's* (sister's) front yard and directly but indirectly addressed my mbambeh and Nyango Mofvungu.

"You are not fooling anyone by your pretend disguise when you say, 'those with the hilly homes,' for we all know who you are referring to," Mola Wotany began.

He concluded his concise and well-prepared talk by saying, "Those and that which you see in your dreams, you will continue to see." Mola Wotany was a man of few words and also a man to watch carefully if you had any dealings with him. He was a man for himself and his family and strictly that and was viewed with lots of suspicion by all other adults, though I was not aware that he was ever accused of li-emba; but his romance with yowo was well-known and so was his condescending attitude. He had behavioral attitudes and mannerisms that on the surface seemed aloof but beneath was more like a disguised complex. He was a munyana to watch, and yes, you watched your back while dealing with him.

Nobody came out as he spoke, and neither did he get any response from anyone. But his timing was good. He made sure they were all home and they all heard him. Mola Wotany's wife never socialized with any of the walana of the family and did not bother to attend any of the occasional social functions organized for the clan. She probably knew before she came that she was not welcome, a persona non grata, and as far as I remember, no family member of ours was present at their wedding or marriage, which took place at her family home in their village.

Mola Wotany was a hunter who seemed to have specialized on killing antelopes that abounded on the forest slopes of the Fako. Whenever he went hunting with Mola Miszroli and stayed overnight or sometimes two nights, they returned with at least one antelope and sometimes two. Every member of the clan had a small share. Our best part of a hunting trip is the early evening when they had to divide the kill. We had the opportunity to see a real antelope and even touch it and then watched the slaughtering and dividing from start to finish.

Because they were civil servants, Mola Miszroli and Mola Wotany could only afford to do an overnight hunting trip over the weekend for which they returned home late Sunday evening. Their kill was kept on the *woka* (a stand above the fireplace in the kitchen usually constructed to dry materials, plants or animals) in Mola Miszroli's kitchen, and we knew about it in the morning as we went to school from a cousin either from the Miszroli household or the Wotany household. The sharing was therefore normally done on Mondays after the close of business. We spent the whole day in school, anticipating and being very excited, barely waiting to go home and witness the sharing. I remember vividly that the men started arguing amongst themselves before a sharing began, and these wunyana argued all the way as they divided and as they determined which part went to who and which part went to which family and the quantity apportioned to each family. Mola Majifu was normally the chief butcher if present and Mola Wotany the secondary. We were critical of Mola Majifu not going hunting but being at the forefront of the butchering.

It seemed customary that the eldest person in the family apportioned the meat around the chest area and precisely the sternal region. This special portion of the divide was called the *ekuku* (the sternum and its immediate vicinity). One kidney also followed this sternal meat, then the heart, and then any other possible additions. The ekuku, therefore, was naturally apportioned to my mbambeh who was the matriarch of the clan. By the time I got to my preteen years, hunting by Mola Wotany had stopped, and I wondered why. Though it was Mola Miszroli and Mola Wotany who went for the overnight hunting, we knew the real hunter was Mola Wotany with Mola Miszroli being a support.

When I thought that Mola Wotany had stopped hunting, I suspected that he still went hunting but was not necessarily sharing as he did in the yesteryears with the whole clan and after all things were changing. But I also noticed that his wana were no longer associating with us; or rather, their association with the rest of the village clan was limited. They specifically avoided my mbambeh's house, which they used to frequent.

It later on transpired that Mola Wotany had accused his sister, my mbambeh, of li-emba. He supported his accusation based on revelations from Wat'o wa Yowo. For many years, it had been very easy for him to simply just go up the Fvako, spend a night, and just be a professional hunter and was sure to return home the next day with a *kaweh* (*Taurotragus derbianus gigas*; the hunting species of the antelopes that used to abound on the slopes of the Vako); but increasingly, this became difficult and then even more difficult to the point that he returned home empty-handed without a kaweh several times. He therefore consulted with the Wat'o wa Yowo, and as it turned out, the reason was simple. Before he started having difficulties and eventually not killing any kaweh at all, he had brought back home some kaweh in a couple of trips in which the ekuku was not given to his sister. This angered his sister who ensured and saw into it that he was detected by the kaweh miles away, making it impossible for him to be able to make a kill and, in addition, made him antelope blind.

While Mola Wotany's contemporaries were still able to return home with a kill, the celebrated hunter of our clan could not. Thus, Mola Wotany was the first one in the clan to accuse my mbambeh and, for that matter, to accuse any family member of li-emba. My mbambeh went irate, for he brought Mola Watany up and took him along with him when she went for marriage. My mbambeh originated from Mbeng'a Mboa wo Wonjongo (down Mokpwe Country of Wonjongo) and came to Gbwea (Upland Mokpwe Country) for marriage, bringing along her *ndomeh wa munyana wa moszrali* (younger brother), Mola Wotany. She even breastfed Mola Wotany who was about same age as his nephew, Mola Miszroli. Was the tundey about the folks with the hilly homes a payback? And was the visible anger exhibited by Mola Wotany, because of the tundey, a reaction due to him having a taste of the *ekwakoko* (ground *Xanthosoma sagittifolium*, a cultural dish of the Wakpwes)?

I had mentioned earlier that the hilly homes tundeys surely excluded Mola Majifu, the Palmwiner or Kwacharite, and he had a good relationship with his iyaka and *Mofvungeh*, his sister-in-law. Majifu was not a reliable bricklayer by trade. He was sure to be absent from work after pay for a couple of days, and by the time he got paid continuously for three to four months, he abandoned the job completely and lived a social life of "luxury and plenty," which was short-lived.

During these times of plenty, he would dress very smartly and spend most of his time out of the village and out of town. He returned a broke man to his now customary life of *bachelier* or *celibataire*. The palmwine and the kwacha were, however, ever-present to sustain this way of life. Mola Majifu was close to his older brother, Mola Miszroli, so his household, like a few others, catered to him in times of need. Mola Majifu also tried his hands on traditional medicine and subsequently became a Mot'a Yowo himself, offering his services to outsiders. Family members, especially, and other village folks thought of him as a fake, but his clients kept returning, some in thanksgiving for a problem he solved.

I must add quickly here that Mola Majifu's own yowo was not based on casting out, deciphering, or combating li-emba cases. His was to treat ailments using trado-cultural means, based on the knowledge of certain plant extracts and concoctions, knowledge handed down familial lines. With his initial success, he soon advanced to making huge fires all night and adorning himself with black and red tunics that bore effigies of human skulls on the back and *nkwel'a weh-szrey* (human skeleton) that covered the full stretch of the front with the facial bones approximating to his actual face. His nkwel'a weh-sz-rey effigy had a dagger and a calabash oozing with thick smoke of steaming herbs on either hand. Atop his head was a hat rimmed with multicolored feathers interspersed with selected leaves associated with the job. Around his big fire of wood mixed with dry and fresh herbs, his yard was bright in the thick tropical darkness, and the atmosphere was scented with the herbs that constituted part of the fire.

Mola Jifuman would balance a clay pot over one shoulder full of fresh and dried leaves and some other ingredients on a gentle fire with a gentle stream of thick smoke streaming in the night air and long leaves held with the other hand, dance around his burn fire, chanting mystical and representing and exhibiting all the feature characteristics ascribed to the wa-i-emba nga-nga. At the peak of his career, Mola Ewang'a Moto's son remarked that, "One day, this wona uncle go kill we all for this compound waiti di ee medicine (One day your uncle will kill us all with his medicine)." He had told this to my ndomeh wa munyana.

Mola Majifu was a Mot'a Ewangi (rich man) for about a year, and then he lost all his clients. While his ewangi status lasted, and perhaps for the first time in his life since I knew him, he seemed a respected man, even if only superficially. While he basked in his riches, nothing about him changed. His house and other landed property still bore the hallmarks of poverty and long-suffering and was in very bad need of maintenance and sometimes just an upgrade, now that the means seemed to be available. He returned to a life of poverty he was now very accustomed to.

The reason for his failure or demise, we were told, was because he was not supposed to ask for any monetary rewards or payments for his services but rather allow the beneficiaries to reward you (him) as they saw fit. He collected his fees up-front and jacked them up as his clientele increased in number due to his successes. When he became mystical and was by all accounts successful, we thought he had given his heart to the mo-ka-szreh or the devil. With Mola Majifu returning to his ground state and with the Miszrolis determined to continue being victims, Mola Majifu was suddenly declared a Mot'a li-emba by the Miszrolis, and this had been confirmed by several Wat'o wa Yowo they had visited and patronized. As kids, we did not get to know such things until they overflowed or boiled to the surface. I was visiting with my mbambeh, and on entering her house, as I climbed the external staircase, I called out to her, "Ho ho, Ho ho awe-l'aga (Is grandma there)?"

Wana and Membambeh (children and grandchildren) alike, we all called her "Ho ho"—that was it for all family members, regardless of age. One exception, though, Mola Wotany called her "Neneh" (in reverence to an older sister that played a motherly role in his life; it was a traditional respect adhered to by those who were culture-centric).

So, when I called out to her, "Ho ho," my Mola Miszroli thought that it was Mola Majifu who had showed up and was calling. I was surprised that he could not tell the difference between my voice and that of Majifu. Mola Miszroli shot out of his house like a warring spear and stood at the edge of the fence that separated his property from that of his iyaka and immediately started spilling it out. By this time, I was already inside my mbambeh's house, and I suspect that it must have been someone in his household that told him that Majifu was around. He did not bother to verify whether it was Majifu or not as he started releasing his steam. I figured out he had been waiting for this opportunity for a long time, and this also meant that it had been a while since Mola Majifu visited with his iyaka or, if he did recently, it was in the absence of or without the knowledge of his older brother.

Mola Miszroli went on to say, "Majifu heh, Majifu heh. Wa wu-gu-weh di wa-wi-ti (Majifu, Majifu you have just uprooted yourself. That yowo that you have obtained and kept on the moon will end up killing but you instead. You will not be able to harm me nor any of my family members).”

This was the second time wonya Miszrolis were ascertaining that members of their own family clan were capable of placing themselves physically and in out of body form onto the moon, the first charge being with my iyaka. As a lad, I had wondered why the Americans claimed they were the first to land on the moon when this technology seemed to have been in existence for a long time with my people. I had also thought that the crater on the surface of the moon was caused by a crash-landing of the first of my people when this planetary body was first being exploited for habitation. My people had the old science. Proof: the crater on the elowalowa or gwendeh as my people call the moon has close resemblance physically and otherwise with a larger crater that is found at the summit of the Mokpwe Mountain, variously called Fako, Vako, Mount Fako, the chariots of gods, etc. On the Vako dwelleth *E-fva-szra-Moto* (literally means half man and half rock that dwelleth on Mount Vako), the Mokpwe deity in its Three-in-One composition of human, stone, and spirit. In Efvaszra-Moto's physical form, there is a superior and an inferior portion, but it is not known which one is *Mot'a weh-na-ma* (*homo sapiens*) and which part is *liyai* (rock or stone).

The wise Wakpwes of old never revealed this secret, and thus, it has remained. It is, however, known in high spiritual levels that the most powerful yoworites of the Vakoland or Mokpweland are “crater communicants.” But it was a very rare assertion for anyone to claim to have knowledge of the craters, but what was one to make of this declaration by Mola Miszroli claiming to have knowledge that his own brother Mola Majifu is in possession of this ancient secret? And worse still, using these powers to harm and do evil to his own flesh and blood?

There certainly was more background to where Mola Miszroli was coming from, and because I was not privy to the background knowledge or information, I was at a total loss. At this stage, my mbambeh came out of her house, which was on higher grounds, and softly said to his fuming oldest son and first child, “It is not Majifu, it is Bwanghai.”

As expected, Majifu eventually learned of what the Miszrolis thought about him. They had consulted yet another Nga-nga who told them that the problem they submitted or presented to him was caused by Mola Jifuman. They cited what they termed his experiment with a nga-nga profession. He had to sacrifice or give something for him to have the powers that he used for his yowo business. He chose to use the Miszrolis, thereby excelling as a nga-nga man at their expense.

Majifu waited until he was high on the *liya* (palm wine) a couple of nights later, and then, while stationed at her Iyaka's yard, said all sorts of things he could say about his *ndomeh wa munya wa mombaki* (older brother) Mola Miszroli, and his *monya* (sister-in-law), Nyango Mofvungeh. Jifuman repeated aloud what was considered common knowledge in the family and village. He called his brother a weakling, a woman-man who had been cooked by his wife with the assistance of nga-nga men, and now Miszroli had lost his manhood and was an *efulefu* (an empty worthless man) at the whims and caprices of his molana, his molana's brothers, and his wana. Jifuman concluded his apparently well-rehearsed discussion by saying this: "E-neh yoma ya mo-gwe-gwe wo lay-li mo-fvo (This weakling, your head, has been eaten or you have taken leave of your senses)."

Mola Miszroli got so hurt that he reminded him that the land on which Majifu built his house was a gift from him, and as it stood, he was about to ask him to vacate the property. To this, Majifu said, "Oh kwa-nyi mo-fvo (You are mad, or you must have taken leave of your senses)."

"No-whe-ni-teh weh woka yami no keh nja-mbi (If I see you dare make an effort as to attempt to enter my yard, I will cut you with my machetes)," Miszroli continued.

Very harsh words continued to be exchanged between the two *ndomeh ja wunyana* (brothers) until Majifu decided to leave on his own as he had come. Until their respective deaths, there was practically no communication or interaction. There was only a semblance of cooperation and interaction when their iyaka died and the family had to "unite to give her a befitting burial."

This was the second time the Miszrolis had declared that the celestial moon was an abode in which wa-i-emba kept their yowo and/or hid themselves, making them beyond reach of any physicality and/or any spiritual warfare.

After Jifuman, my iyaka automatically was declared a li-emba woman for several reasons by the Miszroli family: Her close association with her own mother, my being transferred from Nyango Likao's womb to hers by her own Iyaka, and by virtue of the fact of my mbambeh transplanting brain knowledge from the Miszroli kids to me and my siblings. My Iyaka was ripe material for li-emba. Thus, li-emba antagonists of my mbambeh seemed, logically, antagonists of my own Iyaka. At the onset, when the Miszrolis had started peddling rumors of Mbamba being a li-emba molana, of course, the wana in the family did not know except those wana whose homes originated the "facts," and therefore, those wana who were the victims.

My mbamba had once told me in an unsolicited conversation and what looked at time as an out of place conversation that once as we, the children of my mother, became "someone" in society and started to take care of our mothers, she would be automatically accused of and labeled a li-emba molana. It took several decades, and my brain went back to that conversation and even more than what she had predicted.

The wonya Miszroli first trip to Bam'da (Bamenda or Bamendrous North) was one of desperation and frustration and also one determined to eliminate their li-emba enemies in the most physically brutal way. The reasons why the local Wat'o wa Yowo could not harm my iyaka was because my Iyaka's yowo or li-emba was hidden in the *e-lo-wa-lo-wa* (also known as gwe-ndeh; that is, the moon) and this justified why nga-nga after nga-nga they contracted were unable to do any harm to my iyaka. Disappointed then, they turned to Bam'da or Bameda where the grassland nga-nga had the reputation of ruthlessness and immediate action no matter where the li-emba person maybe.

The Bam'da nga-nga were yoworites of vengeance. They were reputed to being so powerful that they made use of the first "drones," even before the Americans. These Bam'da yoworites use nature as their weapons and precisely the weather. Thousands of miles away, at any time of the day and any day of the year, they used thunderstorms and tornados to strike down their targets with mathematical, physical, and surgical precision, and all they needed was the target's name. In an attempt to disguise their involvement, when they contracted the grassland nga-nga, they requested that the elimination be done during the rainy season and at night.

In Buea, September and October are the months for very heavy rains accompanied by thunderstorms, tornados, and lightning. Before that rainy season ended, we lost part of our roof and tornados with their accompanying lights that often brightened the inside of our house in the pitch tropical darkness. Nights were very fearful during this season, and how we longed for the daylight and for the storms to stop. While we thought of it and knew it was a natural occurrence—that is, an act of nature—the Miszrolis knew better and otherwise and were just waiting for it to happen. Well, to their chagrin and disappointment, the season came and passed, and no one was hurt, and there was less talk of anyone dying.

Furious, they marched back to Bam'da to confront their killer nga-nga once as the rainy season was over. He was accused of many things, including incompetence, having been bribed by my iyaka, though my iyaka did not know him, did not know of their arrangement, and has never before been to Bam'da, etc. They thus demanded a refund of the 300,000 cfa they had paid him—the price on my Iyaka's life. The Bam'da Mot'a Yowo laughed at them and then reminded them of his modus operandi that they knew too well. He did this by asking them questions. "Wona bi see and heya tunda weh e cam for ye horse (Did you see and hear the thunder that came to her house)?"

"Yes," they answered.

"How many tunda wona be count am (How many thunders did you count)?"

"Three, four or sum tam e pass (Three, four or maybe more times)."

"Nobi wona sabi say tunda di kil na only man weh e get witch (Surely you know that thunder only kills someone who practices and has witchcraft, correct)?"

"But we sabi say e get witch bicos oda juju doctor don see yam (But we know for certain that she has li-emba because other nga-nga like you have confirmed it)," retorted the wonya Miszrolis (Miszroli family) very angrily.

"Da woman no get witch. I send tunda four tam and di tunda no kil e. If da woman bi get witch e for don die quata-quata (That woman does not have li-emba. If she did, she would have been totally dead after I sent four thunders her way). Wona wan gee me anoda name?But this one go bi na anoda arrangement. But before we tok about a new name, wona go pay me extra money for the extra three tunda dem weh I be send'am. Wona be pay me only for one tunda (You could give me another name for a new contract, but before we discuss this new arrangement, you have to pay me for the three extra thunders that I sent, considering that you paid for only one as per our arrangement)."

Nyango Mo-fvu-ngu who had been boiling inside her all this while had it now right above her eyebrows as she exploded, "You dis graffi yowo people dem wona be tif people, Na so so tif weh you di do, but I go show you say I nobi graffi woman, you tif man, you must give we back ma moni, today na today (In Pidgin, today na today means trouble; You yowo folks from the grassland are thieves, it is thievery that you practice all the time, but I will show you that I am not a grassland molana, you thief, you must refund our payment today having failed woefully in the execution of your contract."

At this point, the nga-nga's first wife emerged from somewhere and joined them at the nga-nga's hut or shrine which was about fifty meters lateral to their private residence. She was a biggish, handsome, and muscular woman with signs and characteristics of hard life written all over her. She was pounding fufu for her yoworite husband when she heard the loud, aggressive, disrespectful, and abusive voice of nyango Mofvungu. She also knew that women from Buea where not as respectful to their husbands as the women from Bam'da. While she understood and respected cultural differences, she was not going to allow and tolerate a Buea woman come right into her home to disrespect her husband and discredit his business.

She came out with the mortar stick she was pounding the achu koko with and placed it on her right shoulder as she moved toward the shrine and consulting hut of her husband. Vapor was still emanating from the end of the mortar stick with some of the sticky pounded achu koko (*Colocasia esculenta*) still attached to it in the form of a drawy icicle.

"Madame, you no go cam spoil me business right here for me own horse, you go pay or you no go pay? And for add'am you no go disrespect my masa right here for we own horse (Madame, it is not acceptable that you come here in our home to disrespect my husband and to disrupt our business. Are you going to pay or not)?"

Mami Akakurokata looked wild and was swirling her mortar stick while looking down menacingly on Mofvungeh whom she dwarfed because Nyango Mofvungeh was shorter but still looked formidable with features like a semipro woman wrestler. Height-wise, Nyango Mofvungeh had the semblance and features of a giant pigmy from the eastern regions of Cameroon.

"Mofvungeh, weh-meh nanu jo-o-weh (Let go the agitation and let us talk things out)," Mola Miszroli said to his molana who now creating a scene and rousing the interests of some passersby and neighbors. In her agitated and excited state, full of adrenaline and ready for action, it did not seem she heard his munyana, or if she did, she ignored him as a *mo-gwe-gwe* (weakling) and proceeded to grab the jujuman by his free-flowing tunic around the groin area.

The jujuman was infuriated and said repeatedly, "A chu-chu faga'a, a chu-chu faga'a!" The yoworite was calling on his ghosts powers for restraining against this Mokpwe molana who looked very menacing.

Miszroli kept on saying, "Weh-meh, weh-meh (Let go, let go)."

The Mot'a Yowo's wife's entry into this sacred hut just moved things into higher gear. She started by pounding on the knees of Mofvungeh with her mortar stick, and as Mofvungeh buckled and lost her grip from the yowo man's tunic, she kept on saying, "Iyaka eerr, na-way-li moa-ngoh (Trouble, my mother, I am dead)."

Once Mofvungeh was on the ground, writhing in pain and with no support from Mola Miszroli, the Mot'a Yowo's wife started to drag her out of the yowo hut via Mofvungeh's kawa (a free-flowing gown normally won by the walana wa Wakpwes). But Mofvungeh was no fufu and neither was she a *butuku* (no weakling or walkover). She mustered whatever strength that was left of her, forgetting her pain and, with both hands, tore into the face of her assailant with her long fingernails. The pain was unbearable as the Mot'a Yowo's wife, Mami

Akakurokata, screamed and repeated over and over again, "Grimba agrichi, Grimba agrichi!"

This seemed like incomprehensible mumbo jumbo by the ordinary by stander, but as she was pulled to the ground by Mofvungeh, she used her superior size to lay atop Mofvungeh and started punching her face repeatedly as she repeated the "Grimba agrichi" chant.

Mofvungeh, with aching knees, a broken nose, and seriously bleeding mouth with possibly fallen teeth, continued to punch and to push away this mountainous load of a molana now above her and about to choke the living daylights out of her. Then she was saying as she continued to fight for her life, "Walimo na Weh-kongi weh Phako, Gra-fiszri wa no'o-wa (Spirits of the Vako, grass landers are killing me)!"

And then the yoworite said, "Wona Bakweri Juju no fit reach for here (Your Mokpwe spirits in your Buea Mountain are too far to have any effect here)." He said it in effect to counter her spiritual invocation of the Mokpwe spirits by this rude and daring Mokpwe molana.

As if her cry for help was heard and acted upon immediately by the Vako Spirits, the heavy weight above her was lifted and tossed to one side as she was pulled very roughly by her hair out of the yowo shrine and onto the rough stony terrain that constituted the outside portions of the shrine. As she was dragged outside via her hair, she felt the stones tearing into her flesh and making contact with her bones. Because of the excruciating pain borne of the dragging out of the business shrine and onto the stony terrain outside, she did not know if it was preferable for the heavy weight of Mami Akakurokata to be upon her or to be dragged on these stones. She figured it felt as if she was *Xanthosoma sagittifolium* (cocoyams used for making Ekwakoko) being grated to make the ekwakoko cocoyam paste, an initial step to the preparing of the delicious dish, a signature cultural staple of the Mokwelis. She screamed, "I beg no kill me oh (Please do not kill me)!" she pleaded.

The thunder-control Mot'a Yowo had a second and younger wife whose quarters was further removed from the shrine. She was returning from a morning errand when she noticed that their yard was filling up with a crowd of spectators all around the shrine. When she asked what the problem was, she was told, "Na Bakweri dem wan kill we for ya (It is the Bakweris who want to come kill us here at home)."

And then another added, "Some Bakweri woman and e man dem dey inside there and wan kill ya masa (A Bakweri woman and her husband are inside the shrine, wanting to kill your husband)."

And another added, "Ya second masa dedey for protect ya masa."

In polygamous homes in the grassland or up country, the first wife who is usually older than all other subsequent wives is considered a husband of some sort. In some cases, the first wife chooses the subsequent wives for the husband, and hence, she is of great authority within such a polygamous institution. It was this second wife, Mami Nyanga, younger than Mofvungeh's own *muana wa molana wa woszro* (first daughter) who salvaged the destruction of the shrine and who now was being begged by Mofvungeh, "No kill me ya, I bi ya mami (Do not kill me, I am your mother [meaning, I could be your mother and I have children of your age])."

Mofvungeh said this as the dragging stopped, and they were somewhere around the middle of the courtyard, the younger second wife standing over her, all the while not saying a word.

"You tink say you be who?" Mami Nyanga asked Mofvungeh. "Who do you think you are?" Mofvungeh was asked.

"No brin we dat wona Bakweri witch for ya (Do not bring us your Bakweri witchcraft here)," Mami Nyanga continued to address Nyango Mofvungeh.

The Thunder-Tornado-Controller's yard was now crowded with neighbors who were chatting excitedly and wondering what the heck was going on. All that they seemed to have known is that strangers from Buea had dared to come upcountry to attack a family of their own and, very importantly, a recognized Mot'a Yowo in their community. But then they argued that if a Bakweri couple from Buea could come all the way to attack or antagonize a feared Mot'a Yowo in their community, then what they were witnessing was a yowo type of battle that has now become phenotype and therefore, these Wakpwes from Buea need to be feared.

As it happens, the Thunder-Tornado-Controller Yoworite had lived in Vakoland as a young lad growing and learning his trade with an uncle yoworite who had a large number of clienteles because of his successes. To assert, therefore, his knowledge of the Vakoland and Mokpwes, he said, "I be don stay for Kuna and I be don stay for Masikin weh I learn ma work and I do fine work for ma patient dem, all dat time (I have lived in Ekona [Kuna] and Mile 16 [Masikin] where I learned my trade and attended very well to all those who approached me for my services)."

He stated these facts and made a point to reiterate them to clearly signal that he was no stranger to people of the greater Buea Metropole and that he had lots of interactions with the Wakpwelis. The Yoworite was commonly known and called Massa Fine Boy by his contemporaries who had at one time worked with him at the Tole Tea Estate in Small Soppo in Buea. Then he had only his first wife, and they had a son, commonly called Fine Boy because he was a handsome baby; he was thus named unofficially after his son. When the reputed and wife protected yoworite was making these pronouncements, he was standing over Nyango Mofvungeh who was now somewhere in the middle of his outer compound, surrounded by his two wives and Mofvungeh's husband, and in the periphery of his compound was the gathering crowd as in came spectators as if in an open amphitheater.

A "Cinq Cent-Scout" had come in and separated the women. He said, "Vous êtes en train de causer des désordres publics et de causer des blessures corporelles les uns aux autres. Cela justifie une arrestation (You are causing public disorder and also causing bodily injuries to each other. This warrants an arrest)."

"Scout Cinq Cent, Scout Cinq Cent," the crowd echoed in unison, knowing that all the armed scout wanted was a bribe and was not interested in all he had said. It was the norm. They were called Scout Cinq Cent, meaning Scout 500, because their standard bribe intake was 500 cfa, but if it was something "more serious," then the Cinq Cent became upped to anything depending on what they deemed was the severity and whether they considered you rich or poor. Bribes received by the scouts and/or the men of arms went by various names—makala parti, choko, country fashion, trente-trois (33), motivation, one-man, and so on.

Mola Miszroli and Thunder-Tornado-Nganga, now out of the shrine and kind of dazed at the turn of events and how quickly everything occurred, approached the policeman, pulled him to the side, and did *makala parti* (bribed him) with him. He left shortly thereafter to the ridicule of the crowd without perturbation, for he just earned himself some cash for wearing a uniform of a law enforcement officer via soft extortion. Everyone knew it was makala parti because Miszroli brought out his wallet and tried in vain to conceal it as he chose the bank notes to give to the officer of "peace."

The two men decided to settle things quickly and quietly without involving law enforcement. They both had lots to lose if this event continued to go public any further. It was bad for business for the Thunder-Tornado-Controller, and like I mentioned before, Mola Miszroli was a church elder in Buea and his molana Mofvungeh the third assistant leader of the "Walana wa Ndi-ngeh" women's group in her own church. Being a leader of the "Happy Women's Group" in a church in Buea and what was now happening in Bam'da was not consistent. The men settled business very quickly, and part of the agreement was that the Miszrolis would leave town immediately. And so, they did.

As the Miszrolis left the crowd and the outdoor theater stage they had created and successfully staged, Nyango Mofvungeh said to her Munyana, "O-weh-li di Mo-gwe-gwe (You are a weakling)," and then added, "O-szre-nje di munyana (You are not a man)."

And Mola Miszroli replied, "O-weh-li di yoma ya woweh (You are an evil and bad thing)."

As they were in transit for the next twenty hours, changing buses here and there to return to Buea, there hardly were any words exchanged between the couple. Details of their mission and drama in Bam'da remained their secret until leaked out when Mofvungeh decided to spill her guts on a friend in their church, and then the chain reaction started. When it got to the official ears in their respective congregations, it was but a matter of time, and they both lost their leadership positions in their respective local churches.

For Mofvungeh, she was all so worked up that her body and soul seemed to be aching for action. No sooner after she lost her women's leadership in church as a third assistant, she met Mola Wotany's wife in the local market and proceeded to provoke her and call her a witch to the embarrassment of everyone. In the heat of the exchange of words between both women, a crowd had gathered, as expected, and even the market master had to intervene with the urge to avoid disrupting the normal flow of business.

While this achieved a temporary peace, Mofvungeh cornered yet again Mola Wotany's wife in another corner of the market where palm oil was sold. She continued her verbal assault on the person of Mola Wotany's wife and then went as far as poking her on the chest, challenging her to a fight. Nyango Mofvungeh used stork fish, or Mokajo as was commonly known, to poke at Nyango Maloke, i.e. Mola Wotany's molana.

Nyango Maloke's crime was simple and straightforward. Mofvungeh saw her in her dream, and she inhabited one of the hilly homes. In addition, Mofvungeh's grandson became ill with fever caused by the malaria parasite, and in Mofvungeh's *dohtor* (dream), her *mo-mba-mba* (grandchild) only became ill after a visit by Nyango Maloke. Before Nyango Maloke was attacked in the Buea Market, Nyango Mofvungeh had done a tundey round on her, which was ignored and considered rantings of a troubled soul if not derangement. But Nyango Maloke was not expecting being accosted in the open, especially in a market setting. She had underestimated Mofvungeh by assuming that some level of decorum was still left in her. It turned out that shame, embarrassment, and making one's self a public nuisance meant nothing to her.

Mokajo is imported from the Nordic countries whole, except for the head, and at one time, there were rumors in Buea that this fish type had but human heads with beard and hair; that was why we never saw the heads. But for those who know mokajo, you will recall that it is some kind of an import super-dried fish and therefore very hard, comparable to perhaps a stone or, more correctly, a piece of dry wood. An average mokajo was also about the length of the upper limb of an adult. Mokajo could therefore be a perfect weapon if one chose to use it as such.

Nyango Mofvungeh decided to use the mokajo she bought for her home consumption as a weapon against Nyango Maloke by using it to poke her in the chest. She poked her so hard that her adversary tilted backward but quickly regained her anatomical position as she was caught by those women behind her. Nyango Maloke, Mola Wotany's molana, was a very quiet woman who seemed to cherish a peaceful life rather than a confrontational one. At least, that is what one saw phenotypically. But evidently, she also knew just too well that "peace at all costs is no peace." So, when nyango Mofvungeh violated her personal space and almost knocked her down, she knew Mofvungeh would stop at nothing. She therefore wasted no time as she caught Mofvungeh off guard.

She swiftly slammed her market bag containing items bought already onto Mofvungeh's face, and as she lost balance and her sight during those temporal and blinding moments and still had the element of surprise on her side, Nyango Maloke stooped and lifted the nearest barrel of palm oil and rapidly proceeded to pour it all over Mofvungeh, starting from her hair down. Mofvungeh now sprawled on the stony and dirty floor of the market, and specifically this portion of the market with its greasy soil, attempted to raise her herself up, mustering all of her strength, and perhaps thinking of the Bam'da episode.

Nyango Maloke was not about to let go of this advantage she had. She launched herself onto Nyango Mofvungeh, landed on her, but Mofvungeh easily pushed her off of herself as both antagonists resumed their respective anatomical positions. Once upright, they were both locked in each other's embrace, pulling of hair, scratching faces, tearing at kawas as Mofvungeh kept muttering unintelligible words, like *akirichacha, mifiareh, sokosoko, angwarachiria*, etc.

None of those words were Mokpwe, Pidgin, French, nor English, except perhaps some spiritual invocation known only to her and her peers. Nyango Mofvungeh was shorter, fatter, and sturdier—the perfect build for a wrestler—as compared to the lanky and tall Nyango Maloke. Nyango Mofvungeh therefore wasted no time in wrestling down Maloke. The duo rolled over each other interchangeably on the dirty floor of the market, the oil, and the mud coating their kawas and their hair. As they rolled from corner to corner, they clashed into other women's "market" (i.e. the goods they were selling). As they rolled over, the crowd now gathered and cheered as these women exposed what was beneath their kawas.

Nyango Mofvungeh seemed ready for this event, so underneath her exposed kawa, she had a pair of khaki shorts at knee level. Nyango Maloke, on the other hand, evidently ill-prepared, had her underpants exposed to the public, and two men in the crowd giggled and exchanged words excitedly, but a woman next to them turned and said to them, "Eye no di shoot beef (meaning, for your eyes only)."

Maloke, however, determined to put this embarrassment to an end very quickly, scooped a handful of dirty soil and applied it onto Mofvungeh's face, and as Mofvungeh struggled to clean her face and mouth of the dirt they contained, Maloke disengaged herself to effect her next plan.

While rolling and fighting was going on, the Bakweri and Wajili (non-Bakweri) walana were divided in their opinions, or rather, in what should be their role or next course of action.

Some Bakweri Women said, "Let's separate them" and yet others, "Let's leave them alone and then see what will happen."

The Wajili Women said, "Wetin dis Bakweri woman dem wan show we (What is it that these Bakweri women want to show us)?"

"Make we lef dem fight (Let's leave them alone to fight)."

"Dat short one di fine palava (The shorter one is troublesome)."

"I tink say dem don take dat short one for nyongo. Na die e wan die so E-jus di look for man weh e go kill e' (I think the short one has already been given to nyongo. She is just now looking for someone to kill her)?"

They were all hands off then, allowing the fighting women to take their drama to a logical conclusion. Across the palm oil stands was the yam stand. Nyango Maloke quickly rushed over and grabbed a yam almost the length of her arm but slim enough to be used as a weapon conveniently, and despite the protest by the yam seller and the palm oil owner, Nyango Maloke, it seemed, was on auto drive. She took the yam weapon and rushed back to Mofvungeh, just as she was about to straighten her back and ask for help because she could not see. Maloke slammed the yam directly onto her face, and two incisors came flying out as blood splattered, and the crowd went wild with excitement and anticipation of the next move. She hit her again behind the neck and the back as Nyango Mofvungeh lay flat on her stomach, lifeless. The last words she said before she went lifeless or unconscious were, "Ono-way na li-ngi li-emba l'agoh (Kill me with that, you witch). Mami witch di kill me ooh (I am being killed by a witch)."

"Eneh yoma, noo-way i-ba-veh na way (This thing let me kill you so that I can die also)," said Nyango Maloke.

Afraid that she may die or be dead already, a relation of Nyango Mofvungeh who had been watching the saga as part of the crowd became alarmed. She removed her *ya-ngi-szri* (headscarf) and tied it around her waist over her kawa as was characteristic of Walana wa Wakpwe, preparing for some action. She pushed and elbowed her way through the crowd as she exclaimed repeatedly, "Tata koko eh, Neni Moa-ngo (My father, I have seen trouble)! Iyaka koko eh, Neni Mao-ngo (My mother, I have seen trouble)! Gbwea ejeh eh (Buea come and see and be witnesses)!"

As she got to Nyango Maloke, she *kemad* her (she shoved her aside with her shoulder) and then pushed her off Mofvungeh who was still being punched by Maloke who seemed to be pouring out all of her pent-up anger for so long in the face in continuous provocation. Maloke rolled over, and Mofvungeh's relation pinned her to the ground between her lower limbs with her knees firmly pinned to the ground, her thighs acting as vices to Maloke's lower limbs. Maloke did not resist her captivity and confinement, and her captor kept on asking, "Wa-szra di li-mo'o-wa, Wa-szra di li-mo'o-wa (You want to kill her, you want to kill her)?"

Maloke, now alarmed, found herself asking, "Ama-wa ama-wa (Is she dead is she dead)? A-way-li jokeh-jokeh (Is she truly dead)?"

Both walana were now crying loudly in their entangled form as they asked themselves these questions. It looked more like they wanted some kind of reassurance from each other that she was still alive. Two uniformed law enforcement officers who were in the market were entreated by the Market Master to intervene and stem this madness of these walana. The officers complied, and upon arrival at the scene, each fired into the air with their respective pistols, quietened the crowd, and caught the attention of the antagonists. They separated the entangled women. Maloke exhibited a clearly bleeding eye and a right side of the face that was beginning to swell already. Mofvungeh lay almost lifeless to one side. One of the two law enforcers was a scout Cinq Cent, and the other was a "Menofarms Mile Franc." Makala parti was made with the manofarm to his satisfaction while the Cinq Cent was not content with the makala parti that came his way; he wanted more choko. He took the makala parti but insisted on an arrest.

The Market Master a Buea Council or Local Government official made the makala parti because he would rather not have to deal with the judicial scouts and menofarms offices if an arrest was made, which would need his written statement and testimony and accompanying donations or gifts if he was to "clear" his name and avoid making repeated trips to these offices because it just meant more required and expected dictated contributions, donations, or gifts and a waste of time with no justice agenda but an avenue for the scouts and menofarms (the peace officers) to enrich themselves.

As Nyango Maloke was pinned down, the whole market was in chaos. As the walana were fighting, rolling over each other as they, at the same time, were displacing others. Caged and tied life animals were set free and scattered themselves in all directions as the owners and their assistants scrambled to bring them back to the fold. The displaced animals, tasting their freedom ran in a zigzag manner because they encountered humans and other obstacles in each and all directions and, therefore, changed directions all the time, looking for a direction that would lead them to freedom. It was not clear if the marketers were being chased by the freed animals or if the marketers were just running out of fright and the excitement of the moment. This chaos that led to a market in frantic mood was caused by freed chickens from their *kejas* (cages), goats and pigs from their tethering robes, and snakes that managed to crawl out of their cages.

In fact, a freed snake crawled into a woman's market bag, and she picked up her bag unknowingly as she fled from the scene. As she was running away from the scene with her market bag strapped to her shoulder, the snake, in an attempt to free itself from what seemed like a second prison, hoisted its head out of the open bag, and its head was dangling above the woman's shoulders from behind. Oblivious of what was happening, she was simply interested in running as far as possible away from the craziness that was taking place in the market. She never understood why everyone, and everybody was making way for her or was running away from her.

This molana eventually exited the market premises and was headed to her home that was just 200 meters away from the eluwa (market). On her way home, she continued to observe that everyone one she passed or approached seemed eager to make a clear path for her. This did not really register because she was moving very fast and sometimes running just so that she could get home. As she approached the perimeter to her home, she slowed down naturally with almost a sigh of relief. Certain members of her family were in the front yard, and instead of them welcoming her home, they all dispersed as she called after them. She called the oldest child in the group in particular.

"Li-wo-ndeh, Li-wo-ndeh, mameh ewan-ge-ya (Liwondeh, Liwondeh, why are you folks running)?"

"You have a snake on your shoulder," the youngest of them, Likowo, replied while hiding in a safe distance.

At this point, Nyango Njoh-leh, turned her head over her right shoulder, and the *gbwawa* (snake) licked her jaw. She fainted.

Despite the makala parti, Nyango Maloke was arrested for attempted murder but, two days later, was released by the scouts without charge because the Market Master and many other women streamed to the scout station to testify on her behalf. Also to avoid a court case, Mola Miszroli settled with all the market women whose "market" was spilled or destroyed as a result of the fight instigated, orchestrated and executed by his molana as arranged by the Market Master. Miszroli also did makala parti to the menofarms and scouts involved with the case. Their only complaint was that the amount was small and reminded Mola Miszroli that if they decided to write an official report, this was going to be a court matter, and it would mean jail time for Nyango Mofvungeh and a huge fine.

"Nous vous faisons une faveur (We are doing you a favor)," the menofarms said.

When lower market street scouts take a case up to the upper market street scouts, they are considered good and worthy scouts because they are ensuring that upper market street-chop scouts get their own share of the makala parti, and these types of consideration and loyalty on their part ensures that they remain being posted as lower market street chop-chop enforcers of choko. It was "scratch my back, I scratch your back." It was the lower market street scouts that encountered and interacted with the market or main streeters.

Mofvungeh was rushed to the hospital where she remained in a coma for two weeks and then woke up suddenly. Mofvungeh and Maloke attended the same church (when Mofvungeh was excommunicated from her former church, she joined her husband in his church, which was the Church attended by Nyango Maloke), so when Mofvungeh was able to return to church three months after the market event, she demanded that Maloke be sanctioned and excommunicated from the church because of what she did to her, almost killing her. The pastor referred the issue to the elders who returned a verdict of self-defense on the part of Maloke and, therefore, a no guilty verdict. Instead, the elders went further to demand that Mofvungeh be of a Christian behavior henceforth or be removed from the church. Specifically, she was barred from holy communion for one year, and if she involved herself in any unchristian behavior within the stipulated period of time, she would be expelled from the church.

Mofvungeh cried foul and instead left the church before she was booted out. She thus left her second church and joined her third church in Buea, the church'a Mio-dor, also known as the Do Me I Do You Church. This was a very liberal church that prided itself of having an open-door policy where all are welcomed, but despite their reputation, Nyango Mofvungeh was received with lots of skepticism. The Buea Church'a Mio-dor was also very tolerant with parishioners that wore spiritual protections prescribed and designed by Wat'o wa Nga-Nga. Thus, their members wore charms, talismans, and even carried small bundles of calabashes filled with yowonized concoctions tied around their waists. They looked like cowboys with gun belt bands around their waist for their shorthand pistols. The pistol, in the case of the Church'a Mio-dor faithful, was the calabash. Some members of the church'a mio-dor simply wore their yowo as necklaces.

Once, as Nyango Mofvungeh returned home from the hospital, recovering rapidly from a coma, Nyango Maloke was moving out. She had been transporting her belongings by night from her husband's home back to her family home as she returned to her husband's from police detention. On her last night, as she made the last trip passing down by our house, she called out to my iyaka, "Mo-szro-ni, Mo-szro-ni."

My iyaka was a younger woman as compared to her, so she normally just referred to her by her name. Such occasions were rare because she normally did not interact with the rest of the family, but it was difficult for her not to maintain some level of interaction with my Iyaka when she made the occasional trips down past our house. When my Iyaka responded, she said, "Imba Na'a ti-mba o litumba l'ami (I am returning to my family)."

"E-li-ya-nay litumba la-nyu (You people should stay with your family)."

"A-nu-di mo-ka-szreh a-weh-ni ma'a-da may-ni. (It is in this family that satan has his abode)."

My Iyaka then responded, "Weh-deh di gbwamu Nyango Maloke (Go well, Nyango Maloke)."

"Mo-ka-szreh ao loo (Satan has great powers). Wa-moh-moh o-weh-ni e-veh-veh eki, mba-veh szroh (You are lucky you have an alternative to this madness and evil that has befallen us. how about me)?"

My Iyaka murmured to herself. Her frustrations and resignation could not be any more evident.

Nyango Maloke was a childless, tall, fair-skinned molana who minded her business and kept to herself. She did not associate with her in-laws in any way and made frequent trips back to her family that were located east of our clan, about two miles away, in a village called Molikiliki, a stony and hilly village. It seemed to me, therefore, that the only reason she was a target was because she was one of those that inhabited a hilly house. Mofvungeh had seen her in dreams or yowo visions as being responsible for the illness of her *mo mbambeh* (grandchild) who suffered from persistent fever caused by the malaria parasite (Plasmodium falciparum) and transmitted by the female *Anopheles* mosquitoes, a very common occurrence, especially in the rainy season when there is an abundance of standing freshwater pools for breeding. Nyango Maloke was also blamed for Mofvungeh's continuous ill-health state, and Mofvungeh, seeing Maloke in her dreams, even when she slept during the daytime, was also a problem. Nyango Maloke's isolation from the family was itself a recipe for being a li-emba molana.

Nyango Mofvungeh and Ho ho were blessed with children, but not Nyango Maloke. The childless molana thus became a target.

My mbambeh too had her own problems with li-emba. As she grew older, she became a sickling with pain just about all over her body, especially her hands and legs. She barely slept at night and outright had a case of insomnia. But as she lay awake at night when others were sleeping, that is when the wa-i-emba came to bewitch her. She described scenarios of some heavy thing failing in the ceiling and movement back and forth in the ceiling. I thought it was rats and cats playing survival games in there, but what did I know? My mbambeh did not accuse anyone within the family for her li-emba woes, the family for which she was the clan's matriarch.

By this time, I was living with my mbamba, providing her with some sort of physical protection and some level of company. It also meant that I heard lots of things that made absolutely no sense to me, but I somehow was obliged to sit and listen. I knew we had lots of rats around, but so were the cats also that would gladly feast on the rats. So, what my mbamba was describing as bundle of "witches" falling onto her ceiling with a large voice, I will describe more like a cat trying its luck and pouncing onto a rat for a meal. My Mbamba's sickness was attributed to lots of people around, mostly other walana. The "bundle falling" onto her ceiling was the medicine they used to inflict the illnesses on her.

My Mbamba was recipe for bewitching as she has herself told me and went further to say it was a matter of time before it was my Iyaka's turn. The reason why wa-i-embas were out to get her was simple. She has successful children that cared for her and made her life good. When she was suffering with them, no one helped. Now she has become a target of jealousy and hate, folks wanting to kill her. Her general state of ill-health, the dreams or "visions" she has been seeing, and the things (li-wa-nya—a small clay pot containing an assortment of biotic and abiotic collections that are characteristic of wa-i-emba toward a target and as revealed by the nga-nga) were all irrefutable proofs. Like I earlier said, what she knew was a li-wa-nya dropped on her ceiling right above her bed, I thought was a cat and rat dinner game for life. She was surely disappointed when I did not confirm several times that what I heard or was supposed to have heard was something in connection with yowo.

Successively, her wa-i-emba culprits were a third or fourth cousin of hers, an elderly jet-black molana that called her Neneh. Neneh is reverence for a younger sibling to an older female sibling, i.e. a title of respect. This molana called Jej'a Njoku, had her own house next to Ho ho's to the east side, and it was only a footpath or less than half a meter wide that separated both their properties. She was an in-law brought into the clan by a great-grand mola we never knew but only heard of. Jej'a Njoh-ku, I could see, tried all in her will to be and remain respectful and at the same time bear the burden and shame of being labeled a witch.

As it happened Jej'a Njoh-ku did not only end with Ho ho; she extended her bewitching to Nyango Mofvungeh who too suffered greatly from her hands, her health, children not doing well at school, children, and grandchildren being sick and so much more. Thus, Ho ho and Mofvungeh teamed up in their early morning tundeys a couple of times addressing Jej'a Njoku, not so covertly bewitching them, and directly making reference to her very dark complexion, her mannish as opposed to feminine physique, her elevated house, her travels and foreign mannerisms.

Njej'a Njoh-ku spent all of her youth and most of her adult life in Calabar in the Federation of Nigeria and only returned to the village from which she technically exiled herself during her retirement age. She came back with ideas not so accustomed to the village and was the first villager in our portion of the village to start a small commercial business. She had a house built of stones in sloppy terrain. Thus, the architecture was such that instead of doing lots of filling on the south side, rather small stalls were made intended for a poultry or a piggery (pigsty, pigpen). This stone house, similar to that of Mola Moliszr'a Moto, was never finished just like Moliszreh's. However, her own stone house was bigger, well-planned, and seemed to have had a plan from the outset, not just a big hall with partitions as seemed to have been the case with the Moliszra house.

Whenever Jej'a Njoh-ku was a target of tundey by Ho ho and Nyango Mofvungeh, I was uncomfortable for the next couple of days passing Njej'a Njoh-ku's roadhouse and greeting her when we both knew that I came from a home that considered her a witch and called her out to it repeatedly and openly. How I wished it was not so because I seemed to feel the shame, embarrassment, and isolation and the other things that came with it. Ho ho and Mofvungeh could not be wrong because they had consulted with Wat'o wa Yowo and also had their *dohtors* ("visions" or dreams) as ironclad proof. My mbambeh had seen and heard me greet Nyango Njej'a Njoh-ku as I passed her house, and on my return, she asked me, "O-szra wi oma ogo molana di ano-la'a li-emba (Don't you know that it is that woman who is bewitching me)?"

There was no answer on my part because I knew exactly why she asked. I stopped greeting Nyango Njej'a Njoku if my mbambeh was in sight and within earshot. It did not take long before Njej'a Njoku knew that I avoided her gaze and pretended not to see her when Ho ho was around. Once, as I pretended I did not see her and was hurriedly passing by, I lifted my head for one split second, and our eyes locked. I was indeed conflicted. Could I also attribute my own problems to witchcraft? Because for sure, I had my own problems.

As time went on, Ho ho's list increased to add another molana who lived in the east side of the village and who was the wife of a relatively distant relation of hers. But before Jej'a Njoku and the east village molana, Ho ho's list of bewitchers included the two wa-i-embas with the hilly homes. Comme d'habitude, and as expected, Ho ho delved deeper and deeper into the world of the Wat'o wa Yowo who removed liwanya after liwanya, prescribed remedies, only to return again and again to remove another one, perhaps planted by the Mot'a Yowo himself previously. They knew my mbambeh was rich for a village woman, so nga-nga after nga-nga were determined to have their share and their cut of the cake. Her source of cash or funds was what was called in Pidgin "Elephant Beef," and as the saying goes, "Elephant beef nodi finish" (Elephant meat is limitless and unfinishable).

She bought sacrificial animals as demanded by the nga-nga, alcoholic beverages, clothing, and other accessories, plus the huge fee that came with sleeping out in the dark cold nights in a makeshift tent or, better still, in the goat or fowl house. I must also mention that she cooked elaborately for them like one does for a feast. We were sure to eat specially made delicious, expensive, trado Mokpwe food prepared by a master chef, my mbambeh, our Ho-ho. They made a fortune out of her as her misery skyrocketed and as her foolery remained hidden from her. She was, however, adamant in believing that several women have a cohort determined to make her suffer because her children were successful and rich, and she would quickly add that when she was suffering to raise them, they did not help, and now they are dangerously jealous and wanted to kill her.

In this chat between my mbambeh and me, she also predicted that once, as we finished schooling and became financially viable, making our iyaka economically comfortable, she would become the target of wa-i-emba and she would also be accused of li-emba. My mbambeh, in her wisdom, could not have been more predictive. My iyaka became a mue-mba (witch), just as her children became economically viable to take of her necessary economic needs with spare change and once as a modern house with technological gadgets were made available to her.

The ill-health and all the other misfortunes suffered by the Miszroli family increased, and so were the culprits and the li-emba club within the family enlarged.

The persistent problems for the Miszroli family were ill-health, children performing poorly at school, graduated children not getting jobs, and their eldest daughter and child of marriage age not getting a husband. Somehow, Mofvungeh convinced Ho ho to accompany her to a Mot'a Yowo and took along with them Mofvungeh's oldest son. There were three things they had to find out—why Mofvungeh's oldest son was not passing his higher exams, why he had problems at his current job, and why this son had a persistent cough that caused lots of concern for the family.

It is noted that this son was a chain-smoker, and you could smell the tobacco scent emanating from him or his breath far away and the familiar "pop" cough sound. When they got to the yoworite, they mixed some concoction and gave him the drink, and he was apparently supposed to have vomited the mixture without problems. He failed to vomit the mixture, his eyes bulging and popping out like a toad's, and he complained of stomach discomfort. They returned from their secret mission without details, but it was not long before Mofvungeh started spilling out her guts.

It was a matter of time before the clan knew the real reason for this secret yowo trip by the trio. Before this trip, Nyango Mofvungeh had made some other yowo trips consulting with nga-ngas about her son. These earlier trips to the wato wa yowo determined and concluded that the woes of Mofvungu's son were directly attributable to the nefarious bewitching activities of Ho ho. To secure iron-clad proof, the yowo man they visited to find out had insisted that Ho ho be brought to him and that he was going to prove it. Now Mofvungeh is accusing Ho ho of directly wanting to kill her son shamelessly in front of her by blocking her son from vomiting the Kwa-weh concoction that he was given.

Kwa-weh was a fruit that was used to determine witches and wizards in Mokpweland. Extracts of the fruits were made, and the accused made to drink it. If the accused did not vomit it, then he or she was guilty of li-emba, and the muemba (witch or wizard) was exiled from the village. They were normally exiled to Voo (Limbe), which means "far." Voo is lower Bakweriland at the coast of the Southern Atlantic Ocean. I therefore do not understand why the kwaweh was not given to Ho-ho but rather to Mofvungeh's son. And by Mokpwe culture, as it concerns spiritual matters of li-emba, the guilty one was Mufvungeh's son and not my mbambeh.

Mofvungeh had finally established that Ho ho was a muemba and she, Mofvungeh, had the latest and very direct proof that Ho ho was a witch. She also made it known to any willing ear that the reason why her daughter was not getting a husband was because Ho ho had covered her face with a black cloth, making it impossible for prospective wunyana to see her face and therefore ask her hand in marriage. To compound the problem, Ho ho's son that is Mofvungeh's munyana also had seen some visions like his molana of Ho ho, so it was not just her daughter-in-law accusing her but also her own son for tormenting and destroying his family.

Mofvungu, once tundey buddies with Ho ho, now could not stand each other as Mofvungu did not spare any chance of telling any willing ear what a mueba molana Ho ho was and how my mbambeh has tormented her and her family. Ho ho and Mola Miszroli too now became estranged. Mola Miszroli contended that if Ho ho did not have li-emba, then it was his son, Mola Majifu, who was wearing her image and going out with her in spiritual li-emba disguise to bewitch people; that is why the Wat'o wa Yowo always saw her as a molana muemba. This was his best-case scenario, i.e., if Ho ho was not the one truly seen by these Wat'o wa Nga-Nga who had continuously seen her as the molana bewitching the Miszroli family. Mokweli powers are limitless, especially in the realm of spirituality. A strong Mokpwe nga-nga, yoworite, or muemba could "wear" another person's visage or image and look phenotypically identical. Underneath will be another person with the powers while externally will be another person, an innocent person who will be the one seen, who will be blamed and take the fall. It takes an equally very powerful nga-nga to unmask the real power or person beneath the phenotype.

Thus, Mola Miszroli, not being very comfortable accusing his iyaka of witchcraft, had an alternative "theory." It was Mola Majifu that was wearing her mother and *wu-szra-na* (go out) with her when he wanted to bewitch someone, and since as Mola Miszroli was cocksure that Mola Majifu was a muemba, this was a plausible alternative, placatory enough for the two walana very important in his life.

Mofvungu succeeded in turning a *muana munyana* (son) against an *iyaka* (mother) after she had succeeded in turning this muana wa munyana against his *ndomeh wa munayana moszrali* (younger brother), *ndomeh wa molana moszrali* (younger sister), a *molalo* (uncle), and many others outside the immediate clan. Ho ho was eventually removed from her home of long years by his muana, the Mola Blokeh, and resettled to another part of the village where he had his property. Mola Miszroli's siblings were distraught and concluded the best way forward was to not say a word or even call a family meeting concerning this issue because it would have been "bloody," they said, if they addressed their brother and their sister-in-law.

Between Ho ho and the Miszroli family, there was enmity till death. She had absolutely no association whatsoever with Mofvungeh once as she was relocated until her death. Mola Miszroli was Ho ho's oldest child in our village, so after her relocation to her younger son's property in the other side of the village, Miszroli sometimes passed by to say "hello" to his mother. Mola Blokeh banned Nyango Mofvungeh from ever thinking of setting foot onto his property. Mola Miszroli, the oldest of the family, became estranged with his whole family. But they had not seen the end, and their list of wa-i-em-bas had to increase. The Miszroli search was far from being over. Mofvungeh remained a major player and a center-stage personage.

CHAPTER 7

Rza-ngo Ekumut'a Njila

Mo-fvu-ngeh was known as far away as in Bam'da (a.k.a. Bamenda or Bameda), and while the rest of our village knew her or had heard of her, her tu-ndey and targets were limited to our part of the village and very specifically within familial territory. But why should that be enough when she continued to be a victim?

Mola Wotany had a *mbu-nda* (friend) that lived on the eastern lower elevation of our village, called Mola E-ku-mu-t'a Njila. Szra-ngo E-ku-mu-t'a Njila was a soft-spoken man who had retired as an Animal Control Officer for the City of Buea. He dressed even when not on duty in a paramilitary style, and we as kids thought of him as some sort of a Mbeh-lay or a policeman. Shortly after his retirement, Mola E-ku-mu-ti's molana, Nya-ngo I-tor-tor-weh died suddenly. She had returned from the market and was seated just outside the door of her kitchen, starting to prepare a meal, when she slumped and died almost immediately.

When the news broke, the whole village seemed to have been affected and also seemed to have been taken by surprise. The first villagers who reached Szra-ngo E-ku-mu-ti's home and happened to have touched the body of the just deceased declared that it was still "warm." This warmth was to be an integral and central part of the narrative that followed in relation to this sudden death.

The warmness of the body and the blood that oozed out of her nostrils were key and cornerstone factors related to her death. The in-law relationship between the E-ku-mu-ti and I-tor-tor-woh families from the first day of their marriage could best be described as tortuous. They had been married for twenty years, and within this period of time, the I-tor-tor-woh family had spared no opportunity to remind Szra-ngo E-ku-mu-t'a Njila that he came from a li-emba family and therefore should watch out and make sure nothing happened to their daughter. The I-tor-tor-woh family had objected vehemently to their marriage, but I-tor-tor-woh was the decider and I-tor-tor-woh was the first daughter of their family, considered at the time of her marriage to have been long overdue. It was an uncomfortable conversation in their family and the village at large. Walana (women folks) were sure to comment, each time she passed by, in whispers, using sign language, or just by the nod of the head in her direction. She was called names in her village like *Yu-mba ya Molana* (Barren woman), *Mu-nya-na-Molana* (a man-woman).

When Szra-ngo E-ku-mu-ti and Nya-ngo I-tor-tor-woh had their first mua-na, they named him Ngum'a Mboli. This literally means small goat, but in Vakoland, it is not allowed and accepted to translate names because names have certain significance and they may be related to events, thus servicing as historical facts in an oral trado-cultural society. Our village is situated at the foot of the Fvako and borders the rich, luxuriant, thick multispecies forest that flows upward right to the base of the Fvako where it stops and gives way to the rock that constitutes the Fvako. Villagers grow their crops in this forest, and the principal crop is *Xanthosoma sagittifolium*, that is, cocoyam, known in the Mo-kpwe-li language as Ndaa. This is the species of cocoyam with the arrow leaf elephant's ear, and which is a staple of my people, the major raw material for E-kwa-koko, the traditional dish of the Wa-kpwes.

Because the forest is a continuous ascending hill with different gradations of elevated altitudes, the location of farms was designated and named in relation to its nearness to the village (meaning more south bound) or in proximity to the base of the Fvako itself. In ascending order, we had Nkor-toh, Mbo-li, Wheli, and Szra-wa. Without exception, nkor-toh farms were occupied and owned by villagers who had their properties bordering the forest; it was hus the mbo-li elevation and above that accommodated the village mix.

Mbo-li literally means goat. Farms at this elevation were always sure to be visited by range goats from the village, especially from goat owners that dwelled next to the forest frontier. These folks with their properties next to the forest always had a *nkor-toh* or fence, that confined or restricted their free-range domestic animals from getting access to farms. These did not always happen, and the goats somehow found themselves happily eating the succulent leaves and other edible parts of farmed *ndaa* and sometimes the *meh-kor* (plantain) and *mba-szri* (maize) that constituted the multispecies mixed crop farm method of the villagers. Another reason why it was mostly the mbo-li and not the *ngo-wa* (pigs), *nya-ka* (cows), or *meh-leh-ngu* (sheep) that were the trouble was because it was common for mbo-li owners to take their goats to mbo-li elevation and tie them out there for most of the day so that they could feed on the rich vegetation. It was common for the mbo-li to lose themselves and seek for the crop plants that made for a better meal. Villagers that farmed the mboli area, therefore, were resigned to sharing their crops with the mboli.

It was common to hear farmers say, "Na-wu-szra-na di ma-meh i-mboli i-no li-yea-li (My harvest will depend on what is left for me by the mbo-li)."

Nya-ngo I-tor-tor-woh, though heavily pregnant, still insisted on going to the bush (meaning farm) despite protestations from her mu-nya-na, Szra-ngo E-ku-mu-ti. But E-ku-mu-t-i's in-laws saw this as punishment for their daughter and often came to the residence of the E-ku-mu-ti's, accusing their *mo-nya* (in-law), their daughter's mu-nya-na, of wanting to kill their daughter. All attempts for Nya-ngo I-tor-tor-woh to defend her mu-nya-na by being emphatic that it was her decision meant nothing and totally ignored at all times.

It was *Li-woh la Gbwaa* (Wednesday) which is an *e-lu-wa* (market day) in Buea. Nya-ngo I-tor-tor-woh had no plans for marketing; instead, she was expecting some visitors from out of town, determined to pay her a visit before she gave birth. Among these, her expected in-laws, were her favorite brother-in-law and his molana. These were Szra-ngo Nji-ya Wu-wa and Nya-ngo Mo-ti-ma Szroh-ngoh. Szra-ngo

Nji-ya Wu-wa was a *vou-vou* (pounded cocoyam) addict, and Nya-ngo I-tor-tor-woh wanted to please him by preparing the vou-vou with ndaa from her own farm. She had the other things she needed for the meal, except for the cocoyams she needed to get from her farm. When she was leaving that morning for her farm, her mu-nya-na, immediate neighbors, and walana with roadside houses that she had to pass by asked her about the wisdom of going to the *wa-nga* (farm) in the first place and by herself at that stage of her pregnancy. She brushed it aside lightly, saying it was but a brief trip and to the mbo-li farms that are not far. An elderly roadside molana had observed and concluded that, "O-vhe-li ma-ni-ya (You are stubborn)."

To which Nya-ngo I-tor-tor-woh had replied, "Na-li-ti di li-li-ta na-szro-ka mo-szrio (I am only pregnant, not sick)" as she continued on her way.

Gradually, she reached her wa-nga and started the search for the cocoyams. She had hardly harvested any when she felt sudden contractions, and by the time help came, her water broke already.

"Eh-jay eh, Eh-jay eh, Eh-jay eh (Help, help, help)," she yelled to the top of her voice. In the Mo-kpwe language, "Eh-jay eh" literally means "Come, oh" but practically means "help needed;" that is, an emergency situation. She continued her cry for help, "Eh-jay eh, Eh-jay eh." She knew that though most walana where in the e-luwa and the wu-nya-na had gone to work that some walana like her, a few like her, were in the wa-nga at this time, and therefore, she just needed to shout as loud as she could for her to get help and assistance she needed.

It was about fifteen minutes later before the first responder arrived, and when she did, her first responsibility was to sound the alarm to attract other walana as a matter of urgency. In characteristic Mo-kpwe-l'a Molana style, she horned and trumpeted without these instruments but with her mouth, tongue, and internal airways, and beating her palm against the exhaled air from her mouth produced the desired sound, "Wu-lu-lu-lu, Wu-lu-lu-lu, Wu-lu-lu-lu!"

This sound production worked by the same principle of the tympanic membrane vibrating from air from the external auditory canal.

The *wu-nya-na* (men) who were in their wa-nga and/or domiciles near enough to hear the walana alarm sound recognized it immediately as danger or something with grave consequences that needed immediate attention not only of the walana but also the wu-nya-na. In accordance with the custom and expectations, any mu-nya-na who hears an alarming sound must immediately summon other men to the spot where the assistance or attention was needed. Like the walana, the wu-nya-na also had their own summoning signature sound, and this time, it was the turn of Szra-ngo Mo-nyeh mo Wa-nga to sound the summon. His name literally means "farm soil" if one is permitted to do a *mot pour mot* or *mot-a-mot* translation. He was one of the most successful farmers in the village and was reputed for spending long hours in his wa-nga (farms), almost daily with few exceptions.

He returned late sometimes at the early hours of the night or late evenings when the wu-nya-na were already congregated in palm wine joints, socializing, and winding down for the day. Because he was a very likable personality in the village, more often than not, as he returned home late, especially during the weekends, his buddies would invite him for a "one-man"—that is, a drink of palm wine—before he reached home. It was known that after his long hours in his wa-nga, when he entered his home, he would not venture out for the rest of the day, except if it was an emergency. Thus, Szra-ngo Mo-nyeh mo Wa-nga was permanently coated or soiled with *wa-nga mo-nyeh* (farm soil) and small twigs and sometimes thorns attached to his bush clothes.

The mental picture commonly conjured of him was, therefore, a mu-nya-na in wa-nga apparel, which included Tchang shoes (reinforced rubber made sandals, also known as nke-nja shoes in Pidgin), clothes covered with multiple layers of dark brown volcanic soils, and such clothes that are not washed because they are wa-nga clothes. The wear that covered his lower limbs was an intricately balanced combination of pieces that were specific in their area of coverage. There could be no mistake; otherwise, it would lead to some less honorable parts of the lower limbs being exposed.

The trousers (pants) were only meant to cover the area from the thigh downwards. Shorts number one was meant to cover one half of the gluteus maximus only, where the trousers could not protect;

and shorts number two was meant to cover and protect the other half of the gluteus maximus not covered and protected by shorts number one; then came "shorts" number three. Shorts number three was for all practical purposes like a short waist apron whose length was limited to halfway down the thighs. It was not meant to cover anything behind; its main purpose was to cover and protect the groin area of the lowest part of the axial region of the body.

Szra-ngo Mo-nyeh mo Wa-nga also wore a "rubber gun" (catapult) partially around his *li-woh* (neck), locked under the armpit and trailing down to and over the left thigh. A Li-nyio-ngoh is a rubber gun in Mo-kpwe, usually used to shoot, and with the intent of killing *vheh-noni* (birds), usually midsized and small-sized vheh-noni; Mo Wa-nga was adorned by a hat generously containing, minimally, five conspicuous holes that efficiently aerated the head that was sparsely haired. The ta-mba (hat) had a band around just where the head fits and just before the rim. This band was used to tuck in parts of certain plant species and the feathers of certain vheh-noni species.

The plant or bird species tucked into the band of the ta-mba had special meaning to the tucker. For example, Szra-ngo Mo-nyeh mo Wa-nga was the lead village hunter in terms of killing the Kaa-kah Woe-mbey (*Corvus albus*; Crows). He thus had feathers of these crows tucked halfway around his ta-mba and on the right side of the ta-mba, identifying him as a Kaa-kah Woe-mbey, killer champion. Another phenotype characteristic of Mo Wa-ngeh was his wrist bands. He had *ma-szrey-ku* (a band with attachments) around both wrists, and on these bands were attached cowries, skulls of small vheh-no-ni, small calabashes, and the temporal plant leaves attached to the bands. With his machete and the load of firewood on his *mo-fvoo* (head) and ndaa in his *li-kwe-nji* (a men's backpack made of cane) carried on his back, Mo Wa-ngeh was representative of a typical *Mot'a Wa-nga* (farmer) and a typical *Mot'a Wa-nga wa Mbowa* (typical farm villager).

Mo-nyeh mo Wa-nga may not have been his real and original names but rather an evolution of names based on his profession and common phenotype. It was common to hear words like: "Don't be a Mo-nyeh mo Wa-nga;" "You look like a Mo-nyeh mo Wa-nga;" or "Are you a Mo-nyeh mo Wa-nga?" etc.

"Wo-wey, Wo-wey, Wo-wey Mao-ngoh eh, Mao-ngoh eh, Mao-ngoh eh."

In the village code of arms, these words were not uttered ordinarily, and yes, they were very rarely uttered; and when they were uttered, it was a call to arms. It was to the attention of all the wu-nya-na, from preadults and above, except the very old and the infirmed.

In the village, all teen boys and older men were spurred to action anytime these calls were made. Yes, they were calls and more like calls to arms. The men (wu-nya-na) would drop whatever they are doing and hurriedly pick up their war gear, guns, machetes, sticks, or wood made for mortal attacks, etc., and head at once to the trouble spot. No questions were asked. This rapid response was automatic, and it did not discriminate. Whether someone had been your enemy or not, whether you were talking to someone or not, and whether the family concerned was liked or not, at times of such emergencies, there was real unity.

When the young and older men were ascending the hill responding to Mo-nyeh mo Wa-nga's summon, in their mist were some walana also. In particular, there was one molana by the name Nyango E-veny'a Kaylay, an almost skinny molana with ever-lanky features that actresses and models well wish to have. Nyango E-veny'a Kaylay was ebony and jet-black in her complexion and served as the official and unofficial midwife of the village. Nyango E-veny'a Kaylay was "sure to go," it was commonly said in the village because no matter the time of the day or night, when duty calls, she was sure to go.

Every child in the village who was not born at the local Gbwea (Buea) Clinic run by the government and who was delivered at home was sure to have been delivered by Nya-ngo Kaylay. Nya-ngo E-ve-nyeh would not accept any form of compensation for her work whatsoever. She would not even allow the grateful family to pay for the materials she used for the delivery. Once, though, she delivered a baby for an in-law that was a neighbor as well, and when pressed to accept some form of gratitude, she asked that she be allowed to name the child. Permission was granted immediately, and she named the baby girl she delivered Li-mu-ngeh after her own i-ya-ka (mother). That was the only known compensation attributed to her in her life-long career as a needed village midwife.

On several occasions, the *walana wa mbo-wa* (village women) wanted to make her their "Chief" in recognition of her pivotal role in the village and the joy she had brought to many families, but she would not accept. Nya-ngo E-veny'a Kaylay was in the *e-lu-wa* (market) when the alarm bells started to ring. Somehow, she was reached, and she abandoned her shopping basket and picked up and assembled from the e-lu-wa an emergency delivery kit and headed one way toward the call. When the others in the ascending crowd saw her, therefore, with her small bundle of necessities, they began to think that this emergency was labor-related, and this started a conversation entirely from a different perspective.

All attempts by the wu-nya-na to get any information from Nya-ngo E-veny'a Kaylay failed. She scarcely talked, even in normal circumstances. Being a midwife, she sure did know of the dangers associated with a delivery gone bad or not well-attended to. While therefore her presence might have been some sort of a relief to the wu-nya-na, her heart was throbbing as she wished her legs could carry her to the laboring molana faster than they did.

She started humming first to herself, then quietly, but those very close to her could hear, and then she started singing loudly.

Njen'a maya szri-li-ngeh a wana eh
Njen'a maya szri-li-ngeh a wana eh
Njen'a maya szri-li-ngeh a wana eh
Njen'a maya szri-li-ngeh a wana eh

Soon the song was picked up by all in the group headed up to the laboring Nya-ngo I-tor-tor-woh. The song translated meant, "Who will deliver a child and not be happy, oh children?"

Even before they got to her, Nya-ngo I-tor-tor-woh and the first responder molana Nya-ngo Baita Mo-fveh were singing along once as they could hear the advancing choir. The advancing team headed up toward the mbo-li farms and, led by Nya-ngo E-veny'a Kaylay, could be properly described as a mobile emergency delivery team cum choral group. This goodwill group had the benefit of being dominated by *mbe-szra ja wana* (male youths) who were on holidays at this time and therefore a ready help in communal village affairs. The *ngoh-ndors* (young women or female youths) were not normally village-community active-centric but were very quick to make fun or "reprimand" a mbe-szra who was deemed not responding to the call of village wide community needs.

While the singing meant that help was on its way, that the village had been mobilized, the singing also alarmed and startled some of the *nya-ma ja wa-nga* (bush or wild animals) whose quietness and tranquility was being disturbed and private space being invaded. This benevolent group was passing by a ndaa farm when a counted ten *kwai* (*Francolinus camerunensis*, i.e. the partridge or bush fowl) flew from different corners of the farm to the neighboring forest. Kwai were and are still a major avian pest of ndaa farmers but trapping and or hunting them down was a near impossibility if not a mystery. My people the Wa-kpwes describe the kwai as "Wu-wa ja wa-wu."

Translated, it means the "devil's fowl." But why devil? Because kwai had a disappearing formula. You could spot them one second, and the next they are gone, practically disappeared with no trace, even with the most well-trained dogs. The kwai chicks were not left out of this disappearing prowess. For the chicks, it explained that all they do to evade detection is lie on their backs and hold a leaf by their beak as a cover, and that automatically makes them "visionary" and "olfactorily" nonexistent to a hunting party. As part of a hunting village team, we occasionally caught some kwai after visiting with some *wa-mba-ki* (elders) of the village. One thing is certain, though: there is no avian group associated with the Fvako that is as tasty as the kwai; every Mo-kpwe-li knows this for a fact.

When the kwai flew away as the village group advanced, the event generated some talking points among about half of the advancing group. So, while half of the group continued singing and edging forward in the narrow and winding bush path in a single file, others continued the forward march but now focused on something else.

"We have saved this farm from the kwai."

"It is only for a little while, for they will return before you know it."

"We are really disturbing the peace of these bush animals with our singing."

"We are really scaring these animals; they must be wondering what is happening."

"It is not the singing that scared them. After all, we always hear kwai sing early in the mornings and in the evenings as other birds do, so kwai are used to singing."

"So why you think say dem run, waiti make dem fly away (So why do you think they ran and flew away, then)?"

The exchange continued.

"Na people like you and the oda one dem for here, waiti wona bad voice (It is folks like you and your likes in this group with bad voices)."

"Mornin mornin time, you drink pamie, you drink kwa-tcha and now when you think say you did sing na croak you di croak, like frog. (Still in the morning hours of the day, you have drunk palm wine, and you have drunk kwa-tcha [corn beer] that have affected your vocal cords, and now when you think you are singing, you simply croaking like a frog. that is what scares the kwai.)"

"Sing na sing, jus like wata na wata (Singing is singing, just as water is water)," they declared defiantly.

"We no dey here na for competition (We are not here for a competition)," they emphasized.

"Ee better for drink pamie and kwa-tcha than for smoke mba-nga (It is better to drink palm wine and kwa-tcha than to smoke mba-nga [mbanga here meaning *Cannabis sativa*, leaves of the marijuana plant, also known as 'joint' or 'weed')."

"Di man na really li-emba this, I beg no bring me that your li-emba for ya (This is really witchcraft, please do not do your witchcraft to me here)."

"Ah nodi brin any li-emba, na you get li-emba yaa because li-emba dey for wona family (I am not bringing any li-emba. It is you that has the li-emba because there is li-emba in your family)."

"Na so wona di waka di spread dat Mofvungeh-Li-emba thing for dis village (That is how you walk around the village, spreading the Mo-fvu-ngeh-Li-emba Syndrome)."

"Waiti I do you (What have I done to you)?"

Younger folks used the word *li-emba* or sometimes *Mu-emba* instead, not necessarily in literal or practical terms; in other words, they do not really mean what they are saying but rather register their displeasure, disagreement, or irritation with you. On the other hand, if adults used the words *li-emba* or *mu-emba*, they meant it literally and practically. These were loaded with words or adjectives that were not used lightly. Their pronouncement or utterance had heavy and sometimes grave consequences on both sides in the short or long-terms.

These exchanges sometimes between two or more mbe-szra continued, increasing in its intensity and degree of heatedness progressively.

With young people and at this rate, it was headed for some fist punching by the warring parties.

"Mo-toh-wu szra-wu (All keep quiet and let's concentrate on the task ahead of us)," Nya-ngo E-veny'a Kaylay intervened before it got out of hand. She was a respected woman, the only woman in the group, and old enough to be mother and grandmother to each and every one in her human convoy on foot. The singing resumed with all the participants once more, and the discordant notes could not be mixed. Folks who had already breakfasted with palm wine or kwa-tcha or both, as the case maybe, sang even louder as the team approached its destination.

When the Nya-ngo E-veny'a Kaylay foot convoy reached Nya-ngo I-tor-tor-woh mo E-ku-mu-ti, there were three primary responders there already. Nya-ngo Li-kor-woh l'Enjema, the very first responder who called and summoned the village for help and who first heard Nyango I-tor-tor-woh E-ku-mu-ti's cry for help; Nya-ngo Ngow'a Matoe, a village molana who insist on going to her wa-nga, especially on holidays and other days when just about all of the villagers were at home; and Szra-ngo Mo-nyeh mo Wa-nga, the first male responder who got the emergency alarm from Nya-ngo Li-kor-woh l'Enjema and then conveyed same to the wu-nya-na folks.

The trio earlier responders had built a hurried makeshift partial tent without a roof and with a U-shaped architectural design. The open end was facing northward and therefore hidden from a southern position or advance. The walls and shade of the tent made of wood pillars, broad surface leaves of *Musa* plants, *Xanthosoma* plants, and others and also *e-szra-nja* (also known as wrappa; a piece of cloth tied around waist once or twice and that flows right down to the ankle areas of the lower limbs). It was typical of a Mo-kpwe dress code for both walana and wu-nya-na, one difference between the wu-nya-na e-szra-nja and walana e-szra-nja is that it is a one huge continuous piece for men that could go around the waist two or more times (as a consequence a Mot'a Mu-nya-na wa Mo-kpwe [a Mokpwe man]) in trado-cultural attire, will have a huge heap and fold of cloth around his waist that resembles the waist band of a Japanese sumo wrestler, and to a large extent, an overall semblance of a longer version of a Scottish kilt.

Walana, on the other hand, typically will prefer to have two pieces instead, tied one atop another. Because a Mokpwe molana's e-szra-nja dressing was normally of two layers or two pieces, in cases of emergencies, such a molana could afford to donate, spare or give one of such layers of her e-szra-nja to the needy, while still being properly dressed, with the remaining one. The Nyango E-ve-nyeh convoy came from the south end and was stopped beyond fifteen meters to the tent. The two walana primary responders where stationed inside the tent with the laboring I-tor-tor-woh, while Szra-ngo Mo-nyeh mo Wa-nga was stationed outside, sort of keeping guard and ensuring that the mbe-szra did not come too close to the delivery tent.

Midwife E-veny'a Kaylay quickly extricated herself from her group and dashed immediately into the delivery room. While the midwife and her assistants were judiciously working on the emergency delivery, Mo Wa-nga too went to work with the mbe-szra. Leaving three behind to stand guard, the rest went with Wa-ngeh into the neighboring vegetation to select, cut, and bring back appropriate materials for the design and making of a shoulder-borne stretcher to transport back to the village, the *iyaka* (mother) and *mua-na* (child) that were the center-stagers of this rapidly developing event. They needed sticks, robes, leaves, and soft grass and brain ingenuity to make an "air ambulance" that will contain and sustain mother and child back home without further incidence or drama. This was a delicate task, and there was no room for error, and it was an emergency.

While the wu-nya-na were in the wa-nga, looking for and collecting materials for the custom design air-ambulance, the baby was delivered. The three sentries left behind heard the cry of the neonate and, almost in unison, "Mu-nya-na ka Molana (A boy or a girl)?" they asked.

"Mua-na wa Mu-nya-na (A boy child)," came the reply.

Then they called out after their comrades in the bushes, "Ae Mua-na amaja eh, Ae Mua-na amaja eh (The child has come, the child has come)!" they cried out.

"A-vheh-li di ma-meh (What is it)?" came back the response from the bushes.

"Mua-na wa, Mu-nya-na (A boy child)," the reply went back into the bushes.

Then the singing and dancing started again in the bushes and around the delivery tent.

Ima
Njen'a maya szri-lingeh
A wana eh
Njen'a maya szri-li-ngeh
A wana eh
Njen'a maya szri-lingeh
A wana eh
Njen'a maya szri-li-ngeh
A wana eh

Approximately translated the jubilant singers are asking

"Who will give birth to a child and not be happy?"

And as if answering their own question, they will kind of reply

'Oh Children"

This will be repeated over and over

As a signal to stop, the lead voice or singer will say

"Tu tu tu tu"

"E-mbo-wa eh"

"E heh". The jubilant singers will respond

At the "E hey" the singing stopped

The group will respond in a way to say we hear you loud and clear, though it was more like the chorus of the *mo-szro-koh* (song).

Tu, tu, tu, tu
E-mbo-wa eh
E-hey

This stoppage signal could hold for good, but if anyone went ahead and intoned the song again, the singing started all over until it was stopped by another stoppage signal of:

Tu, tu, tu, tu
E-mbo-wa eh
E-hey

Making of the transport ambulance and giving mother and child some time to stabilize meant that the homeward journey did not start till early evening. By this time, Szra-ngo E-ku-mu-ti Njila was at hand and some other close family members. The convoy too was well-supplied gastronomically, for it was a long day for them, though the young men did not seem to mind, liking the adventure. They eventually got home in one piece; the air ambulance survived the journey. There was no singing as the convoy marched down into the village because by custom, ancestral spirits that inhabit the forest and that normally come out at night are at variance with singing and the noise that singing produces is a disturbance to their peace. The villagers knew better than to attempt to vex the ancestors gone before.

There was the village crowd gathered outside the E-ku-mu-ti residence to welcome the wonder bush baby and the brave and strong or perhaps detrimentally stubborn mother. Amid the applause, when they all arrived, there was some light singing, especially by the walana. Some were praising the ancestors gone before for their gift, safety, and save delivery of the gift while others were praising God for saving the lives of the mother and child.

This wa-nga birth occurred eighteen years ago, two years into the marriage of E-ku-mu-ti and I-tor-tor-woh. Two days after the event, E-ku-mu-ti's *szra-ng'a li-wa* (father-in-law) and two of his brothers (Meh-la-lo meh Li-wa) visited the E-ku-mu-tis and requested a meeting with their son-in-law in the backyard, under the large tree, normally reserved for talks among wu-nya-na. Once there and after the first keg of palm wine had been dawned, the three in-laws vented their displeasure about the wa-nga birth and blamed E-ku-mu-ti for allowing her wife who was in such a state to still be going to the farm. This was considered cruel on his part and unacceptable, and being a crime, it came with consequences.

At this point, Szra-ngo E-ku-mut'a Njila was beginning to boil inside him. And he asked them,

"Ma-meh ya-szra

(What do you want)?

Ma-meh ya-szra li-gbwe-ya

(What do you want to do)?

Li-szru-wa di e-je-le-leh a-nu

You are starving for the lack of meat at your homes, that is why you are here. He stated as a matter of fact.

"Na-szra weh-ni mbo-li toh ngowa lay gbwa"

I do not have a goat or a pig to slaughter and give to you people

"Mi-ano na meh-vili ndi meh ko'oki oh lou-nga"

Your stomachs (hearts) are full of crookery, dishonesty, and ulterior motives

"Na-ngeh, ya-nji-yeah oh ndawo y'ami"

Now get out and leave my house

Eku-mu-ti ordered and concluded

After E-ku-mu-t'a Njila had ordered his in-laws to leave his property, half an hour later, they were still there as it had turned into a quarrel and a shouting match between him and his in-laws. It was dark already, and wu-nya-na in the neighborhood had come to see if they could settle these differences between these *mo-nyas* (in-laws), but once as the neighbors got there, they took the side of their neighbor, E-ku-mu-ti, and accused the in-laws of extortion and thievery tactics and therefore repeated the call for their immediate departure. "Making profit of a near unfortunate event that happened to your daughter is very disgraceful and cannot be rewarded or patronized, so you hungry *mo-nyas* (in-laws), leave our village!" a spokesperson for the E-ku-mu-ti support neighbors surmised.

And then he was challenged by one of the in-laws, "Wa-veh Nje (Who are you)?" he said. "Wa-veh nje," when used, is normally meant as a challenge and or a belittling terminology.

The challenger in-law got his answer with a straight punch right in the middle of his face that broke his nose immediately as blood started to ooze out down his nostrils. Then it was a free for all fight, pitching the four protecting neighbors versus three extortionist in-laws. Punches and insults were exchanged for about five minutes before E-ku-mu-ti returned from a quick dash into his nda-wo to return with his gun.

E-ku-mu-t'a Njila was a retired law enforcer and also a small-time village hunter; he thus had and knew how to operate firearms. He fired the first warning shot into the air of a dark and relatively quiet night, which illuminated the dark atmosphere above, and then got their attention, and then he yelled out "Yeh-ndeh (All of you, go)!"

As he said yeh-ndeh, he fired the second shot into the air, and at this, the party of seven fighters disentangled from each other, ran in all directions, scattered all over E-ku-mu-ti's backyard, and eventually climbing or jumping over his hedged fence into the night and out of E-ku-mu-ti's property and, therefore, out of harm's way. All other spectators who too were assembled outside the hedged fence watching the outdoor drama by the wu-nya-na, all also ran away and took cover, avoiding any stray bullets that may come their way.

The three in-laws regrouped about 100 meters away from E-ku-mu-ti's yard and decided to return and give him a verbal piece of their minds. They debated among themselves for about fifteen minutes before coming to a resolution. They had decided fifty meters away from his home was safe and, in the darkness, hiding behind trees and the two available pillars was protection and safe enough from E-ku-mu-ti's shots.

Then they began, shouting at the top of their voices, not only for E-ku-mu-ti to hear them, but also for the whole village to hear them. It was their method of Teh Tu-ndey. Then they started, "E-ku-mu-ti o-vheh-ni li-emba (E-ku-mu-ti, you have witch [you are a wiz-ard]). O-vheh-li di Mu-emba (You are a wizard). Wai-ti li-ya (You are stingy). O-vheh-li di Moto wa wo-weh (You are a bad and evil man). Wa-szra lo'owa mua'na-szru (You want to kill our mua'na [child]). Wa-szra li-gbwaa mua'na-szru oh Nyongo (You want to give our child to be killed by nyo-ngo)."

As the word *nyo-ngo* was being finished, a third shot into the dark night air by E-ku-mu-ti brought about peace in the village for the rest of the night.

One of the in-laws was heard saying, "E-szra no-li-ya (You people should not leave me alone behind). E-ku-mu-ti ama kwa-nya (E-ku-mu-ti has gone mad [gone crazy or taking leave of his senses])."

A unicellular protozoan parasitic disease that is a constant in our village was the *Plasmodium* species, the malaria parasite that caused the malaria disease, which was normally characterized by hyperthermia. The malaria disease is no respecter of persons, age, gender, social status, nga-nga or no nga-nga, mu-emba or not, etc. Two years into Ngum'a Mboli's life, he fell gravely ill with an infection or disease that was characterized by very high temperatures, a fever that was associated with loss of appetite and little or no movement. Some said it was the usual and customary malaria that plagued the community all the time, especially during the rainy season, and while children are the main targets, adults are not spared either. The medications that were given to the child did not seem to help, and the child was in this state with little respites now and then for two weeks.

The maternal grandmother of Ngum'a Mboli then decided to pay a visit at the request of her daughter to help out in any way possible. Before Nya-ngo I-tor-tor-woh's mother showed up. She first of all consulted with a Mot'a Yowo who made it clear and without difficulty that it was E-ku-mu-ti himself that was responsible for the sickness of his son, that E-ku-mu-ti was in Nyo-ngo, that E-ku-mu-ti was under pressure from the nyo-ngo secret society to "give" (meaning to kill) his son, and that considering that he failed the first time to kill this child, he was given a second chance to accomplish that which he did not accomplish the first time. Nya-ngo Mo-szra-iye, I-tor-tor-woh's mother, did not confront Szra-ngo E-ku-mut'a Njila with this information. She narrated the information to her daughter instead, avoiding a direct confrontation with her son-in-law.

"Mu-nyan' ami a-szre-jeh di mu-emba (My husband is not a wizard)," I-tor-tor-woh said matter-of-factly to her iyaka when Nya-ngo Mo-szra-iye had finished her narration. She had chosen to brief her daughter when E-ku-mu-ti was out of the house.

"Eh mua-na a-weh-ni di nya-mbeh ya Mot'a weh-na-ma (The child has a normal human sickness)," I-tor-tor-woh stressed the point to her mother.

"Szre-keh omo-gbwa ma-iye (You do give him medications, yes)?" Nya-ngo Mo-szra-iye asked the daughter sarcastically.

I-tor-tor-woh replied to the affirmative by the nod of the head only, knowing where the "logic" was headed, and now wondering how she may be able to convince her otherwise.

"Ma-meh nde-nga-teh a-szra li-ya szro (Why doesn't he get well then)?" Nya-ngo Mo-szra-iye made the obvious conclusion.

I-tor-tor-woh had no answer. She kept silent for some minutes, then she asked her iyaka, "Na weh-li di Mu-emba (Am I a witch)?" The mother seemed taken aback and did not respond immediately.

"Ja-iye (No, you are not a witch)," she replied to her daughter.

"Neh o-wie o-ma na-szreh-nje di mu-emba (How do you know that I am not a witch)?" I-tor-tor-woh asked the mother, Nya-ngo Mo-szra-iye.

"Na wie e-wa-nja o-weh-li di mua-n'ami (I know because you are my child)," Mo-szra-iye said to the daughter.

At this, I-tor-tor-woh walked away from her mother after gazing at her intently for about five seconds and went and was occupying herself in her kitchen. Mo-szra-iye followed her into the kitchen after a while and declared that she had come with medications (portions) from a Mot'a Yowo, one to be administered to her mua-na (Ngum'a Mboli) and the other to be administered to her mu-nya-na (Doo-hu E-ku-mu-t'a Njila; Doo-hu is the pet name a Mo-la-n'a Mo-kpwe gives to her husband). I-tor-tor-woh thanked her mother and took the child's medication from her, which she administered to the child later that evening, but the medication for the husband she did not touch and did not acknowledge and feigned no knowledge of it all.

Two days after the mother and daughter talked, the mother reminded the daughter again of the medicine she brought to be used on the husband, in case she forgot about it. There was no response from the daughter and then Nya-ngo Mo-szra-iye said, "O mo'oka wor-ngoh (Are you afraid of him)? Ah-mo nji-szreh di mo-gbwe-gbwe (He has turned you into a weakling). Ah-mo'olah li-ngi li-emba lay-ni (He has bewitched you with his li-emba)," she concluded.

That evening, while in her room, preparing to sleep, Szra-ngo E-ku-mu-ti appeared and stood in the door of Nya-ngo Mo-szra-iye room, blocking it and with his machete in his right hand. He said nothing, and nothing was exchanged between them, and while he seemed to have stood there for a few minutes only, it seemed like eternity for her mother-in-law who seemed practically frozen anatomically and physiologically. Before Szra-ngo E-ku-mu-t'a Njila returned from his wa-nga, the next day, during the early evening hours, he was informed that his mother-in-law left the village in a hurry in the morning. It must have been after 5:00 a. m because E-ku-mu-ti left the house at 5:00 a.m. if he had farm duties to be accomplished.

About twenty years into their marriage when Nya-ngo I-tor-tor-toh E-ku-mu-t'a Njila was in her early fifties, and Szra-ngo E-ku-mu-t'a Njila was in his mid-sixties, I-tor-tor-woh suddenly died in the middle of the day and in the presence of her husband, "in broad daylight" as it was narrated in the village over and over. Sudden deaths of "healthy" persons in the village were considered mysterious and suspicious, and it did not matter in the manner in which it came; and even more so if the persons were considered not to be of dying age, and this "age" was subjective between adults and especially between the younger and older persons.

Sudden mysterious deaths were attributed to Nyo-ngo that originated from Tontino Land. It was a characteristic of rich people. But then slow deaths and even "expected" deaths that befell anyone considered not to be of dying age were also attributed to Nyo-ngo or Li-emba. The words "cause of death" are alien in our culture, post-mortem autopsy procedures to determine the cause of death existed not for a variety of reasons. Ignorance is a main problem, capabilities of the local medical facilities, and high costs. It is commonly said if through a postmortem you knew what caused the death of your loved one, that would not bring the deceased back, but you must have wasted and used up valuable funds that should instead be channeled to the funeral. And, yes, my people spend a lifetime's fortune for funerals, being more generous with funds after the death of a loved one than spending on medical care when the individual was struggling with an illness.

Another common victim of death is poisoning. Phenotypically, my people know symptoms of poisoning, regardless of how the poison was administered. Thus, they knew deaths were caused by poisons, and along that came knowledge of who was responsible for the poison because this must have already been revealed when the deceased was still alive by nga-nga. There was no need, therefore, for an autopsy.

The most popular cause of death which required no medical procedure was death by Nyo-ngo and or Li-emba. Like death by poisoning, this cause of death was easily decipherable just by anyone, young or old, male or female, and especially by adversaries or enemies. But evidential credence for this was the deciphering of the nature or cause of death as determined by Wat'o wa Yowo or Wat'o wa Nga-Nga. Their determinations and conclusions of the cause of death were ironclad and written on solid rocks. These nga-nga told you who killed the deceased and proffered a reason or reasons why but not the real cause of death. Thus, my people were not really interested in cause of death but rather who caused the death. This was the professional domain of the Wat'o wa Yowo, a domain and a business they protected murderously.

The verdict was out. Szra-ngo E-ku-mu-t'a Njila killed his wife via Nyo-ngo. His being at home when it happened, the sudden nature, and the blood oozing out of I-tor-tor-woh's nostrils all fit well into the narrative.

"Ah-mo-toh di vhe-yey (He beat her with sticks, thus the bleeding and suddenness of death)." He had to be at home, and it had to be urgent, for if it was not her, then it could have been him. E-ku-mu-ti himself would have died mysteriously. E-ku-mu-ti had over-delayed the giving of one of his own to nyo-ngo while he had been benefiting from the nyo-ngo. These delays and postponements saw him right to his retirement, but then it was now or his own life.

E-ku-mu-ti had no sympathy in the village. The village opinion found him guilty, and guilty he was. Initially by word of mouth, it was decided and circulated in the village that no one should attend the funeral services and let him "eat" his kill. But then out of respect for the deceased and the deceased immediate family members, it was thought that according to the deceased, her last rites in respect and honor was the right thing to do. But even at this, the funeral was very poorly attended by village standards, but death is a community issue involving all adults because at death, all differences are put aside except those differences for which the belligerents have said, "Na-teh no kwe-li (Until death, there will be nothing between us)." "Na-teh no kwe-li" was an oath, one that was not broken.

In the Mo-kpwe tradition, the third day after burial was the day of Szra-Szra. Szra-szra is the final burial ceremony in which the spirit of the deceased is finally severed from the human living world. All relationships with the living are severed, and the ceremony includes special songs chanted and sung by professionals in the culture who will, in due course of the ceremony, lead the spirit of the deceased out of its nda-wo and cast out into the dark to meet the spirits and take its rightful place in the spirit world. When this spirit is cast out into the dark by a trado-culturally versed person, the deceased name is not to be called again by those inside the house who have to follow the ceremony to its logical conclusion. The szra-szra ceremony is actually two ceremonies, which begins on day two after death, and it is concluded on the third day after death. The separation of the spirit ceremony takes place on the night of day two, and it is restricted to family members only. Day three after burial is an elaborate ceremony that includes nonfamily members but mostly includes village members only, unlike the wake and burial ceremonies that is open to all from far and near.

Before the szra-szra day, Szra-ngo E-ku-mu-t'a Njila went house to house and door to door in the village, reminding his village comrades and kinsmen that his late wife's szra-szra was the next day and that they should not forget to show up. Szra-szra in the village is not the type of event that you have to invite anybody, especially the young people, for they will come invited or not. The third-day szra-szra ceremony is an early evening event, a feasting event mainly of eating and drinking.

On the morning of the third day, the day of the final szra-szra, animals are killed or slaughtered, mainly *ngowa* (pigs), *mboli* (goats), and *nya-ka* (cows). The slaughtering of a cow or cows was a symbol of social status; it was thus not a common animal that was usually slaughtered for szra-szra. The animals that were slaughtered were used to cook the meals that were to be consumed later that evening. The slaughtered animals were normally from the children of the deceased, siblings of the deceased, and in-laws of the deceased. Rarely and occasionally, an animal to be slaughtered could come outside of these boundaries. The slaughtering of the animals was done by the youths of the village, sometimes accompanied by some elders.

Any slaughtered animal is divided into four approximately equal portions. One portion goes to the donor of the animal, one portion is used for cooking the meals to be eaten later in the evening, one portion is left with the immediate bereaved family, and the one portion is divided to the village. The village portion is subdivided into three sub portions; one sub portion is roasted immediately and downed with palm wine and beer by all those present at the slaughtering.

The second sub-portion will be divided to take home by all those present. These were called the Wa-Teh-meh, meaning the bystanders, and the last sub-portion was apportioned according to families, whether present or not. Thus, a bereaved family did not have to invite anyone for a szra-szra. It was "looked forward to" because people came invited or not, foe or friends, so if anyone had to "campaign or solicit" for attendance, this was speaking volumes from a village custom perspective. It is noted that by village standards, Szra-ngo E-ku-mu-ti was a well-to-do man, a man of above average social status by way of means.

As E-ku-mu-ti left one house after house, "making his appeal" for attendance—yes, appeal for that is what is was—behind his back, the comments were not similar but identical.

"Li-ya-na ae szra-szra ya-ngoh (Stay alone with your szra-szra)," they would say as they had said during the burial just two days ago. "Li-ya-na ae-mbey ya-ngoh (Stay alone with your corpse)," they had said when they refused to participate and give Nya-ngo I-tor-tor-woh a benefitting burial.

The *szra-szra* (the two days after death ceremony or ritual), like the *kwe-li* (funeral) was poorly attended. E-ku-mu-ti was isolated in his own village, treated as an alien and a social outcast and a thing to be feared and dreaded.

When *wana* (children) ran away from him anywhere they met with him in the village since after his wife's death, he would ask them "Ma-meh na gbwe-yi (What have I done)?" He would say this not necessarily addressing the wana, but it seemed more like asking himself the question and addressing the village, him wanting to know why he was being ostracized.

Those who were not very versed with the Mo-kpwe language called him "Li-emba man or Nyo-ngo man," while those versed with the Mo-kpwe language simply referred to him to as "Mu-emba," meaning wizard or, more correctly, a "Killing Wizard" or a "Homicide Wizard."

E-ku-mu-ti had to mourn his wife and also come to terms with the treatment he was getting from the village of his birth and where he had lived all of his life. A son of the village, son of the soil, or a wo-nja ya mbo-wa—this meant that both of your parents were natives of the village or natives of the locality. You were a free-born, a "title" that often came and was invoked with bragging rights and upper handedness.

Mo-fvu-ngeh seemed to have gone underground since her last movie as the major character at about the same time that E-ku-mu-ti was still mourning his wife and trying to come to terms with his new position in the village or, better still, how he was viewed in the village and how he was going to live his life going forward in an environment that now seemed hostile to his very presence. E-ku-mu-ti got very sick two years after the death of his wife, Nya-ngo I-tor-tor-woh and he received treatment for the malaria parasitic protozoan disease. In the village, malaria was treated using local herbs, a tradition that is traced right far back and that was preserved and communicated through an oral tradition, just like many other traditions that are customary in the village.

The herbs used for the treatment were a mixed concoction composed mainly of roots, rhizomes, small branches, and leaves of *Carica papaya* (paw-paw; papaya), *Cymbopogon nardus* (fever grass; citronella grass), *Psidium guajava* (guava), *Mangifera indica* (mango), ma-njue-li, mai-ja ma njo-mbeh, and ma-ngoh-ngi. Cut into pieces, they were immersed into a metallic container containing *maliwa* (water) for a total volume of up to 5,000 liters. This container with a lid was mounted onto a *li-yoh* (fireplace) made of three huge stones stationed in a triangular format. This fire assemblage to boil the plant mixture was normally set up behind the house. The plant mixture was allowed to boil for three to four hours with occasional stirring using a befitting wooden stirrer.

The boiled plant extract mixture for the treatment of the dreaded malaria parasite worked in several ways. The first step is, the sick or plasmodium parasitized underwent a tou-mba or la'a tou-mbeh. The container with the steaming mixture was placed on the floor between the legs of the patient, who sat on a low wooden stool. The pot or herbal container had a stirrer for stirring the plant parts in the pot to release the most amount of heat as possible. The patient, concoction pot or container, the stool, and the stirrer were all covered under an old blanket. The blanket covering was to ensure that no heat escaped so that all of the wet heat that emanated from the stirring of the pot was concentrated onto the body of the malaria-infected patient. The patient stayed in this confinement for two to three hours. The stirring of the pot every fifteen to twenty minutes or so was required to as to maintain and sustain the continuous flow of wet heat onto the body of the patient that was being tou-mbaad. While adult patients did the stirring by themselves, younger patients had an adult do the stirring for them periodically. Temperatures under and within the "blanket room" could sometimes exceed 40°C at times and had led to some patients collapsing, especially the wana and the very ill. The principle behind a wet sauna is tou-mba-based. The blanket makes the enclosure (sauna room), the pot plant mixture and containing solution provides the wet steam, and then the malaria patient trapped inside.

Wana (children) never opted for tou-mba or la'a-tu-mbeh because it was a torture once as you experienced or tasted it the first time. Nevertheless, despite its "torturistic" nature, it was a miracle cure, for it worked just about every time, except if the right plant species and mixtures were not assembled and, in the case, where the patient was not suffering from a malaria infection but another ailment. For example, a li-emba-induced malaria disease cannot be cured by the la-a-tu-mbeh process because the patient will not have the *plasmo-dium* parasites in his or her mai-ja (blood), that is cured by the tou-mba process. The hot sweating that resulted from the la'a-tu-mbeh was cure to the malaria disease.

After the la-a-tu-mbeh, the patient bathed with the now cooled water. The bathing was without bath soap, and after the bathing, no towel was used or allowed to dry the body; the body was to be air-dried only. The last stage of the tou-mba cure was drinking the liquid (solution) mixture of the tou-mba extracts. After the la'a-tu-mbeh, the mixture in the pot was strained or sieved and the liquid filtrate collected was divided into two portions: one for bathing and one for drinking. The tou-mba patient drank a cup of this moisture warm (usually recommended) or cold three times a day, e-lay-lay (morning), moe-szray (afternoon), and ngom-bay (evening), until the mixture was finished. It was customary to share some of this tou-mba drink with other wana of the litumba (family) and specifically wa'a-na wa nda-wo (children of the household). The sharing of the tou-mba drink to the other wana wa litumba was a prophylactic preventive measure. Normally within three to five days after the la-a-yu-mbeh and the drinking of the extract mixture, the patient got well, and the malaria parasite eliminated from the patient's mai-ja. If it was malaria, this tou-mba process never failed. The "torture" and the awful tasting mixture drink paid off until the next malaria bout, which was about twelve months away and around the corner, just waiting and biding its time. It did not seem as if our immune system was capable of developing antibodies or some other form of protection against the Plasmodium parasite perhaps because of the ability of the blood parasite to undergo antigenic variations. The traditional tou-mba treatment of the malaria disease therefore became a "periodic constant," one that was known by the ancestors, the walimo gone ahead.

The malaria parasitic disease was at its apex each year during the rainy season when there was lots of standing water everywhere and when temporary freshwater ponds abound. The disease is transmitted by the Anopheles mosquitoes, specifically the females that need a human blood meal for egg production. At the heart of the rainy season (July, August, September), the mosquitoes breed on leaves, discarded tires, open tins and other containers, road and roof gutters, shores of relatively large water bodies like streams, fishponds, etc. The height of the breeding season coincided with the malaria epidemic each year, though the disease was there all year round. The all year hot and humid tropical climate and the availability of aquatic habitats for breeding meant that there was no shortage of high populations of the invertebrate vector host.

Vio-ngu, as the Mo-kpwes call mosquitoes, are the blood-sucking enemies of the people and associated with misery. Western medications for malaria were not effective because the parasite was sure to develop resistance to a new drug no sooner than it was introduced into the population (looked like a case of antigenic variation). Drugs like the quinines, for example, chloroquine and mefloquine, fansidar, and later sulfadoxine-pyrimethamine, all proved ineffective against the dreaded malaria.

Before the advent and introduction of western medications in the treatment of malaria, Wa-kpwes have been battling with this disease that they could not see but that they knew was there and needed protection from. In Mo-kpwe Land, there are two types of Wat'o wa Yowo or nga-nga. There were the Wat'o wa Yowo specialized in treating ailments using herbs, knowledge passed down orally for many generations and for certain specific illnesses. The secrets for treatment rested with particular families, and they guarded these secrets jealously.

Then, of course, there were the nga-nga whose specialty was spiritual affairs. Because malaria was not a "specialized" disease, everyone in the village was a potential patient. Everyone was a potential target for female Anopheles mosquito sucking with their painful proboscis when they pierced the skin to reach the blood vessels for blood.

The nga-nga who had the first secret of treating malaria with natural plant extracts freely shared their knowledge as a matter of security and survival for their local communities, and therefore, as the Mo-kpwe communities spread, elders in each nuclear family knew the recipe. Or in the rare event no one in a nuclear family knew the recipe and the administration, then a neighbor or, better still, some other family member gladly stepped in to play this part of nga-nga.

When the mixture was considered done after three to four hours, it was brought down from the firestones with the lid on so as to maintain the steaming temperature. The patient was seated on a chair, specifically a stool that was slightly higher than the metallic pot with the boiled plant extracts. The pot with the concoction was positioned between the legs of the malaria patient, and the patient was then covered with one or two blankets that enveloped all three occupants—patient, stool, and pot. The blankets flowed to the ground, leaving no escape route for any heat from the pot. The stirrer stick was left inside the pot, and the patient was required to—as often as the patient could—stir the pot so as to release the heat vapor that contained the medicinal extracts of the plants assembled.

The patient stayed in there for thirty minutes to one hour. The patient came out drenched in hot sweat. This hot sweat that dripped from the patient took away the malaria disease just as normal sweating takes away heat energy from the body. This process is called "tou-mba" in the Mo-kpwe language. The patient that undergoes the tou-mba process does not wash off whatever it is that evaporates onto the patient's body. Such a patient is only allowed to have a bath till the next day. For the next seven days, after the tou-mba process, the only drink of the patient was that strained from the tou-mba pot. It was rare and very rare that a patient was cured seven days after the tou-mba. In fact, patients started feeling better the evening after the tou-mba, for the tou-mba was normally done late morning or early afternoon.

If a patient did not feel better or get well seven days after the tou-mba, then they turned to western medications or went to the hospital or just simply declared that it was li-emba or nyo-ngo; then nga-nga were visited, and the person responsible was revealed, and a then new chapter of the illness began. Tou-mba was normally not administered to children. Once a child of about ten years of age was administered the tou-mba process, and he ended up collapsing, most probably due to heat exhaustion.

Szra-ngo E-ku-mu-ti had been sick on and off for about a month but was almost bedridden for the last one week, so his sister, Nya-ngo Mu-ema mo Gbwamu, left her own home and family to come nurse her *ndoh-meh wa mu-nya-na wa mo-mba-ki* (older brother). She had asked some neighbor mbe-szra in the village to help her fetch the required plant species and in their right quantities, which they did for a handsome compensation, including food that she prepared. This was the second day after the tou-mba and E-ku-mu-t'a Njila thought he was beginning to regain his strength and had even asked his *ndoh-meh wa molana wa mo-szra-li* (younger sister) to cook his favorite dish for him, which she did with all her pleasure.

With the sister's urging, E-ku-mu-ti made an effort to get off his back and sit on the bench he had on his veranda overlooking the rest of the village. He felt good and relieved, breathing this fresh air again and feeling once more like a *Mot'a weh-na-ma* (human). After about thirty minutes sitting out there, he was getting tired, and Nya-ngo Mu-ema mo Gbwamu said it was okay, that he could return and rest on his bed and emphasized that the recovery was a gradual process. Just as he was making an effort to stand and go back inside, then came Nya-ngo Mo-fvu-ngeh.

"E-nay yoma ya mu-emba a-szra waa (This killing wizard, won't you die)?" she spat out the venom in her. "O mo-owa mo-la-n' a-ngoh, na-geh i-mba di wa-szra lo-owa (You have killed your wife, and now it is me you are wanting to kill)," she continued to spill out her guts with hate and murderous facial expressions. While she seemed a little incoherent because of the afvoh-afvoh she had to take to calm her nerves and build her confidence and make her bold enough to face her killing wizard adversary, she was, however, composed and effective in the delivery of her message and standing her ground.

Af-voh-voh, which was estimated to be about 180 proof went by other names like afo-fo, "push-me-I-push-you," kai-kai, and so on. It was considered an illicit gin and, therefore, a contraband by the government, though it continued to flourish as it was made in the bush distilleries and served "discreetly" alongside palm wine and kwa-tcha in alcohol parlors (social parlors) normally associated with the low-income bracket, the main streeters. Locally made, it had been argued that it was a colonial economic ploy to kill the local distillery industry in favor of gins that were imported from Europe and particularly France. They argued the alcoholic content of their af-voh-voh did not make it any better a killer of the people than the alien gins permitted to be sold.

After "independence," the ban on afvoh-afvoh continued alongside the existence and serving of this alcoholic beverage. There have been cases of some very serious stomach ulcers that have been associated to af-voh-voh drinking by village regulars, though the argument was that there was no proof. Social alcoholic parlors were a backbone and support of the immediate local or village economy. There were three categories of producers and suppliers—palm wine, kwa-tcha, and afvoh-afvoh. Secondary producers and suppliers were the kanda, achu, fufu-corn, and kwa-koko; the tertiary group in this line of business supplied the cigarettes, bitter kola, kola, cookies, and candies.

Outside these social alcoholic parlors were strategically located street businesswomen. They provided roast fish, roast plantains, roast plums, and miodor and mboh-mboh-lor. Sometimes the kwa-koko came from the street, if not served inside. The af-voh-voh business was, therefore, an intertwined economic activity, a keystone species as the biologists will put it.

The families of Szra-ngo Wotany and Szra-ngo E-ku-mu-ti socialized occasionally but only on an identical gender basis, meaning the men visited with each other and the women did same. I do not recall anytime that either couple made a trip together for a social visit. That is, Nya-ngo Maloke visited with Nya-ngo I-tor-tor-woh, while Szra-ngo E-ku-mu-ti visited with Szra-ngo Wotany. These two families were very withdrawn from the village community as a whole and from a social perspective.

These were very obviously loner families, so it was not surprising that the loner families were friends and made an effort to socialize with each other. Their strangeness, thought to be shrouded in mystery, seemed to have made them collectively prime candidates for li-emba and nyo-ngo.

While the village thought that Nya-ngo Mo-fvu-ngeh had at last returned to her ground state after staying in the excited state for so long, she knew no peace while externally, the village was at peace from her, or so it seemed. For close to two years, Mo-fvu-ngeh had been inflating like a balloon and because she was of short stature, she had the phenotypic appearance of an engorged tick on the skin of a dog, being a semi-endoparasite feeding on its host's blood. In our community, people got nicknamed easily based on physical deformities that they suffered; for example, "O-ngo wa Mu-endey" or just simply "Mu-endey." These meant that the person had one type or another of a lower limb deformity; for example, it could be knuckle knees or K-legs as we called it in Pidgin English, in which case the person will be called "Ma-boh-ngoh;" or it could be victims of the polio virus that deformed both legs or just one.

You could be called "Mo-fveh" if you had a large head or "Ma-szro-ngeh" if you had a noticeable problem with your dentition, for example, permanently missing a tooth or teeth, teeth not well-aligned, canines or incisors that were not well aligned, and sometimes attempted to extrude themselves out of the mouth like a *Ngow'a wa-nga* (hog or bush pig), and so on. Nya-ngo Mo-fvu-ngeh was being filled up with some fluid, for there was certainly fluid accumulation going on inside her, so she became swollen like a sponge that had soaked some water. Her state of edema was phenotypically holistic. Mo-fvu-ngeh thus became "Michelini," meaning like a Michelin tire, "Li-ngu-lu," like a tire, or "I-tor-lor-l'a vfla-wa," a female toad laden with eggs as commonly seen during their breeding season, all about the village, carrying the males on their backs.

Younger folks preferred the Michelini name while the older and more Mo-kpwe-centric ones preferred using the I-tor-lor-l'a vfla-wa.

Phenotypically, Nya-ngo Mo-fvu-ngu mo Mi-szro-li nee Makala ma Toe-mbeh could appropriately be described as short, fat, round, and with a characteristically shorter and broader bantu nose. Nya-ngo Mo-fvu-ngeh had been sick for a while, and as she got progressively inflated, being engorged with fluids, she had gone from one yowo man to another, moving from one nga-nga house to another. The verdict was unanimous; it was Szra-ngo E-ku-mu-ti who was bewitching her.

"No-whe-neh o doh-tor jami (I see you in my dreams)," said Mofvungeh. "Oh wor-ti wo-szro wom'a molana wa-ngoh (You wear your wife's face)," she continued. "Oh mo wu-szra-na, di na-wi i-ma o-wa (You go out with her, but I still know you are the one. Such a poor disguise)," she "revealed" in mockery. "Ma-meh nde-nga-teh wa-szra li-vfu-mu-leh Moto a-way-li (Why do you want to resurrect a person that is dead)?" Mo-fvu-ngeh asked E-ku-mu-ti, accusing him of necromancy.

E-ku-mu-ti, under normal circumstances, was a mystery in the village. His name E-ku-mu-ti was an attestation to that. The Wa-kpwes have three spirit types—E-ko-ngi, Mo-li-mo, and the E-ku-mu-ti; an encounter with any of them was not a good sign at all, for they were known to terminate lives of *wat'o wa vheh-na-ma* (human beings), the visited, or those they came in contact with. When a person died and resurrected in the spirit, the spirit returned as either an E-ko-ngi, a Mo-li-mo, or an E-ku-mu-ti, and such returns were normally for revenge, in "games" of death or life.

In the Mo-kpwe culture, while some names may seem meaningless—for example, Wolowa, meaning toilet, Dima (blindness), Wo-szro-ngi (enema), Mai-ja (blood)—there is always a story or event behind each name, good or bad. Thus, the name that one bears is revealing for those who know the culture. Why would anyone bear the name E-ku-mu-t'a Njila? Njila in Mo-kpwe is a lion; therefore, for a mot-à-mot translation, this Szra-ngo's name was Spirit Lion. Lions kill and eat their prey, so a spirit lion kills its prey spiritually and eats the prey spiritually. These spirit types were exclusively associated with evil and death, being agents of the devil. Szra-ngo E-ku-mu-t'a NJila was therefore a Devil Lion; that is the premise Mo-fvu-ngeh was coming from.

E-ku-mu-teh's sister, Nya-ngo Mu-ema mo Gbwamu, was busying herself in the kitchen, excited and happy that her ndoh-meh wa mu-nya-na had started his journey through recovery, after the tou-mba process, when Mo-fvu-ngeh arrived around midmorning and stood about twenty-five meters away from their house, hauling to the outside the venom and bitterness that was accumulated in her and which she must now vent to avoid an implosion.

"Oh-szro-wa toh eya (Say not a word)," Mu-ema said to her brother, E-ku-mu-ti. "Na mo'o-wa-neh (Let me talk to her and handle this). Mo-fvu-ngeh Makala ma Toe-mbeh," she called out as she came out of the kitchen and stationed herself in the veranda where E-ku-mu-teh was seated. "E-neh yoma witi na I-tor-lor-l'a vflawa (This thing that is swollen like a toad, she vomited with anger)."

"Nje-neh or-ghe-leh oma o-whe-li (Who do you think you are)?"

"Wa-veh Nje (Who are you)?"

In most Mo-kpwe villages, women are brought in for marriage from another village, sometimes far and sometimes near. Mo-fvu-ngeh was brought into the village from another village that was west of out village and who were considered of a lower social stratum. This was a tiny village between Gbwa-szra and Wo-kwao-ngo (in Greater Gbwea), easily missed when passing by, except when pointed out to you locals. Thus, the daughters of the village were not friendly and, dare I say, sometimes openly and directly hostile to in-laws who brought disorder and discord into families and, therefore, upsetting the social order of the village. Mo-fvu-ngeh, to say the least, was not popular among the walana in the village. She knew that and knew better to keep her distance. She was not a member of any of the women's social clubs in the village that kept the village alive with their annual social activities, especially their singing and sometimes acting and dramatic presentations in the open air for the entertainment of the village.

"O-szre-nje di molana (You are not a woman)," Mu-ema declared, continuing her initial affront on Mo-fvu-ngeh.

"O-vhe-li di mu-nya-na aou-tu a-wor-ti ae kawa (You are a short man)." In kawa, that is a man dressed like a woman.

"O-szra-wi ma-meh de-ga-teh o'oka mo-ngo mo-szri-yio mo li-li-ta (You do not know why you are suffering from this disease of 'swelling')?" Mu-ema mo Gbwamu asked Mo-fvu-ngeh.

Nya-ngo Mo-fvu-ngeh mo Makala ma Toe-mbeh was known and characterized as being lazy. Every molana in the village had crop farms and the crop farm duties were shared along gender lines. The exception was in the Mola Mi-szro-li household in which the wu-nya-na assumed all the duties while the walana were onlookers. To the "defense" of Mo-fvu-ngeh and her wana wa ngoh-ndor (female children), they were constant targets of vhi-emba (witches and wizards) and therefore anatomically and physiologically, they were always too ill to engage in any physically demanding manual labor. What Mola Mi-szro-li tolerated was attributed to his wife having "cooked" and subdued him with medicine from Wat'o wa Yowo, and now Mi-szro-li was a skeleton and shadow of himself, a puppet at the mercy of Mo-fvu-ngeh.

In Pidgin English, it was said, "Ee doh charm i-masa (She has charmed her husband)."

And in Mo-kpwe, "A-mo li-szreh yowo (She has fed him with charm [love potion] put in his food)."

Village farmers were, for the most part, subsistence farmers. They farmed primarily to feed the families, livestock, and other domesticated animals. Any excess left was then sold in the local markets. The usage of what came out of farms was the exclusive domain of the woman and among the village women, how much one was able to sell in the local markets in a sustained manner and year-round, was a measure of hard work, and economic autonomy on the woman's part. Mo-fvu-ngeh had never been seen selling *Xathosoma sagittifo-lium* (cocoyams or *Koko* in Pidgin) in the local Buea market or any other local markets within the Buea Metropole, and this was not surprising. While she attributed this to her ill-health, others thought otherwise—laziness and a charmed husband who had spoiled her.

There were, however, non-apparitional sightings of Mo-fvu-ngeh in faraway markets selling Xanthosoma sagittifolium. The fight sighting was in Voo (Limbe), then it was Ekona Leh-lu, and lastly, Tikowa (Tiko). These are towns outside the Buea Municipality, so when the first sighting was reported in the village, the Roman Catholics in the village thought it was a Mo-fvu-ngeh apparition, though she was not a Catholic. When the second and third sightings were reported, then it was clear that these were no apparitions but a real *Mot'a vhe-na-ma* (real human being).

For a while, walana in the village had been complaining about a possible night harvester or perhaps a spirit harvester. They had found *Xanthosoma sagittifolium* dug from their farms when they arrived very early; that is, before 6:00 a.m. While farm owners had to battle with kwai and other pests, now they had a human or spirit pest to contend with as well. So, when the "apparition" sightings were confirmed as a result of multiple sightings, rumors had it that Nya-ngo Mo-fvu-ngeh was the invisible spirit woman that was the non-contributory partner to other farmers at harvest time.

Surveillance at night and very early hours of the day yielded no fruits, so some of the *walana wa mbo-wa* (village women) went to a Mot'a Yowo and "spoiled" their farms. *Spoiled* here means fortification and protection of their farms; that is, they obtained medicine from the nga-nga with instructions on how to plant it in their farms, such that anyone who stole from the farm caught a disease with characteristic phenotypic symptoms. Only the women who planted the medications knew what the symptoms would look like. When such symptoms started manifesting externally, they became vindicated, and among the adults in the village, the news spread in hush-hush tones.

Nya-ngo Muema mo Gbwamu was a daughter of the village, married in another village; it did break her heart that these foreign women were tearing the social fabric of her village.

"Ma-meh nde-nga-teh ou-ngeh-li na-nu (Why are you so swollen)?" she asked Mo-fvu-ngeh. "Or-ngeh-ley o-ma i-szra-wie (Do you think we do not know)? Eh mbo-wa ya-szrey eh-wie (The whole village knows). E-neh yoma ya mwui-weh (This thief, she finally landed). A-njia-na e-ke-szro ya-ngoh a-nu (Get out of here with your evil secrets and evil deeds)."

E-ku-mu-ti had a female *Sus scrofa domesticus*—that is, a sow— that had just delivered ten piglets, and it was let out of confinements at about midday or noon so that it could range in the yard with its piglets. E-ku-mu-ti had a large compound which was all fenced; therefore, the gate was open. The sow was not able to venture outside its owner's property. E-ku-mu-ti normally locked the gate before letting the sow out, but on this day, Mo-fvu-ngeh was approximately ten meters from the gate as a one-man central stage caster. While Mu-ema mo Gbwamu was engaging Mo-fvu-ngeh, E-ku-mu-ti decided to go let out the pigs that he had not been able to release for the past couple of days because of his ill-health and, therefore, was determined to do so today.

When the sow came around the front of the house with its piglets and saw Mo-fvu-ngeh, it immediately charged toward her. It might have been charging to get through an open gate that was next to Nya-ngo Mo-fvu-ngeh mo Makala ma Toe-mbeh. It is also known that sows are very aggressive and are chargers when they are with their piglets. They are offensive in the protection of their young. The sow did not venture out of the limits of its yard. It turned to return to its piglets once as it arrived at the gate and as the intruder fled.

"Mao-ngoh eh (Trouble oh). Na way-li (I am dead). Eh Ngow'a li-cmba y'ama E-ku-mu-ti ya no-owa (E-ku-mu-ti's bewitched killer pig is about to kill me)!"

Mo-fvu-ngeh was narrating and begging for help at the same time as she retraced her steps back to her part of the village. Mo-fvu-ngeh forgot and abandoned her well-rehearsed and carefully planned longtime mission and instead was now running away from it in an attempt to save her mortal life. Mo-fvu-ngeh's residence was at the middle elevation of the western hilly portion of our village while E-ku-mu-ti was at the eastern lower plateau valley of the village; thus, Mo-fvu-ngeh had to run southwest and then north, a total distance of approximately 300 meters. This was a long distance for someone who was physically ill, even if they just had to walk.

Mo-fvu-ngeh combined "running" and walking fast without looking back once until she reached her destination, entered her house, and closed the door behind her. All the way, she was narrating her story of E-ku-mu-ti's bewitched and devil-possessed ngo-wa trying to kill her. She did not seem to know that there was no ngo-wa chasing her, that it was all in her mind, wishful thinking.

As she passed people on her way, they commented, "Dis witch woman don craze (This witch has gone mad)."

"Dis tif woman don craze (This thief of a woman has gone mad)."

"E-ngeh yowo ye-ni e-ma mo kwa-ni-szreh (Her love for medicines from yoworites has made her go mad)."

"Mo-ngo mo-szrio mue-ni, mo kwa-ni-szreh (Her illness makes one take leave of their senses)."

It was the middle of the rainy season. Our unpaved village footpaths were coated with black slippery mud and pools of water at the sides or right in the middle, if there were any potholes. Mo-fvu-ngeh did slide and fall several times before she got home. She was drenched in mud all over and resembled range village pigs playing in a mud pool, their favorite play place.

The word *Kor-weh* in the Mo-kpwe language means "dangerously evil," and this word was not lightly used, and neither was it used often. It was a rare terminology that beginners of the Mo-kpwe language would not be familiar with. To be called a Kor-weh, therefore, was no compliment. Mo-fvu-ngeh was a Kor-weh and a *Yoma ya Wo-weh* (a dangerous thing) to be avoided, like one with a contagious plague.

CHAPTER 8

Hunter and Hunted

There was a *Mo-ku-szra* (widow) that lived south of the Mi-szro-li property, and they shared a common boundary. The Mo-ku-szra family had just moved in, so to say, to a property that seemed abandoned for many years as we grew up as kids. Evidently, the owner of the property did not care or did not have the means to care for it, and we never knew who this person was. When this mysterious person passed, his remains were brought to the village for interment. Then we, as kids, learned that he was based in Voo (Limbe) where he worked and lived with his *li-tu-mba* (family).

When he passed, they used the unfinished house he had started, which was next and south to the Mi-szro-li's for the funeral and, eventually, for burial, and then his li-tu-mba moved in—his *mo-la-na* (wife), three *wa-na* (children), his *ndo-meh wa mo-la-na* (sister) that he took care of when he was alive, and two wards of his wife. This abandoned property was made up of an unfinished house with a roof and was enveloped by a thick bush that could make a good hunting ground. We were scared of this bushy yard for another reason because we were informed that there were two *szroh-ngoh* (graves) in this property that were normally covered by the bush. We did not know who was buried in these szroh-ngoh because they were not part of our li-tu-mba, and that is what made these graves mysterious and fearful.

An immediate friendship was struck, and the Mo-ku-szra's li-tu-mba and that of the Mi-szro-lis were very close and did lots of things together, both *wa-mba-ki* (adults) and *wana* (children). The Mo-ku-szra and Mo-fvu-ngu were experts in downing other *ma-tu-mba* (families) especially the wana of other matumba. My siblings and I had our own fair share. I considered this to have been some sort of a complex behavior, covering up something and pretending to be normal superficially. What could it have been? Both matumba had similar problems—adult ill-health and poor educational performance by their wana. These negatives in their lives were attributed to li-emba from their immediate neighbors. While the mokuszra did not go out to "teh tu-ndey" with Mo-fvu-ngeh, she was part of the grand plan and was well-aware and informed of the when, where, who, what, and how.

"Small pikin cutlas di sharp for mornin tam (This is a common pidgin language adage, which literally means hot stuff gets cold really fast)."

Nya-ngo Mofvungeh's modus operandi toward li-emba and nyo-ngo was simple and straightforward—Kwe-li; that is, death to the wa-i-emba or nyo-ngo wu-nya-na and wa-la-na. That is why she would not hesitate to employ "thunder-control" jazzmen from grassland up country to strike down her enemies. She was thus nicknamed Methuselah. The reasoning was that because she desired death for others and let her, therefore, live forever. Nyango Mofvungeh had not succeeded in killing any of the wa-i-emba, and her problems were still there and increasing. So, while she was not about to discount any of those she had accused previously and tried in vain to kill, it was now time for her to look elsewhere for additional culprits. She desired *mai-ja* (blood) and revenge many times over to prove her strength and ruthlessness.

Anthropologically, the origins of the Wa-kpwes is Wo-mbo-ko (a land situated behind the Vako), and they are reputed for having strong or powerful Wat'o wa Nga-Nga. Mofvungeh's return trip from Womboko turned out to be an unusual finding. The upland Wakpwes inhabit the foot of Mount Vako to the south while Womboko is situated on the other side of Mount Vako to the north. When Mofvungeh visited with the popular and renowned Mot'a Yowo in Womboko known as

Makala ma Toe-mbeh, she returned home, perhaps never before so energized and so ready for action. She seemed very determined to win this envisioned battle if for nothing other than to compensate for the lack of any success with her in-laws thus far.

The summary of her trip to Womboko was that the serpent under the roof was the Mokuszra Molana, and Makala ma Toe-mbeh quoted specific known instances and events that backed up these claims. For example, an old textbook of Mofvungeh's son that was missing just before an exam, turned up by the szroh-ngoh of the Mo-ku-szreh's munyana, and Mofvungeh's son failed that exam. The Mokuszra was also very big and fond of spices and had recommended a certain spice for the Miszroli litumba to put in their soup. As it turned out, the mokuszra provided the spice and assisted Mofvungeh in preparing the soup. Both matumba ate the soup, and while all of the Miszroli litumba members suffered some digestive system discomfort, including a running stomach after eating what they all called a delicious soup, the mokuszra's litumba was just fine.

Many more instances were quoted of specific events that were known only by both matumba. This soup event had another twist. It was further interpreted as the widow trying to steal Mofvungeh's munyana—that is, Mola Miszroli—and that spice recommended, provided, and put into the soup by the Mokuszreh Molana herself was actually a charm meant for Mola Moliszroli. Mola Moliszroli did not suffer any of the symptoms experienced by the rest of his entire household after eating the delicious soup.

The relationship between Mofvungeh and the Mokuszreh, Nyango Li-szro-ka, went from very good friends to worst enemies overnight, and the whole village was just watching to see what was going to happen next. Immediately, though all forms of interactions between the two families stopped and there was an uneasy calm between these two adjacent matumba. Nyango Mofvungeh ensured that she shared her findings with the whole village by narrating her story, standing in her balcony, overlooking the Nyango Liszroka house, and ensuring a time when she knew the Mokuszreh was in and as well as just about all of the neighbors.

As mentioned earlier, as wana, the Liszroka property was really more like a haunted house, a good one for a Halloween treat. It was roofed with aluminum sheets, walls of blocks and cemented floors. It was an unfinished *nda-wo* (house) surrounded by bushes outside and the rooms clustered with vegetation and creeping reptiles. At a time when an average house of the village was made of wooden boards or "plank houses," as we commonly called them, this Liszroka setup with a barely noticeable szroh-ngoh of an unknown (as far as we were concerned), and also because not even our parents seemed to know made this property so close to home very uncomfortable. When the mysterious owner of this property was brought to the village dead and for burial, we were confused the more, and this further increased the mystery we associated with this ndawo.

As wana, we thought we remembered that the poorly attended szro-ngoh was that of the owner of the property, so therefore, when it was said that the property owner's remains were being brought here for burial, that only increased the mystery. Did this munyana die twice? And whose remains were in the abandoned szro-ngoh in this property? My immediate litumba were specifically five houses north of this haunted property, so this was more of a problem to my cousins, the Miszroli wana whose property was next and adjacent to the Liszroka's than it was for me.

While this property was not inhabited, snakes crawling from there to the Miszroli property was fairly frequent, which led to sometimes clearing into the mysterious property just so that maybe it will minimize the cross-boundary movement of the creeping reptilia. The death of a Szrango Miszroli's dog had previously been attributed to a snake bite, a snake that originated from this bushy property. But all of a sudden, after the owner's death, this "bush" became very lively with humans and accompanying activities. We wondered whether the owner of the property being alive was a hindrance to this liveliness, which took his absence for this "full of life" to emerge.

As Nyango Liszroka settled in her new property, from nowhere— at least, as far as we were concerned—there were rumors, wicked rumors at that, for a molana who had just lost her munyana.

The Miszrolis had dogs used as security, especially at night, companions when they went to their farms or bush as we commonly called them, and occasionally for hunting. Nyango Mofvungeh was in her kitchen, taking care of dinner for her family, and in this case, she was alone, which was a rare situation because her kitchen seemed crowded as she made dinner most of the times, getting assistance from household members and teaching home domestics at the same time to especially the daughters of the household. In addition, when cooking or preparing dinner, she could also do with some human company, humans she used as "whipping boys", howling and dishing out orders every so often. In her crowded kitchen, Mofvungeh normally inserted herself as the central figure, even if there were other wam-baki or adults there, like the occasional presence of Mola Miszroli her husband, during dinner preparations. Mofvungeh ensured that the narrative of the crowded kitchen was about her, around her, and was concentrated on her. The reaction of the crowd around her was often times of silence as she rambled and ranted in self-aggrandizement.

Dogs normally would not enter the kitchen except in the rare occasions where their presence was needed; for example, the occasional treat that was fall-out from the cooking—the head of a fish, bones, scales, and other entrails that may not be desirable for the cooking. In which case, these human undesirables were treats for the *gbwa* (dogs). These gbwa treats were presented in two ways. The dog was called to the kitchen, or the treat was placed outside of the kitchen at the spot that was used as the feeding lot for the dogs. The reason why placing these treats out there was not a good first choice because it meant the stronger gbwa got to get all the treats, and it also led, for most of the time, to fighting among the gbwa.

Calling an individual gbwa by name, therefore, ensured that the said gbwa got the treat, and this treat was to be administered under the watchful eye of the benefactor. Nyango Mufvungeh did not have any treat for any of the gbwa this cooking period, so it surprised her to see one of the gbwa named Meh-ke-lou rush into the kitchen, growling in a low frightened pitch and with its tail between its legs, an act of submission and great fear. Mehkelou the gbwa rushed into the kitchen and took up a position behind Mofvungeh.

Mehkelou was a male gbwa and sometimes a dominant male gbwa from another household passing by could bring about such great fear to another gbwa. But this had never happened to Mehkelou, the dominant gbwa in the yard, and if it was another gbwa, there would first be some loud barking followed by some fighting and then a retreat if need be. There had never been a retreat with Mehkelou face-to-face with another gbwa. So, what was it? Certainly, a *Mot'a weh-na-ma* (a human being) with a menacing weapon, but if it was a Mot'a Weh-na-ma that was approaching, then the Moto would have spoken. So, she asked, "Nje-neh a-weh-li a-nga (Who goes there)?" There was no answer.

It was getting dark, and Mehkelou was still growling fearfully behind Nyango Mofvungeh, and by now, she had stopped her cooking, and some sort of fear was now creeping up on her. She knew her son was home, so she called out to him, "E-li-wa-li-wa ae Tu-mba-na!" And when there was no answer, she repeated the call in a higher and louder tone, "E-li-wa-li wa a-we-li a-nga? Is Eliwaliwa there?" No answer.

Now fully alarmed and the adrenalin levels in her blood rising to unusual levels, she stretched her hand and got hold of a machete tucked away at one corner of the kitchen and decided to venture out of the kitchen instead of waiting inside for what now seemed like a dangerous situation. She stepped outside of the kitchen with Mehkelou following close by, and as she saw nothing, Mehkelou led the way to the *ndawo ya wu-wa* (chicken or fowl house). She followed fearfully and trembling as she simultaneously was calling after Eliwaliwa ae Tumbanah. She reached the entrance of the fowl house, shaken and not entering. Mehkelou started barking very loudly and continuously, a warning that whatever it was, was inside the ndawo ya wuwa. But what could it be? And could she take the chance of going inside the ndawo ya wuwah?

The wuwa had just settled down to rest for the day. It was early night, and they were roaming all day; it was their rest time. Strangely, though, there was no noise coming from the ndawo ya wuwa, so what was it? She was now getting fully scared as Mehkelou became even more restless and barked even more furiously. Then Mehkelou started making a dash to the entrance of the ndawo ya wuwa and almost immediately backed away as it barely entered the ndawo ya wuwa. At this point, a large *vhe-yi* (viper) started to crawl out of the ndawo ya wuwa as the retreating Mehkelou continued its barking. As the *gbwa-wa* (snake) headed for the entrance to Nyango Liszroka's wolowa (toilet), Mehkelou was in pursuit but at a safe distance, evidently knowing the formidability of the legless reptile it was engaging. The gbwawa finally entered Nyango Liszroka's wolowa through a liovah (door) that was, for the most part, only partially lockable so there was no problem gaining access. Mehkelou did not enter the wolowa but stayed outside, barking, as if to say, "I know you are there, and I will be watching out for you!"

The vheyi practically disappeared once inside because a search thereafter did not reveal the presence of any gbwawa, and while the Miszrolis swore they saw the gbwawa, the Liszroka litumba lightly dismissed it as some kind of an illusionary hallucination, meant as an affront of some sort on their family.

As the gbwawa left the Miszroli property for the Liszroka's, Mofvungeh, shaken and having deciphered what was happening, decided to sound the alarm which should later justify her actions or, rather, reactions. While the mortal danger was in her imminent vicinity with an easy striking proximity, Mofvungeh was frozen, and her bonds were only loosed when the danger was distal from her.

"Tata eh, wa-iemba wa no'o-wa (My father [or ancestors], witches are killing me)." Gbwawa di womi oli no'o-wa. (It is a snake they have sent to kill me)."

Transfixed and continuing with her shouting and instantaneous interpretation of the situation, she did not dare to attack or confront the snake. Eliwaliwa ae Tumbana, her *mua-na wa munyana wa mo-mba-ki* (oldest son), came to the scene just in time to see the tail of the legless reptile disappear into the wolowa of the Lizsroka litumba. Mehkelou had done its job, warned Mofvungeh, smoked out the danger, and chased the danger out of their property to that of Liszroka.

"I-ya-ka, gbwa-wa wo-szro-mbi? (Mother, were you stung by the snake)?" Eliwaliwa ae Tumbana asked.

"Szreh-ke-teh Gbwawa, Moto (It is not a snake, it is a human)," Mufvungeh replied. "Nawi nje-neh (I know whom)," she added.

Eliwaliwa ae Tumbana eventually was able to lead back into the house her transfixed iyaka who seemed to be now speaking incoherently but planning her revenge attack at the same time. This was a "near-death" experience for her, and she was visibly much shaken.

When he settled and calmed her down some, he asked his iyaka, "Neh o-wi-ye-li o-ma szreh-ke-teh gbwawa (How do you know it was not a snake)?"

"I-mba na-szreh-ni Moto, ne-ni di gbwawa (I did not see a human, I saw a snake)." Eliwaliwa ae Tumbana added as he probed deeper.

"Ogo Molana di a-we-ni wo-ngo gbwawa (It is that woman who has that snake)," she responded. She was pointing to the direction of Nyango Liszroka's ndawo, so Eliwaliwa knew exactly what she was insinuating or rather stating as a fact. "Ah wo'o-mi di olija lino szro-mba (She sent it to come and sting me with its poison for death)."

While the village was learning of this event, the "Molana" in question was an open secret; it was known she was the most recent adversary, and the stage was being set for a big-time confrontation. It was a matter of time, an uneasy calm before the storm. Mofvungeh left everyone in the village guessing with anxiety and anticipation. It was once more Mofvungeh, a "comme d'habitude" sort and a déjà vu, the center-stager, the victim, the attention seeker, etc.

The chance came sooner than later as was expected by most in the village. It was barely two days after the "Mofvungeh-Gbwa-Gbwawa confrontation." A female dog owned by the Miszrolis was called Li-wo-weh. It had gone to the Lizsroka's property and specifically their kitchen and tried to help itself to some meat that was temporarily displayed awaiting its preparation. Nyango Liszroka had just returned from the market and displayed her market purchase on the kitchen table. She returned to the main house to change and probably catch her breath before she started cooking. On her return to her kitchen, she stumbled on Liwoweh who had pulled the meat down from her table and was struggling to eat the raw meat that was now on the uncemented floor (dirt floor) of her kitchen. She quickly pulled the door of the kitchen closed, trapping Liwoweh inside it, and she did so very quietly. She then called her son from his room.

"E-ko-lo-ko-lo, ja eh (Ekolokolo, come)," she called out. "Ekolokolo i-ma ja eh ka-szri ka-szri (Ekolokolo, I say you should come quickly," she said in a louder voice. "Mameh o-gbwe-ya E-le-ma oszra ta-neh Lija ka-szri ka-szri Ye-tay-na nyio-ngeh Ao we-le-teh (What are you doing that you cannot come quickly when you are called by your mother?" she said with clear irritation in her voice.

When Ekolokolo finally arrived, she instructed him with an urgency in her voice, "E-ndeh o-ja-neh weh-yeh i-ti-yeah e-neh gbwa (Go bring some sticks. Let's beat this dog)."

"E-ma-la ae nya-ma Na'a-di weh lu-wa O li-gbwi-na e-ngo-nya (It has eaten the meat I bought from the market to make soup)," she added, still holding onto the door of the kitchen to prevent the gbwa from leaving.

The obedient son, incensed by the fact he was being deprived of meat and soup by a dog, was cursing and muttering words as he rushed to the fence that served as property boundary and was quickly able to cut, with his hands, four whips or canes, as we commonly called them. These were elastic or twistable whips that inflicted maximum pain permissible by their structural design with the added advantage of not being breakable.

Ekolokolo knew that it would be foolish and fatal to attempt punishing a gbwa corporally while being in the same room with the dog and, worst of all, locked in. The gbwa would certainly protect itself by attacking and fending off its assailant. He cut his mo-lo-ngoh cane (as we called structurally unbreakable whips) long enough so as to avoid close proximity with the beast. He returned, panting, as his iyaka asked how he intended to proceed with teaching the dog and its owners a "lesson." He was going to launch his punishment via the window instead, and there were two windows, so he would alternate from window to window, as the case may be, ensuring that the canine had no hiding place. At the same time, he would use these windows as his own shield from the fury of this bitch.

"Toh mameh wa-szra li-gbwe-ya, Way gbwe-yeh kaszri kaszri (Whatever you plan to do, do it quickly)," Nyango Liszroka urged his son, Ekolokolo.

With some minimal manipulation, the poorly constructed windows of their kitchen could be opened from the inside, even though you were outside. The trick and hard one was going to be how to maintain the windows closed and make them an escape proof route for this *gbwa mui-veh* (thieving dog). When Ekolokolo returned, their very first task was to find a way of letting Nyango Liszroka out of the kitchen, but without the trapped gbwa, for her iyaka would be become a target of the gbwa when its punishment started.

He cracked open the first window and could see the dog making all efforts to tear off the remainder of the meat or skeletal muscle still attached to bones. It certainly had and was still having a good meal at the expense of him and his family. He had to close the south window and go to the north window that was closest to the gbwa. He opened the north window gently to the apparent obliviousness of the enjoying gbwa. He lifted his mo-lo-ngoh cane and struck as hard as he could around the abdominal region of the animal from a dorsal position. It groaned with pain and then quickly moved away from the source of the annoyance and pain but still carried with it a bone between its teeth.

Ekolokoleh changed positions, used a stick to poke it out of its hiding that was beyond reach of the molongoh, and when it was exposed, he lifted and then landed the molongoh again hard on the torso region of the canine. It groaned with pain again, and this time, left and dropped its trophy. It moved quickly to the other side of the kitchen, seeking where to hide, out of reach of its now apparent or, more correctly and obviously, assailant. In the course of hiding deep and securely, the gbwa had to displace items in the kitchen and bring down certain others, the beginning of a chaotic kitchen.

"Whe-ni e-geh gbwa E-no bu-li-szreh-neh Eki-szray-ni y'ami (You see that dog scattering my kitchen)?" Nyango Liszroka said with bitterness and anger. "Ya'a-nu gbwa-na veh Na mio-njoh (The gbwa is also breaking my plates)!" Nyango Liszroka said bitterly.

E-ko-lo-ko-leh increased the pace of the punishment, and now the dog, Li-wo-weh, was physically in distress and anguish and determined to free itself from its captors and punishers. Liwoweh did this by a continuous cry of pain, "Ha-wou, ha-wou, ha-wou!" and darted back and forth, left and right, and into all corners of the kitchen, just so that it could free itself. By this time, the Liszroka's kitchen was in total shambles and everything on the floor.

Mehkelou got the distress message from Liwoweh and ran to the scene of the danger immediately and figured out what was going on. Mehkelou started barking incessantly to the top of its voice, advancing menacingly toward Nyango Liszrokeh and then backing off in an effort to get her to open the door and let Liwoweh go free. Nyango Liszrokeh had to use her body to block the door of the kitchen, without which a simple push from Liwoweh would have shattered it and let the captive free. Nyango Liszrokeh had a big stick in her right hand while securing the door with her left hand from the outside. Each time Mehkelou had made a menacing advance toward her, she had raised the stick in a ready strike position, which thus far had held the attack canine at bay. A Mehkelou dash at Ekolokoleh did not also work; it was met with a strong handed molongoh across its face, which left Mehkelou temporarily writhing with pain as Mehkelou joined Liwoweh in the "Ha-wou, ha-wou, ha-wou" chorus.

The "hawou hawou" sound was typical of the "Mokpwel'a gbwa." Mokpwel'a gbwa means Mokpwe Dog or Bakweri Dog. Based on molecular evidence, dogs are descendants of the gray wolf (*Canis lupus*) domesticated about 130,000 years ago. The Mokpwel'a gbwa was a breed of dog (*Canis lupus familiaris*) that is thought to have genes very close to their ancestors. Due to their size, athletic nature, and viciousness, the Mokpwel'a gbwa are used primarily as security and hunting dogs. Trophically, they are no-non-sense carnivorous mammals that eat their *aves* (bird) prey, holistically. These dogs made the "hawou hawou" sound when they were inflicted with serious pain as to when they were being punished, restrained one way or another or when they hurt themselves.

It was now getting very rowdy. The two gbwa competing with each other at a loud call for help and the Liszrokas having to cope with a fast-changing situation found themselves shouting at the top of their voices in an effort to effectively communicate with each other.

At this commotion, other members of the two families who were home were now drawn to the scene, and all knew what was happening. The Miszroli parents were not at home, and Nyango Liszroka made a conscious effort not to engage in any verbal exchange with the Miszroli children. It was enough for the wana of both families to engage each other or rather to exchange words.

"Dis witch ting dem, wona wan kill we dog (These witches and wizards, do you want to kill our dog)?" the Miszroli children said.

"Dis witch pikin dem, wona nodi gee wona tif dog chop (These witches and wizards of children, don't you feed your thieving dog)?" replied the Liszroka children.

When he arrived at the scene and without any waste of time, Eliwaliwa ae Tumbana rushed toward the kitchen door of the Liszrokas and quickly kemahd Nyango Liszrokeh out of the way. *Kemah* is to knock someone off with one's shoulders, using all one's might and was a favorite offensive tactic among my people, especially the mature adults who were apt at fighting. One obvious reason for its favorability was because it enabled you to use all of your strength and energy and bring pressure to bear on your target or subject. Nyango Liszrokeh easily fell over, not being a match of the masculine strength accompanied by the testosterone rush, and clearly, Eliwaliwa had the element of surprise on his side because as later was revealed, Nyango Liszrokeh was not expecting, and neither did she think of just one moment that Eliwaliwa would dare attack or assail her as she thought of the mother figure she had been to them and the bonded friendship that existed between Ekolokoleh and Eliwaliweh.

Was it all a dream or was this actually happening? She said to Eliwaliweh, "Owa di ono kay-mi Oszreh na-nu (Are you the one knocking me to ground like this)?"

"Weh-meh ae gbwa yeh-ndeh (Free the dog)," Eliwaliweh replied.

Nyango Liszroka, now sprawled to the ground, was dislodged from her attachment as she let go of her grip of the door. As the door showed semblance of ajar-ness, Liwoweh lost no minute to find its way out just as Ekolokoleh reached for the door and maintained its closure with a tight grip, determined to keep Liwoweh captive and continue with the punishment. As Ekolokoleh attempted to close the door, Liwoweh's head was already out of the door, so the closure attempt meant that Liwoweh's neck was caught in this process. Its head out and the rest of the body in meant excruciating pain with a renewed vigor of "hawou

hawou hawou;" and then at this instant, Mehkelou lurched forward, planting its front paws on the chest of Ekolokoleh, knocking him off the ground. Nyango Liszroka and mua-na Ekolokoleh on the ground, Liwoweh freed itself, and as Mehkelou pinned Ekololokoleh to the ground, Liwoweh quickly did same for Nyango Liszrokeh, preventing her from rising from the ground. Both dogs proceeded to inflict bite wounds on their captives and assailants, making their captives and assailants now the hunted.

At this stage, the Miszrolis became frantic and were doing everything in their powers to free the Liszrokas from the fury of their dogs, for this was degenerating into something beyond control and with serious consequences if not stopped now. Calling back the gbwa by their names did not help. As the Miszrolis were trying to restrain their gbwa, the other Liszrokas got into the fight. The other Liszroka children entering the fight did not help. Most importantly, it hampered the efforts of the Miszrolis in their attempt to disengage their dogs from feasting on human flesh as they now had as their prey. Thus, the Miszrolis children were fighting on two fronts—fighting and fending off attacks and punches from the Liszroka children and at the same time struggling to disengage their now dogs gone wild. The scenery was a pile of humans upon humans and dogs sandwiched by the humans.

By this time, a good proportion of the village was already assembled, witnessing this saga/drama and commenting excitedly while obviously enjoying this free and open amphitheater theatrics that was now a constant, a deja-vu, and a comme d'habitude as long as the Miszrolis were concerned. The only surprise was this was too close to home, and where could this be headed? These two families were like blood families, only indigenous villagers knew they were not and, therefore, how could this be happening?

Nyango Mofvungeh and Nyango Liszrokeh had for a long while been joint attackers. They were a formidable duo in attacking others in the village, making derogatory statements about other children and families and knowing who the witch and the wizard was and knowing who was not. They were also very determined to confront overtly and subtly. Nyango Liszrokeh seemed to have preferred a more subtle but obvious approach, sometimes a polite approach. But as it has been said before, "polite" rudeness or accusations could be more hurtful than the direct ones sometimes.

In our town of Gbwea, we called tax collectors "messengers." Messengers of our local council wore paramilitary-like uniforms, and with their batons and heavy Germanic boots, it gave them some air of authority and importance. They saw themselves and oftentimes acted like some kind of a local police force. One of their biggest weapons was the whistle they blew to bring order and or to call attention to themselves. Two tax collectors, appropriately dressed, came to the Miszroli-Liszrokeh scene and blew on their whistles repeatedly until all could hear them and paid attention to their presence. They ordered all the fighters to disengage immediately as they approached the scene, blowing their whistles repeatedly and brandishing their batons in the air as weapons that could inflict pain. The humans disengaged; they ordered the dogs to be tethered and that these dogs should remain on their leash. There was to be a human case between the parties involved, but in the meantime, there was to be immediate action toward the gbwa.

After separating the protagonists and restoring peace to the village, the tax collectors returned to their office and reemerged in the village about four hours later. They brought papers serving both families and summoning them to appear before the native court on the appointed day and time with any witnesses they may have. In addition, the messengers came with two metallic cages and "arrested" the two dogs Mehkelou and Liwoweh. It was known that it was the last time anyone saw the dogs again. They were to be put to rest for having spilled and tasted human blood.

Mofvungeh who had not been around during the free show, was home when the gbwa were arrested, and she wept openly and bitterly like a muana as the dogs were taken away for good, recalling how Mehkelou just days ago had saved her life from a "snake-witch death." She went on to say that this was all orchestrated by Nyango Liszroka so as to leave her without protection from her "snake" and other physical harm. A small crowd had also gathered when the dogs were arrested and aimed for the maximum effect with the attention it brought; it was time for Mofvungeh to attack and finish this molan'a li-emba.

"O-no molana wa li-emba (This witch). Oh mo'o-wa munyana wa-ngoh (You have killed your husband). Mameh o-na-szra-na (What do you want from me)?" Mofvungeh said, addressing Nyango Liszrokeh as she wiped out the perspiration that had broken out from her face, and she felt the perspiration from her armpit draining down the surface of her skin.

"O-ma-keka li-no-wo'a-na mu-nya-na w'ami, Di o-szra-ta-neh (You have tried to take my husband, but you failed)." Na-ngeh waszra linowa Na gbwawa wa-ngoh, Oszra taneh (Now you want to kill me with your snake but again failed). Way-nga-szro wa-kay-li di i-gbwa jami (So now you are passing through my dogs to get me, having them out of the way).

"E-neh yoma (This thing) No'o-ntoh na weh-yeah (I will beat and pound you with sticks). No'o-way na li-ngi li-emba la-ngoh (So as to kill you with that your li-emba). I-szro no-wa na-teh no-kwe-li (Me and you until death)," Mofvungeh continued. "I-mba di naloma lo'o-wa (I will kill you first)," Mofvungeh seemed to have concluded.

By this time, Nyango Mofvungeh was not just soaked in sweat with her kawa hugging her body, but she seemed to have developed some annoying dry cough that interrupted her so frequently that she had to repeat herself when she thought she was not understood or when she thought her emphasis was not clear.

By this time, all of the Liszrokas were indoors. The village crowd had returned to their respective businesses, lamenting the sure and impending death of the Mehkelou and Liwoweh, gbwa they had become accustomed to for years and were part of the village community, contributing to the overall security, especially at night. They also knew that the Liszrokas were going to win the case eventually because animal cruelty was not a big thing in our village, but animals inflicting wounds and tasting human blood had to go and had to be put to rest. Even Mofvungeh's wana, who had been an integral part of the free show earlier in the day, retreated into their home and respective rooms, trying a replay of the day's events while trying to rationalize their behaviors and analyzing to see what they could have done differently and where they might have gone wrong. It was all still fresh and confusing and needed time to be digested. Thus, their Iyaka's attempt to recreate or reenact the scene of earlier in the day in her terms and conditions, imaginary or actual, did not resonate with any of them.

What just happened and what was happening? Perhaps for once and for the first time, Mofvungeh had no audience. It did not take her long to note that she was really talking to herself, and because she was one not to be ignored, she considered this lack or absence of an audience unacceptable and at least a betrayal by her own family. Her husband, Mola Miszroli, who had just returned home, and knowing too well the gravity of what had just happened, totally ignored her and did not even bother to urge her to "Weh-meh," the usual "let go" that was characteristic of him to his molana. Mola Miszroli had only one question to ask his son, Eliwaliwa ae Tumbana, at the right moment several days after the open-air drama.

"Mameh nde-nga-teh, Mameh nde-nga-teh (Why son, why)? How could you let things degenerate so low and to such an extent in my absence? Where is the Muana Munyana wa Mombaki in you? What happened to the first male child status, responsibilities, and expectations?"

The boy would know these were loaded statements and that they were to be followed by consequences somewhere down the line. Eliwaliwa ae Tumbana now saw himself as a destroyer and not as a uniter and a leader as he wished to be and as he knew his ta'a-teh was looking up to. He had since been haunted by Nyango Liszrokeh's question to him when he kemad (knocked her to the ground using his shoulders) her to the ground.

"What about your relationship with my son?" she had asked him and then added, "What about what I meant to you before now?"

Eliwaliwa ae Tumbana had been asking himself one question over and over and again and again. "Mameh nam'a gbwe-yeah (What have I done)?" These were the words of a seemingly tormented man whose world, in a flash, had just crumbled before his own eyes.

Mofvungeh was a fighter, physically and yowo-wise, and she did both fights simultaneously or one at a time, depending on the situation. She had the build of a molana Mokpwe wrestler, called a Ngumumina or Ngumese—short, stout, sturdy, with an expanded spade-like, flat-like bantu nose, enough to suffice three wato. Mofvungeh became very active in consulting with new and "more" powerful yoworites in determined efforts to win her battles spiritually, if she failed physically. She consulted with a known yoworite from Mavaja and then proceeded to Likombe. These were villages in West Mokpwe Land, reputed for their spiritual prowess as was related to issues of li-emba. She wanted a long-suffering illness for her victim that was to culminate in an agonizing death. The manners of death she specified could not be fulfilled in Mavaja alone, so the Mavaja nganga referred her to a competent colleague in Likombe who could fulfil that which he could not.

Despite the expense, Nyango Mofvungeh paid and returned home with her assortment of prescriptions and what she needed to do. She did her "planting" in the deep of the night and then waited for the results. Her plants were carefully buried next to Liszroka's kitchen, and a footpath shared by both families alone.

While she was waiting for her "plants" to be fruitful, she grew very ill and was having lots of nightmares and dreams in which she was being attacked and about to be killed by wa-i-emba. She and her husband quickly arranged and brought in a yoworite to uncover the li-emba molana or munyana as the case may be who was responsible for her maladies and punishment. For the first time, Mofvungeh preferred to rather deal with this li-emba issue quietly as opposed to the tundey and confrontational style. Over the years, she had changed her tactics and outgrown old methods of engagement.

The nganga came on a Friday night. They normally came on Friday or Saturday and stayed overnight in the open or attached to the kitchen. The yoworite she brought in was from Ekona Lelu. His reputation preceded him as he was also a member of the "Oba-szri-jo," a yowo cult that aimed to unmask witches and wizards and that also revealed "spiritual" secrets and provided also spiritual insights to matters of the village. Oba-szri-jo was a juju or yowo that originated from cultural peoples found at both sides of the border of southwest Cameroon and Nigeria. Thus, on the Cameroon side, it was indigenous to the Bayangis and on the Nigerian side, it was indigenous to peoples of Cross River State, particularly the Effiks. Outside these borders, cultures, or peoples and inland, the Bantu groups of Barondos and

Bakweris "bought" this yowo from these alien cultures because they needed it for the good of all and for the protection of their villages.

Not all Bakweri or Mokpwe villages had an Oba-szri-jom cult group. For villages that did not have them, they "borrowed" from the villages that had for a price to come perform some special duty and accomplish a specific mission usually in the presence of the entire village, in the village square, called E-wo-k'a Yowo, meaning yowo square. The Oba-szri-jom of the Wakpwes was bought from the Bayangis, and therefore, its priests and practitioners spoke the Bayang language once they were adorned with the Oba-szri-jo tunic.

In Mokpwe terminology, the adorning or wearing of the chief priest tunic was called "a-gbwa," meaning to "climb." But because the Wakpwes did not understand the Bayang language, there was always an interpreter and translator who communicated with the assembled village crowd. Surely, Oba-szri-jo was alien to the Wakpwes because Mokpwe Wato wa Yowo operated only at night, devoid of spectators. Also, the tunics worn by the presiding priest were a mixture of black and red with bells and mirrors interspersed. An additional oddity as compared to Mokpwe Wato wa Yowo was the "head crown." The cloak of the Oba-szri-jo had a hood. This hood was a wood-carved head of an extinct reptilian shape, a very long snout with gigantic canine teeth depicting a carnivore predator. The artistic design of the mask won was a combination and mixture of human, crocodile, lizard and dog-like features, atop a neck that was about half a meter long and about 20 centimeters in radius.

The Oba-szri-jo ekale or juju did not come out very frequently. It was a rare occasion and when he did. It took several hours for the "show" to be completed. For the ordinary eye, it was a show, but it certainly was a complex spiritual process that took a while to accomplish. Because of the length of time that it took, it made it possible for anyone interested to attend, even if this meant you had to travel to another village to witness the event. There were special drumbeat sounds and special horn-blasted sounds that signaled or announced that an Oba-szri-jo exposure was in progress, and these were loud enough to be picked up by neighboring villages.

Participants from far removed villages could also be present if they chose to because sometimes, the day of the event was communicated by word of mouth in advance, or if it took people by surprise, there was still enough time (two to three hours) for one to arrange to be there, if you got the information. There were at least four Oba-szri-jo practitioners for each event. The chief priest wearing the cloak and deciphering the problem, the translator, and at least two others whose sole business was to guard the chief priest and to ensure that he ended up at the Ewok'a Yowo to reveal his findings in front of the whole village audience.

When a priest is "caught," or rather possessed by the yowo spirit, he will start chanting in tongues, and in the Bayang language, in this spiritual mode, he is no longer a human. He has now been totally transformed to the *E-li-ngeh* (spiritual) realm. At this point, immediate members of the Oba-szri-jo group will be called. When they arrive, they will perform the necessary rituals and then take him to the Oba-szri-jo (obasijom) shrine where they will do some more work on him, culminating in him wearing the Oba-szri-jo cloak.

At this point, the priest in Elingeh form will start running around the village, going to specific points and places all meant to fully prepare him for his revealing mission. As the possessed priest runs about, he will be followed by his guards, one drummer, and one "horner." The drummer plays some light music, while the "horner" blows on an antelope's horn, and the bells on the possessed priest's cloak clicking as he runs; all mixed up, this produces a harmonious combination that informs all that Oba-szri-jo is in process, demanding quietness from all.

The juju will roam around the village for at least two hours before eventually arriving are the Ewok'a Yowo to the welcoming embrace of all present, the hands clapping and frenzy of the drummers that were stationed at the Ewok'a Yowo welcoming the chief priest in sacred music whose meaning is understood by them only. The Oba-szri-jo will circle around the Ewok'a yowo at least once, and then it will start to communicate in the alien language that was translated to the village assembled.

What we normally heard was, "E-sa-meh" from the priest and "Ogoja" from the translator. "Esameh ogoja, Esameh ogoja." It seems this was repeated over and over or rather this is what we wana heard repeated over and over.

Then the priest would continue with some long narration that we understood not, but left enough gaps or spaces so that his assistant, the translator, could do the translation in real time.

However, if a family personally or privately invited or paid for the services of Oba-szri-jo, then their yard became the open theatre.

When Oba-szri-jo was first introduced into Mokpwe-land, it was respected and much sought after yowo. It performed a wide range of services, li-emba cases, communication with the dead, illnesses, etc. As time passed and the original priest and practitioners transitioned, the next generation of practitioners gradually became corruptible; thus, the group passed from incorruptible to corruptible. The Oba-szri-jo ekale of certain villages had become totally corruptible, and generally, villages did not seem to trust their own Oba-szri-jo. The chief priest of Oba-szri-jo in a neighboring village went so far as stealing *meh-koh* (plantains), and this ended up as a bad rap for the entire institution. It was the beginning of the end of Oba-szri-jo in Gbwea villages.

I already mentioned that Mofvungeh became seriously ill after the Miszroli-Liszroka episode, and because Oba-szri-jo in surrounding villages have been compromised and discredited for bribery and corruption, Mofvungeh's choice of an Oba-szri-jo yoworite from a faraway country was an attempt to eliminate any possible corruption. Mofvungeh brought in an Ekona Lelu yoworite who combined normal Mokpwe Nga-nga methods and the Oba-szri-jo methodologies. This was what made this Mot'a Yowo a very powerful one but also very expensive. It was said that he used all three kinds of Mokpwe Spirits in his work.

These were the Ekongi, Ekumuti, and Molimo or Elimo. Ekona Lelu is faraway Mokpweland, a land that most of us in the village only knew existed and as its name meant a faraway land. This "farness" increased the chances of the nga-nga being a good one and also meant the folks Mofvungeh wanted to catch would not be able to bribe him;

and also, she was going to take her wa-i-emba by surprise and therefore inflict the maximum damage.

The nga-nga worked tirelessly all Friday night, breaking Saturday. Saturday, at about midday, the yoworite finished his job of chasing and digging until he eventually trapped the Li-wa-nya that had been running all night long under the ground, like an underground train, in a liwanya (clay pot). He cracked open the liwanya after covering it with an assortment of leaves, spittle, and chanting.

These were the contents of the liwanya:

- Head skeleton of a chicken;
- The hair or fur of a mammal;
- A human tooth;
- An *Agama agama* lizard that was still breathing slowly and described as the driving force that brought about the locomotive displacement of the liwanya in the underground terrain; that is, the subterranean driver;
- A piece of white cloth;
- A snake tooth or fang;
- Assorted fresh leaves;
- An egg shell;
- And a host of other articles that were not readily identifiable.

Some thick dark smoke was exuding from the liwanya as the yoworite was doing his extractions and handing them over to an assistant who carefully laid them in neat rolls as the yoworite continued to chant his mystical words. When the yoworite finished eventually, it was time to announce his findings, the significance of each, the li-emba person responsible, and the next action to prevent a replant.

At this point, the Mot'a Yowo started shaking, and before long, he was speaking in the Oba-szri-jo tongues. He was quickly whisked away by his associates, and the normal signature tune drumming began, and as expected, this started drawing a village crowd and possibly others into the Miszroli yard. There was commotion and unintelligible words diffusing from the nga-nga house, punctuated by some singing, and after about sixty minutes, the possessed and adorned nga-nga man from Ekona Lelu, now an Oba-szri-jo ekale priest, was led out of his "shrine" and brought over to the waiting crowd that now circled the "underground recoveries." It was necessary that the yoworite made his revelations and pronouncements on the recovered items in a state of "infallibility," and that meant he had to wear or be under the oba-szri-jo cloak, what was called a-gbwa in the village.

Speaking through the interpreter and translator and moving around the small theater area available, guarded and closely followed by his attendants and assistants and being aware of the accompanying silence and expectation, all eyes fixated on him, he started, "Owa Nyang'a Mofvungeh Di o'o-ni Li-ni liwanya (It is you, Nyango Mofvungeh, that planted [buried] this liwanya)."

"O-ma mameh eh (What did you say)?" one of the adults present asked the Yoworite from Ekona Lelu through his translator. The interrupter was ignored.

"Liwanya l'a-ngoh lini (This is your liwanya)," he repeated himself, pointing to Mofvungeh.

Everybody seemed confused and was wondering if they heard well or if this was some kind of a joke on the part of a yoworite who was hired to be paid. A hire cannot turn against his employer.

All eyes now turned to Nyang'a Mofvungeh who seemed as if in a trance, who seemed fixed and very confused. When she did not a say a word, then Mola Miszroli said to his molana, "Way-nga owa di Ono la'a li-emba (So you are the one bewitching me?"

"Mameh nde-ga-teh Waszra li-no wu-lu-wa (Why do you want to betray and expose me)?" Mofvungeh asked her Munyana.

"Szre-keh i-szro Wa'a wa-keh di i-ma li-ka (Wasn't it the two of us who buried the liwanya)?" Mufvungeh asked her munyana, Mola Miszroli.

At this, the whole village assembled busted out in exclamation of wonder.

"Wooooooo."

"Na wa ooooooooh."

"Na wa ya ooh."

"Jay-ja eh."

"Ta-ta eh."

"Ta-ta koko eh."

"I-ya-ka eh."

"Jen-ni vay-neh, Jen-ni weh-ya."

"We see son ting."

In wonderment, there were exclamations, in Bakweri and in Pidgin English, of complete disbelief and complete astonishment at the turn of events. It was the first time a hired nga-nga had turned against his employer.

When the voices of the crowd died down and determined to make her point, that her husband was party to the underground mobile liwanya, Mofvungeh proceeded to say, "Nageh waszra lino Vimba o ngi-ndi (Now you want to throw me under the bus in the presence of the crowd)."

"Na-szra wie mameh o'o-wa (I do not know what you are talking about)," Miszroli said. "Li-ya-na e-ke-szru ya-ngoh (Stay with your witch)," Mola Miszroli said to his molana as he stood and left the assembled crowd and returned to his house. Before he left the village crowd, he said one last thing to his wife, "O-weh-li-di kor-weh Nde-ga-veh na yoma ya woweh (You are a thing to be feared, a thing not to be trusted, and an evil thing)."

The drama and theatrical Miszrolis were once more center stage and the talk of the village. A molana in the crowd shouted to the top of her voice, "Eweli di weh-ma weh woweh (You two are bad things and you are also evil)!

"Wa ta-ngeh-ya ogo Mola, wa Ekona Lelu nanu (Considering the turn of events, do we expect the Miszroli litumba to still pay the yoworite from Ekona Lelu)?" another village woman asked.

"Moto wa yowo wa woweh ono (This is a bad and an inefficient nga-nga)," another molana said.

"Ama vanga ewolo yeni (He is a spoiler for himself who has spoiled his own work or trade). Na e-geh y'ama i-veh-veh nga-nga (And that of other fellow yoworites)," another observer added.

After many decades of patronizing yoworites and spending millions of francs, Mofvungeh vowed that she was never going to use their services again. By this time in the village, Mofvungeh or Miszroli became an adjective used to describe persons who exhibited traits of discord, social strife, and evil intent.

While Mofvungeh had given up the services and hiring of Wat'o wa Yowo, it did not mean that she did not still need their services. However, at this point, her son has also become a nga-nga and called just plain "Nga-nga" by his peers and friends. Nganga was still living with his parents and used his room as a consulting room for his clients. While family members did not take him seriously because of familiarity, his clientele grew steadily, very soon to include his iyakeh, Nyang'a Mofvungeh.

Nga-nga, Mo-fvu-ngeh's *mua-na wa mu-nya-na* (son) had gone through a number of names by his peers in the Li-bi-yeah clan and the village as a whole. When he was still under ten years of age, he was called Goal Keeper Okala or just simply Okala. Emmanuel Okala was a star of the Nigerian National Football (soccer) Team and was African Footballer of the Year in 1980. Okala was therefore big news in the African Sports Arena and a pride to the Igbos of Onitsha, his hometown. Nga-nga adopted this name because at this time, he was the goalkeeper of our village soccer team; then Nga-nga transitioned to be called Onana Elundu, oftentimes just Onana or Elundu.

For many years, Onana Elundu was principal defender of the Cameroon National Football (soccer) Team, so while Nga-nga was not a defender himself, goalies like him would love reliable defenders for a good game. Onana Elundu was in the order of defender Ndumbe Lea before him and David Nangoh of Prisons Buea Social Football Club: another transitional name he went through was Nya-meh Makoko. This name was derived from the most reputed Mot'a Yowo that lived on the eastside of our village, next to the village graveyard. He was said to have been seen carrying out live conversations with the dead in the deep of the night as he roamed the graveyard. He was only normally consulted if clients had problems with the dead and wanted communication with the dead.

His own yowo was in the practice of necromancy. He was therefore a necromantic nga-nga, feared in the village and even by his own immediate family members and, by extension, his own family members too became feared wato by virtue of association and proximity, also genetics. His family was generally isolated in the village, and this carried over to his kids at school.

At a very young age, Nga-nga was aspiring to be a Mot'a Yowo, therefore strong yowo figures shrouded in mystery were a fascination to him. At one time, Nga-nga was called Yoveh; that is, the bird dove. One of our favorite activities in the village was going hunting, and as a litumba, we collectively hunted partridges, which we called bush fowl. At some point, Nga-nga extricated himself from the boys hunting group and became a solo hunter, obsessed with bringing home doves. Boys in the village who were bird hunters using catapults or "robber guns," as we call it in Pidgin English, knew that doves were a difficult kill, but Nga-nga had staked his reputation on these difficult kills and thus made a reputation for himself.

As Nga-nga grew older and started his own family, he settled down as a farmer and as a Mot'a Yowo. Nga-nga thus seemed like the last of his many adoptive names.

Nyang'a Mofvungeh developed an abnormal physiological condition; evidently, water and other fluids were accumulating in her body, a form of holistic edema. Hospitals and clinics and numerous forms of traditional medications failed to make any headway. Naturally, Nyang'a Mofvungeh brought her problem to her son to find out who was the cause of her swollen body. The son obliged and followed the normal protocols and procedures of nga-nga. He dug out yet another liwanya and extracted the contents and laid them out in neat rolls. He did not bother to explain the significance of each of the contents but simply went on to reveal the source or the owner of the mobile underground liwanya. While aliens have aero-saucers, my people have subterranean liwanyas. These are just technologies of different types.

"Lini Liwanya liweli di la-ngoh (This liwanya is yours)," Nganga said to the iyakeh, Nyang'a Mofvungu.

"Ta'ata eh ono muana ono szra-mbo-leh way-wo'oka (My father [or ancestors], this child you have disgraced me in the open," said the mother, Nyang'a Mofvungeh.

"It is the Liwanya you buried to harm Nyang'a Liszrokeh that has now turned against you," Nganga said. "We will need a he goat, a white dog, a red cock, and a bag of salt to do what is necessary to li-mi-szreh it." Limiszreh means to quench it. Limiszreh is a terminology not lightly used and used very frugally among the yowo practitioners. Limiszreh, which is meant to "silence" or to "make go" a spirit trapped in the body of its dead host, is a very tricky business. This task is normally undertaken by a superior spirit residing or possessed by a yoworite. If this task is too much for one yoworite, then it calls for a synergetic effort. For a spirit without a host causes havoc to both yoworites and *wato wa wehnama* (humans).

Mofvungeh self-exiled herself from the village after the ceremony was performed and went to live with a close relative of hers in a neighboring village, Szro-f'a Wonganga and then, in a little while, moved overnight to Woteva, a faraway village we only heard of this time to live with a maternal cousin of hers. Her welcome was, however, short-lived as she was booted out of the relative's house and her husband, Mola Miszroli, summoned to come claim and carry his "cargo" home. Thus, after a brief absence, Mofvungeh returned, and the sigh of relief by the villagers, especially her immediate neighbors, all seemed not only far-fetched but also an illusion. Mofvungeh's problems and those of her family continued, and her own health was beginning to deteriorate with very visible swollen features. Mofvungeh went blind, thereafter, coupled with almost total paresthesia.

CHAPTER 9

E-li-mo ya Sasse

When I grew older and graduated primary school, I went to secondary school or college, as was commonly known. My college was a very prestigious one for various reasons. It was called Saint Joseph's College, Sasse, commonly referred to as Sasse, the village where it was located. Sasse was a more or less anglicized pronunciation of what the Wakpwe locals called and pronounced as Szra-Szreh. It was the epic achievement for any young man of my age group because of its reputation and the graduates it had turned out over the years.

My clan was one of a select group of Mokpwes in the Buea area that were given the opportunity to represent the Mokpwes at this citadel of education in Anglophone, Cameroon. Admission was based on brains and economics, and the word *sasse* was used variously to mean big book, English grammar guru, educated elites, high social status, perhaps rich, etc.

In our Libiyeah clan, I was the seventh in line to represent us as scholars of this great institution, two of my uncles having paved the way earlier. Sasse is the Harvard of Anglophone, Cameroon, and ex-students of the institution are called Sobans. These are very productive fine men scattered the world over and are very productive citizens in Cameroon and anywhere else on planet Earth that they find themselves.

When I entered Sasse, I was housed in the central quarters and put in the dormitory called Saint Christopher, St. Kitts for short. The Sassians and future Sobans called the St. Kitts house the "Bourgeois Dormitory" or simply "the Bourgeois." While we were in the "Bourgeoisie," we practiced "socialism" or "Communism," two terminologies we used as alternatives. This meant that aside from your very personal effects, every other thing that you had was shared property and ownership. For example, we all had buckets with our names written on them when it was time for using buckets, e.g. cleaning, watering, etc. As a member of the house, you used the first bucket closest to you, except if you had a choice or were selective. The same went for the hoes and machetes that we used for farm and yard work. Bathing and washing soaps that were left in the washroom, as well as toothpaste and toilet tissue, automatically became communal property to be used by anyone and everyone.

I was admitted to Sasse from Presbyterian School Buea Town in the year 7819, and my matriculation number was 1228. In our time, the lead history instructor was Master Amueh Osangeh, himself a Soban, educated at the University of Lagos in Nigeria. Our preparation for the General Certificate of Education (GCE) was in World Affairs and, therefore, it was Master Amueh's job to prepare his minion comrades to excel in this subject at or during the GCE exams. This was a smart historian well-versed with world affairs and always pitching the "rich" or "bourgeoisie" ideology versus the "socialist" or "communist" ideology. We called our instructors "masters;" it was a strict tradition of the college, and yes, master was also the way we addressed the principal.

Master Osangeh, we came to conclude very quickly, was ideologically a "socialist" but seemed to long being or living as a "bourgeoisie." When we covered Russians and the Mullahs, he was quick to note that the Mullahs were powerful and rich as compared to Bakweri Molas who live a life of "Luxury in Poverty" (In strict terms, Mola in the Mokpwe language means maternal uncle. There are no paternal uncles in the Mokpwe language, for they are considered of equal status as a Ta'a-teh or father and thus called. In a loose manner, Mola roughly translates to Mister, a title, an identifier for a Mokpwe person, an honor, etc.).

That was an affront to us, the Mokpwe pupils in the class, but there could be no retaliation because he was the master and us the pupils. Master Amueh was smart and hardworking, and good results were obtained at the GCE exams in history, year after year, under his tutelage. He was soon promoted to the position of Discipline Master or Master of Discipline, which was shortened to MD and, a few years later, had another promotion as the new Vice Principal (VP for short), a post newly created. We were happy for him, and as he entered the class to teach on his first day after his promotion, we all stood and clapped for him. We normally stood up when an instructor entered the class. It was the rule and the tradition, but on this day, it was with clapping and all smiling faces. He seemed very touched and perhaps showed some emotions, a rare thing for an African man, especially in the presence of his students.

Shortly after his promotion as VP, it was rumored that Master Osangeh had bought a car. No instructor had a car, except for the principal who used the Sasse school bus and the school pick-up truck for his personal use as well. So, when the news had it that the VP had purchased a car, there was anxiety in the air. We wanted to see the car, we wanted to know if he could drive, and after the excitement, we would have wanted to know where this socialist got the funds to buy the car; and furthermore, we would "ask" him if he had now joined the bourgeoisie that he so criticized. And yes, in those days in Sasse, owning a car was a class attribute, it was a luxury and was not seen as a necessity.

Before the VP came to class that morning, there was a drawing on the board of a car and driver, the driver being the lone person in the car. The car had just passed a woman and a child strapped to her back in our African tradition. The woman was pleading for a ride, and the driver of the car put his hand out of the car and just simply waved at her while he continued with his car ride. The drawing had two shades; the green shade occupied by the woman and her baby and the red shade for the car and its driver. The respective shades were captioned "socialism" and "bourgeoism," and combining the two captions was "sasseism."

This was a mistake and miscalculation on our part. When the VP entered the class to teach, we all stood up as expected, and normally, we also sat when the instructor told us to. He entered the class, and I think he sensed that there was tension in the air, this time not one of excitement but one of quietness and fear. He glanced at the board and then immediately asked, "Who did this? What does this mean?"

There were no answers to his questions. He immediately retreated to his office and came back with Mo-loh-ngoh canes, whips that inflict maximum pain on human flesh without breakage. When he left the class, we all knew why, and at this point, a debate ensued as to whether those who did the artistic ideology show should own up and spare the rest of the class some whipping, but at the same time, we all knew that a collective punishment was better and lighter, for if it boiled down to a few individuals, it may not be only whipping but it could also be suspension and even the possibility of dismissal.

We got whipped very well, and there was also some tongue lashing, and there were no sell-outs. And as it happened, there was no car for the VP. Silently, though, I think he realized that we imbibed and analyzed what he taught us and that any contradictions in him were also noted critically.

Before this collective class show, I had a run-in with the VP. The VP was nicknamed Chiang Kai-shek; this name existed before we came to Sasse, and we came to know why this name ourselves as we spent more time with him in the classroom. When we studied China, it was more like the socialist versus the bourgeoisie, Chiang Kai-shek representing the bourgeoisies and Mao Tse Tung representing the socialists and the masses. In his presentation of these materials, which took weeks to cover and in which he did not have to look at his notes, except for the occasional glance, VP Osangeh practically and literally sang Chiang Kai-shek praises. He knew he was called Chiang Kai-shek behind his back.

Senior History students of our bourgeois dormitory—that is, forms 4 and 5 (tenth and eleventh graders)—thought and concluded that our bourgeoism went hand in hand with the socialist attributes of this beloved dormitory. That was what the VP was doing to himself. However, the acclaimed history instructor found these bourgeois and socialist characteristics incompatible based on the China history lectures. The VP himself seemed contradictory and perhaps confused sometimes, but you dared not point that out—you would be roast meat. Master Amueh professed socialism and was fiercely critical of riches or the bourgeois because everything rich was ill-gotten and—or sometimes, it seemed—in the wrong hands. He had once described the father of a student in his class as "an illiterate bourgeois."

Mola Mbul'a Kaweh was a local Mokpwe Businessman in Buea and one of the richest people in Buea, and while he did not have much education, he was still a very successful businessman, but as per the VP, he did not deserve this because he was an "illiterate." The VP bathed in anything that had to do with aspects of riches associated with him, and rich "students" got to know how their parents made their riches, oftentimes illegally and often from the backs of exploited masses.

After these successive promotions, which we all welcomed, I had asked him in class one day, during one of his lectures in which he, in characteristic style, dwelt on the masses, peasants, ruling class, in general, social stratification how he felt now that he was wearing well-tailored three-piece suits and his administrative position that now placed him among the ruling elites of this great and most renowned institution. I regretted that question. The whole class went dead as he seemed to have stopped briefing for a while and started quietly moving toward me without a word and with a clenched fist. When he was at arm's length from me, he licked his knuckles, moistening them, and then "cracked" my head thrice. We had just returned from an "outing week" in which we were required to cut low our hair. I had a skin cut and I was skinny, so my skull bones were literally exposed. The barrier provided by my very thin skin above my cranium and forehead was very minimal.

When the MD and now VP cracked my head three times, the dead class now erupted in unison in saying, "Stars." It was our way of saying that one was in great pain and in an apparent confused mental state. Did I really see stars? Perhaps yes and no, but the pain and disorientation I felt were not imaginary. My classmates became in absentia immediately after saying, "Stars." Later on that day, the junior students that were below our class on the ground floor claimed that they heard a sound that sounded like a wood against metal. The three cracks (a crack is a knock on the head with the knuckles) were in quick succession, and I went dizzy. The only reason I was not sprawled on the floor was because I was sitting, and part of my chair was under my personal desk, which gave me the required support.

The class and its contents spun for a while, and then gradually, I returned to reality. Whatever he said during this my period of "absence," I did not hear. When I could hear and understand again, the bell rang, and it was change of period, albeit it was time for another class. Within these ten minutes of intermission during which another instructor came into the class for another subject, some of my friends came to my desk, some sympathetic, some thinking I deserved it for being so bold, others proffering a course of action, etc. I was just looking at them all, not saying a word nor communicating in any form. I was gazing into the atmosphere, trying to process what had just happened and so quickly, though some thought I was still dazed and suggested I go to the sickbay.

It was VP Chiang Kai-shek's duty to ensure that any student who decided to answer a question on China in World History that it was the one that had to do with the Chiang Kai-shek character, vis-à-vis, his relationship with mainland China. He literally sang his name.

Master Osangeh's promotion and rise to power in Sasse was not well-received by some, and before long, they started visiting nga-nga against him. He was absent from campus for months one term, and it was rumored that he had gone insane and taken leave of his senses. There was even much talk that he was now referring to chickens in his village as his students. We felt very sad for him, also that he just got married.

Master Amueh comes from an ethnic group that was known to be well-grounded in yowo business, so eventually, he got cured of his condition and returned to campus later, a very subdued man. Shortly, he resigned his position and left the institution, partly because the hierarchy of the institution beyond campus could not continue to stand by while he criticized them frequently. He was a victim of yowo and was also an ideologue, even if in ambiguity sometimes. Like Master Amueh, you had to have been a student resident in the St. Kitts

House to determine whether this hall of residence was a bourgeois one or a socialist one. To the outside world, though, we were the bourgeois and the communists.

Saint Joseph's College Sasse was an all-boys school, and the favorite sports was football or soccer. There, existed other teams and individual sports like basketball, handball, lawn tennis, martial arts or karate, and volleyball. There were also track and field events like cross-country races, short distance dashes and relays, long and short jumps, javelin, shot put, hurdles, etc. The other sporting and athletic events were more or less for external representation of the school and were intensified or emphasized only in preparation of the annual school competitions leading up to the eleventh of February of each year and commonly called Youth Day. It was in commemoration of the day La Republic du Cameroun and the Sovereign State of the Southern Cameroons "decided to come together as a Federation of Equal Status to form the United Republic of Cameroon," a two-state federation of equal status. It would have been cumbersome for the school authorities to attempt to organize Inter-House Competitions for all of the sporting activities, and Inter-House Competitions were ongoing, cutting across terms.

Inter-House or Inter-Dormitory Competitions in football were in four categories—minor, cadet, junior, and senior. This system was designed to accommodate all classes from form 1 to form 5. The system was also designed as a recruitment ground for selection into the school football team that represented the school externally. The minor team was for the form 1 students, the cadet team for the form 2 students, the junior team for the form 3 students, and the senior team for the form 4 and form 5 students. Occasionally, though, there was some overlap, albeit a second year or form 2 student playing in the minor team and a form 2 student playing in the junior team. Retrogressive or downward mobility were to accommodate the *bebelacs* (weaklings or faint of hearts) or simply those who were not good at football but were interested and had to be accommodated somehow.

Upward or progressive mobility, on the other hand, meant you were good at football to play for the next level, regardless of your age and size. Remember, classmates are not equal to age mates, so sometimes, an upward mobility may be a combination of skills and age. However, it was primarily a matter of skills.

In my first year and first term, I was confined to the minor team in our St. Kitts dormitory. My skills as a footballer at the minor level were above average. I must also add that my going to secondary school was delayed one year after I graduated from primary school with my First School Leaving Certificate (FSLC). I was, therefore, at least one year older than an average classmate of mine, and there were also others who were probably five to six years my senior in the same class. In our first few games at the minor level, I was deprived from being the captain of the team because a form 2 student who could not measure up to play for the cadet team was in the minor team, and he was a good player, though it was evident that I was better. Seniority in class took precedence, especially if there was evidence of skills and competence.

In the Sasse tradition, a "Plebian" or pleb (which we pronounced as "prep") meant that you were a freshman, and in your first year, you had no voice; you all were called "pleb." Being a pleb meant you obeyed all instructions that came your way, and you could only "grumble and stay." For the most part, the nemesis for plebs were the promoted plebs or the form 2 folks. They could not wait to do what was done to them and were visibly excited to exercise real power after enduring for one year.

Before the end of the year, however, I became the captain of the minor team and featured in some of the cadet games. We went on to win the Minor Teams' Championship Cup, elevating our bourgeois status on campus. Out of six houses, we beat St. Thomas Aquinas to take the cup. In my second year, I played for the cadet team and junior teams and, in my third year, played for the junior and senior teams, and by the end of my third year, I had started training with the college team and actually was fielded in two games, defending the college, one at home and another an away game. I was a defender, sometimes a little too rough.

In Sasse College, there is an *Elimo* (ghost) story that had been in existence a long time before our batch that lingered around all of our five-year stay in Sasse and has continued lingering around decades after our graduation. This Elimo was called "Eyaboweh," and its origins and mission were not clear as there were many stories associated with it, handed down generation after generation in the oral traditions of the school. Every dormitory had experienced Eyaboweh's presence one way or another, and the very mention of the name Eyaboweh, especially at night, brought about silence and fear and forced all and everyone to take cover under their blankets.

While Eyaboweh seemed like a legend, it still was able to put fear in us. We had one student in the bourgeois dormitory who was a class ahead of mine. He was big, a loner, and his classmates barely talked to him. Normally, conversations in residential halls are among classmates with interclass conversations being sporadic. So, if anyone was not engaging in conversation with his classmates, it did not only make the loner lonely and isolated, but it resulted in others being suspicious of you, thinking you were a weirdo. The student named Eyaboweh sweated a lot and had some dermatological problems and as expected, kept to himself all the time. I did not know his relationship with his mates during class or academic activities, but his classmates in the socialist dormitory avoided him at all costs. I do not know if he knew he was called Eyaboweh because this was a hush-hush name behind his back when he passed by a group of students, not only from St. Kitts.

Eyaboweh was an Elimo. Was this the spirit that had now taken flesh? 3r was this just another sick and wicked joke characteristic of preteen and teen boys? And yes, Sasse boys were wicked. They gave nicknames that were thought to be fun but which in hindsight were just outright wickedness and torture.

When I started playing for the cadet team, Eyaboweh was also a member of this football team squad. Initially, my position in the cadet team was as a substitute, and I had no voice because I was a pleb, and they were promoted plebs. Oftentimes in house teams, we had a maximum of, say, thirteen jerseys for eleven players, and as time went on, some went missing, and we barely had eleven or less for the whole squad. In one of my very initial games with the cadet team, I had to replace Eyaboweh, and that meant that I had to wear the jersey he used, all soaked with his sweat. I wore it, went in, and played. It was after the game that I knew he was called the Elimo and that none of his classmates could ever use his jersey. I was a pleb, so I had to use it. It worried me some but perhaps not very much.

After his second year in Sasse, the Elimo Eyaboweh was let go, having been found wanting and lacking in his academics. Some hypothesized that it was because the principal knew that he was an elimo or was involved with the spiritual world, that was why he let him go. Our principal had the reputation of having some special spiritual powers, not from a biblical perspective but from the other world, and based on this, he knew and could tell students that were involved in yowo practices. The elimo dude, Eyaboweh, had his own real name, but very few ever mentioned or called it. I do not remember that I knew it, but I said hi or "how naa" to him now and again, and he called me by name, asking how I was doing.

"Bwanghai, how are you?" he would ask, oftentimes after I had initiated a hello. When he talked to me to the hearing of others, they whispered to my ears when he was gone that I should remember he was an elimo, the Eyaboweh. The elimo dude was a reserved fellow and did not seem to have any friends, not even among his classmates. He was, however, a subject of admiration when it came to farmwork or housework. Whatever was assigned for him to do inside and outside the dormitory was done meticulously and quickly too. He also had the tendency of sweating profusely and would help junior and weaker students finish their work if he saw them struggling. Normally he did not ask them; he simply just went their portion (a piece of land that you were allocated or assigned to take care of for at least one academic year. The care could be and included clearing, weeding, picking up trash on it, caring for crops, etc.) and would start clearing or weeding, as the case may be.

In one of our cadet matches, two substitutions were made simultaneously. Eyaboweh and one of his classmates were leaving to be replaced by another classmate of theirs and myself. The exits had to surrender their jerseys which we, the replacements, had to wear. Because of the hot tropical heat, it is difficult to think of wearing an undergarment before your jersey, so for the most part, the hygienic aspect of adorning a sweaty jersey from another comrade was not giving second thought. I, however, realized that the other replacement made a very conscious effort to ensure that Eyaboweh's jersey did not end up with him. I saw him whispering with his classmates that were at the sidelines but could not really hear or understand what they were saying. As members of the same house or dormitory, we congregated together during games or inter-house competitions. However, despite our natural and expected house congregation rooting for our house team, we still always maintained subgroupings based on academic seniority or categorizations.

I saw that these form 2 dudes were looking at me as I wore the jersey—Pupils of Form 2 were called promoted plebs or promoted foxes as the preference may be. Yes, a freshman in St. Joseph's College, Sasse was called a plebs, which was pronounced and thought to be "prep." *Plebeian*, also spelled as *plebian* (Latin *pleb*—plural *plebes*), was a member of the general citizenry in ancient Rome as opposed to the privileged patrician class. In our history classes taught by Master Amueh Osangeh (a.k.a. "Ndelenism" a socialist-oriented scholar), he used the word *proletariat*. The proletariat is the class of wage earners in an economic society whose only possession of significant material value is their labor power. A member of such a class is a proletarian. Thus, in St. Joseph's Colege, Sasse, we used the terms *plebeian* and *proletariat* as synonyms and sometimes as alternatives, depending on whether you were talking history or whether you were simply emphasizing and exerting class social stratification within the Sasse system of power-social stratification.

Another name that was used also by our masters (we called our instructors *masters*—this was easy to comprehend in an exclusively male teaching and nonteaching staff, not until in our lifetime in St. Joseph's College, Sasse, a female instructor was employed to teach us English. So, what were we to call her master, mistress, or something else) was "foxes." Foxes were freshmen that is form 1, and promoted foxes were form 2 pupils. I could care less. I went to the field and played as expected and later washed the jersey and handed it over to the house sports captain as required. I was still puzzled as to the mystery behind the jersey on that day on the field.

As time went on, I got to learn more about Eyaboweh. He was always dodging, albeit breaking bounds and leaving the campus without permission and spent lots of nights not sleeping in his bed. It was also a matter of time before we, the newcomers, learned that the whole school knew him as a wizard. His "spirit" had been "seen" many times in the bourgeois dormitory, tormenting his enemies and sometimes in neighboring dormitories. Thus, no one wanted to joke with him at any point in time and certainly wanted no association whatsoever. It was also said that the college principle who himself was considered mystical knew of Eyaboweh, and this was exemplified by an end of term warning "for bad conduct" without specification.

By form 3, Eyaboweh was dismissed for academic and conduct reasons. But before he was dismissed, I had an encounter with him. I was in Dorm-B of our bourgeois house, like Eyaboweh, and one night, I was tossing about in my Vono bed, unable to sleep. We slept in pitch darkness, except for security lights from the exterior that permeated the interior of the building via the glass windows and also an almost dim lighting in the corridor that separated Dorm-A and Dorm-B as we called the two sections of our hall. First, I noticed all lights went off, but there were dim rays from afar, reaching and entering our dormitory, so this meant it was a local blackout restricted to our hall. Then the lights came on again after flickering for about ten minutes. But within these ten or so minutes, the darkness in our dormitory turned bluish, then reddish, these colors alternating with the flickering lights.

In the course of these bizarre lighting patterns, I thought I saw a whitish figure moving selectively to certain beds and kind of bending and watching over the loud snoring and sometimes loud farting sleeping comrades. I initially dismissed what I was seeing as just my mind playing some tricks, but after scrubbing my eyes several times and pinching myself to ensure that I was awake and alive, I then concluded that what I was seeing was "real." I was not clear on what I was seeing—a human, male or female or just something moving with the silhouette of a human. Whatever it was, it was coming toward my direction and a decision had to be made immediately, since I did not want it briefing over me, and I do not know what had happened to those this "thing" had visited already.

I was now conflicted. If this thing was an illusion and then I took any action that woke up the dormitory, what would the house and school think of me thereafter? And how would that affect my stay in the house and school long-term? If this thing was "real" and I accosted it, what would be the consequences on me? There was no time to continue theorizing, and by this time, the thing was upon me, gazing down at me with piercing, gazing, bloodshot eyes that seemed to be darting from point to point. The Elimo's breathing was like a hissing of a gas exiting a tube in a physics or chemistry laboratory.

At this point, I was sweating with a dry throat, and words could not come out of my mouth, for I longed to scream. At last, my voice returned to me and was able to come out, and I heard myself say in successive languages:

In the Mokpwe language: "Mameh (What is it)?"

In Pidgin: "Na wai-ti, Na wai-ti I do you (What is it, what have I done to you)?"

In French: "Pour quoi moi (Why me)?"

Pidgin French: "Na wati (What is it)?"

In English: "Depart from me you evil one."

As these words came out of me automatically, I was also lashing out with all my four limbs at the "Molimo's" torso region with all my might and strength. At this point, the Molimo bent backward, responding to the weight and force of my lashing out and creating a small distance between us, allowing me to get off my bed. As this was happening, beds that had been previously visited all came alive, and in unison or chorus, the shouts started.

"Eyaboweh!"

"Eyaboweh!"

"Eyaboweh!"

And others were shouting, "Put on the lights!"

And yet others, "Call Pa!"

We called the principal Pa because he was like a father to us all, and very sternly, he treated us all accordingly. The senior students rumored that he used *Cannabis sativa* (also known as marijuana, mbarga, nga-nja, weed); his eyes were always red and sunken, and he always looked and behaved like one that was high on something. The junior students thought of him simply as a no-nonsense administrator burdened with the education and security of hundreds of students, most of whom were from privileged backgrounds. All attempts to light personal torchlights failed and considering that the main lights in the hall of residence were controlled from another dormitory by the timekeeper, that was not a very useful and helpful option for folks who wanted lights immediately.

As the cries and shouts continued, the light controller seemed to have been alerted, and the lights were put on, but somehow, while our mates in Dorm-A got lights, we in Dorm-B, the action spot, had no lights.

"Switch the lights on!" the plea continued.

"There are lights in Dorm-A," others added.

Somehow, those who tried to switch the lights on all failed as our dormitory continued oscillating in blue and red lights with a "whitish" presence in each illumination.

By this time, the whole Dorm-B was awake and most of Dorm-A, except the very heavy "dead" sleepers because we were separated by a corridor or hallway that was about four meters wide and about thirty meters long and not soundproof. The Molimo now started heading for the door to try and escape, but the door was blocked and jammed by those fleeing and others from Dorm-A who wanted to come and see or perhaps assist to capture this spirit that had been tormenting folks of the St. Kitts house for so long and the whole college, for that matter. The Molimo therefore double-backed now, attempting to use a window as an escape route. I followed it and from behind kicked what I thought or looked like the legs without feet, all covered in a whitish garment. I did not feel that I kicked anything, but I thought at that instant I saw an *Nkwel'a weh-szreh* (a skeleton). It seemed to have halfway bent forward and then immediately seemed to have vanished. I kept the nkwel'a weh-szreh observation to myself.

There was commotion everywhere in our dorm, and comrades ran here and there, huddling together and if they could see the Elimo. Shouts of "Eyaboweh" and overt crying of the smaller and younger students was evident. Lights eventually came on in our dorm. It took a while because lights were centrally controlled by the "timekeeper" who happened to be in a neighboring dormitory. With lights came relief with the obvious questions. "What was it? Where did it go to? How did it leave? Will it come again? Are we safe in this dorm? Etc." There was another question or questions that needed to be asked or discussed, but this could not be to everyone's hearing.

Small groups formed, talking in hush-hush tones, looking and or pointing to my direction with the nod of their heads and mustering words that I could not decipher.

This was all a dream to me. As the days went by, I began to feel uncomfortable on my right toe, the leg I had used to attempt kicking the Elimo. When it went real bad and the toenail began showing signs of separating itself from the rest of the toe, the pain grew worse. I could not discuss this with anyone. I went to the sickbay and told the nurse it was due to an injury I sustained on the football field, and the nurse's response was more like "Sure" or "Indeed." He gave me aspirin and bluish solution dressing.

By the time we went home for vacation, the nail had fallen off; my toe became infected and painful. I could not wear covered shoes and kept even more to myself after this episode.

After this episode, conversations on campus went like this: Eyaboweh is an Elimo that has remained legendary for decades and perhaps since Sasse started. No one has ever made an attempt to confront it and never has this elimo come to life almost assuming human format. But who was this junior student who had the guts and the apparent ability to confront this legendary elimo physically? An elimo that has tormented students of all dormitories? "Who was he? Or rather, what was it?"

I went home during the holidays and narrated an abbreviated version to our village kids who wanted to hear college stories. They came back the next day and said, "We mami dem say na lie say you kick devil (Our mothers say it is not true that you kicked a devil)."

My response to them was "Na wati be lie (What is a lie)? Dem be dedey (Were they there)?"

Then I showed them my toe and asked them to compare it with the other toe and their toes, but an older one who was about four years younger than me said, "You sure say nobi jiga (Are you sure it is not chiggers)?" That was meant to be a deflator blow.

And then they started arguing among themselves, for and against. My *ndo-meh wa molana wa mo-mba-ki* (older sister), Nyango Ngow'a Imbolleh, a couple of days after hearing the narration, decided that she would henceforth call me Mola Kik'a Molimo or Mr. Kick Devil (Mr. Devil Kicker). Village kids came around me, time and again, asking for stories. Though the older ones had decided my stories were "lies," that did not deter them from being part of the listening party. It was not uncommon for parents in the village to ask me when we met face-to-face in our village paths or roads if my stories were true. They normally got no response from me except showing my respects by greeting them appropriately.

CHAPTER 10

E-fvu-meh

As kids growing up in our village, our most favorite sport activity was football or soccer. Football was also the passion of our town, Gbwea (Buea), and was also a regional and national passion. We organized intra-village tournaments among ourselves and, during vacations, sports-loving rich folks or the local government organized inter-quartier (inter-quarters) football tournaments. At the local level, all Gbwea residents were united under the town's premier soccer Team-Prison Social Club of Buea, simply called Prisons. The town's support for the team was almost fanatical, and it seemed the personal property of everyone and at the same time collective property.

The cofounder, first president, and initial sustainer of Prisons Social Football Club Buea in 1967, was Justice Samuel Moka Lifafa l'Endeley who later became His Royal Highness Chief Endeley IV, the Paramount Chief of Buea, and the Paramount Chief of the Wakpwes. His specific given names at the coronation were Nakuveh and Naliomo. The other cofounder of "Prisons" as the football team was commonly known, was Richard Titang, the Director of Prisons. Ni Richard Titang was a quality paramilitary officer and an ardent football (soccer) enthusiast, under the Ministry of Territorial Administration.

Prisons Buea became an avenue for the recruitment of warders or wardens, and this was exploited to the fullest from east of the

River Mongo. Thus, shortly after the team's creation and founding, it was the first premiere league team that was the dream of a "United Cameroon." That is to say, it was a team that reflected the bicultural nature of the country, representing respectively those of English and French extractions, the Anglophones and Francophones. Thus, from east of the Mongo, initial heavyweight names that were pillars in the team included Nammeh Bella (who went on to become the national goal keeper for the Indomitable Lions of Cameroon and also played professional football in Europe and North Africa), Eszromba, a formidable right winger and header of no measure, Etond'a Yeye, a center-forward with incredible dribbling skills that brought the whole field alive in cheering and excitement, especially the children; and there was Njava, a defender of great build and physique, very effective in stopping adventurous attackers, capable of creating havoc around the goal mouth area. Then there was E-szru-ng'a Tai-tay, the sprinter, with incredible speed to the annoyance of defenders and the fear of the goalie of the opposite side.

The Wakpwes were ably represented in this formidable team by David Nangoh, the full back defender and team captain and oftentimes the coach as well; Tiya Efvumeh, the half-left back defender; Joseph Nwambo Ewokem, a man short in stature but very effective as the right-half back defender; Joseph Njuma, tireless midfielder and goals assists; Goalkeeper Tanga, a man short in stature but very agile as goalkeeper, and his assistants John and Akuwo; and Humphrey Musenge (the Berliner), the youngest of them all and an attacker full of youthful wonders.

Musenge was the darling of the kids. We crowded around him after each game and especially if he scored. Then, Musenge was a tall, very light-skinned lanky youth with lots of promise as a professional footballer.

In our village, which overlooked the Prisons Stadium, we had two of these initial pillars and stars of the Prisons team. They were Tiya E-fvu-meh and Njava. Younger folks in our village who became players in this team shortly after were Kulu Ngembu—who eventually played for the Cameroon Junior National Team—and Victor Lyonga, a.k.a. Molehleh. In later years, we had Stephen Wose—an attacker of unrestrained mannerisms but a nightmare to his opponents—and Moleya Tilili—the cool headed and very calculative full back defender—alongside Ngonja, a right-half back defender who, like Ewokem and Tanga, was vertically challenged but very formidable on the pitch.

Then even further down the line, our village produced the coach of the team in the person of John Livena Matute, a.k.a. Coach or Dee. Coach was a trained physical education instructor with the ministry of youth and sports (a.k.a. use and spoil, as they were commonly referred to). Our village had very long and intimate ties with Prisons Buea.

Tiya Efvumeh and Njava were defenders. Njava was the half fullback and Efvumeh was the left half-back. Njava was our Douala Mbedi cousin from Douala, and we, the Mokpwes, being Mokpwedi Mbedis. At some time, the Douala Mbedi defender was a tenant in my *Mba-mbeh wa molana wa evaru ya nyango's* (maternal grandmother) house and married to a local Mokpwe Nyango from the eastern part of our village. Njava was tall, muscular, and athletic and a good defender who normally would bulldoze attackers either by blocking them, felling them, and or dispossessing them of the ball. In the event he could not dispossess them of the ball, that was when the fullback and captain of team David Nangoh came in to clear with a fine finish. Njava could, however, never be trusted if Prisons was playing a Douala based team, especially Oritz Douala and Leopard de Douala (this was true of the other players from east of the Mungo whenever a Douala or a Yaounde based team was being played). They were his Douala brothers, and oftentimes, the Douala team came to our yard just before the game, visiting with Njava and using my Mba-mba's yard for their warm-up.

We were the envy of the village and the town as they spoke Douala and French. With a Douala team, however, it was more like a given that Njava would cause a penalty one way one or another that led to a goal or he would make his defending sloppy or something that would eventually lead to a decisive goal and usually toward the last minutes of the game. We, kids, all knew of that, picked earlier from the adults and then watched out for it intently during games ourselves. It was blood is thicker than water.

Njava, during the last minutes of a game when it was tie or Prisons was leading by a lone goal, would jump as if to head the ball in defense and would clearly hit it with the hand, so openly that it had to be a penalty. Usually, the whole stadium grumbled in disapproval and disappointment of his disloyalty to his team in favor of his home team. There were many advocates who thought and opined that players from east Cameroon be left out of the line-up whenever Prisons was playing a team from their "home" for which it was known they had a weakness for betraying the Buea people. He played for Prisons because the prison's department employed him in Buea as a warder or prison guard. You could see his Mokpwe Molana waiting on the visitors with all enthusiasm and happiness.

At such times, they all spoke only in Douala, though occasionally in French. Like I must have said before, Njava was biggish, not as large as a linebacker of the likes of American Football, but his position on the soccer field was more or less the equivalent of the linebacker; he was what was commonly called the "Four" because he wore jersey number four, and that was the number for that position. His position was also called the "stoppeur," meaning he stopped any advances by the attackers of the opposing team.

The job of the fullback or libero wearing then jersey number five was to come and tidy up any wreckage left behind by the stopeur. The libero was like the quarterback. We were close to him as kids because, like I said, before he was a tenant at our Mba-mba's house, and our Mba-mba's front yard was the common playground for us all, her *May-mba-mba* (grandkids). So Njava talked to us, and we talked to him, and this raised our social status in the village and in school because we were associated with this star.

However, Njava's stay in our yard was probably under two years. He moved to the warder's barracks where the government provided him with housing like his other comrades who were from out of town. This was the official story. But after he left with his wife, we started hearing other stories. Njava's Molana was a grown-up woman who should have had lots of kids of her own. But she had no kids, and there did not seem to have been much communication between her and her parents. The long and convoluted story was that a Mot'a Yowo had revealed to her that it was her Iyaka (mother) who was responsible for her barrenness and suggested that she leave the village.

Her family home was about one and half miles east of ours and the warder camp they relocated to about five miles south of their family home. As preteens, we blamed Njava's *Nyango wa liva* (mother-in-law) for being the driver behind this relocation. She took away something from us. Njava's Nyang'a liva had wanted her daughter to marry a local villager or a Mo-kpwe from another village. When this did not happen and the daughter decided instead to marry Njava, there was bitter exchange of words between *Nya-ngo na Mua-na* (mother and child), and the mother refused to bless and attend the marriage ceremony. They did not seem to have forgiven one another, and in the village textbook, this was recipe for li-emba, exploitable by others out of the immediate litumba (family) involved to settle scores or to sow discord.

But not to worry. We still had our own indigenous star with us, our own homeboy. In our west part of the village, we had three main clans, the Litumba la Maykomba, the Litumba Liszrali, and our own the Litumba la Li-bi-yeah. We were the largest of the three, at least numerically, and while it was not in our DNA to venture out of our clan geographical confines, other kids of our ages were attracted to us. Thus, our homes and play yards were more or less village playgrounds.

Tiya Efvumeh, the town's hero and our village champion, wore jersey number three, which meant he was the left halfback defender. He was an above average defender notorious for his rough play. His notoriety for rough play was known nationwide among the premier league circles. I remember one rough play that ended up with a serious injury, precisely a profuse nose bleeding that he had inflicted deliberately onto an offensive opponent player. The game was in Buea, and it was nearing the end when Efvumeh sprang his legs like a horse with his hands pivoted down on the floor of the field for support and hit the opposing player right in the face. This dude was lucky that it was not his eyes and perhaps some part of his body that could have been more delicate.

The attacked dude was bleeding profusely, but ironically, the referee did not sanction Efvumeh for this overt and uncalled for rough play that resulted in such serious injury. The crowd roared in support with chants of "Efvumeh, Efvumeh" or "Tiya, Tiya." It was obvious why the referee did nothing; he feared for his own life. Football referees had been killed before via physicality by angry supporters, especially those of a home team. Kumba Town, a.k.a. K-Town, was very notorious for its "wildness," a behavioral characteristic that was attributed to its very metropolitan nature that included Nigerians and folks from the French-speaking parts of Cameroon. Even as a preteen, I was very disappointed at the recklessness that could result to a permanent damaging injury and perhaps death.

But he was our hero/star, and he knew me by name and never waited for you to greet him. Whenever you met in the village or outside the village, he would call your name first and greet you. He would always say, "Moighai, you well?" or something of the sort which, to me, meant much. I also mattered in the life of a star and was known by a star. The benefits of being known by a star did not end with his greeting me. Whenever there was a game, us small kids went and stood by the entrance of the field. We did not have money to pay and get in, so we stood there with the hope that an adult who bought a ticket may take you by hand and take you in with him or her. Sometimes the officials keeping the gate waited until about halftime, then would start sending in small groups of us kids into the field, systematically or haphazardly. This was a nice way to get in but also meant you missed a good chunk of the game.

It was also common to steal your way in if the gateman was not looking or was distracted, trying to stop some other kid from entering. During big games, police were brought in to man the gate, and therefore, we dared not try playing pranks. With "wicked" policemen manning the gates, you could wait out there till the end of the game. There was an alternative, though, but riskier. The Gbwea stadium (Buea Stadium) was, for the most part, in bad shape and in need of repairs. That meant that the walls of the stadium had some spots with holes big enough to contain a squeezing child or sometimes simply jumping over the wall and running and mixing yourself with the nearest crowd. This was the favorite entering mode for teenagers who did not stand much of a chance to be let in via the gate.

Efvunmeh's nephews who were my playmates called him Pa Efvumeh, not necessarily because he was an "old man." In our Mokpwe culture, we do not have a paternal uncle. Your paternal uncle is your *ta'a-ta* (father), and you address him thus. Your maternal uncle you called Mola. The Maykomba clan had at least four of them working as warders, two brothers, Tiya Efvumeh and his *Ndo-meh wa mu-nya-na wa mo-mba-ki* (older brother) and their two nephews. Efvumeh got the job as a warder like most of them in the prison team primarily because of their athleticism. The Maykomba clan and our clan occupied the western and first portion of our village.

We were only separated from the stadium by the main road and the grounds outside the frontage of the stadium. Our village was on a hill while the stadium was situated on relatively flat land at a lower elevation. We could stay at home and watch the whole game from start to finish, for there were less than seventy meters between our village and the inside of the stadium, the higher elevation providing us with an additional advantage. The prison team entered the field via the front gate, normally atop an open back Land Rover. They all stood up, clinging to the railings, to the applause of their fans that were essentially the whole of Buea Town. Applause for them started once as they were sported from a hilly part of the road that descended onto the first portions of our village and at the border between the Presbyterian School Buea town and our village. It was thus continuous applause from the hill, past our village portion, and onto the entrance of the field. They could be seen all the way along this route.

Occasionally, though, the prison team entered the field via the back, jumping over the fence and parting bushes, then coming to the open to the applause of all. I wondered at first why they would want to pass through the back, and as I grew older, I came to learn that they did what was determined by their Mot'a Yowo. There were times when Efvumeh dropped off the team's vehicle down the road as they headed to the field. He would then make a quick dash up the hill to his house and then later rejoin them in the field. It is not known why he could not just continue with his mates on the field. It was commonly rumored that he came home to take his "ring," one he ordered from India. He had to wear this ring before playing but did not necessarily take it to camping.

His achievements as an athlete seemed to have all been attributed to the Indian ring he had. This ring ordered from India had yowo powers, and this was the main driver, the driving force of Tiya Efvumeh. If Pa Tiya had to enter the field on foot, it was our lucky day; he gathered us all, his nephews and neighbors, and marched us in without a word from the gatekeepers. However, by foot, I mean through the main gate. If they did it on foot through the bushes from the government primary school adjacent to the field or from anywhere jumping in rather than entering with the vehicle, it spoke volumes. You just had to be by some adults, and you get the gist.

This fence or wall jumping was mostly during the early season when heads of a white dog, red cock, and black goat had been buried in the center of the playground as directed by their Mot'a Yowo. This normally came with the promise of a better season ahead. The Mot'a Yowo for the team was a "respected" man in town for those who knew him. They talked a lot about him and his "powers."

Tiya Efvumeh, the rough defender and local hero, lived less than two hundred meters northeast of our house. He was the last of many children, and his father died when he was a young man, perhaps in his twenties. His dad was an old man and very old by our wana standards, and we scarcely saw him, perhaps occasionally and from afar. Because he was very old, and we could not talk to him, and neither could we have a close-up of him, we considered him mystical, and our parents did not help. It was said that he owned a black mamba, some sort of zoomorphism.

There was a stream we normally crossed to go to our farms. We had first to traverse the Maykomba clan grounds and hit the forest. About one hundred meters into the forest was a stream between rocks that flowed southbound into what seemed like a very deep ravine. This stream was only visible for perhaps a total of seventy-five meters. It seemed to have suddenly emerged from underground, from the edge of some thick forest, and then escorted and guided by large rocks on either side into the deep that started with another thick forest. We could hear it gush down the steep dive.

The part of this stream exposed seemed like a clearing amid a dark surrounding forest. When it rained very heavily and persistently, the stream overflowed and was unpassable or uncrossable. If we were on our farms and it started raining very heavily, we were sure to more often than not start a premature return journey home. Alternatively, we waited at its banks for the volume to subside before crossing. The problem with waiting was that it always ended up with nightfall and the dread that came with it.

This stream was called Uleh. The water was cold and clean, and it was generally believed that it originated from the mountain that was several thousand meters northward. Proof of this was that even when it did not rain in the village, sometimes this stream overflowed its banks when we could see that there was rain on the mountain. Our village was at the foot of the mountain. The Uleh water was premium water for drinking, especially considering its characteristics.

We had other farms northwest of our village that also required the crossing of a stream. This we called the "forest stream." Forest because these farms were located in an environment where forest trees were planted; that is, pine trees. The quality of the forest stream water was nothing as compared to that which was contained in Uleh. We drank from the forest stream and were very comfortable with it. The conditions at both streams were almost exact opposites.

Eszrong'a Maykomba, Tiya Efvumeh's ta'a-teh, was said to use this Uleh environ as an abode for his black mamba. Our parents had seen it time and again based on their conversations we picked, and there also seemed to have been lots of small talk in the village time and again when it was said that the black mamba had delivered babies. This mamba was special, not just because it was owned by this *monuni mo Moto* (old man), but it was also said that whenever it delivered, it brought forth snakes of other species. Hence, the proliferation of snake types in this environ. We kids were not allowed to go that route by ourselves, but I did so several times by myself as I got older and saw nothing.

As kids, though, whenever we were approaching this area, we were encouraged and instructed to make loud noises so that if this snake was basking itself on the large rocks, it would crawl back into its hiding house. We also knew that this old man would die the day this snake was killed, for it was always the case.

Tiya Efvumeh as a footballer had lots of influence on younger future footballers of our village origin who eventually became players of the most cherished team. Later on, after a couple of years, Tiya Efvumeh became the full back defender and captain of Prisons Buea. He was followed a couple of years later by Kulu Ngembu, another defender and captain of the team. Kulu, who ended up playing for the Cameroon Junior National Team, was followed by Moleya Tilili, a fullbacker and team captain, and finally by Stephen Wose, an attacker and team captain. Other younger players were to follow, like Ngonja and others. To crown it all, John Livena Matute from the village became the head coach for the Prisons Team. Our village, therefore, contributed significantly to the social and economic life of Buea via football and via Prisons Social Football Club of Buea.

CHAPTER 11

Snake Hunters

As we got older, we lads in our clan went hunting. We hunted mostly Kwai (*Francolinus camerunensis*), also called partridges or bush fowl, and occasionally rat moles or the giant African rat (*Cricetomys sp.*), and once we caught a local fox species. Our hunting formation was simple and as established as a pecking order. The older ones in the team, usually two or three, and *gbwa ja mo-fvao* (hunting dogs) went into the forest and did the active search. The other members of the team, usually the younger ones or an older team member who has no *mofvao* (hunting) experience, were stationed strategically around the periphery of the target hunt area. The periphery hunters were more like sentries, and their duty was to watch out for any game (mostly bush fowl, in our case) that would fly out of the target area due to the hot pursuit and make sure you saw where it landed.

You must be able to provide this information accurately, for the next stage of the mofvao and its success depended on the accuracy of the sentry's information as to the precise location of landing. The duty of the in-forest hunting team, including the gbwa ja mofvao, was to frighten and disturb the kwai or game and put so much pressure on it that it would be felt compelled to fly out of habitat. The overall reasoning that kwai are heavy *Weh-nor-ni* (birds), and though they can fly, they can only do so for a comparatively short distance, and by our repeated experience, we knew and estimated that if a kwai flew more than two times, putting enough pressure to ensure that the rest times in-between flights were as short as possible, then this tired the kwai.

A tired kwai will not fly. It will only run on the ground if disturbed, and running on the ground we counted on, because a kwai running on the ground, be it on open grounds or fields or under a thick forest, was no match for the gbwa ja mofvao and their *wato* (human) counterparts. It was therefore very important that sentries like us tell immediately where the fleeing kwai went to, and then we all took our positions again and repeated the same maneuvers. We repeated these maneuvers as many times as it took until we caught the kwai or sometimes, after just the first maneuver, the kwai disappeared, and many a times, we returned home empty-handed.

There were two reasons for the disappearance or inaccurate information from the sentry or just simply the disappearance of the kwai. For the most part, we attributed a "disappearance" due to inaccurate information, but based on oral traditions from our parents, kwai are called "wuwa ja wawu;" that is, the "devil's fowl." Being the devil's fowl means they can disappear, and their disappearance modus operandi was quite simple. The kwai just simply picks up a "leaf" and holds it between its beaks and then lies on its back. When that happens, then it becomes invisible to us, the living. Thus, the gbwa and wato will search in vain.

Signs that our team was actively engaged in hunting were the very quiet sentries at the periphery of the target area and hustling inside the target and surrounding areas. There was the gbwa and wato pushing bush out of their way as they made a pursuit. There were the barking gbwa when they came face-to-face with game, and there was the wato chant repeated over and over and over, "Leh-mbeh leh-mbeh leh-mbeh. Leh-mbeh leh-mbeh leh-mbeh." Roughly translated as, "Catch it, catch it, catch it."

This was urging the gbwa on, making them relentless in their pursuit. The senior *wa-szro-nge-li* (hunters) also had the responsibility of redirecting the gbwa if they knew that the game had changed position within the target area.

Also, very indicative of our mofvao in action was the mai-wo won by the gbwa ja mofvao. Maiwo was a small dry empty calabash tied onto the *li-woh* (neck) of the gbwa ja mofvao. Inside the calabash were *ma-nyai* (stones), *weh-szrey* (bones), or *ma-szro-ga* (teeth), depending on the seniority and hunting prowess of the gbwa mofvao. When the maiwo had to be filled with either weheszrey or maszroga, it required some special chanting ceremony, normally not witnessed by wana. The maiwo we wore on our gbwa ja mofvao were selected and made by wa-mba-ki in the clan.

The maiwo served a couple of purposes and essentially served as a bell that indicated movement. The different maiwo made different sounds, and thus, we could use these sounds to differentiate between the gbwa ja mofvao. We could thus tell which gbwa was or which gbwas were active and the direction that their pursuit was taking inside the forest. Thus, as a sentry, you got to know when the game was approaching your jurisdiction of influence and information. Sometimes we were required to communicate to the principal *mosz-rongeli* (hunter) or *waszrongeli* (hunters) that the pursuit was toward us; this way, they steered the other gbwa to the right direction if they were concentrating on the wrong spots. Also, if two gbwa ja mofvao seemed to be headed in different directions, efforts were concentrated on the direction or lead indicated by the senior gbwa ya mofvao; that is, a gbwa ya maiwo ma maszroga will be given preference over the other gbwa in terms of following a lead.

We had some gbwa ja mofvao that were not adorned with maiwo, not because of a shortage of maiwo but because these gbwa stayed with us, the sentries, and occasionally, they and their sentry did the actual capture and killing of the *nyama wanga* (game). These were the younger gbwa or they could be older dogs not well-versed with the act of hunting or perhaps not just acquainted with the act of "locomoting" in thick vegetation. Initially, when we started mofvao, we used to urge and try to force these non-maiwo gbwa to get into the forest and be part of the chase, we thinking they were weak gbwa. For in our village, gbwa were used for mofvao and security. They could be used as pets when they are puppies. More experienced hunters in our clan, however, corrected us, stressing that these *gbwa ja mea-nday* (foot dogs) could be very handy at times.

One unforgettable day, we were returning from an unsuccessful hunting trip, and as we got to Uleh, the gbwa ja mofvao became very agitated and broke loose from our company and into the thick dark forest area. We had never gone hunting in this area for obvious reasons, but we thought on this day that our luck for a special small game animal was at hand and very close to home. So, the gbwa all swarmed into the forest, and we stood at the periphery, urging on with our special hunting tactics and chants in Mo-kpwe: "Leh-mbeh leh-mbeh leh-mbeh. Leh-mbeh leh-mbeh leh-mbeh."

We urged them on as was the customary call to signal hunting in progress. We knew that it was not a Kwai by the judged behavior of the gbwa. We adorned the necks of the gbwa with maiwo (a small calabash-like shell that contained small stones tied to the liwoh of the gbwa. It served as a bell and enabled us to locate, mentally and otherwise, the position of the gbwa. With kwai hunting, there is normally a short period of ground surface running and then a flight, then another surface chase, then a flight. If a third ground chase was achieved, it was most certainly sure to be the last.

The gbwa seemed to have been concentrating, and their produced sounds seemed low-key and strange. So, we knew that our nyama was not a kwai, so what could it be? After about twenty minutes since the homeward bound chase began, there was movement toward the clearing, and the sounds we heard clearly signaled a gbwa in distress. Nobody could dare say what we all seemed to be thinking, but one thing was certain: we intensified our calls for the dogs to come back to us as in a retreat, but that is not the type of order you expect to be obeyed by a gbwa that was on the chase; it was therefore a waste of time but better than doing nothing. Almost unexpectedly, the thick dark forest seemed to have given way in between the peripheral portion occupied by us, and then our three gbwa ja mofvao practically leapt out of the forest with Major, the captain and oldest of the pack, leading the way with a mba'a-mba (*Dendroaspis polylepis*) wrapped around its abdominal region and gbwawa's neck region between Major's teeth. In a twinkle of an eye, our mofvao team of six was scattered, and it became "Everyman for esef (To your tents oh wa-szro-ngeli [hunters]; To each his own)."

In our village, the two most feared and dreaded snake species are the *veh-yi* (viper) and *mba'a-mba* (the black mamba). The Gaboon viper (*Bitis gabonica*) is a viper species found in the rainforests of sub-Saharan Africa, where our village, Wonya-Lyonga, is situated. Like all other viper species, it is venomous; it is the largest member of the genus *Bitis,* has the longest fangs (five centimeters), and the highest venomous yield of any snake. The mba'a-mba (*Dendroaspis polylepsis*), on the other hand, is a species of extremely venomous snake, a member of the snake family Elapidae, a native of Vakoland. Stories and tales of dread and accounts of actual encounters with these reptiles abound among our people, and each one of them is meant to put fear and dread in you at all times.

These were mortal enemies to our people and time and again made good dinner, if the one encountering was lucky. Of the two species, there were more frequent encounters with the mbamba as these reptiles seemed "domesticated" in their search for food, being drawn to homes that reared wuwa or chickens (*Gallus domesticus*). In Leh-lu Mokpwe Country (Upland Vakoland), these two reptiles were also associated with zoomorphism. An encounter with any of them was thus difficult to interpret, if it was natural or a chance occurrence or if it was a zoomorphic occurrence, a fellow villager, meaning to do you mortal harm.

We fled in all directions, shouting and crying for help, and ended up at the opposite end of the clearing. Our *mua-nya-gwa-ru wa wambaki* (older siblings) among us decided that we were not going to leave the gbwa there at the mercy of this brutal reptile. After tumbling over each other, we returned shortly like an aftershock and tried in vain calling the name of a dog that was clearly easily losing it, now on the ground, and the gbwawa that seemed to now have a clear upper hand was unwinding itself from its adversary to return to its fortress.

"Major, Major, Major!"

"Major, Major, Major!"

We were not really calling the gbwa, for it was obvious that we were witnessing death of the gbwa right before our eyes. We were instead calling for help from anyone who could hear us and who could help. The gbwa we used for mofvao as a team was contributed by three households—my Mola's household of the lower third, my grand Mola's household of the hilly upper third, and my immediate family household of the plateau. Major was the only gbwa mofvao we had for a very long time, and the responsibility to take care of Major was that of Ndiv'a Molimo and myself. Ndiv'a Molimo, a.k.a. Tanko, was too young to be part of the mofvao team, so he was not present, and that was a blessing. For I am certain that if he was present, he would have attempted to face and attack the gbwa in an effort to save Major. This was a nightmare as I seemed transfixed, seeing this drama unfold before my very eyes.

The other gbwa could not help, barking from a safe distance, and we did a good job of calling them to ourselves to at least save some of them. The gbawa and we were in shock and seemed dazed. Major seemed eventually to have given in, on the floor of the forest clearing, lying on its sides and breathing with difficulty. We continued shouting and calling for assistance. Our calls were in vain, though we were very close to the village. The nearest clan to this scenario was the Eszrong'a Maykomba clan, and evidently, no one heard us, or if they did, we were simply ignored; "every man to himself."

The venomous poison of the mba'a-mba had finally and quickly dealt its ultimate final blow, and Major went breathless, at which point, the gbwawa around Major's torso started to untie itself in an attempt to free itself from Major. All this while, Major had the neck region of the reptile in its mouth, and despite the large diameter of the mba'a-mba, it seemed obvious that Major's canine bites had gone deep enough to touch the vertebral column, which accounted for the large volume of blood that was spurting out. Though, I must add that, we did not know whether the blood we saw was from Major or from the gbwawa.

When Major let go off the gbwawa because its strength was failing, it untangled itself and attempted a quick dash back into the thick, dark, mysterious-looking forest but could hardly distance itself by up to a meter from Major who lay breathless, at which point, I dashed toward the gbwawa as other members of the mofvao team called after me to come back, saying the gbwawa was at its most dangerous now, but the adrenalin was in control and not me. Once I got close enough, I raised the machete as high as I could and, in two quick successions and with all my might, targeted the liwoh region of the mba'a-mba, severing the head region of the reptile, and then proceeding to cut and launch attacks on the other parts of the gbwa-wa's body as blood was spattering on me until I was stopped by hands way, way more powerful than me.

"Livam so e do die (Let go, it is dead)," they said.

At this point, I turned my attention to Major, and to my amazement, Major was still breathing, even if just barely.

"Major di brif (Major is still breathing)," I declared.

They did not share my enthusiasm, so I proceeded to take Major home.

The language mode of communication within our clan varies and is dependent on the two communicants. When wana spoke or communicated with wambaki—that is, elders or parents—the language of communication was in the Mokpwe language and so was communication between parents and elders of the clan.

The language of communication between wana was dependent on whether wambaki were present or not. We had the option of communicating in the Mokpwe language or the languages in which we were taught in school, i.e. the English language, or if we could, the French language. However, in the absence of wambaki and or out of their hearing range, we normally communicated with each other but in Pidgin English. Our mates outside our clan but in the same village spoke in Pidgin among themselves and with their wambaki. Outside our clan, we followed the same pattern. We spoke to wambaki only in the Mokpwe language. Thus, unlike our contemporaries who grew up under similar conditions and in the same village, we can proudly understand and speak the Mokpwe language fluently.

However, communication with our gbwa followed a different pattern. In our clan, dogs were communicated with and spoken to only in the English language, and this was true for the wana and the wambaki. Somehow, the gbwa only "understood" English, but when we took them for mofvao, the mofvao language was in Mokpwe. For example, the familiar "Leh-mbeh, leh-mbeh, leh-mbeh" would, in

Pidgin English language, translate as "Catch'am, catch'am, catch'am (Catch it, catch it, catch it)."

Unlike with other families outside our clan but around our clan with close proximity, they spoke Pidgin to their gbwa, and further removed away from our own portion of the *mbowa* (village), the language of communication with the gbwa was in Mokpwe. When we go hunting, we are met and accompanied by our sympathetic ancestors who are gone before us. They hunt with us and guide us in our hunting. The ancestors gone before us understood only the Mokpwe language. It will thus be an insult, disrespectful, and a waste of time communicating in another language. There were times when we made repeated back-to-back hunting trips (three to four in a row), without a catch. That was when the *Walimo* (spirit ancestors) were annoyed with us for one reason or another, and we had to do some ritual as directed by our parents to appease them.

After the appeasement, we started "catching" again and returned home with a hunting game. To be in the good books of the hunting Walimo, after every catch, some specific part of the animal must be given to the Walimo before we, the *wat'o wa weh-na-ma* (mortal beings), devoured our own share. As wana, we had wondered and grumbled among ourselves why these walimo had to depend on us for a share of the catch when they catch and kill as many game animals as possible without any assistance. But we could not voice this aloud for fear of annoying and vexing them.

Though I was the youngest of the hunters, it was ultimately my duty to carry across my *liwoh* (neck) and over my *weh-tu-li* (shoulders) the dying gbwa; and yes, it was also our gbwa and has been my companion for many years, and the loss was more of mine than any other in the mofvao team. Major was a big gbwa, so I was helped to place it across my neck, and it took sheer will, shock, and adrenalin to bear this weight of Major. The consensus was that I should not bother carrying Major home because Major was going to die before we got home. Major had to get home, and I took him home where he died, even before I could explain to my parents what had happened.

On Major's final journey home, I kept on hoping some miracle would happen and the gbwa would survive, and I also thought if only my iyaka would take upon treating it and directing us on what to do as its caregiver, that it was all going to be well. I just needed to get home with Major and hope that my iyaka was there, waiting for us. Thus, on my way, I alternated or rightly dashed.

"I beg no die yaa, you go well (Do not die, it will be all right once as we get home, you will get well)! Gbwa ya-szru o-szri-wa (Our dog do not die). Notre chien ne meurt pas."

That was the last of our hunting team, and patriarch Mola Eszrong'a Maykomba died about three months later as was predicted by our parents. We still, however, had to walk through this bush path to go to our farms. There did not seem to be an alternative, at least as far as we were concerned, and also, it was the only route we knew, and that had been used by our parents and our *mbamba-szru wa molana* (grandmother). We still saw the shed reptilian skins time and again and also the empty eggshells which signified that a new batch of legless venomous creatures were roaming about. I was not blamed for this unfortunate event by the mofvao team, not that I was looking to take the blame. Our belief in zoomorphism was reinforced by two neighbors—Mola Ewang'a Moto and Mola Eszrong'a Maykomba— both owners of mba'a-mbas, both died within months of their mba'a-mbas being killed.

The patriarch of the Litumba la Maykomba must have been over a one hundred years at his death, easily the oldest persons that we knew that lived in the village. Physically displayable wealth, evident success of any nature, extreme poverty, and older than usual are all ingredients and attributes of yowo, making you a generic yoworite that does not harm anyone but is there to serve you, a Mot'a li-emba, the poor form of yowo that made you boiling jealous and drove you to cause hardships and other forms of ills to your victim without killing them, and you remaining poor, angry, and bitter; and Mot'a nyongo, possessing yowo that kills close family members for the sole purpose of enriching the giver at the expense of the dead or given that are now working ghosts. The dead by nyongo were given to nyongo and therefore, while they were "dead," they still existed as working ghosts or spirits. These ghost workers work for those they were given to, that is, their "buyers." They were employed as ghost workers through a nyongo death.

Because Mola Eszrong'a Maykomba was really old, he was automatically feared and branded a yowo man. While Mola Eszrong'a Maykomba was never said to have killed anyone, nor had he been reported to have bewitched anyone in the village or elswhere, that he had a mba'a-mba was enough. Every precaution was therefore made to ensure that as wana, we never went anywhere near Mola Eszrongo, the patriarch of the Litumba la Maykomba.

CHAPTER 12

Transitioning of E-fvu-meh

Our ace football team was called Prison Buea Social Club; Prison because the team was originally started as a private club in association with the correctional and prisons department. In the early years of the team, the top players were all correctional officers or warders, some brought in from different provinces or regions of Cameroon. This will seem to suggest that they may not have been necessarily trained as warders but rather athletes of great repute. The prisons department under the ministry of territorial administration was a government department, and therefore, its employees were state civil servants.

Prisons Buea was therefore a football club with a mix of cultures. There were the Anglophones and Francophones, and among the Francophones, we had star players from the Littoral, Central, and Western regions or provinces. The two Anglophone provinces were ably represented and formed the core of the team. From our province, the southwest, the Mokpwes from Buea dominated and made us very proud. In my village alone, we had Tiya Efvumeh as the main man, then Joe Njuma, and the upcoming junior players like Kulu Ngembo, a.k.a. King Kulu, and Victor Lyonga, a.k.a. Molehleh; and also in our village, we had our Douala cousin and in-law, Francois Njava, the able stoppeur and half fullback defender. In "Las Town" and Bonaberi, we had David Nangoh, who was the captain and full-back defender, and Joseph Nwambo Ewukem, the right halfback defender.

The team had many goalkeepers at different times, including one from Douala, the Littoral province. Nammeh Bella, a Douala native kept for Prisons Buea, and like Njava, his fellow Douala comrade, he too could not be trusted when Prisons played a Douala-based team. Bella went on to being a national and an international star, making a productive career in football and sometimes dabbling in sports with national politics. For many years, Bella was Cameroon's number two goalkeeper at international events, like the FIFA World Cup and the African Cup of Nations.

As time went on, most of these stars left the team. Bella's contract ended, some were getting old, some got transferred to other parts of the country when they could no longer be productive footballers, etc. In the southwest, Prisons Buea was the only Division I team throughout our childhood days. It was indeed sad to watch the dying giants and icons. It was Prisons Buea that opened the southwest to an influx of Francophones who used sports to see the Anglophone heritage of the country, and being that their destination was Buea, it made us see these folks and their fancy cars and mannerisms.

Thursdays and Sundays were cherished days during the league season. The dreaded and inevitable happened, and our beloved Prisons Buea was relegated to Division II. By this time, the team was a skeleton and shadow of its former glory. All but about two or three of the original stars were still with the team, among them Joe Njuma and Tiya Efvumeh.

Tiya Efvumeh stayed on to play as a Division II player while the rest of his contemporaries retired or relocated. Tiya Efvumeh became the captain of the team, now playing as fullback defender, no longer the left halfback position that he had occupied for so long, and that had brought him fame near and wide. By this time, the town became a second division football or soccer town, and perhaps we began losing interest, but Prisons, as we commonly called the team was our team, and soccer was our passion, perhaps the only thing that united a town that was becoming the more and more diverse, and my people, the Wakpwes or sons-of-the-soil, as some called them, progressively were assuming minority status. However, this also meant that we were exposed to the other many second division teams that were scattered all over the southwest province or now called southwest region.

There was disappointment, and the enthusiasm for the game had also waned for some but not for Tiya Efvumeh, the football addict and enthusiast. While for some of us it was the glory, fame, and exposure it brought to Tiya Efvumeh, it was rather a passion as he became a major force behind the sustenance and maintenance of Prisons Buea as the name and past glory sought to be preserved. Prisons Buea remains to this date a name and club with fond memories for folks of my generation and who are original Buea townies.

Football players of Prisons Buea lived and survived through the mercy of their god. They often sustained serious injuries due to rough and hard plays and very little or no proper medical attention. I doubt medical insurance was an option, and if it existed, was it implementable when needed? We knew that the players survived mostly on painkillers that were supplied to them by the management. The very strong folks like Tiya Efvumeh were not really bothered about or paid much attention when it came to any form of medical attention. The strongman did not need it. It was said that he had complained that the day he would die, no one will know because it is generally felt and thought he did not need any medical attention.

While Prisons Buea was some hot Ekwakoko (the cultural identity dish of the Wakpwes or Bakweris), I was still in primary or elementary school. One morning, we came to class, just getting to be on our own. For the last weeks, our teacher had been coming to class without teaching because he was preparing for his own exams. He used class time to study while he urged us to "study" on our own. He was a young man that looked old, and I had my doubts from the day we entered his class if this teacher was versed in what he was supposed to be teaching.

Hailing from the northwest province, he spent most of his time sucking up to certain of our classmates who were from his village or province, especially those with parents with high social status. In turn, they "sang" his praises and protected him from any noise that may come from the class with the potential of intruding on his concentration. His faithfuls were the older pupils and those pupils with known high familial social status. I was a no-nothing, or as we commonly said, a "natin-man." I boiled inside me in vain, and nothing changed.

Though I did not know how to pray or what I prayed for, I negatively prayed for his exams anyway. The only interaction we had with our teacher during such weeks was when he came to the floor of the class to beat the noisemakers. Noisemaker victims were either a list he compiled secretly while he sat upfront, studying, and/or a list compiled by his handpicked class prefect. This beating of noisemakers looked more like some sort of recreation or a short break away from his studying spent on whipping pupils.

There was nobody you could complain to in school. The headmaster was equally a happy whipper of pupils. In fact, the teachers all seemed to have been in some kind of a "whipping" competition, and we, the male pupils especially, took the brunt of it at a stage when you are called a senior primary pupil; that is, from class five to seven. You could not complain at home, for then it would be seen as a sign of *mo-gwe-gwe* (weakness), especially being a "man-boy" or *Mot'a munyana* (a male child).

Coupled with pupil-pupil bullying, school could be hell, and indeed, the fainthearted abandoned ship and took to some other trades or vocations, including large game hunting that abounded at the foot of the Fako Mountain.

We were quiet, "studying" on our own, and I do not remember seeing our class teacher, Massa Wanji, walk out of class, but on reentering, he said, "Wa-ah! He was my classmate!" within earshot of the whole class. I thought Teacher Wanji looked far older than the athletic Efvumeh and could not think that they were ever classmates. It was also a clue that Teacher Wanji actually grew up in Gbwea and perhaps was born in Gbwea as well, though his loyalty like others of his kind was with the grassland, and this fierce loyalty was palpable. But then, who says classmates are age mates? It was just like comparing Akabateh Akabateh Square with myself.

One of his favorite pupils then asked him what he was talking about. The privileged pupils could speak in Pidgin to him, but not the others, for if you dared, it would attract some sort of punishment, often in corporal form.

"Please, Sah na waiti," asked Akabateh Akabateh, the oldest pupil in the class who had already started using the razor blade on his face. Akabateh Akabateh was also known as Akabateh Square or just simply A2. Sometimes, he acted as if he had a mental problem, and therefore, Akabateh Square became associated with mental instability or someone not to be taken seriously.

"Tiya Efvumeh the footballer is dead," Teacher Wanji declared. "Wa-ah! What a loss," he concluded.

I knew I was dreaming based on what I had just heard, and yes, it was a dream. Our school was less than one hundred meters from our residence, and Tiya Efvumeh's residence was about another mile northeast of ours.

Later at home, I got the details. He died in his sleep. He was found dead in the morning with blood streaming down his nostrils. This was Monday, and very early in the morning, he was rushed to the hospital when he was discovered. The team had an out-of-town game on Sunday, and Tiya Efvumeh had a head-on collision with another player. It was not taken seriously, though he complained of headaches. He was given some painkillers, and he returned home and went to sleep.

The village was quiet and in mourning, especially our portion of the village. I do not know how long before he was buried, but the days before his funeral, a good number of his former and current play teammates streamed into the village and camped in his yard where they told us, kids, stories and adventures they had with him. He was given a Catholic burial with all the traditions and a full mass entourage. I remember vividly the mass-boys (mass servers) and their bright white and pink wear and the smoking incense as they led the funeral procession from the road up to his hilly residence and final resting place.

It was difficult to fathom that Tiya Efvumeh died, but though it was evident that he died, we were also a community that was very spiritual from many perspectives. Thus, there was hope that Tiya Efvumeh would be raised from the dead, somehow, one way or another. He was too young and too much of a village and town hero to just die like that. Tiya Efvumeh evidently died in his early thirties because I heard him being compared with other great men that had lived before him. I heard many times words like, "Jesus died in his early thirties. Great men do not live for long."

A nephew of Tiya Efvumeh lived out of town, precisely Muyuka. His name was Mola Livanje or just simply Molali for short. Molali was one of several nephews of Tiya Efvumeh that was older than their *Mola* (maternal uncle—Tiya Efvumeh), for Tiya Efvumeh was the youngest and last child of Patriarch Eszrong'a Maykomba, and Patriarch Eszrong'a Maykomba was still alive, blind, bed ridden and just hanging in there, being the oldest person in the village. Tiya Efvumeh was the jewel of his aged *ta'a-teh* (father), they were the Jacob and Joseph as in the Old Testament Bible. When he was informed of the death of his muana, he cried softly, and for days, his face was full of tears as he stopped eating.

Molali was the *muana wa munyana mombaki* (oldest son) of Tiya Efvumeh's *ndoh-meh wa molana wa mombaki* (older sister), and because he was older than Tiya Efvumeh, he simply called him Tiya, instead of Mola Tiya. For in the Mokpwe language, a paternal uncle is called Mola, though Mola is also used otherwise, for example, mister, respect, title, or just simply identifying a Mokpwe male. Tiya Efvumeh did not have a problem with his nephew calling him by name, though this was considered disrespectful from a traditional perspective. Molali arrived from out of town forty-eight hours after Tiya Efvumeh had transitioned and had to pass by our yard to go to their clan and family yard. I was working on our yard as he was passing through and heavily saddened by the incessant wailing and cries that came from Tiya Efvumeh's house by walana who seemed to cry incessantly and endlessly since Tiya Efvumeh passed.

Aside from the wailing and crying that came from the bereaved home, the rest of the village was silent, especially our portion of the village. We only spoke in hushed tones, both wana and wambaki, for we were bereaved. I do not know whether Molali saw me or not, but that did not matter. But I know he did not acknowledge me in any form. When he was but a few meters away from me and now hearing the wailing and weeping from their family yard, it dawned on him at last that his Mola Tiya Efvumeh had actually died. He said, "Weah! Tiya a-way-li Njor-keh njor-keh (Truly, truly, Tiya is dead)," and then started mumbling under his breath indecipherable words that translated to weeping, but he could not do that directly or openly because in our village, wunyana do not cry.

It made me sad to see him so saddened, and it also annoyed me because he seemed to be implying that my hope that Tiya Efvumeh will be raised from the dead was being dashed. He was expected to know better for two reasons—he was an older person and that he also lived and was coming from Muyuka. The Mot'a Yowo that rumors had it had been contracted and charged with Tiya Efvumeh's resurrection (or jerop for die as it is said in Pidgin) was from Muyuka and went by the name Ma-nya-ka. How could Molali not know of this renowned Mot'a Yowo who had been contracted by his Eszrong'a Maykomba clan to bring back to life Tiya? But I knew he certainly knew of Ma-nya-ka, if me a natin-man could know of him, but to cut Molali some slack, he was not resident in the village and perhaps he was not aware that the Mot'a Yowo Ma-nya-ka had been contracted but that it could also be that Molali did not have faith in this Ma-nya-ka's spiritual powers.

I remember, though, when I had asked if Manyaka had ever resurrected anyone, I did not get a clear answer, just as I could not know for certain that he had been contracted. Molali was a "Johnny Just Come;" that is, a JJC. What did he know? Whether wishful thinking or not, I held onto it. Like a cricket in the winter, I waited and waited in anxiety and anticipation for word that Manyaka had come and done his magic and had vumuled (resurrected) the efvuma (football) hero. The wishful thinking and hope against hope increased my agony and pain for this loss. Manyaka never came not to the best of my knowledge, or if he did, he did not succeed. I did not know what to think about him. I was disappointed.

Still wanting some reassurance and perhaps as a last resort, I approached my iyaka. "Szre-keh wa mo-wa Wama Manyaka Amo vumuleszreh (Did they not say Manyaka was going to resurrect him?" I stuttered.

When she did not respond immediately, I knew I had to qualify my statement and/or indicate the source of my information. "Nor-di Liveneh Amo weh (That is what Liveneh said)," I quickly added.

Without looking up from the nda'a (*Xanthosoma sagittifolium*; cocoyams) she was peeling and cleaning in preparation for dinner, she had asked, "Owi Moto away-liSzri a vumuwi (Do you any *Homo sapiens* that have died and then resurrected?" She said these words without reprimand in her voice.

"Err., yes," I said.

"Njeneh (Who)?" she asked.

"Eh mua'na w'ama Ta'a-t'I-wo-ndeh (The child of God Almighty)," I answered her very confidently.

"Mameh e-weh-li Li-na'a lay-ni (What is his name?" she asked.

I thought her lips and jaws twitched or moved in what looked or seemed like a small smile. My iyaka was a no-nonsense molan'a Mokpwe; smiling with her wana was not part of her duties. Was the apparent smile a trap or some kind of an amusement?

"Ye-szru (Jesus)," I said.

Some seconds again elapsed. Then she asked, "Oweh-li o-veh-vehMoto owi away-li Szri a vumuwi (Is there any other human or person that you know who died and then resurrected?" my iyakeh asked.

We had learned about photosynthesis and osmosis in school, and I had come back home with a show and tell attitude, an attribute that was known not to be characteristic of me. Before the end of that day, my smarty head was spanked hard enough to keep my mouth shut. So, it was therefore in my own interest to be really smart here by not being smart or, more correctly, by not playing it smart with my iyakeh.

"Ou-leh teh wato wa Ka'a-ti ya Lowa O-szray-nje (If we exclude people from the Holy Bible or God's Book, there is none)." This answer was meant to cover me in two fronts. Going to Sunday School was mandatory in our ndawo, and understanding what was taught was also required because you were quizzed when you came back home and there was no room for you not giving the correct answers as asked.

"Nga-nga Manyaka a-szray-nje di Loweh (The yoworite is not God)," she said. "Nde-nga-veh Tiya Efvumeh aszray-nje di Yeszru (And also, Tiya Efvumeh is not Jesus)."

That was the end of the conversation. It did not make me feel any better, but it was a closure, an acceptance, and a letting go. The Manyaka and resurrection story originated from Kelleh, my cousin, and propagated by Liveneh, my brother. Now that I had hit a wall with Liveneh and my iyakeh, perhaps I could still go back to Kelleh and hear something that was an illuminant.

About a week after his death, I saw the religious procession led by the mass servers (or mass boys as we commonly referred to them. The mass servers were the Ndoko boys, extracts from the unmistakable light-skinned devout Catholic family, from the Buea Town Catholic Parish, who were ever ready to serve, a service-minded attitude that followed them to Saint Joseph's College, Sasse.) in white and pink of the Catholicism tradition, the priest, the casket borne by Tiya Efvumeh's football comrades, and flanked by men in warders' uniforms followed by close family members, then officials of the prisons football club and the department of correction and prisons, then the Gbwea Town and other out of town sympathizers ascending our village hill after the funeral mass, commending his spirit to the Lord God.

The location of Tiya Efvumeh's residence was on the east of the upper hilly level of our portion of the village; thus, the procession had to ascend from the lower third, through the middle plateau portion, and then finally to the upper third hill country. Joe's remains actually traversed the topo-geography of his village in his final journey, the same walking he had done on foot many a time and repeatedly when he was alive. I knew, therefore, that it was finally over. The long and suspenseful wait and all the hopes and anticipation all now seemed nothing but wishful thinking. Hopes were dashed, and reality kicked in.

As the funeral procession ascended in silence, it went past Mola King'a Walana's house. Mola King'a Walana was the oldest brother of Tiya Efvumeh. As Tiya's former football colleagues slowly followed after his remains in the coffin, Tiya's niece by the name Namondeh, who was the oldest daughter of Mola King'a Walana, said, "I di see all other player dem di waka pass, osa Pa Tiya dey (I see all the other players passing by, where is Pa Tiya)?" she asked.

Tiya Efvume was Namondeh's paternal uncle, which qualified him as a father. Thus, she would refer to Tiya Efvumeh just as she would refer to her own dad, Pa or Ta'a-teh. She broke into an open wailing, and I felt very sad for her.

Immediately following Efvumeh's death, our *ndoh-meh wa munyana mombaki way-va-ru ya nyango* (older maternal male cousin) by the name Kelleh told us, the younger ones, that a Mot'a Yowo was being sought who would come and resurrect Tiya Efvumeh. He was the origin of the "rumor," the rumor about Manyaka from Muyuka with the apparent reputation and or capability of being a "resurrectionist." Manyaka was well-known to be tough on treating mai-szreh (twins) with their mystical powers. All roads led to Manyaka if a family had any mai-szreh problems. I must say, however, that before now, I did not know that this Manyaka man was associated with resurrection powers.

I clung onto this hope tenaciously and believed it might come to pass. It was now over. He really was gone and gone forever. I never had a way of finding out if my ndo-meh believed what he told us or if he was just pulling our legs. He seemed very serious, though, and this was a big loss for us all, so why would he joke about something of such magnitude or importance? If you were wise, you did not question or confront an *ndoh-meh wa mombaki* (an older sibling), especially when they too were in a mourning mood, when they too were hurting. Several months later, I summoned the courage, and when he was in an apparent good mood, I asked him, "Nobi you be tok say Manyaka go wake-up Efvumeh (Did not you say that the yoworite Manyaka was going to resurrect Efvumeh)?"

"Shut up ya mop (Shut your mouth)! Wheda e-cam or e-no cam Wheda e wake e-up or not Na me ibi di jazz-man Manyaka (Whether he came or not and whether he resurrected him or not, am I the yoworite Manyaka)?" He shot out these words from his mouth with a warning of a spanking and kicking if this seeming interrogation or confrontation continued.

The Prisons or correctional department in Cameroon is more like a paramilitary force. At the end of the religious rites at the grave, and just before the grave was to have been covered with earth, stones, debris, etc., there was then a mini parade and gun salute in his honor by fellow warders or correction officers. The officer-in-charge then took over the ceremony. He shouted orders that were followed as the well-performed parade brought tears and wailing from the crowd assembled. The walana wailing very loudly seemed to have been blaming someone or some people for his death. But who were they blaming? The team management? At the end, the people lined themselves on the other side of the grave, facing the crowd, and their guns aiming for the sky, ready to fire as a final farewell to a local champion and hero and one of their own. The lead officer, who was the Chief Warder, gave the command thrice for firing, and each time, not a cricket sound emanated from the nozzles of the officers' guns. For each unsuccessful firing into the air, the mass servers, that is, the Ndoko boys, made the sign of the cross, and the crossing of themselves was done very rapidly, and we all wondered what that meant.

"W'ano wat'o wa kata."

(These Catholics), a Mokpwe molana in the crowd observed. In our village, those of the Roman Catholic Church were a significant minority.

Embarrassed and frustrated, the lead officer went over and took one of the guns from a subordinate officer, manipulated it, and fired it himself. He too tried twice with no success. They gave it up. At this point, the village *wa-szro-ngeli* (hunters) who too had prepared their own village farewell salute to a worthy muana of the village who had brought honor and recognition to the village, and who himself was a mo-szro-ngeli (hunter), gave him a six-gun salute in doublets—that is, each shot was actually two shots—fired at the same time. The village was silent, and all sobbing kept to minimum, for it was announced that crying during the firing would compromise the whole exercise and defeat the purpose of the gun salute.

Tiya's spirit had to be associated with and combined with the shots as they departed from the living. At the last shot, there was open wailing, the casket was lowered into the grave, and the filling with earth began, and the crowd started to disperse in silence, some in tears.

When the paramilitary force failed to succeed in firing even one live shot into the air after their brilliant but short parade in honor of our village hero, there was murmuring aplenty, and when we returned home later and as the days passed by after the hero's burial, I seem to have gotten two sides of the failed gun salute by the correction officers. One was incompetence on the part of the officers who did not check their firearms to ensure they were functional, and the other version was attributed to Li-emba. Tiya Efvumeh was sending a coded message saying he was killed via Li-emba and not a game accident, as it seemed.

Nyango Mukuszra, Tiya Efvumeh's widow, stopped talking to King'a Walana (King of Women) on the same day that Tiya died, accusing him of killing Tiya through Li-emba. King'a Walana was the oldest *ndo-meh wa munyana* (brother) of Tiya Efvumeh. King'a Walana was also a warder or corrections officer. He was the first of four from the Eszrong'a Maykomba clan in this line of profession.

Two days after Tiya's burial and for about two weeks thereafter, King'a Walana woke the village up early every morning at approximately 5:00 a.m., crying loudly, mourning the passing of his *ndomeh wa munya moszrali* (younger brother). Perhaps I should add here that King'a Walana was the one taking care of their ta'a-teh, Patriarch Eszrong'a Maykomba, who had a room in King'a Walana's house and was attended to by the polygamous household of King'a Walana. King'a Walana was bound to trado-cultural duties as the first muana wa munyana to be primarily responsible for their parents in their old ages. King'a Walana did his crying and mourning in his backyard where he climbed and sat on the plateau of a rock that was used variously by his family. This was my first time knowing that a *munyana* (man) could also cry, for we were always told, especially by our *iyakas* (mothers), that, "Mot'a munyana a-szray-ya (A man does not cry)." They would say they had good reasons for that from a cultural and sociological perspective.

King'a Walana's crying was enough proof that he killed his ndomeh as the whole village now seemed to know and have concluded. He was crying because he gave his ndomeh for Nyongo. Nyongo was a form of li-emba where you "gave" (killed) someone, and you were compensated monetarily for it. Humans given in Nyongo were referred to as "Cow way no get tail;" that is, a tailless cow. This "given" could come in many forms—a road accident, a heart attack, an attack by a domestic or wild animal, attack by bees, venomous reptile attacks, and even from human hands in the form of a physical altercation, etc. This was the rich form of Li-emba. When you gave someone for nyongo, the dead person went to "work" for their buying masters, mostly in their coffee and cocoa farms. These coffee and cocoa farms were owned by the Jangilites whose farms were situated mostly in the plateau parts of Cameroon, but also anywhere that they made their home in the English-speaking parts of Cameroon.

King'a Walana, it was said, was seeing Tiya working and suffering, and this broke his heart and, thus, the crying. The li-emba oriented or attuned villagers hated King'a Walana for killing Tiya, and the Eszrong'a Maykomba clan was divided. Camps were formed and enemies created. Once a united family, now a divided family. King'a Walana and his ta'a-teh, Patriarch Eszrong'a Maykomba, cried and mourned the passing of Tiya Efvumeh, his *mua-nyua-gweni wa moszrali* (younger brother), asking why death would choose such a young soul and leave them, the older ones, alive.

King'a Walana had also been struggling with his own health for several years now, which had significantly affected his physical fitness. The rest of the Eszrongo Maykomba clan too was mourning, but their bitterness and anger was geared toward King'a Walana who "killed" Tiya Efvumeh via nyongo. Tiya Efvumeh's ndomeh ja walana (sisters) did not associate with the nyongo "hypothesis" which was headed and very strongly fronted by Nyango Mokuszra, Tiya Efvumeh's molana (wife) left behind to mourn him.

With the clan so divided, it made it very hurtful, not allowing folks to grieve as they see or saw fit. While King'a Walana killed Tiya Efvumeh, he never became rich. This was strange and against the norms of nyongo after a very high-priced sacrifice.

Perhaps I should also add here that there was another version to Tiya Efvumeh's death. I had mentioned earlier that Tiya was said to have a "ring" he ordered from India. On that fateful day, when he had this collision on the football pitch, it is reported that that "ring" fell and all efforts to locate the ring failed, and thus, Joe returned home without his ring. We knew that if you wanted supernatural powers, the place to get it was from India. It was first Oku in the northwest and then Ijebu-Ode in Ogun State, Yoruba land in Nigeria, but it would appear spiritual powers are attainable from India; so, if you could, it was India one way, and we as kids had more faith in "Indian Jazz" than those attained from Africa for many reasons.

We saw lots of Indian films or movies long before Harry Porter, and we could see what Indians could do with all these "powers," so you did not have to convince us about Indian power; we saw it and we knew it. Indians could fly and disappear, they could turn a *Mot'a wehnama* (human being) into any animal, e.g. snake, frog, etc.; they could just say the word, and your body would be so badly afflicted, etc. With the same ease that they turned humans to animals and/ or inanimate objects, it was just as equally simple if you went to the right Indian Mot'a Yowo for a reversal of whatever was changed.

As likers of football, we also knew that India had been banned from the FIFA World Cup Soccer events because some years back, the Indian National Team trashed their opponents a hundred goals to nothing. The Indian players wore slippers or flip-flops instead of the normal soccer boots (Football boots, called cleats or soccer shoes in North America, are an item of footwear worn when playing football. Those designed for grass pitches have studs on the outsole to aid grip.), and the Indian players simply flew from one part of the field to another in the course of the game. They were thus banned. Proof of that was that since we started following World Cup soccer, India had never been represented.

However, we also knew that it was a matter of time before the Indians that gave you these powers asked you to pay for it because they always did in due time. You mostly paid with your life or the life of a close loved one. Tiya had refused to give his molana, Nyango Mokuszra, or any of his *wana* (children) when approached, which meant he had to go; that is, he was going to be the sacrifice, and so it was. Tiya's power associated with the Indian ring served him only as a first division player. It served him well, and now it was payback time.

I was wishing my people also had powers that would enable them to confront the Indians. The disappearance of the ring was the definitive sign, and he knew it. Tiya was "seen" a couple of times around his grave and on some of the village pathways. When he approached his *mbou-nda* (friend), King Kulu, whom he had literally mentored to be a footballer, the frightened young man rebuked him, saying, "Tiya na waiti na me I kill you (Efvumeh, what is it, am I responsible for your death)?"

When Kulu narrated the story, he was convinced that he missed an opportunity in which Tiya was attempting to convey a message. Kulu felt disappointed in himself and cried bitterly for having turned away his friend and mentor. Kulu, also known as King Kulu, saw Tiya again a few more times, but this time, Tiya gave him his back. He could not see his face, and they could not communicate. There were times in the village where nightfall was not to meet you outside and when it was concluded that the deceased star's spirit was in torment and roaming the village. I was a man with lots of wishful thinking but capable of doing nothing. I was a no-nothing. I had thought his spirit could be "caught" and the Indians be made to restore him to life. So, what Manyaka could do, these Indians could do. Or could they?

The "seeing of Tiya Efvumeh" by King Kulu many times was also interpreted as proof that he was given to nyango. His spirit was roaming, wandering, wanting to be put to eternal and final rest. That was the job of a Mot'a Yowo, Mola Mokpwel'a Maija, a reputed yoworite from the Mokpwe Village of Wo-nya-Mo-ngoh, a village dominated by Christian beliefs but also home to one of the most trusted and feared Nga-nga in upper Mokpweli-land. In a night ceremony, after all of the *szra-szra* (ceremonial rituals made for the dead to bid them a final farewell and to make them acceptable to their ancestors gone before them and that they are going to meet) had been made, Mola Mokpwel'a Maija performed his yoworite ritual in the deep of the night around Tiya Efvumeh's grave, a spiritual ceremony in which Tiya Efvumeh's spirit was *li-mi-szred* (quenched). Tiya Efvumeh's spirit was not reported seen by anyone thereafter, and life in the village now had the semblance of returning to "normal."

CHAPTER 13

King'a Walana

The patriarch, E-szro-ng'a May-ko-mba, died shortly after our gbwa-wa hunting experience and shortly after the death of his "Joseph," Tiya Efvumeh. The transitioned Mola Eszrong'a Maykomba left behind to mourn and miss him were five wana—Mola Likokeh, Mola Njay-njay, Nyango Likoweh, Nyango Litakay, and the oldest Mola, King'a Walana. Unfortunately, the patriarch had to bury his Joseph a few months earlier before he transitioned, and it was said that Tiya Efvumeh's death was contributory to the patriarch's own "early" exiting of this physical world.

He died as the oldest person in the village, almost unknown by the younger generation who kind of knew of his existence but had never set eyes on him. His age was estimated at over a hundred years old, for there were no birth records kept at the time he was born, and one's exact age was not a necessity in the carrying out of business in his earlier active days. Proof of his old age was that he had no friends, and no one in the village told stories of their childhood or things done together some years back or in a previous younger life. He could well have been a living ancestor.

However, my Libiyeah clan had earlier predicted Mola Eszrong'a Maykomba's imminent death after the killing of his mba'a-mba in our last hunting expedition. Officially, I do not know how they factored in the death of the patriarch's Joseph as related to the patriarch himself, for otherwise, this connection of a muana dying and causing and or accelerating the *kweli* (death) of a parent seemed already well-established and as an accepted norm within the clan and the village as a whole. Patriarch Eszrong'a Maykomba could not even participate in any of the funeral activities toward Tiya Efvumeh's funeral because of his advanced age, blindness, and other physical constraints that come with old age.

The patriarch was estimated to be a hundred plus and some years, for he was born at a time when birth certificates were not issued and when no official birth records were kept, but rather, events were used to estimate their ages. Mola Eszrong'a Maykomba died, leaving behind *may-mbamba* (grandchildren) and *ti-mba may-mba-mbeh* (great-grandchildren). All of his *wana wa wunyana* (male children) married walana and raised their families within their Maykomba landed property limits. The *wana wa walana* (daughters), however, got married and left, divorced, and then came back to their ancestral and childhood property where they built their own houses and continued to raise their individual nuclear families. Some of their own wana were now adults with their own families.

The Eszrong'a Maykomba clan was a large one, bubbling with lots of youthful life that brought spotlight onto the village via sports in the person of Tiya Efvumeh, the footballer and defender with Prisons Buea, but also brought a peculiar spotlight to our part of the village due to the origins and behavioral mannerisms of Tiya Efvumeh's molana and Tiya Efvumeh's two *may-nya may walana* (sisters-in-law).

I occasionally and intermittently hung out with three of E-szrong'a Maykomba's *May-mba-mbeh* (grandchildren), boys of about my own age, our interactions being mostly playing football (soccer) together. Two of these wana wa wunyana were from the Mola King'a Walana polygamous nuclear family, and the other one was from the Mola Likokeh nuclear family. The King'a Walana boys were Bwido Matoe and Woszro wo Ngowa, a reserved formidable attacker in our village football team with great dribbling and scoring skills. The Likokeh boy was Nammeh, not much of a footballer but was very supportive of group social activities and events. Nammeh had three older *ndoh-*

meh ja walana (sisters); they were all "married" with their own wana but were living with their parents in the Mola Likokeh family home. Nammeh's ndoh-meh ja walana were separated from their *wunyana* (husbands) for various reasons and then returned home with their wana as was customary with Walana wa Wakpwe.

Nammeh's oldest *ndoh-meh wa molana* (sister) was a mo-ku-sz-ray; that is, a widow. The story was told that she "killed" her *munyana* (husband) and the method or circumstances of her killing her munyana seemed to vary. One version had it that she had a *njuma* (fight) with her husband, and in the course of the fighting, she beat her munyana with her *maszronga* (teeth) around the *liwoh* (neck) region, which led to serious bleeding, and by the time the munyana was rushed to the *ndaw'a weh-tu-nay* or *nga-nga* (hospital) and was attended to, he died.

Another version had it that on the course of the njuma, Nammeh's ndo-meh wa molana grabbed at the munyana's groin with both *maah* (hands) and, with all her might, stuck there until the munyana's cry for help was yielded to by neighbors who came to the rescue. In our culture, a munyana does not *eh-ya* (cry), and a munyana does not also readily show that he is in *mo-szri-yo* (pain), neither does a munayana ask for help readily, for these were all signs and exhibitions of a public display of *mo-gwe-gwe* or *wolokoness* (weakness).

Consequently, when Nammeh's *monya wa munyana* (brother-in-law) was calling for help from his neighbors to rescue him from his molana, neighbors did not take it seriously, and the neighbors also knew that their presence would be an embarrassment to this munyana. Evidently, by the time the neighbors took it seriously and came to his aid, it seemed too late; he died four days later in the nga-nga. A third version was that Nammeh's ndoh-meh wa molana had li-emba. She had killed her munyana so as to inherit all of his property. This is a version that was advanced mostly by the *litumba* (family) of the deceased munyana. Either way, Nammeh's ndoh-meh wa molana became stigmatized in the village. She was looked upon as a killer or a li-emba molana or commonly both, and this was used against her by her adversaries any time the opportunity arose.

Nammeh's ndoh-meh wa molana's name was Nyango Namondeh Ewondeh nee Likokeh, and her munyana's name was Szrango Ligbwea

Ewondeh. Szrango Ewondeh, originated from the Mokpwe western village of Likombe, western vis-à-vis Gbwea. Szrango Ewondeh was in the employ of the Cameroon Development Corporation (a.k.a. CDC), an agro-industrial corporation that occupied a good junk of Fakoland at the expense of the Wakpwes and that served as a milk cow for the Cameroon Government. Ewondeh was a middle-ranking official with the purchasing office of the corporation stationed in Tikowa (Tiko). He had been sick for months with an undiagnosed disease, and the CDC Cottage hospital could not be of any assistance. His family thus took him back to their village of Likombe to pursue traditional medicine since the *mokala* (white man) medicine had not done any good. He had to be relocated to his village with his whole family, his molana, and five wana.

Ewondeh's parents and the Ewondeh litumba as a whole were not very keen admirers of their daughter-in-law, Namondeh, whom they generally referred to as "o go molan'a Gbwea," meaning "that Gbwea woman." When it was time to temporarily relocate Szrango Ligbwea Ewondeh to his Likombe Village, for traditional treatment, the Ewondeh family was divided as to whether his molana, Nyango Namondeh, should accompany him or not, for it was the position of some litumba members that Namondeh had her hands one way or another on the sickness of their son and brother and that her presence in the village would interfere and or delay the healing of Ligbwea.

In the end, feeling not wanted and with other practical and socioeconomic considerations, Nyango Namondeh decided that she would be visiting with her wana to see Ligbwea instead of moving the whole family to Likombe. She was an elementary school teacher at Tikowa, and their wana were in nursery, junior, and senior primary, schools all in Tikowa. Ewondeh was moved into their Ligbwea Ewondeh house in the village, a joint property with his molana Namondeh. Namondeh was visiting with the wana every two weeks, and they spent their weekends with Ligbwea. Three months after his relocation to the village, Namondeh decided to pay Ligbwea a visit in the middle of the week, at night, and without the children.

Ligbwea was caught in the company of another molana, a village girl under very compromising circumstances. The village molana exited the ndawo via a window when the commotion began, and then it was now left to Namondeh and Ligbwea. A sickling put under such physical stress of brutal fighting with an enraged molana was thought to be very contributory to his death. After Ligbwea's death and funeral and then the szra-szra ceremonies, Namondeh and her wana were declared persona non grata in Likombe and ordered to leave immediately. She was not recognized as the Ligbwea's mokuszra, and the wana were also not recognized as Ligbwea's own. Namondeh and her wana were also stripped of any claim of the property in Likombe village.

Overnight, therefore, the Mola Likokeh family had to get their daughter and meh-mba-mbeh out of Likombe, affording Namondeh the opportunity to mourn her husband in a civic environment with her wana. The Ligbwea Ewondeh family argued that while Namondeh could not kill their son via li-emba, she had to do it physically, taking advantage of a very sick man, sickness she was responsible for. All attempts by Namondeh and the Mola Likokeh litumba to assure the Ligbwea Ewondeh litumba that this unfortunate incident was not meant to be and that it was not planned and that it was fully regretted fell on deaf ears and did not hold any water and simply did not fly. If for anything, it only helped to fuel the anger of the in-laws and villagers of Likombe.

Two of Patriarch Eszrong'a Maykomba's children were prison officers or correctional warders (wardens)—the oldest, Mola King'a Walana, and the youngest, Mola Tiya Efvumeh, commonly called Pa Tiya (many years later, two of their nephews followed suit and also became correctional officers). What these two ndomeh ja wunyana also had in common was that they were wife beaters. Mola King'a Walana was a plumber by trade, and among all of his ndomeh ja wunyana and among all the wunayana in our portion of the village, he was the only polygamous munyana. He was thus nicknamed King'a Walana; that is, the king of women.

King'a Walana had two homes in the village about one hundred meters apart from each other. Each housed a molana. He lived in the lower building which was of a mixture of stones, mortar, and wood and which never seemed to have been able to see a completion date. In addition to these two walana he had in the village, his very first molana lived in another far-off village called Wokwai. I never knew where it was but knew it was far away. Wokwai was one of those southeastern villages of Mokpweli-Mbowa, vis-à-vis Gbwea. It would, however, seem that at least two children from this "first" marriage lived with him in our village at any point in time, and there was the back-and-forth movement of the children now and again between our WonyaLyonga Village and the Village of Wokwai.

There was another muana wa munyana who lived with Mola King'a Walana. He begot him with a molana he never married. Therefore, directly under Mola King'a Walana's roof was a complex of group genes. His ta'a-teh, his most elderly molana, and the wards she brought with her, at least two children from the Wokwai molana at any point in time and a child from an *Iyaka* (a mother) we never knew.

There were the occasional visitors who came to stay, temporarily but perhaps semi-permanently, whose connection with the family I never knew. In King'a Walana's house, there was one of his muana wa munyana who was a playmate of mine. We played football together in representing our portion of the village and sometimes as the flag bearers of the village football team, the WonyaLyonga Warriors. Nammeh was his name, and he was easily the best dribbler of our football team. We fondly called him I-kom'a Loko after the ndima (blind) and talented guitar musician we had in our village.

King'a Walana was a plumber by trade, training that my *mbamba wa evaru ya nyango* (maternal grandmother) used as a handyman. He was sure to come back to fix the same problem over and over, even when he bought new parts to fix the problem. My mbambeh grumbled bitterly behind his back. There was continuous plumbing taking place at my mbambeh's, just like the familiar yoworite visits. It looked as if these two professions were competing with each other, only that the yoworites drained thousands of times more cash than the plumber. There seemed to have been a faulty flushing toilet all the time and blocked sinks in the kitchen.

While King'a Walana had the village reputation as a wife beater, it was not known that he ever raised his hand to *ti-ya* (beat) his eldest wife who was perhaps about his age group and who lived with him under the same roof. This molana of his was called Nyango A-szra-tor Nyakeh, was very quiet, and barely raised her voice, even when talking. Though she was married in WonyaLyonga, she never socialized in WonyaLyonga. She came from a neighboring village, Wondongo, and she had to walk past the WonyaLyonga graveyard to return to her village. This graveyard was a common burial ground for both the Wondongo and Wonya-Lyonga villages and it also served as the boundary for both villages. It would seem that she visited her village perhaps every day or just very frequently.

Nyango Aszrator Nyakeh was a yumba molana; that is, she had no kids of her own and apparently the only molana in King'a Walana's life that was barren. She, however, came with what I should think were a niece and a nephew that lived with her as her wards. These were her errand boy and girl as she would hardly ask another child to do an errand for her.

King'a Walana's second legal molana was from another village called Wokwaongo, and she seemed the youngest of all of Mola King'a Walana's walana. She was lanky and very obviously taller than her *munyana* (husband), King'a Walana, and was also taller than all of the other walana whom she met already as walana for the *Kinge* (king). Nyango Moh-tor-wu mo Wana had some two vertical tattoos on each cheek, running down her face, poorly mimicking the very large tattoos of the Yurubas from Nigeria who lived in our town of Buea. These marks on her face were sure proof that she was not a molana from our village. These marks seemed an object of conversation amongst adult walana in the village time and again as one could easily hear them comment about them when passing them on the road or sometimes on the rare occasions when the village assembled for something.

Nyango Mohtorwu mo Wana had her house built on a rock on a hilly location, making the house very visible from afar. Nyango Moh-tor-wu mo Wana had asked for a separate house as a condition for the marriage when King'a Walana had asked her hand in marriage. Our nuclear family residence was just about fifty meters southwest of Nyango Mohtorwu's house.

Nyango Mohtorwu was some sort of a loudspeaker parrot-like molana. Her *wana* (mouth) would always talk to the annoyance of the gentle, soft-spoken, and ill-looking King'a Walana. This younger and very energetic molana was at least one and half times bigger than Kinga Walana, but the *Kinge* (King) somehow managed to be able to be the beating man whenever he deemed it necessary.

This large-mouthed woman with vertical marks on her cheeks (characteristics attributed mostly to the Yorubas from Nigeria and the Munchis who lived in Gbwea, for these were alien traits) also knew how to cry loud. King'a Walana normally went on his beating exercise late at night, the earliest time being about 9:00 p.m. when we were sleeping already, so we followed the events in bed. The rock plateau and elevated position of Nyango Mohtorwu mo wana's house made the sound drama that emanated from her ndawo during the relatively quiet nights, except for the chirping crickets and breeding *weh-toh-loh-loh* (frogs or toads) very vivid. Before the *njuma* began ("fighting"), which almost immediately turned into *ti-ya* (beating), anyone awake in the surrounding houses, especially those of us who were downhill, could tell there was a storm brewing. I never heard King'a Walana's voice, but you heard Nyango Mohtorwu mo Wana boasting, "Na-szro'o-ka woh-ngoh (I am not afraid of you)," she would say. "Waveh njeh (Who are you)?" she will continue daring him.

"Waveh o-weh-li di munyana (Are you also a man, she will continue, mocking her munyana)? Nu-mue-leh ima na-weh-li di molana wa Wokwaongo (I will show that I am a woman from Wokwaongo)."

And the posturing and daring would go on and on, and we knew the setup and therefore just waited for the encounter to begin. These were our movie nights while tucked in bed, our brains recording every bit of it while enjoying at the same time.

Such nights, my *iyaka* (mother) would come to our room to see if we were sleeping or awake.

"Bwanghai, Moighai," she would call. "Bwanghai oma naga (Are you asleep)?" she would ask. When I was younger, I actually would answer saying, "Err nama naga (Yes, I am asleep)," but not until my *ndoh-meh wa munyana wa mombaki* (older brother) told me what a fool I was.

When the quiet King'a Walana decided to go for the offensive, it normally started with walls of their plank (wood) house shaking, the shuffling and falling of household items, and eventually Nyango

Mohtorwu mo Wana crying to the top of voice, "King'a Walana a-no'o-wa eh (King'a Walana is killing me)!"

"You will kill me today," Nyango Mohtorwu would continue to say and say some more as much as she could before the inevitable that she knew was coming.

Whenever we heard, "O-noway yawono (Kill me today)," it meant King'a Walana was now at full attack, paying her for all the words she had said, daring and mocking him, and also paying her for the main course of the fracas. This phase was normally followed by the children crying, pleading with their *ta'a-teh* (father) to spare their iyaka.

Nyango Mohtorwu mo Wana had three children—two *wana wa walana* (daughters) and one *muana wa munyana* (son). The muana wa munyana was the oldest muana for Nyango Mohtorwu mo Wana and playmate of mine. He too was in the village football team as a minor substitute, not a real force to reckon with like his *mua-nya-ngwe-ni* (brother), Nammeh. His name was Bwido Matoe. He was named after his grandfather, the Patriarch Eszrong'a Maykomba, and therefore, most of time, he was simply referred to as Maykomba.

The *wana wa walana* (daughters) coming to their Iyaka's aid would pick up their song where they left the last time there was a beating of their iyaka.

"Ta'a-teh o-szro-wa iyakeh (Ta'a-the, do not kill iyaka)!" they would plead in singing. "Ta'a-teh weh-meh iyaka (Ta'a-ta, leave iyaka alone)," they would continue. "O-wio-ma a-weh-ni wana ya nde-neh (You know that she has a large mouth), Di o-szra weh-ni li mo'o-wa (But it is no reason to want to kill her). Awehli di nya-ngwa-szru (She is our mother). Nde-nga-veh, a-weh-li di molana wa-ngoh (And also, she is your wife)."

The daughters, Maliy'a Tuwi and Wio-leh mo Va-nghe-li, would continue their mantra until there was intervention from other adult members of the Eszrong'a Maykomba clan. I would think intervention only came within their own clan because I do not remember any of the adult males in our clan heading out there to separate a fight as would have been expected. It was left as an internal or intra-clan family affair.

While Maliy'a Tuwi was petite and dark in skin tone, her younger sister Wioleh mo Va-nghe-li was plumb and very fair-skinned, like Bwido Matoe. Maliy'a Tuwi stopped going to school by class two or three at the primary level. Though an early elementary school dropout, she could still engage in a conversation in Pidgin. Wioleh mo Va-nghe-li, on the other hand, did not seem to have ever been enrolled in school, and thus, her only mode of communication was through the Mokpwe Language, the language spoken at home.

We had asked Bwido Matoe a couple of times why he never came to the assistance of his iyaka as his ndomeh ja walana did each time their ta'a-teh was on the offensive. His answers could be summarized as him being "Eh mua-na w'ama Ta'ata," meaning "I am daddy's boy, or I am a man." Bwido would also add that "Dis woman dem, their mot don too much," meaning women talk a lot. "Na di tok-tok di kill ee (It is the too much talk that is killing her [meaning her mother]," he would add.

Bwido's ndomeh ja walana, while reputed for coming to the assistance of their iyaka anytime and every time their ta'a-teh came to the attack, are also known to have turned against their iyaka sometimes in the absence of their ta'a-ta. Between Maliya and Mo Vangheli, Mo Vangeli was the younger of the two ndomeh ja walana. In one of the night njuma, after their ta'ata had been made to return to his quarters by internal family intervention and mediation and when all seemed quiet and their iyaka was still barking and blowing hot air, Maliy'a Tuwi said, "Iyaka waveh e-neh wana yo fveti (Mother, you have a large mouth and you talk too much) And then mo Vangeli added, "O-loma di na gbwa e-szro-veh maszroga (You bark just like a toothless dog or a paper tiger)."

And then and in unison, "O-szra weh-meh nanu (Why do not you let go or why do not you leave it alone)?" they both added.

At this, their iyaka went irate and responded angrily, "Yu-gbwa di may-titi (You smelly filthy rags)! Na-ngeh eweh-li di evaru yama szra-ngw'anyu (Now you are on your father's side)! Ya mo ti-mba-na di ebo-szra (You are now supporting, backing and taking your father's side). Mombaki O'o-wa-teh, yu-mbeh i-ngi wana janu ju-gbwa (When an adult is speaking, you shoot your smelly mouths)!"

The punishment she had just received from her husband and their father she had to vent out now on them, for they dared to reprimand an adult and their mother. This was really a disappointment for her, coming from own daughters. The boy, her son, had been lost to the father. Was she now losing her girls to their father also? What was she doing wrong? What had she done wrong?

In our village, Nyango Mohtorwu mo Wana was the most vulgar of all the adults and shamelessly so. She could be very insulting and vulgar to both adults and children at anytime and anywhere, without inhibition. In that same token, her two little girls, Maliya and Mo Vangeli, were the most vulgar children and most insulting children of the village. While their spoken Mokpwe was poor comparatively to other children of the village, they spoke very advanced Mokpwe when it came to insults and vulgarity. They were kids to be avoided, and for the most part, they kept to themselves, barely venturing out of the confines of their immediate roofs. Their older ndomeh wa munyana, Bwido Nathaniel, dealt with this situation with frequent slaps and knocks on their heads whenever any tried to throw their venom his way.

Maliya and Mo Vangeli were kids to be avoided, and parents in the village made sure they instilled this into their wana, but perhaps that was not necessary because they kept to themselves, maybe sensing the deliberate efforts of other kids to isolate them by staying away from them and/or distancing themselves from the duo sisters. These sisters could insult anyone with taboo insults and words in the Mokpwe culture. All wondered and doubted how they could be so well-schooled in the negative in an environment where they seemed like fish out of *maliva* (water).

King'a Walana eventually died of ill-health after suffering for many years and seemed to have shrunken in size to the bare minimum. A few days before his death, his Wokwaongo molana came to our clan's territory to chat with her Wokwaongo sister who was Nyango Mofvungeh. I remember her saying she thought King'a Walana was going to die the night before because he was talking "Lokor-lokor" and "Tuwa-tuwa," speaking gibberish in an uncoordinated manner, not making any sense at all.

At least three years before Mola King'a Walana died, it was evident to all in the village that he was not doing well health-wise. If you did not see it, you probably overheard adults talking about it. He was very scarce, hardly seen, then he would be seen going to work for about a week. Then he would disappear again for months before making another attempt that was supposed to signal an improvement or a back to normalcy of life. It was evident he was suffering from a wasting disease. The relatively short stout and sturdy munyana was progressively getting smaller and smaller each time he was seen in public, which was rare.

As mentioned before, King'a Walana was a warder and was commonly seen in his heyday marshalling prisoners in the village who came to work to earn money to feed themselves. Our Gbwea Town was a well-known town associated with the Corrections and Prisons Department of the Ministry of Territorial Administration. Gbwea had three prison posts called "farms." To the northwest of our village was the upper farms, to the southwest of the village was the west farms in association with the Boastal Institute (a juvenile correction center), and to the south of our WonyaMongo Village were the lower farms that served as the main and central authority, housing the seat of the overall superintendent of the service, and was also the center for the hardened criminals with jump suits initialed "CC," which meant Condemned Criminal. Condemned Criminals were destined for execution in the gallows within the center's confines.

Word usually spreads in town just before an execution. Only one execution was carried out in public, and they used the football stadium which was used by the Prisons Buea Football Club. The person executed by firing squad was a Nigerian prisoner who had "accidentally" killed a police officer who had gone to arrest him for a crime he had committed. The execution drew a large crowd, and we learned that all attempts by the Nigerian Government to have the then Cameroon President, Ahmadou Ahidjo, a.k.a. Grand Camarade, to commute the sentence to life imprisonment without the possibility of parole failed. While we were told at home not to watch it, for it was bad luck, we managed to sneak out somehow and, from somewhere, watched the firing squad.

The following football season, Prisons did not win any game at home, playing in that Buea Town Stadium. It was the start of Prisons relegation to the Division II League later.

The three correction prison centers in Buea were called farms because, either currently or in the past, the detained inmates were engaged in farming activities that involved crop growth and production and animal husbandry. The upper farms were nearest to our home, and we used to go there to buy fresh *ma-nyo-ngeh* (cow milk), *wiono* (*Discorea rotundata*; yams), and *mba-szri* (*Zea mays*; corn), depending on the season, and as announced or advertised to the public. We, in our part of the village, normally knew when such sales took place because of our connections with the farms by virtue of family members or village members working with the department. This idea of farms associated with prison departments in Gbwea started with the German and then British exploiters who wanted their prisoners of locals to be able to feed themselves since they, the jailers, could not afford to feed them. Their prisoners had to fend for themselves.

In addition, these farms operated by "prisoners of conscience" (for the most part), extracted from the local population, served the needs of their creators. They provided the exploiters with fresh milk, vegetables, meats (cow, pig, chicken), eggs, etc., at absolutely no cost to them. When the management of the prisons and farms were taken over or passed over to Cameroon Administrators after "independence," the purpose for creating and maintaining the farms was continued, but just like every other thing, it was a matter of time before it could no longer be maintained. The land was still there and fertile, being volcanic soil, but crops could no longer be grown, and then emphasis changed on production of animals, milk, and eggs. This too was sustained for a couple of years and then finally died.

A primary reason why the crop production failed was that, unlike the European exploiters, the indigenous Cameroon administrators did not care about the gastronomic needs of their prisoners. Prisoners became personal properties of the Chief Warder of the center or farms. All crop harvest became that of the Chief Warder. The Chief Warder sold to the public what he and his family could not consume, and all the funds went into his private pocket, meaning the cash received from the sales was shared. He passed some of it up to the food chain of his superiors. None of the farm produce was used to feed the prisoners who labored on these farms, from preparing to plant, the planting, then maintenance, and finally harvest and sales. The prisoners did the sales under the watchful eyes of the warders.

Laborer prisoners saw themselves being used by the Chief Warder and his associates with the knowledge of higher-ups as far as possible. Prisoners became a moneymaking industry for the Chief Warder. Before long, the starving prisoners learned their lessons. During harvest of the crops they have grown for the Chief Warder, even under the watchful eyes of the junior warder officers out in the field with them, a substantial proportion of the harvest "disappeared," unknowing of the watching warders, or they knew but turned a blind eye, knowing what was happening.

The harvester prisoners would later on in the evening escape from their quarters and retrieve their hidden harvested crops from nearby bushes. Retrieved harvested crops were for two purposes—sale to the nearest local population, which included our village, and cooking for the stomachs in their cramped quarters at the end of each day. These two options or activities had many problems. Within their cells, cooking forward and eating alone or with some selected friends, food meant officially for all prisoners was not acceptable. Also, selling food to the outside local population that was officially meant for all inmates to eat was also not acceptable. It was viewed as the over-exploitation of the inmates by the Chief Warder who was outside the cells and certain "Chief Prisoners" inside the cells who too were just an extension of the untouchable Chief Warder.

The Chief Prisoners had therefore two enemies or adversaries—the Chief Warder, externally, who would know that they "stole" from him and then the fellow inmates who saw them as fellow oppressors with the Chief Warder gang. Certain "Chief Prisoners" were exposed to the Chief Warder, and this resulted in isolation, physical lashing, and in some cases, an extension of their prison term with charges like "escape and return." The crop farms collapsed eventually.

As the years progressed, the subsequent Chief Warders abandoned crop production as an economic venture and dwelt more on animal husbandry, but before long and adapting to the changing styles and tactics of inmates, who played mouse and cat games for the greater share and ownership of the animals raised and products from the animals like the *ma-nyio-ngeh* (milk) and *may-yo* (eggs), the Chief Warders abandoned the smaller animals and animal products production in favor of raising only the *nyaka* (*Bos Taurus*; cows) and for their meats only. Currently that is their main business.

Prisoners who worked in the piggery, poultry, and in the milking of the cows, invented ingenious ways of disappearing whole animals and large quantities of animal products, for which they found ready markets in nearby villages like ours. The villagers patronized them for a number of reasons, though they knew what they sold were "stolen" goods. Short bargain and relatively cheap, the prisoners needed to eat and stay alive, and by patronizing them, you were ensuring their livelihood and keeping them alive. Surrounding villages of "farms" had suffered a lot in the hands of prisoners who constantly invaded the villages and stole from homes and yards anything they could and then taking their loot to another village for a quick and cheap sale, just so that they could buy food and eat and also be able to afford other basics of life, not available within the prison walls. Our home had been a victim of prisoner burglary in which all of my college supplies were stolen and other household items at a time of "rentrée scolaire" (back to school).

Cows are bigger animals, more difficult to "steal" and to dispose of in a "village market" clientele. And nyaka without the milk and cheese meant that Chief Warders "alone" owned the industry and the economics that come out of farms. More recently and currently, the nyaka that are reared in farms are completely and totally not the property of the department of correction and prisons. The cows are 100 percent owned by private individuals in conjunction with the Chief Warder. It is a total private business run and operated in public properties and using prisoners as laborers for private profit.

The managers and owners of this business stretched from the Chief Warder, the local operator to Ewonda, at the table of prominent and influential party and government top civil administrators who are above the law and can do and undo. As children at the elementary school level, we kind of all desired to be Chief Warders, judiciary scouts and menofarms, ports officials, political party bosses, and a government big man or perhaps open a Pentecostal church. It came with the prestige, the money, and the power, all seemingly unlimited. They were the top echelon of society and occupied the high table everywhere, including churches.

It was not only the prisoners that were associated with the farms' economic business that needed to survive. When the government became too broke to provide the basics for prisoners, including their daily food, Ewonda decided that prisoners be allowed to venture out of their prison yard to work for people and families privately so that they earned some money for food and other basic necessities. Prisoners who had families or relations that could support them had no need to hire themselves out as ready hand laborers.

This did not seem like an official policy sometimes, but there was no way that it was not known to the highest levels, for it was very open and known. Prisoners for manual labor were accompanied by warders to do jobs—mostly manual jobs—at government facilities and private facilities that would have paid the corrections department. This official work was done in the morning and all afternoon up until three to four hours past noon, then the prisoners were "free" to go do private jobs to earn a living. The "free and private job" moments were not occupied by warders watching over the activities of the inmates. Sometimes these free periods for the prisoners started in the morning, perhaps when the prisoners were not assigned any duties or rather when there were no duties to assign them. Whatever the case, the free periods had a limit; they were all to answer present on "campus" by six hours after noon, unfailingly. Otherwise, it attracted some punishment, including being deprived of your "livelihood freedom" and being isolated.

This freedom meant that prisoners worked as domestic servants, yardmen, farmhands, and general repair people to families in need in nearby villages and communities. This also increased the crime rate, especially stealing incidents in these villages. The cheap labor notwithstanding, it was a matter of time before nearby communities mounted complaints, requesting that the prisoners be kept in their cells.

When Mola King'a Walana felt better intermittently and returned to work, we saw him walking and accompanying prisoners that he brought to the village, sometimes to do some work in his yard or house. King'a Walana was a *Mot'a aou-tu* (a short man), and with his long battle with sickness, he had lost lots of weight and therefore was a petite man with curved legs. The prisoners that he marshalled into the village to do work all were bigger and healthier than him. We normally pitied him, thinking if he was attacked by any of them, he could hardly defend himself. He would walk slowly behind them, not talking, and barely even answering audibly when greeted. Most of his strength had gone, and we wondered whether even the gun he carried would have been or was of much help to him if the prisoners wanted to stage a run or if the prisoners decided to rough handle him as they did occasionally to some of the warders.

Mola King'a Walana did not die before Tiya Efvumeh's molana and *Mokuszra*, Tiya's mother-in-law, and Tiya's sisters-in-law showed him and his litumba what they thought of them, vis-à-vis, Efvumeh's death. But whether Mola King'a Walana was sick or not or whether he was near death or not, Tiya Efvumeh's Mokuszra and her family were to still continue with their plan. It had to be done, for it was unstoppable.

When word had reached Mola King'a Walana that he was being accused of having Li-emba and that Nyango Mokuszra and her litumba had concluded he killed Tiya Efvumeh by giving him for Nyongo, King'a Walana cried bitterly.

He said in reply, "Nyang'a Mokuszra awi di Tiya na Mot'a munyana (Nyango Mokuszra only knew Tiya as an adult, as a man). I-mba na mowi na muana (I knew him as a child). Nde-nga-veh na ndo-meh wami moszrali (And also as my kid brother). Mua-nya-gw'ami moszrali ah way-li Nde-nga-na I-mba eh mo-mbaki (My kid brother has died before me, the older one)."

He was not recorded to have ever addressed this issue again for the remainder of his life. His illness, the passing of his father, the passing of Tiya, and now these outlandish and preposterous accusations all took a deeper toll onto his already fragile health, and his downward spiral had no return signs. He died a very sad man. The Nyango Mokuszra Litumba had visited with many nga-nga and yoworites in the manner and order of Szrango Ma-nya-ka, but only this time, the emphasis was a Mot'a Yowo capable of killing someone who was guilty of killing another person via Nyongo. At their first stop, they were told that Mola King'a Walana was a higher-up in the nyongo realm, meaning it needed more than the ordinary and standard procedure to get to him. This meant a cash price commensurate with work that needed to be done. The Mokuszra Litumba was said to have visited other killer yoworites with the hope of getting one that was affordable.

Nyongo killings were associated with riches. That was not evident with Mola King'a Walana, but the agony he went through was very evident. Was it true that men did not cry as we were told and being brought up to believe and be?

"Mu-nya-na a-szray-ya" (A man does not cry).

Nyango Mokuszra explained the continual poorness of Mola King'a Walana after killing her munyana like this. She was told by yoworites that after seeing Tiya Efvumeh toiling in the cocoa and coffee farms owned by ghost businesspersons from the plateau regions of Cameroon, he refused to take their money and demanded that they rescind their agreement or contract. The businesspersons told him politely that there was no rescission in their business, so he either had to take the money and enjoy and live big or he remained with that guilt all his life.

CHAPTER 14

Nkwel'a Wana

Koff'a Moteh, also sometimes called Talameh, had long suspected that the early death of Nkwel'a Wana's kids may not have been due to natural causes. But he had no way of proving it. Ours was a society in which establishing and documenting the cause of death was either not known, not a priority, or perhaps due to lack of knowledge. For the most part, most deaths occurred at home, and for infant kids, they were buried almost immediately after it was established that they had died for certain, and there would be no crying. Oftentimes, the mother attempted to cry or sob. When this was seen or heard by the *wambaki* (elders) present, they would immediately hush her down and emphatically state that, "I-szra-szra luwa a-nu (We do not want any crying here)."

Naturally, I always wondered why this apparent hurried burial, sometimes even before family members in close proximity even knew. That is, if a family member, say, went to their farm in the morning to return in the evening, and this infant died in the morning or early afternoon, it is very likely that the family member would only be told of the burial on arrival later. When I had asked my iyakeh why this custom was, she had said, "Wa weh-li di wana wa wo-weh (They are bad babies). Nde-nga-veh o-szra-szra li-ta-ti-szreh wa-li-mo (And in addition, you do not want to annoy the ancestors gone ahead)."

On questioning her further, I learned that "spiritually bad kid" could mean more than one thing. It could mean the dead infant decided to return to where it came from either because it was missing its kindred "back there," especially if it was a *mai-szreh* (twins); the other, "annoyed of being left behind" will insist that the earthly born one returns. Otherwise, there could be some dire consequences. For example, it could be that the born maiszreh would be a sickling and would not be treated kindly by its *litumba la wat'o wa weh-na-ma* (the human family), which would lead to an early death; or just simply that the neonate found out immediately that there was lots of misery in this physical world and especially the house it came through and judged it was not worth it to continue to stay.

So, if a bedeviled infant decided to go back at a very early age, if for anything, it should be a cause for joy. Weeping or any signs of emotional attachment may mean it will go and come back during the Iyaka's next pregnancy, and yes, our village walana who lost a kid at infancy seemed to have just turned around and were pregnant again. There were physical proofs that some kids had "gone" and "come back," and naturally, a family wanted to know whether the next muana after an infant death was a *mo-ti-mba* (a comeback or returnee). Bodily marks were put on the dead infant before burial. It could be a chopped piece of *li-toe* (ear), removal of some tissue from the *mbu-szra* (back) or *lou-nga* (belly) area in a triangular manner, and/or it could be simply chopping off part of a *njo-nor* (finger or toe).

Very commonly also, an x-shaped tattoo was made to the lateral of the torso region. The marking of the dead infant before burial was normally done with incantations and other rituals us kids were not allowed to see. The village nga-ngas made their living this way.

When the next child was born, its body was critically examined to ascertain if it was a mo-ti-mba or a mo-fve-nya; that is, a fresh or a new child. If a born infant was deemed a motimba, the nga-ngas went to work to ensure that it did not return a second time or, in the case of its early death, they ensured that there was no third return route for it to the earthly world. This involved an elaborate yowonized (spirit-filled) all night long ceremony, which was very scary for us kids. There seemed to have been some cases of multiple mo-ti-mbas, and the nga-ngas had explanations for that and worked even harder.

Alternatively, an infant death could be the work of the *wa-li-mo* (spirits or ghosts gone ahead) who were the spiritual ancestors that took care of the wat'o wa weh-na-ma. Crying will mean a challenge to their authority and knowledge. Since as kids were gifts from them, displeasing them would not be wise as an infant death was considered a "recall" from the powerful and wise beyond.

I had asked my iyaka for proof that the wa-li-mo were associated with babies born. She had lots to say. For example, when my *mbam-beh wa evaru ya nyango* (maternal grandmother) died, my *ndo-meh wa molana mo-mba-ki* (older sister), by the name Ngoweh Imbolleh, had a first muana less than a year thereafter. When the congratulatory songs were being sung.

"Fvo-boh-woh eh Fvo-boh-woh. Fvo-boh-woh eh Fvo-boh-woh (Congratulations, congratulations)," they sang and then gave thanks to my Mba-mbeh jeah-ni lo'o-mba o ti-mbi-szrey (We have seen the bundle of joy you have sent back to us the living). And given the semblance or likeness between the infant and its *ti-mba-li-mba-mbeh* (great-grandparent), it was concluded that it was she my Mba-mbeh who had returned. Words were actually directed to her through the other ancestors. In our culture, when you thank someone through another person, it is considered a worthier way of conveying your thanks, for at this time, you will not only be the one doing the thanking but your emissary also.

The wato wa wehnama thus sent their thanks like this:

"E-mo-weh-ya ma Nje-ni lou-ba Ma-szro-ma szrai-szrai (Tell her that we have seen her parcel and gift, and we are very grateful for it)."

This message is normally sent through other walimo. It is addressed to her via emissaries who, when they deliver the message of thanks, will also be thanking her and will be witnesses that the *wat'o wa weh-na-ma* (*Homo sapiens*) were grateful and not ingrates.

Then they will continue, "A-gwe gbwa-mu (She has done well). Ma-szro-ma Szrai-Szrai (Many thanks)."

They will then proceed to describe certain physical characteristics or phenotypes on the child that are identical or similar to the ancestor *E-li-mo* (spirit) that was the generous "gifter." This was normally the job of the walana; the wu-nya-na did not seem very particular about a birth, not that they were not concerned. For walana, it brought them together and brought about reconciliation in cases where reconciliation was needed. For example, if the molana who delivered the muana had made some enemies and, say, was not talking to some other molana or just barely did, when the "enemy" came to celebrate the birth of the child, it was "all sins forgiven." Their differences were not talked about, and all returned to normal; a new and clean page in their relationship was started.

In lots of families among the Wakpwes (Bakweris), there are lots of kids who are either Mo Timba on their own rights or Mo Timba as in one who had already lived a full human life before within the family or perhaps a child who died as a *mbe-szra* (male youth) or *ngoh-ndoh* (female youth). Oftentimes, these *Wa Timba* or *Wa-ti-mbe-li* (the "Returns or the Comebacks" or the returnees) were given names to reflect this spiritual status of theirs and were often treated differently with respect, fear, and suspicion—all of these or any combination of these. Sometimes their naming was related to the "assumed before life" they now represented in mortal form.

For example, while Ta'a-ta or Ta'a-teh means father, a child could be named Ta'a-ta, inferring that a Ta'a-teh who transitioned either Ti-mbaad (returned) or O-maad (sent) the born child. Alternatively, or in cases where a born-child was not a Ti-mbaad (a returned), he or she could still be given the name of an ancestor gone ahead. In which case family members were always reminded of the special status the mua-na (child) had in and within the family. Wa Ti-mba wana related to or associated with a gone before person of high social status had many privileges in their immediate family circles. When however, a Mo Timba of high social status found himself or herself (very rarely) being a much younger sibling, he or she normally found himself or herself at a lower pecking order among the wana of the family, albeit among his or her own siblings; these often led to problems of sibling rivalry.

The Wa Timba normally held in high esteem were normally males and rarely females. This seems to be related to a culture that was "patriarchal." The Wa Timba played their cards well and took every advantage there was, especially as they grew older and got comfortable with the protection and preferential treatment. The Wa Timba only occupied their real pecking positions at home in the absence of their parents. They assumed their rightful and accorded positions otherwise. This was because siblings did not seem to buy into this Mo Timba and Wa Timba notion; it was for the elders of clans and families and the custodians of the traditions and customs of my people, the Wakpwes. It was these returnees or early "exiters" that were commonly called by those without our Wakpwe people as "Oba-njeh."

"Oba-njeh pikin"—in Pidgin, it meant you were a returnee. You were feared and left alone for the most part, but oftentimes also, it was a disadvantage, especially as it concerned folks outside your immediate and extended family. Folks older than an oba-njeh would taunt them and sometimes physically assault them, daring them to do their worst.

It would therefore seem that in Koff'a Moteh, also known as Talameh's mind, Kwel'a Wana had been an inadvertent or calculative beneficiary of the culture of her people and the profession of nga-ngas. Like was said before, Nkwel'a Wana was known as a woman who had lost at least four known kids as neonates, and this drew sympathy her way from some quarters and suspicion from other quarters. Nkwel'a Wana had an excuse or explanation for the deaths of her children—it was Li-emba. When it happened the first two times, her mother took her to pay a visit to a Nga-nga, and it turned out that it was her *Mbamba wa evaru ya szra-ngo* (paternal grandmother) that was responsible. This strained their relationship, and her iyaka and Mba-mbeh stopped all forms of communication and socialization.

Nkwel'a Wana and her iyaka had gone in the early morning to her Mba-mba's house, did not enter, but rained her with insults of witchery and evil tendencies, standing in front of her door, daring her to come out for a snake beating. This was a social stain in our culture that was hard to do away with. It also had credence because it came from within, meaning it came from members of the same family. You see, the way li-emba goes, it mostly works only among family members; that is, if someone in your family has li-emba, he or she is only able to practice it on close family members—close meaning genetically, proximity wise, and/or in-law-ship. Candidates for li-emba-ship were normally young prosperous persons, especially from a financial perspective, and then the other natural group were the older folks. For the older folks, it went either way. If you were materially poor, you were a prime candidate for li-emba, and also, if you were materially comfortable, you also were a prime candidate for nyongo.

Nkwel'a Wana fairly frequented our village, so one had the opportunity of seeing her pretty often in good times and in the not so good times. The mental picture kept of her was a one molana group or company. She normally had at least four kids in her company each time she was seen: The one she *ba-baad* (strapped to her back with a piece of cloth) and usually the youngest, two by her side connected to her by the holding of hands and one in front of her by a few steps. All of these wana would range in age from zero to about six or seven years old. The oldest one who walked or marched in front of her seemed to have been insulted and shouted upon at all the way because the muana must walk and lead the way as expected. Insults to such a muana oftentimes was traced back or related to an uncaring or absentee father or a baby daddy, as commonly referred to in the United States.

This one molana company walked a distance of at least three kilometers one way to get to their destination. The hardest part seemed to have been once they entered our village because of the recurring hills and short-distance intermediate plateaus. Whenever Kwel'a Wana was sick, she became a Nkwel'a Weh-szray; that is, a skeleton. She was characterized by a long bony *liwoh* (neck), shrunken jaws, and protruding predator-like incisors, with lower limbs too emaciated to carry or support the above load. In this state, the conspicuousness of her behind and chest load became magnified several times and very palpable. As Nkwel'a Weh-szray, it was only her thin skin that covered her *weh-szray* (bones) that could be counted and named from the external, especially her clavicles (collar bones) and scapulars (shoulder blades), all component bones of the pectoral girdle of the upper limbs that practically could be seen jutting out of her *nkwel'a weh-szray* (skeleton) being restrained only by the integumentary system (skin).

I must point out that Nkwel'a weh-szray's one molana company did not seem to always progress naturally and biologically for a reasonable length of time; that is, a complete one molana company was made up of five persons, one adult—Nkwel'a Weh-szray—and four wana. A specific and named company of this description or nature lasted for less than a year before the wana composition changed, a decrease, and then an eventual increase back to the company of five; that is, an iyaka and her four wana.

Let me also mention that her one molana company brought anxiety and anticipation and provoked conversation in just about all families that lived along her path of the "great trek," a trek that started from Las Town going past the Buea Town Market, through the Government School Buea Town, past the Cinema Hall, and then onto the middle lower elevation of the Wonya-Lyonga Village, passing through the properties of the Ekos, Liszrambehs, Njumbehs, Esongamis, and then the Malangehs and Maykombehs, and then ascending the hill to our portion of the village that was situated at a higher elevation. She would not only shout at the three wana (the two by her side and the one in front) that were struggling to make the long and difficult walk and the keeping up with her adult longer strides, but it was also common for her to pick up "quarrels" with them as if they were adults or teenagers, should anyone dare to complain and/or make a statement not acceptable to her.

This wrangling between iyaka and wana was a familiar scene all the way from Las Town to WonyaLyonga, a terrain characterized as stony, hilly, and windy. Once a Ngoh-ndoh (lass) who was actually a relative of Nkwel'a Weh-szray is reported to have said to Nkwel'a Weh-szray, "Chei Sista you nodi shame you di quarrel waiti small pikin dem (Ah, sister, are you not ashamed to be quarrelling with the kids)."

Nkwel'a Weh-szray, without hesitation, had responded, "Ou-gbwa, na small pikin dem dis (You smelly girl, are these kids? Dis old papa and mami dem way dem come back for worri me (These old men and women who have returned for the sole purpose of worrying and troubling me)."

Then the Nkwel'a Weh-szray had continued, "Osa dia papa dem dey, way na me one dem di trouble-am (Where are their fathers that I am burdened alone with them)?"

To this, the Ngoh-ndeli relative by the name Etond'a Ndolo had responded, "Na only you sabi osa dem papa dem dey (It is only you who knows where their fathers are)."

This conversation was getting into Nkwel'a Wana's inner perimeter, a place you do not want to be in. Her briefing rate was elevated, and she was clearly irate, considering the immediate strain of the stress associated with making this WonyaLyonga trip fairly frequently to visit her ndomeh wa molana wa mombaki who was in marriage with WonyaLyonga. Nkwel'a Weh-szray was Tiya Efvumeh's *ndo-m'a molana wa liwa* (sister-in-law).

Now, clearly annoyed and agitated for being challenged by a Ngoh-nde-li and a younger relative for that matter, she retorted venomously, "Ou-gbwa oweh (You stink, you hear me)?"

Nkwel'a Weh-szray shot back, "Ou-gbwa ma'a-teh-teh (You smell of your own shit in your ass)!" Then she continued in Pidgin, "If ibi sabi osa dem dey, I for di askam (If I knew where they are [the baby daddies], would I be asking?"

Now very agitated and sweaty, she continued, determined to assert her authority over this Etond'a Ndolo. "Look'am eh, make you nodi try me, you small a-kwa-ra a-sha-wo pikin (Do not ever make an attempt to dare me, you little slutty tramp)! You no know say, I-bi ya big sista way you cam di tok foolish for ma front (Don't you know that I am an older sister to you, that you have the nerve to talk nonsense to me, standing right in front of me)?"

In our culture, there is an adage that "Mombaki a-szra totowa nja-nga" or "Mombaki a-szra toe-na" (An elder or an older person is never wrong). What this means is that younger folks in our culture must be respectful, obey the laws and elders, turn a blind eye to anything wrong done by an elder person or person of influence, and the younger folks are also held to a higher standard in every respect. This is a phenomenon also common in boarding secondary schools where senior students are never wrong. The mantra, "grumble and stay," sums it all up. You can grumble, but there is nothing you can do. The normal tendency was for you to wait your turn of being a senior student to continue with the tradition.

"Ya mami dey house (Is your iyaka home)?" Nkwel'a Weh-szray had asked Etond'a Ndolo, intending to report her or lay a complaint for disrespectful behavior and perhaps also intending to put some fear into the ngoh-ndoh so as to abandon her very daring line of questioning. "Na di thing make way you not fit pass First School (That is why you are unable to pass First School)," Nkwel'a weh-sz-ray jabbed Etond'a Ndolo, a younger cousin of hers.

The First School Leaving Certificate was the diploma earned and awarded to pupils who successfully completed the primary or elementary course of study, which took seven years from class one to class seven (Grade 6) that was later changed to class six, reducing the duration by a year. The class one pupils were normally called "Class 1 Koko," indicating that they knew nothing and were just babies. These babies were normally five years of age. Thus, you were considered not to be smart if you could not attain this certificate after writing the national exam. It was some sort of a social shame to you. This became a frequent insult at home and outside.

By this time, Nkwel'a Wana and Etond'a Ndolo have started pulling a crowd, which effectively blocked off the small village pathway. The gathering crowd made no attempt to bring to an end this back and forth; they loved it, and some were actually urging them on from both sides. As we say in pidgin, "Putting fire." While Nkwel'a Wana was busy trying to make a point and/or assert her authority—or was it venting her frustration in some sort of a displacement behavior? —she forgot about her walking wana who one must say was happy to be away from her, even if just for a moment. The oldest one whom we could call the scout leader wandered around and came upon some mboli (*Capra hircus*; West African Dwarf goat feces which he thought was ngoh-do'or [groundnuts or peanuts] as he said later on) and did not hesitate to pick it up and throw it in his mouth. He had masticated a handful of his "ngoh-do'or" before he was discovered or noticed by one of the walana who was part of the gathering crowd.

Another of the Nkwel'a Weh-szray company kids had somehow stumbled on fresh watery gbwa (*Canis lupus familiaris*; domestic dog) feces (in pidgin, we say purge "belleh shit") in the nearby bushes and decided to play the piano on it, occasionally wiping her face with her hands, thereby making a poop coloration on her face. When this was brought to the attention of their iyaka, she reluctantly pulled away from the crowd and her adversary after being kind of scolded by an elderly Nyang'a Mbowa (village mother) who insisted that caring for those kids was her primary responsibility and not public shows as she was apt to doing with persons of her age, older persons, and even as now, younger individuals.

"O-weh-ni lor-nghe-ya wana wa-ngoh (You must take care of those wana of yours)," the Nyang'a Mbowa insisted and commanded.

When the kids were brought to her, Nkwel'a Wana said, "Wona see dis bad luck pikin dem (Look at this bad luck, kids." She attempted to share her frustrations with the rest of the crowd, employing them to be her witness or rather that the crowd had a peak into her troubles and problems with the wana.

"Which kind pikin dem go di go chop shit-so for daytime (What manner of children will be eating shit in broad daylight)?" she had asked in annoyance. "Wona see me ma own bad luck (People see my own bad luck and misfortune right in front of me)."

And then Nkwel'a Wana continued, "Wa-li-mo weh wana wanu (These are devil or evil-possessed wana)."

The Etond'a Ndolo with which she had been warring came forward, took the muana with the poop-coated face with her, stepped into a nearby bush, cut some fresh juicy leaves, and began to clean the muana's face in an attempt to make it poop-free. But by this time, the Nyang'a wana (that is, the mother of the children) Nkwel'a Wana had given each poop associated muana a hard knock on the head (what we called in pidgin "crack") and a solid slap on each jaw, which sent the terrified wana sprawling on the dusty and stony road path. Crying and helpless, Etond'a Ndolo and another village molana, Nyango Matanga ma Kaweh, took charge of the wana and ensured their cleaning. When the walana had finished cleaning the wana, their iyaka ordered them to get going.

"Wona pass go, chop shit pikin dem (Get going, poop-eating wana). Wona di make lekeh say wona nodi chop for house (You wana behave as if you are not being fed at home)?" she continued.

And then somebody in the crowd had asked anonymously, "O jor-keh jor-keh, owa gbwa molayli (For real, for real, do you give them food to eat at home)?"

To which she had responded without even looking or wanting to know who was questioning her. Her immediate reply was, "Ya mami pim yaa!"

This was a Pidgin insult of the highest level of vulgarity, referring to an opponent's mother's genitalia. This was considered very vulgar and associated with *wato* (persons) considered to be at the lowest social stratum. It seemed a favorite of young folks under the booze influence or some other drug or just simply someone wanting to vent out some venom to hurt as much as possible their opponent verbally. Younger folks used it sometimes as a way of getting even with older peers. This insult was also used more frequently by *wat'o wa wunyana* (males) than *walana* (females). In our village, such vulgarity was considered a taboo, and when heard as on such an occasion, it was introduced by an outsider, in this case, an outsider from Las Town.

When Nkwel'a Wana was asked if she indeed fed her wana, she had replied, after the insults and vulgarity, "Which kind foolish dull question bi dat (What sort of a dumb question is that)?" and then continued, "You look'am say na air and wata fullop dem skin way dem big so since way they born dem (Does it look as if they are instead filled with air and water, making them this big as compared to when they were born)?"

She lashed back and then continued to buttress her point and went on the offensive, "Abi na wata or na ekwakoko fullop ya head or na sense (What do you even have in your head? Is it water or *e-kwa-ko-ko* [ekwakoko is ground cocoyams, the main traditional dish of the Wakpwes]? Or it is a brain tissue)?" Nkweleh asked this mockingly and insultingly.

By this time, the anonymous questioner who was known in the village as Mbella Ka'a-keh was quiet, and Nkwel'a Wana clearly enjoyed her upper hand.

"Way-ga ima tu-mba mo-lay-li owa li-szreh (So what kind of food do you feed them)?" another voice, that of Ndu-mbay Elengeh from the spectator crowd yelled out. These questioners were "anonymous" because they did not show their faces to Nkweleh. They rather buried their faces in the crowd, but those near them knew who they were. No one really wanted a direct confrontation with Nkweleh if it could be helped.

Before she could respond, the anonymous voice continued to press on, changing from the Mokpwe language to Pidgin. Ndumb'a Ele-ngeh, known commonly as Ndu-mb'Ele-ngeh, was a very jovial and soft-spoken man in the village who spoke only the Mokpwe language to wana and wambaki alike, except if he knew for certain that you were not a Mokpwe person. Because of his jovial nature and down to earth mannerisms, he was often disrespected and sometimes made fun of by wana. It was not common for wambaki to admonish wana who attempted to be disrespectful to him. I always wondered why. However, we liked him because he had time to play with us kids sometimes for a short while before he went his way, and in our Libiyeah family, disrespect for elders was a no-go red line. This time, however, and perhaps for the sake of the those in the crowd that were not Wakpwe, Ndumb' Elengeh decided to speak in Pidgin instead of Mokpwe.

"Na ka-nda and pap or na garri-fufu and beans?"

Kanda is the tough hide and skin of a cow usually used in the production of leather products, but which is also used as food and, nutritious or not, is a regular in some dishes or menu combinations; for example, *eru* (a vegetable staple of Manyu origin in the Southwest) and *achu* soup (a staple from the northwest grassland fields). Kanda cow, as it is popular known, could also be fried and eaten as a dessert or used as source toward another meal. Because of its toughness and/ or hardness and it being generally considered of little or no nutritional value, it is not normally considered food for wana. Pap, on the other hand, is a semisolid corn meal used as cereal normally fed to wana, the sick, and the very elderly. It constituted a relatively "heavy" starchy meal. Sugar and milk are normally added to pap (for the rich folks and salt only for the poor folks), and therefore, a combination of pap and kanda was not meant as a compliment.

Garri, on the other hand, is a *ma-kwa-mba* (*Manihot esculenta*; cassava, is a tuber tropical crop) product. It's a ground makwamba in powdery cereal form. It could be eaten as cereal by adding sugar and milk (or salt only) or prepared with hot water to make it or turn it into garri-fufu, which would be swallowed with soup, constituting another heavy starchy meal. Eating garri with sugar and milk is common in boarding secondary schools when the students are still "rich," mostly at the beginning of the semester and perhaps after an outing (when students are allowed to go home or out of campus for a whole day and returning in the evening). This normally happens in the middle of the semester. For the rest of the semester, garri with or without salt was a luxury, and students normally walked around campus with bent spoons in their pockets, ready to pounce and partake in a bowl of soaked garri, invited or not. This was very typical of boys who attended the Baptist Boys Secondary School, a.k.a. Bad Boys Secondary School, in Great Soppo Buea.

The Bad Boys Secondary School (BBSS) is now called Baptist High School (BHS), and another reason the Sasse Boys laughed at them was because they ate corn-chaff (a mélange of beans and corn cooked in porridge form), and on special days, pap (a product of Ma-Kwa-mba [*Manihot esculenta* or cassava] that approximated to a whitish custard paste) for breakfast, all the time, and their green and black uniforms made them look like refugees at a time when *refugee* was an alien terminology in Buea and Cameroon.

Garri in cereal form can be eaten with beans. This is a rare combination commonly and mostly among boarding secondary school pupils, especially when they are broke. When students are broke also (which is more often than not), salt replaces sugar in many occasions while milk goes extinct. Eating garri-fufu with beans was an abnormal gastronomic activity or behavior, even with boarding school students. Therefore, a combination of garri and beans was also not meant as a compliment. All of these non-compliments were known by all, and mostly so Nkwel'a Wana who was very sensitive to disrespect and any aspects of belittling or attacking her.

The anonymous contributor carefully chose his combination to make his point. This was no food combination even for adults who talk less of its nutritive value. It was meant as a provocation and an irritant, and it seemed to have gotten her right under the belt, activating all of her nerves. At this point, Nkwel'a Wana turned a blackish-red, and her rate of respiration increased manifold. We thought she was going to collapse after a heart attack as she tried to utter words that would not escape her lips. And just then, an elderly molana, Nyango Li-ngo-lo Litany, came to her rescue.

"E-weh-meh ono muana i-deh na wana weh-ni oma mua-nyan-gwe-ni (Let this muana [referring to Nkwel'a Wana] be on her way with her children to visit with her sister)," she said. Then she continued, "E-szri mo'o-wa anu nji-ya (Do not "kill" her here on the road)."

Nyango Li-ngo-lo Litany talking and her request to the crowd brought about some quietness. So Nkweli took this opportunity to respond to the anonymous questioner. "Dis BonaLyonga Pikin dem wona dull like mor-leh-ngu (Ovis aries) (You these children from WonyaLyonga, you are as dull as sheep). You think say dis pikin dem, dem big-so, say na air and wata make dem fat so (These kids are big and fat, do you think it is because of air and water)? See Li'a-ngeh l'E-szro, you think say na air and wata fullop e-belleh so (Do you think the big belly of Liangeh l'Eszro is due to air and water?"

Liangeh l'Eszro was the name of her eldest son among her travel company of age, about seven years old. He had a potbelly that was approximated to kwashiorkor.

At this mention of "big" and "fat," and with particular reference to Liangeh l'Eszro, there was a loud outburst of laughter from the crowd.

"Dis ya pikin dem way dem dry like stick and bo-nga (Your kids are as skinny as sticks and dry fish [Ethmalosa dorsalis]). And your Liangeh, na kwashiorkor e-gettam (Your child, Liangeh, is obviously suffering from kwashiorkor). Na you foolish and dull nobi we for dis village and you blind too (You are the fool and the dullard, not us in this village, and you must be blind also)."

Then the anonymous voice concluded in pidgin that he knew would be well understood by Nkweli, "Dis Las Town girl-dem eh (These girls from Las Town) Na bad pikin dem (are badly brought up children). We no want dem for we village (We do not want them here in our village)."

These badly brought ups from Las Town are not welcomed in our village, he said in finality.

C'est-à-dire des enfants mal élevés—someone of Francophone extraction in the crowd interjected, seeking clarification and understanding.

Visibly exhausted and obviously very vexed, Nkwel'a Wana must have inwardly and secretly been thankful for Nyango Lingolo Litany's intervention. With her coming into the scene, it would seem this outdoor stage drama would finally come to an end. It looked like an unfair plot or act in a play in which one was pitched against multitudes in a war of words—a one versus many, a village hostile to their in-laws.

Nyango in Mokpwe language is a prefix accorded to a molana in good standing in the village with much respect and sometimes just simply used as respect. Litany, on the other hand, could simply be equated to "brightness." So, for example, a ripe mango fruit would be described as "lingolo litany," and the morning could simply be referred to as "wunya woma tana," which precisely will mean "daybreak" which, of course, comes with brightness.

Nyango Lingolo Litany was fair-skinned among mostly dark brown folks with some actually approximating to "light black." She was thus bright among her people, and it was her style and habit to bring about brightness, even in the gloomiest situations. Yes, Nkwel'a Wana was certainly grateful. For Nyango Litany stood about forty to fifty meters without the crowd, and her static position gazing straight into the crowd and specifically onto no one in particular meant that her piercing eye was reaching each person and at the same time reaching the crowd as a single unit.

Nyango Litany had only one eye, and there was no eye patch covering the other empty socket as we saw in movies; and besides, we also thought that eye patches were only worn by men, mostly bad and powerful men. We could see deep into the eye cavity or eye socket which had been vacated by an eyeball. This cavity, however, was not without an occupant. This cavity was occupied at various times and/ or in turns with a viscous greenish-yellowish fluid that attempted to make its way out of the vacant cavity by forming vesicular-like shapes, or the socket occupant was a less viscous fluid that flowed freely down her cheek and occasionally made its way into the corner of her mouth, and this she leaked very comfortably all the time. It was her right eye that was missing, and because she had the tendency of always leaking it, it would seem that the tip of her tongue was kind of permanently protruding out of the right corner of her mouth, and flies sometimes took advantage of that.

Nyango Litany was more of a Halloween figure in the village for children as her name was used sometimes to scare children. For example, a crybaby could be told to stop crying or else Nyango Litany would be summoned, or the mother would say, "I can see Nyango Litany coming." At the mention of her name, some adjustment was always made.

There were a couple of stories behind this missing eye, but I never got a full version of any, and all of them seemed more like conjectures. From what I gathered; it could have been an accident in her *mo'o-da* (crop farm); it could have been as a result of a fight with her late munyana.

A third version had it that Nyango Litany *ah-ton-dead*; that is, transformed herself into an elimo or spirit via yowo and was roaming the village as a molana elimo. Considering that the realm of *yowo* (spirit living) belonged to the wunyana of the village, this rivalry or attempting rivalry had no place for tolerance. After several warnings from the *walimo wa wunyana* (men spirits or yoworites) that she did not heed, she was attacked, and a fight ensued; but this fight in the yowo world had to be completed in the physical world, and Litany's munyana was given the task of finishing the job, which included incapacitating the eye she used as her path to the yowo world.

Not long after Litany had the fight with her husband, which looked like a "normal" physical fight between spouses, Mola Li-szro-ngeh la Kayma died, and Nyango Litany la Kayma started having an eye problem which led to the ultimate extraction of the eye for good. Nyango Litany la Kayma was accused of killing her husband, making her a li-emba woman.

Another version has it that during the German occupation of the Mokpwe lands, the occupiers formed a small local military or paramilitary force. They used this force to oppress and terrorize and subjugate the local population; that is, my people. Mokpwe wunyana refused to be part of a force that was meant to subjugate them in humiliation. Wunyana from other ethnic groups were brought in, and this local force was constituted. At this point, the wakala (peached-skinned) occupiers stepped back, arming and backing their local, brown-skinned force as they now "rested" while enjoying the African-to-African violence. Nyango Litany was a Ngoh-ndeli, then with a flat chest that seemed without maweh (without breast). She was kind of tom-boyish and with fair skin. The occupiers were more than happy to accept her into the force when she went to them, opting to join.

It was possible that Nyango Litany had Germanic blood. She entered the force disguised as a munyana and also as an informant of the Mokpwe resistance. In her disguise, Nyango Litany was like "Arkansas" Petite Jean. This "man-woman," as we would call her in Pidgin, was designated to lead a battle that was to raid the neighboring Mokpwe village of WonyaMongo. She passed on all the relevant information to the village resistance council, and on the day of the raid, she led her well-armed team into a nice ambush. The fighting that resulted led to the loss of her eye. She was the only human "prisoner" taken alongside the European arms of the local paramilitary force. I had hoped to fully exploit all of these options one day but had yet to succeed.

Thus, Nyango Litany seemed a force to be reckoned with in the yowo and physical world. Either you respected or, better still, feared her from the yowo perspective or from the physical perspective. Thus, when Nyango Litany stood her distance and was gazing at the crowd, we knew this was the end of this midafternoon saga. The crowd was dominantly young folks and women. It did not appear there was any who could dare challenge her or her authority, less her orders. Thus, her stare meant *vamoose* (disappear), as we will say in Pidgin. The vamoosing was for all, including Nkwel'a Wana. This whole outdoor saga took about an hour, and at the end, when we had all vamoosed, I returned home to realize I had forgotten to engage in an errand assigned to me by my iyaka and which was due, like, yesterday. So, when I came in late, she said, "Chei-ye Ou-ki na luka (At last, you made it)."

It was when she said "ou-ki na luka" when it dawned on me that "enjoyment" I just had with the free outdoor movie or drama was about to be squeezed out of me. And she said, "Chei-ye," which could mean many things depending on how it is used in the Mokpwe language. In this case, it meant "you overdid it," meaning you overstayed and without results, which meant severe punishment now or later.

Within twelve months of the roadside drama, the two older kids of Nkwel'a Wana died. These were the wana known by other wana in the village as "Chop shit pikin dem" (Poop eaters)."

I was very sad when we learned of the deaths, though I never learned what killed them or how they died, not that it would have made a difference. Shortly after the second death, I met with Nkwel'a Wana in the village path that ascended onto her sister's place and that also descended to the lower elevation portions of our village. I was descending, and she was ascending, and we met face-to-face. I did not know what to say. So, I moved by the side and stood still in the bushes, allowing her to pass. Before I could say it, I found myself crying. Then I said, "Sista Ashia-ya, for pikin dem die (Sister, I am sorry for the death of the kids)."

She came closer to me and held me close to her bosom and said, "Moighai no cry yaa, ma pikin no cry yaa (Moighai, do not cry, my child, do not cry)."

But that did not help. However, it was a matter of time before she took over the crying, and with the top-hill vantage position, it was more like a public address system summoning all of the people around that portion of the village.

"Ma pikin dem oh, ma pikin dem oh. Dem doh die-oh, dem doh die-oh (My kids, my kids, they are dead, they are dead)," she said repeatedly.

Now a roadside crowd was gathering for another possible drama outdoor show. I got alarmed for two reasons. I was on my way to accomplishing an errand. I would not allow myself the luxury of a repeat whooping that occurred only a couple of months back and at about the same location. Secondly, I did not think I wanted to be the subject of conversation, especially one associated with Nkwel'a Wana in the village. You see, there were stories going around in the village that she may have had a hand in the death of her wana. This was more or less hush-hush talk among adults, which we sometimes accidentally stumbled on. And what did she mean when she called me "ma pikin"? I am not her pikin for sure, and she looked a little bit too young to be my iyaka, and I thought she was about my older *ndoh-meh wa molana's* (sister's) age, Nyango Namondeh.

But what did she mean when she called me her pikin? Nobody wanted to be her pikin because being her muana meant sure early death, and if she really was in a "society" in which she "gave" her children, then I wanted no part of that. I had every reason to run, and so I vamoosed. However, it did not appear I vamoosed quickly enough, for I was seen by some wana who saw different things and saw me in different positions. By the time Nkweleh had started crying loud, she held me close to her anterior portion of body and was kind of rocking me to the left and to the right as she lamented the successive passing of her wana within a year. So, the wana who saw me in Nkweleh's embrace had different versions of my body's position, vis-à-vis, Nkweleh's body. There was the narration and the aspects that dwelt on my jaws and face sandwiched between her *maweh* (breast), and they wanted to know how it felt, and yet, still there were those who thought I had been sucked into her yowo realm, and me being called her muana was a deal sealer.

The conclusion was that I may as well be on my way as a muana of Nkwel'a Wana. These are things that just added to my inner turmoil, and I did not talk much; it boiled inside me sometimes at very high temperatures that led to hyperthermia and ulcerations.

Another thought and turmoil in me was the fact that when Nkwel'a Wana embraced me or rather dragged me close to her bosom, I thought I felt a protrusion about her belly level, but it could have been anything; perhaps she just ate and her food was yet to digest or she ate long ago, but her digestive system lacked the necessary digestive enzymes to break down the food fast. A thought that was deep down in me was that she might be pregnant, but could this be true? And how could it be true when she was clearly in mourning?

I dismissed this thought as quickly as it was generated. For it could not be. Nkwel'a Wana just lost two wana within the last twelve months, and she still had two wana with a cumulative age of approximately three years, and obviously, she was in mourning, though she was not allowed to show it outwardly as a matter of spiritual culture. She, however, seemed subdued after these losses and kind of kept a low profile whenever she visited the village. Low profile does not mean that her presence went unnoticed whenever she visited; it just meant she was less combative, less confrontational, and relatively less loud, but dramatic she was all the time.

With the most recent deaths of Nkwel'a Wana's two wana, Szrango Koff'a Moteh, a.k.a. Mola Talameh, Nkwel'a Wana's Mola could not have been more suspicious than ever and could not have been more determined than ever to prove that an infanticide gene did not run in their family but rather something else. But what was that something else? How could he elucidate that something else? It was a matter of time before it became obvious to all and externally that Nkwel'a Wana was pregnant again, and voilà, my suppressed internal suspicions became vindicated.

Once as it became obvious that a muana was being expected by Nkwel'a Wana, Szrango Koff'a Moteh's routine, schedules, whereabouts, movements, and general behavioral patterns changed and became unpredictable. All those close to him at home and outside wondered why, but there was no answer. Szrango Koff'a Moteh was Mola to Nkwel'a Wana—that is, he was maternal uncle to Nkweleh—and they all lived in the same compound in their Las Town residence.

CHAPTER 15

Njok'a Moto

Before now, Szrango Koff'a Moteh had a pretty stereotypical and predictable schedule and routine. He was a retiree of the local council administration where he worked as a tax collector but was erroneously called a "messenger." His uniform was brownish, and it was always khaki shorts, a matching short sleeves khaki shirt, thick brown socks that were pulled to just under the knee, and a heavy set of matching military-style boots that covered a little over halfway up the length of the leg. We were told this dress type was of Germanic heritage. He also wore a military style fez cap that was blackish. His shirt was sure to be tucked in exposing his broad-banded black belt to which was strapped a baton and handcuffs on either side.

Szrango Koff'a Moteh was a biggish man, an estimated 1,000-pounder, and a 1,000-pounder man in the described attire was certainly not only a sensation but also very unavoidable. Needless to say, Moteh was not a liked man professionally, but this was only among adults and particularly those who were sure not to pay their taxes on time and/or those who did not intend to pay at all for one reason or another. Koff'a Moteh was confrontational and aggressive and, needless to say, a very powerful man as compared to an average person in Gbwea (Buea).

In Koff'a Moteh's days as a Gbwea Municipality Tax Collector, only male adults paid taxes, and as you paid your taxes, you were given a "card" as certification or proof of payment. That card you had on your person at all times, for tax collectors had the right and authority to ask you to show proof of having paid your taxes for the year, and failure to meant arrest and jail time in the Gbwea Municipality's jailhouse until the taxes were paid or until you were bailed.

Szrango Koff'a Moteh was a devoted and liked tax collector to the successive German and English occupiers, for he collaborated with them to humiliate and settle scores with the local population. In all of Vakoland—the Wakpwes, that is—the Bakweris refused to work for the occupiers who had seized their lands and now demanded forced and slave labor from them. When the Wakpwes resisted, the occupiers brought other Africans from outside Vakoland, especially from the northwest, who seemed just too happy to be in Vakoland and even happier to earn some money, even though they were paid a peanuts salary as compared to the work they did and the profit the occupiers made from the Cameroon Development Corporation agrocomplex.

The Wakpwes called the imported cheap slave labor into the Vakoland occupier agro-plantations as Wa-jay-li, a name that later evolved to *Wajili* (meaning strangers). The Wajili could pay their taxes because they worked, and the Wajili and their *matumba* (families) also became "economically empowered" as compared to the sons and the daughters of the soil who would not work for the occupiers that had stolen their ancestral lands and were making profits out of it at their expense. While the Vakolanders never intended to compromise with occupiers, a mutual distrust was established that was palpable. It was, however, a matter of time before there was growing tension between the Wajili and the Wakpwes. The occupiers sat back, engineered, and enjoyed seeing the two brother African populations at each other's throat—the Wajili with the economic power and rising populations, and the Wakpwes in poverty and decreasing populations.

All and successive occupiers of Vakoland had used this divide and rule tactics to subjugate and continue the exploitation of Vakoland. Szrango Koff'a Moteh or Mola Talameh was thus seen and associated with occupiers and Wajili. He was thus considered a *Mojili*—that is, a stranger—and he was truly estranged by his peers in Gbwea.

It needs, however, to be said that the work ethics and or reliability of the Mokpwe workforce left much to be desired by the Cameroon Development Corporation (CDC) employers when the corporation was run and managed by European occupiers. Some Wakpwes knew and therefore decided that a new economic reality was emerging and evolving, and to survive economically, perhaps it was better to be in the occupier's employ. A few Wakpwes therefore had employment with the occupiers.

While these Mokpwe workers were hardworking and good at their jobs, their ties to the culture and proximity to their culture made them not so reliable as employed workers expected to work a full schedule Monday to Friday and perhaps sometimes over the weekend. The Malay (the Mokpwe Elephant Dance) and the *weh-szru-wa* (wrestling) were sociocultural events that occurred over the weekends and was rotatory from *mbowa to mbowa* (village to village). A Mot'a Mokpwe or a Mo-kpwe-li was not to miss a malay event or a weh-sz-ru-wa event. If these Mokpweli workers were actual participants in the malay or weh-szru-wa, they needed to be in camp Thursday and Friday, and aside from being in camp before the actual event, they were required to practice long hours before the event. Thus, to be a team member of malay or a member of the village wrestling team, you could not be away working in the occupiers' plantations.

Finding it difficult to balance work on the plantations and meeting expected trado-cultural appointments and being and remaining an insider in the culture, their occupiers sooner or later found them wanting in their assignments and job. Sometimes a Mo-kpwe-li takes off on Wednesday in the middle of the week, only to return on Monday or Tuesday of the following week and maybe stay for the next one or two weeks not going anywhere but taking off again after, at most, two weeks. The German occupiers who had previously been defeated by the Local Mokpwe Army, led by Kuv'a Likenya and Moudindi mo'Ekeka, eyed the Mokpwe very suspiciously and was not going to be lenient in any way. They wanted the Mokpwe subjugated, and they had an ally in the Wajili whom they assisted in every way.

Divide and rule—a strategy maintained by the British when they took over the plantations, and then with the exit of the British, this strategy continued. "Soldier-go-Soldier-come" is in Pidgin commonly said as "Soja-go-Soja-cam," which practically means the same or more of the same. Soja-go-Soja-cam was exemplified by the Nigerian and other West African militaries, when one military junta toppled another military junta, just for it to be toppled by another group of disaffected comrades in arms, in a circle of military coups d'état. Each military junta gave the nation a variant of the same reasons for overthrowing the previous junta. It was the same strategy, and it was for the same reasons, and the results were identical. The soja-go-soja-cam strategy and concept was well expounded artistically and musically by Fela Anikulapo Kuti, the great Nigerian multi-instrumentalist, musician, composer, and the pioneer of the Afrobeat music genre, and human rights activist. His opposition to the soja-go-soja-cam theatrics and human rights violations and abuses characteristic of military junta always put him at loggerheads with the Nigerian military juntas, earning him jail time. Therefore, for the Mo-kpwe-li man and the Cameroon Development Corporation agro plantation complex, it was soja-go-soja-cam, whether under German management, whether under British management, or whether under Ewouda management, it was soja-go-soja-cam. No royalties agreed and promised to the Wakpwes, owners of Vakoland on which the plantations flourish.

Now the Mokpwe excuse for not being reliable workers under the employ of the occupiers as it related to sociocultural weekend activities did not mean that the Wajili from the grassland were any less inclined to their culture, for they were a very culturally conscious folks. The young Wajili that were brought down to the *szrawa* (coast) via Mamfe in Manyu were loaded in enclosed wagons, an enclosed covering, and blind-transported by night to the plantations in the south in Mokpwe land. These mbeszra ja Wajili had no clue how they got where they were and certainly had no clue how to return to whence, they came, even if they wanted to. That luxury of returning to the village to participate in weekend social activities was of the Wakpwes only. It is not entirely known that the mbay-szra (youths) ja Wajili came to work in the plantations in the Mokpwe land out of their own volition, but the economic and other advantages that followed seemed to have been worth it a thousand and then millions of times over with the passage of time.

Pound for pound, though, I do not know if Mola Talameh would have been considered a Mot'a ngi-nya—that is, a powerful man—but certainly the excess poundage brought about some advantages; plus, also having the law or government on his side certainly made him a powerful man. Because Mola Talameh made more arrests and brought in more taxes than most others of his peer tax collectors within a short turnover period of time, it took Mola Talameh a relatively short time to be appointed and promoted as head tax collector. He still wore his khakis, but this time, they were greenish to distinguish him from the other fieldworkers. Mola Talameh now spent more time around the council building with a small office of his own, a desk, and what looked like an ancient manual typewriter. He went out only to settle difficult cases. He seems to have two stories that made tax defaulters shiver at the mention of his name.

He was reported once to have visited a tax debtor's house, and when he was spotted, the tax debtor shut his doors and refused to open and also refused to talk to Mola Talameh. Koff'a Moteh (a.k.a. Mola Talameh) wasted no time and simply ripped the door from its hinges, flung it behind him, and walked straight into the man's bedroom, lifted the bed, and picked him up from under the bed to the horror and annoyance of the man's family and his buddies. The man's molana and wana had hurled insults at him like "Mot'a Njoh-ku"—that is, Elephant Man, meaning a man of elephantine proportions—"Mot'a Vako," a Mountain Man or "Mboma Tree Man" (in Pidgin) that is a Moto with size proportions of a baobab tree, and went further to accuse him of being a traitor of his people.

At this time, those who worked with the local administration were considered traitors, and not paying taxes was active defiance against the occupiers. Despite their insults and the resistance of his captive in the form of kicks, face spitting, scratching, and a torrent of insane vulgar utterances, the arrested man was hauled outside his house, flung to the ground, and handcuffed after a couple of lashes with the baton, all of these in plain view of his family and neighbors. By the time Koff'a Moteh departed with his captive, he left behind an open house. The main entrance door and the master bedroom doors had been ripped off, and the captive's scanty furniture living room was in shambles with lots of broken pieces as a result of the struggle between the huge captor and the relatively small captive.

Another incidence that made Koff'a Moteh famous, but perhaps not so famous among his people, was a case of an elusive tax defaulter. He had no family and lived alone, and all attempts to catch him at home failed, and he had also skipped his normal "kwa-tcha house" (corn beer bar), making him difficult to find. The elusive tax debtor, however, came back deep into the night one day and tried opening his door just to realize that the door fell backward. He entered and felt his way to where he kept his matchbox and his oil lamp. He had just finished illuminating his parlor and was now proceeding to see, lamp in hand, what the matter was with the door that he left earlier in the day in perfect shape and function. Could he have been visited by thieves? That would be unlikely, for there was not much to steal. It was known by the whole village and his neighbors in particular that he was a man of very little means. What could he have that would be of interest to anyone? And why would anyone be so wicked as to add to his misery?

Mo-ke-ngeh, done talking inside himself, thought it was now time to vent outwardly and address the village and his immediate neighbors in particular whom he thought must know something, had done something, if they had not seen something; for the destruction to his scant property was surely caused by a neighbor of a villager and he needed, therefore, to address the village immediately, even if it was deep into the night.

"I know that you do not want me in this village, and I know that it is one of you who knows my routine. What do I have that you want? Because I keep to myself, you call me Li-emba Man. Because I do not associate with anyone in the village, you call me 'weirdo.' Mameh nay gbwe-yi (What have I done to you people)?" he concluded.

At this point, Koff'a Moteh who had been sitting and waiting in the dark in an adjacent room emerged and answered in response to Mokengeh's question, "E-wa-nja o-szri ta-ngui ee ta-szri (Because you have not paid your taxes)."

The Wakpwes have a deity called E-fva-szra Moto that is half man and half stone that resides on the Vako that is Mount Fako. When Mo-ke-ngeh turned abruptly for an instant, he thought he was seeing Efvaszra Moto, but Efvaszra Moto could not fit into his small thatch house, and Efvaszra Moto was not all flesh. The human mountain that was now approaching and already at arm's length was no spirit, and in a split second, it dawned on Mokengeh that this was Koff'a Moteh. Boiling with anger and determined not to make things easy for his hunter and more importantly not visualizing another life in the council jail, he quickly, and with alacrity, used all of his will and power and slammed the oil lamp into the towering face above him that presented him with a large surface area. Mokengeh also calculated that the glass globe of his oil lamp was broken on one side, exposing a sharp surface. He also knew that the cap or cover to his oil tank was so twisted that it did not close tightly and, at most, only halfway through. He thus normally moved the lamp from one part of his house to another with great care and caution.

If he moved fast, the air passing through the broken globe would turn off or blow out the burning light and/or kerosene would spill. He now knew that these two deficiencies of his only source of illumination could be used as an effective weapon against this gigantic intruder. Mola Mokengeh mo Liwoh, as he was known, also knew that dealing with the gigantic and elephantine intruder in open space would give the Njoh-k'a Moto an advantage, but a mace-like environment with familiarity to him, Mokengeh mo Liwoh, would be ideal and probably turn the advantage to his side. Immediately, therefore, he made his way back into what was left of his house, passing between the legs of Koff'a Moteh, catching him off guard.

Mokenge mo Liwoh had only ventured about twenty meters away from his front door and had to make it swiftly back to his mace. He had entered his house while Njoh-k'a Moto was still struggling to catch up with him, especially taking his time to be able to make it through the relatively tiny door. Mokengeh had put out his kerosene lantern, and the inside of his house was in pitch darkness. There was no moon, and flickers of faraway celestial stars of bodies illuminated the interior of his home via the holes that decorated his thatched roof. Mo Liwoh knew that there was not really any good hiding place in his house, and a level playing field would be an advantage for the Njoh-k'a Moto.

Without wasting time, therefore, he climbed his *woka* (a platform made above the fireplace used as a wood drier). The platform above the fireplace had three strata—from top to bottom the woka, the Keh-li, and the mbaah—nearest to the source of the fire. The chronology of stratification was in accordance with their sizes the surface area covered. The woka and top layer covered the most area, sometimes spanning the entire width of the kitchen and was used for the drying or smoking of the larger items like firewood and was also a good hiding and storage place because of the total surface area it afforded. It was also used as a store for prepared food for safety and to put it out of easy reach.

The Keh-li was mostly used for the drying or smoking of meats and fish and also the palm kernel fibers that were used to light the fire. The kernel fibers that were used to light or start a fire are called ma-tor-veh. When the Wakpwes make the mbar-ga soup used to eat their ti-mba-na-mbu-szra e-kwa-ko-ko, which is grated ndaa (*Xanthosoma sagittifolium* or cocoyams), they boil the mbi-ya, which is palm kernel nuts from mi-nya (*Elaeis guineensis* or palm trees) and then squeeze out the mo-szra-ka (liquid portion) from the surface of the nutshell. The squeezed mo-szra-ka is mostly composed of lipids in the form of fatty acid oil. When the squeezing is done, there is a two-step process of straining or sieving using the perforations of the hands as the strainer or sieve. First, the mixture is separated into two components: the hard nutshell kernels versus the rest. The nuts (containing the seeds) are then removed from the processing kitchen basin. What is left is the mo-szra-ka and surface nut fibers that are further separated by using the perforations of the hand as a strainer or sieve into the filtrate and the fibers. The filtrate, which is the mo-szra-ka, is squeezed out of the fibers through the perforations of the hand. The retained fibers constitute what the Wakpwes call ma-tor-veh, when dried. To form the ma-tor-veh, the wet fibers are dried in the keh-li, and when dried the individual fibers can be separated from each other, making it possible to determine what quantity can be used to light a fire. Ma-tor-veh are used as fuel for starting a fire in place of kerosene. Ma-tor-veh are infused into a pile of dry wood and then lit with a match. Dry ma-tor-veh are very flammable, they are thus easy to light, they catch fire very easily, and in addition, they spread their heat and flammability easily. They thus make good fire starters and therefore a "staple" and necessity in Mokpwe village homes. The mbaah was the smallest component, shaped mostly in basket form and made of elastic cane material; it had a cover with oftentimes a fancy design. The mbaah was used mostly if not exclusively for the smoking or drying of spices.

The Woka was usually a mosaic of sorts and oftentimes so loaded that it became a complicated mace and, therefore, a perfect place for keeping or hiding. Mo Liwoh was a moszrali mo Moto (smallish man), so he quickly carved out a small niche for himself in his woka, hiding from Njoh-k'a Moto. Mo Liwoh's house had three compartments—a kitchen, a living room and his bedroom. The rooms were demarcated with incomplete walls, height wise, and with only one internal door, the one-bedroom door. Thus, a huge person like Njoh-k'a Moto could look over the dividing and adjourning walls to scan the contents of each section.

Mokengeh lay quietly with the remains of the lantern in his hand, the broken glass, and rusted metallic portions of the lantern as his sole weapon of assault against the elephantine and Goliath-like predator. Koff'a Moteh quickly scanned all three internal compartments and did not readily see anything. But because he was himself out of breath, having difficulty walking fast as a result of his weight, he was breathing heavily and also loudly, which would impair or hinder his chance of locating his prey by sound. He had to have some rest and calm himself down.

Mokengeh had used Koff'a Moteh's sluggishness or rather took advantage of it to hide and take cover. His heart was pounding as loud as possible as Koff'a Moteh continued making his rounds over and over, sure that Mokengeh was there and that it was a matter of time before Mokengeh gave away his hiding place. As the tension increased, Mokengeh was now thinking if it was a wise idea for him to have taking cover in his home; perhaps he should have instead abandoned his house completely.

Koff'a Moteh thought he heard a sound somewhere in the bedroom, so he opened the door and entered, groping in the dark and being thankful for the minimal illumination provided by the stars. He entered the room and saw nothing, but then there was movement, and with a room so scant, the only hiding place that seemed logical was under the bed. He moved closer and said, "Wu-szra onomua-n'a etoe (Come out, you small rat). No'o-wa yawono (I will kill you today)." He waited, and nothing or no one came out.

"Oszra ta-neh li-wa-nga li-na-ka (You cannot run faster and past me). Na-mo'o leh-mbeh (I have cornered and caught you)."

Koff'a Moteh grabbed the *li-nor-ngoh liszrali* (small bed) with his left hand and flung it past him, exposing his trapped prey.

"Hmmmmmmmmmm! Haaarrrrrrrrrrrrh! Hoo hoo hoo!" It was a canine with shiny eyes, exposing the entirety of its canine teeth and ready to pounce at this intruder.

Koff'a Moteh was taken aback and was totally surprised; not the first time this evening, though. He stepped backward, but the gbwa did not charge at him. Mokengeh had a gbwaa, a relatively small breed in the manner of a Chihuahua and also very malnourished. It thus seemed devoid of any energy and will to attack anyone, perhaps wanting instead to be fed.

"O-no Mo-kpwe-l'a Gbwa di o-weh-ni (You can only afford to have a malnourished and a weakling gbwa)?" He mocked and taunted Mokengeh whom he knew was still and certainly inside this house. When the word *Mokpwel'a gbwa* was used, it described a malnourished, hungry, tired-looking, and sickly dog that was not expected to harm anything, not even a fly.

Like I mentioned before, woka was a favorite hiding place and sometimes home for many different animals, *may-mbala* (*Felis catus*; cats) *and weh-toe* (*Rattus spp.*; rats) included. As Mokengeh lay almost breathless but with a heart pounding louder than a school bell, it would seem, he was also motionless, and as he watched Koff 'a Moteh destroy his bed and now at the verge of injuring or killing his gbwa, he had to change plans and quick too. He felt trapped by his own planning and was now regretting it. Mokengeh heard a light breeze of air blown across his face starting from the lip region but remained still, and without moving any part of his *nyio* (body), he moved his eyes laterally to find himself eyeballing an etoe. He stayed still, still ignoring the *etoe* (rat) until the etoe decided to leak Mokengeh's lips, starting first with the sensory sensation generated by the etoe's whiskers.

Mokengeh wasted no time lashing out at the etoe with his free *li-yaa* (hand) that was holding onto his weapon of defense. He missed the etoe and scattered the wood around him as the woka rocked back and forth.

Mokengeh had revealed his position, and now Koff'a Moteh who was still in the bedroom now hastily headed toward the woka area. Mokengeh raised himself partially and called out to his gbwa, "Mao-ngoh ma May-ko-mba! Mao-ngoh ma May-ko-mba! Leh-mbeh leh-mbeh leh-mbeh! Leh-mbeh leh-mbeh leh-mbeh!"

He called out to his gbwa and then urged Maykomba, the gbwa, to attack this intruder as it would play a game in the bush during hunting. Maykomba charged from behind as Koff'a Moteh was stretching his *maah* (hands) to grab Mokengeh. Mao-ngoh ma Maykomba stuck his sharp canine teeth into the large behind of Koff'a Moteh, and as Koff'a Moteh turned behind him to dislodge this annoyance that was inflicting so much pain on him and becoming an inconvenience and a distraction, Mokengeh had to act fast.

Njoh-k'a Moto dislodged Mao-ngoh ma Maykomba by pulling or rather extracting Maykomba from his *mbo-ndo* (the buttocks or gluteus maximus muscles) by holding and pulling violently at Mao-ngoh ma Maykomba's midsection. Mao-ngoh ma Maykomba was skinny and boney, so it was an easy grip around the abdominal region. Maykomba was, however, extracted along with some tissue *ya nyam'a mbo-ndo* (gluteus maximus tissues or flesh) and *maija* (blood). Mao-ngoh ma Maykomba was violently hurled against the wall, then the floor, and clearly, Koff'a Moteh had the intent of seriously injuring or just outright killing this obstacle. Mao-ngoh ma Maykomba landed on the dirt floor with much pain that was accompanied with, "Ha-wou, ha-wou, ha-wou," the sound that gbwa make when in serious pain.

As Mola Koff'a Moteh turned around, fixing his attention on Mao-ngoh ma Maykomba, Szrango Mokengeh mo Liwoh, from his vantage point at a higher elevation, jumped onto Mola Talameh from behind, enclosing his *liwoh* (neck) between his *may-ndeh* (legs) while Mola Talameh's large *mofvo* (head) rested onto the abdominal region of Mokengeh. Mokengeh tightened his grip by crossing his may-ndeh across Mola Talameh's chest and wrapping his left hand across Mola Talameh's liwoh. Mokengeh mo Liwoh kept his right hand free, which he used to hold onto very tenaciously his assault weapon, the broken kerosene lamp made of pieces of sharp-edged glass and rusted sharp-edged metal. His left hand around Koff'a Moteh's neck was like a vice tightening the joint as much as it could be tightened. Taking full advantage of the surprise, Mola Mokengeh mo Liwoh started pummeling Njohk'a Moto's face with his weapon with the intent inflicting maximum pain and damage, for this was a life and death matter.

Mokengeh was a smallish man but very agile also, and many people did not know it he was a member of the Malay Group with high-ranking status. In Vakoland (Fakoland), the Nga-nya and Malay are the highest social groups associated with spiritual power. While the Nga-nya was born from the Malay, it quickly rose to prominence. Thus, the Paramount Chief of Buea, who is the Paramount Chief of the Wakpwes, is the head of the Nga-nya while a Prince from the Royal Court (usually the senior Prince) was the head of the Malay. There were four dancing components of the Malay reserved for ranking members:

- The Mom'a Njoh-ku (the male elephant, reserved for the top-ranking members);

- The Mua-l'a Njoh-ku (the "female" elephant, one step below the top echelons);

- The E-kwa-ng'a Ti-ta'a (the big-headed costume ekalay or juju);

- The Mo-szre-keh (smallest in size and the least adorned with a comparatively simple costume of all the higher echelons and was the lowest rank of the upper ranks).

These *weh-ka-lay* (plural for ekalay) decreased in size in the order listed, and they were all adorned with costumes, making it difficult to tell the Moto behind the costume.

The Mo-szre-keh was the darling, especially of the wana. He thrilled them with his very skillful movements that matched the equally tantalizing drumming. The spectator crowd went wild with cheering, the singing along, and the movement of parts of their bodies as they partially danced along with the Mo-szreh-keh.

The Weh-ya-mbeh was a lower level non-ekalay dance component of the Malay that composed the new recruit young men. They danced open-faced but with lots of coloration on their faces and body that would still make it difficult to tell who was who. The Weh-ya-mbeh were not masked and not necessarily only new recruits or rookies. There were long-serving malay members who did not advance to the higher *yowo* (spirit) level of the society but had established themselves as Weh-ya-mbeh forever.

It is the weh-ya-mbeh component of the malay dance composite that ate the raw *nda'a* (*Xanthosoma sagittifolium*; cocoyams that are cultivated as food crops belong to either the genus *Colocasia* or the genus *Xanthosoma* and are generally composed of a large spherical corm [swollen underground storage stem] from which a few large leaves emerge; the Wakpwes normally cultivate the genus *Xanthosoma, Colocacia* only as a last resort and because it is very easy to grow with very low maintenance) and *meh-kor* (*Musa spp*; plantains) and also ate the raw and live chickens in the course of the dancing. The weh-ya-mbeh also ate blazing fire and trunks of fresh plantain and banana plants.

Depending on the village that was doing and hosting the Malay dance, females could be included. This was, however, rare. The female dance society normally associated with the Malay dance was the Malowa. The walana also adorned their almost top naked bodies like the weh-ya-mbeh, being of many colors; they danced alongside the weh-ya-mbeh sometimes. They normally led the overall dance party, followed by the weh-ya-mbeh.

Upon the arrival of the weh-ya-mbeh, the *walana wa Malowa* (the Malowa women) were normally surrounded by the weh-ya-mbeh; thus, there were the drummers ringed by the Malowa and the Weh-ya-mbeh in the outer ring. The Malowa leaves eventually, followed by the weh-ya-mbeh, to make way for the ranking masked weh-kalay. The different components of the malay made the whole.

Mola Mokengeh mo Liwoh was the main Moszrekeh of the greater Gbwea Malay group. Members of the Nga-nya and Malay were respected and feared sometimes; membership, however, was never publicized. It was thus not readily known who was and who was not a member, and if for some reason you knew that someone was in the Malay group, knowing their level or rank within the society was a secret among them; this was not shared with non-members. It was only afterward that it was known that Mola Mokengeh mo Liwoh was the principal Moszrekeh in the Greater Gbwea Malay Society.

While Mokengeh was hiding, he put off his kerosene lamp, but now, just before his attack on the predator attacker, he lit the lamp, intending to use the kerosene light as a weapon to burn as may be required. Njoh-k'a Moto, having gotten rid of the irritant gbwa, now was faced with his real adversary and prey that was proving not to be as easy as he had thought and who he must confess thus far had been more ingenious than expected. Determined to detach Mokengeh from his strong hold, he stretched his hand up to grab Mokengeh's neck, and with his big and expanded hands, his hands easily surrounded Mo-ke-ngeh mo Liwoh's relatively small and bony neck; and tightening his grip, he tried hard to pull this neck attachment his way.

He did not succeed at first. Mola Mokengeh mo Liwoh had a good grip and given that Szrango Njoh-k'a Moto had to stretch to reach Mokengeh's neck, this was additional strain to his muscles and heart, and frankly, he was also getting tired, the strain of carrying his weight under what seemed like strenuous physical exercise. Njohk'a Moto took off one hand from his grip to rest it and then try again, and while he was doing that, breathing heavily with strain, Mokengeh used the opportunity no matter how brief to inflict some more damage on his predator's face and also to solicit once more Mao-ngoh ma May-ko-mba's assistance one more time, even though he did not know whether May-ko-mba was alive or dead.

"Mao-ngoh ma May-ko-mba! May-ko-mba! Mao-ngoh!" he called out in rapid hurried succession. "O-mo leh-mbeh o yoko! O-mo leh-mbeh o chor-lor-lor (Grab him in the groin region)," he repeated and urged Maykomba, his only source of assistance.

Mao-ngoh ma Maykomba, evidently with a spinal injury, dragged itself with pain, its hind portion of the paralyzed body pulled and dragged itself with the last traces of energy and will left, and when close to Njohk'a Moto, leaped and inserted its canine teeth deep and tight onto the chor-lor-lor portion of Njohk'a Moto and, with a full mouth bite, pulled with the intent to rip off or detach this portion of the body from the rest of Njohku's body.

Njohk'a Moto screamed in pain, "Na way-li eh (I am dead)!"

And at that, Mokengeh urged Maykomba, "O-mo Leh-mbeh! O-mo Leh-mbeh! O-szri ki-ki-meh-leh (Hold onto him, hold on to him, do not let go)!"

May-ko-mba was clearly in control, for it had a mouthful of the complete assemblage of Noj-k'a Moto's lo'o-mba ya yo'o-ma (genitalia) and chewing on them or exerting any physical pressure on this lo'o-ba meant excruciating pain. May-ko-mba's grapping and biting put tremendous pressure and pain on the pudendal and cavernous nerves as well as the ilio-inguinal and genito-femoral nerves of the scrotum or scrotal sac. It was a humbling experience for Njoh-k'a Moteh, and for the first time in his job as a law enforcer and tax collector, his own vulnerability was made apparent as it flashed in his face in the hands of what he had considered a small fish assignment.

The pain was unbearable, so Mola Njohk'a Moto had to let go of his superior attached foe to quickly deal and finish the inferior attached foe once and for all so that he could concentrate on his primary prey without distraction. Freely using both hands, he held Maykomba in the midsection as he had done earlier and, with the other hand, slapped Maykomba's head region, targeting the eyes and ears with as much force as was possible. Maykomba, in great pain, let go off Szrango Koff'a Moteh's chor-lor-lor, and then Mola Koff'a Moteh lifted the whole of Maykomba above his head and then slammed it very hard onto the three large stones that were used to support the pot above the fire while cooking. Mao-ngoh ma Maykomba was disabled permanently as it lay helpless and barely alive between the fire stones.

Mola Mokengeh mo Liwoh used this vantage position to try to inflict as much damage as possible and tightening his legs around Koff'a Moteh's *liwoh* (neck) meant that his predator could not easily shake him off without destabilizing himself. While La Moteh (Koff'a Moteh was simply called La Moteh by those close to him whom he called his friends) concentrated on Mao-ngoh ma Maykomba, Mokengeh had La Moteh's head and face all to himself, even if for just a few minutes. Without much ado, Mokengeh mo Liwoh launched the lamp onto La Moteh's face with all his might. Mokengeh launched his weapon onto his attackers face twice in quick succession as the flame became extinguished, and there was the sound of shattering glass, and the smell of kerosene filled the enclosure.

Mokengeh directed his assault weapon onto the top of La Moteh's mofvo, then lateral to the sides to include the ears and eyes, and as he ventured to plaster his weapon straight into Njohku's face, his predator blocked the oncoming assault by covering or shielding his face with his forearms. Njohk'a Moto's head seemed to be on fire, his ears were ringing, and he was dizzy and could not hold himself in an anatomical position. To shake off his tenacious prey, a prey that now seemed the hunter or attacker and that seemed to have the better part of him thus far, he decided to go on a spin dance with hands outstretched like a helicopter propeller. He spun his upper body portion as vigorously as he could.

In this spin state, Mokengeh mo Liwoh was free of La Moteh's grip or pressure, but he also knew that if he was dislodged from his strong hold by the spinning pressure of his predator, his dislodgement and fall could be catastrophic. He had, therefore, to abandon ship on his own terms for a safe landing. Njohk'a Moto was making an uncoordinated zigzag pattern, like a drunken njohku, just doing anything to be able to dislodge Mokengeh. When La Kovie neared his bedroom door, he dropped his assault weapon, loosened and then untangled his lower limb grip on La Moteh's neck, then jumped, landing on his feet safely like a *mua-mba-la* (cat).

The interior of the small thatch house now was pitch black like a typical tropical night, but there was the smell of kerosene, and shortly thereafter, smoke could be smelled; and before long, a small fire was simmering, concentrated on an old termite-visited plank or board used as part of the walls of the house. The house was an old one, and both the walls and the roof were great recipes, providing the right conditions for a full-blown fire. In what seemed like a life and death struggle, the Mokengeh mo Liwoh weapon flew out from his hand after dislodging attempts by Njohk'a Moto and made contact with burnable materials; it was a recipe for fire and, therefore, the stage was set for one.

Njohk'a Moto needed to stabilize himself as he had now started bleeding in the head region. When Mokengeh jumped off La Moteh, the Njohk'a Moto seemed poised to spinning himself onto the floor of the house. Once, as La Moteh fell, he quickly pulled himself up and sat on the dirt floor, taken totally unaware of an underestimated prey that left him zoned out. While he was still trying to re-coordinate himself, he found himself also thinking of Mokengeh launching a surprise attack on him in the darkness, considering that this was Mokengeh's turf. Though he could not see, he could feel there was some fluid dripping down into his right ear, coming from his right eye. The pain was growing, and the leaking eye seemed to be losing its vision.

La Moteh, the predator, needed to let go of his prey if only for a little while so that he could adjust and then deal with Mokengeh once as for all. But was that a good strategy? Because now his prey had been let go; or rather, the prey had freed himself because he relaxed and had to abandon his grip on it. As Koff'a Moteh, a.k.a. La Moteh, gave in to his dizziness due to his spin dance, he fell face-down on the dirt floor. Mokengeh wasted no time bailing out of his house. As La Moteh was struggling to gain his balance and figure out what had just happened, Mokengeh headed to the door that led to his sleeping room and wasted no time climbing out of the house through a small window just above his bed. He knew he had to run for his dear life, not only from Koff'a Moteh, the traitor tax collector, but he also knew that he had to save himself from the smoldering heat which would result from the fire now brewing and which would soon engulf his house.

As Mokengeh bailed out of his own house through the window, the weakened La Moteh made a beleaguered effort to chase after him, but that was not enough and could not have been enough to stop Mokengeh mo Liwoh. Njohk'a Moto stood by the window of Mokengeh's bedroom, or what was left of it, gazing into the thick night darkness as Mokengeh parted shrubs and tree branches, out of reach of his predator and out to safety and freedom. Njohk'a Moto was irate and humiliated as he returned to the parlor and kitchen portion of Mokengeh's house which it now seemed he owned. He saw that Mao-ngoh ma Maykomba was not dead, barely alive, so he grabbed it by the skin behind the neck and tossed it to the corner of the wall which was now fully ablaze for Maykomba to roast to death. Mao-ngoh ma Maykomba did not utter a sound, but its hair and skin burning brought a quick end to its life as its external anatomy changed from brown to black.

As Mokengeh mo Liwoh made his way into the bushes, northwest of his home, he sadly noted that perhaps he was seeing his house and other belongings for the last time. His belongings and house at this time were irrelevant, and he should not be wasting his time and thought processes on materialism; his immediate focus should have been on his escape and survival. All the while, Mokengeh made no attempt at alerting the neighbors of anything being amiss, so when he catapulted out of his house for the last time and disappeared into the thick darkness of the night, it was without any attention to himself or any attention to the fast and dramatic events that just unfolded in his house for the last thirty minutes or under. He knew his way around, even in this pitch darkness. He would hurry and take refuge "there," and from "there," he would watch safely in clear view to see what happened. It would also be an opportunity for him to at this time to determine his next course of action.

As Mokengeh neared safety, he had spare time to start doing some expansive thinking. He had two common insults in the village. He had a *ndawo ya ngo-nja na kalawoli* (a house made of wood or planks and with a thatched roof), and he was also a *mor-kor-yoh mo Moto.* A *mor-kor-yoh* in the Mokpwe language could mean a bachelor, but more precisely, it means a relatively old man that is not married. To compound things, he lived alone, with hardly any sign of visitors or some external family members visiting. To crown these circumstances, there was every sign that he was a man in want of some of the very basics of life. Nobody seemed to know how he survived, but he was known to be a very peaceful man, minding his own business, and he sang with a beautiful bass tone some nights when he returned full of kwa-tcha.

His lonely life and isolation were characteristic attributes of Li-emba. While he ran for his dear life, he time and again glanced over his shoulders to see if Koff'a Moteh, the human fvako, was in hot pursuit. He was relieved not to see him in pursuit. For cautionary purposes, he did not run in a straight pattern to his "there" or hide-out, though he was sure that in this pitch darkness and nearing to midnight, there was no one out there watching him. He reached his "there" and lay on the misty grass belly down but with very attentive ears. He could hear his heart pouncing and his labored breathing. He had thought he was high with the three full plates of kwa-tcha he drank before coming home, but certainly his stomach was full, and it seemed miraculous that he could run so fast like a *kaweh* (*Neotragus pygmaeus*; the royal antelope is a West African antelope recognized as the world's smallest antelope) in hot pursuit by a *gbwa ya mofvao* (hunting dog).

His "there" or hideout offered him a vantage position to see his yard and ndawo and the neighboring parts of the village. By the time Mokengeh was secure and safe in his "there," he looked down onto his village and particularly his ndawo to see that the entire roof was almost engulfed in flames and the dry ngo-nja (certain palm tree leaves matted together into sheets or mats used for roofing), providing just the right conditions, as were the dry boards that made the walls. What happened to his assailant? he wondered. By now, this part of the village was wide awake and alive, and folks were streaming toward what was once his house. There was confusion as attempts were being made to put out the fire and, of course, his immediate neighbors also knew that he was home and trapped in the fire. He did not sound the alarm that Njohk'a Moto was an unwelcomed visitor to his home; he just quietly fought back and rescued himself from the occupier tax collector. The village was to figure it out for themselves, sooner or later.

Before Szrango Koff'a Moteh knew and saw that Mokengeh had escaped, he was very desperate to find him. By the time Mokengeh's assailant knew what was happening, that he had lost grip of his prey, the predator's first instinct was to search and smoke out its prey. Trying to feel his way in darkness, in unfamiliar territory and in pain, was no light task for him. The pain and the injuries were secondary for now; his finding his prey was paramount. There was no way this Moto Moszrali (small person or little man) could outsmart and disgrace him like this. It would be the talk of the town, and that would diminish his authority, and he could not afford it to be another Goliath and David story. Mokengeh had to be found and optimal punishment inflicted.

He had a problem, though. It seemed he was searching aimlessly, and he now just seemed to realize that there was smoke everywhere and there was fire, especially on the roof above him and walls behind him. This meant that his search was limited only to those parts of the house that were fire and smoke-free. As his thoughts were racing like an athlete climbing the Gbwea Mountain or the Vako, he wiped the perspiration that was running down his forehead and onto his eyebrows and then almost immediately realized some perspiration had run down his cheek and jaw and now was seeking admission into his mouth from the right side. He licked it, and it was salty-normal sweat.

A few moments later, sweat from his forehead had succeeded in entering his eyes and more into his mouth. It did not take him long thereafter to realize that the "sweat" was not pure sweat; it was mixture of sweat and blood, his own blood in his eyes and mouth. Later on, he was to realize that the blood in his mouth came from a cut pinna, and the blood in eyes came from a gaping wound near the center of his skull. What he did not apparently realize was that there was fluid oozing out directly from his eye, but because it was not bloody, there was no cause for worry.

His bleeding, his fading sight, the pain, the smoke, and the increased flames meant it was time for him to vacate his enclosure, but how could he with all those villagers assembled outside? The last straw was when part of the roof above him collapsed and the wall behind him, and he said to himself in Pidgin, "Make man take shame comot (Ignore the shame and humiliation, stop playing the hero, and play safe by saving yourself)."

He just stepped out of the blazing house as the red-hot roof was caving in, with his left hand clutching onto his left eye as a mixture of bloody fluid oozing from his eye blinded it with excruciating pain. When he emerged, the assembled village crowd went dead silent and at attention. No one in the crowd uttered a word; nor did Njohk'a Moto. As he made his way out of the village in silence, he practically thronged on both sides of the village path. The onlookers parted their ways for him as he approached them. It was just before he left the scene of the nightmarish events that a four-year-old by his mother's leg remarked, "O-ngoh o-ngo Mot'a Njohku (Behold the elephantine man) Na maija o-li-szro lay-ni (With a bleeding eye) Na maija o chor-lor-lor (And blood in his groin area)."

The Njohk'a Moto did not seem to have heard these comments as all in the vicinity held their breath. He continued his forward progress, and after about twenty meters, he turned abruptly and started heading toward the direction of his descriptor. The crowd fled as if faced with a wounded lion but for the mother and her child. Njohk'a Moto approached them, and when he was close enough, the child's mother said, "A-weh-li di mua-na (He is but a child)."

About five meters away from the woman and her son, the Njohk'a Moto again abruptly turned and resumed his final exit from the village. He did not say a word to the molana nor to the mua-na. As he departed, the mua-na again asked, "Ma-meh de-nga-teh ae-ya (Why is he crying)?"

In our village, while children were apt to speaking pidgin among themselves, the tendency was to speak in the Mokpwe language when addressing an adult and especially a *nyango* or *szrango* (a parent, mother or father). When a muana spoke in pidgin and a mombaki spoke in Mokpwe, it meant that the muana had to speak in Mokpwe. That much was understood.

Mokengeh lived in Wo-nya-Mo-liyo (a village that had a burial ground or graveyard that was feared by all wana in villages around the vicinity of WonyaMoliyo. As wana, we did not look at the graves when passing, for the graveyard was by the roadside at an intersection that was used by at least five villages, so you could not miss it. You not only did not look at the direction of the graves; you stopped talking, you stopped breathing, and if by some mistake you pointed out the graveyard to someone, you had to bite your fingers as self-punishment; otherwise, you would be visited by *walimo* (ghost spirits at night; among wana, whenever this graveyard was approached from any direction, the older wana who knew the history told the younger ones what to do and what not to do, or it was just simply a reminder; whenever we were at a safe distance away from the grave, which was almost always breathless, then we started breathing and talking again).

When finally, Njohk'a Moto had to leave Mokengeh's house and village, he left a WonyaMoliyo village all awake and alive, talking and speculating excitedly about the rapid and strange events of the night. The previously quiet sleeping WonyaMolio village was now wide awake. La Moteh also left behind him a burning house whose fire contained the charred remains of Mao-ngoh ma Maykomba. When the villagers had finally dispersed well after the early hours of the morning, and when Mokengeh's house had practically been completely burned to the ground, it was time for Mokengeh to also go.

"Mo-szre-keh hoh hoh szre-lay hoh. Mo-szre-keh hoh hoh szre-lay ho. Mom'a njoh-ku a-ti-mbay-lo-bo-ka szre-lay hoh. Mo-szre-keh hoh hoh szre-lay hoh," he repeated this three times. While in our village, most Mokpwe homes speak English to their gbwa, Mokengeh communicated exclusively in the Mokpwe language. Thus, while many of us wana thought that gbwa only understood English, Mokengeh made it loud and clear that it was not the case.

This was a Malay song, and Mokengeh mo Liwoh was a Moszrekeh in Malay. He danced as he sang in his hideout, bidding farewell to this comrade, Mao-ngoh ma Maykomba, and then when he was done, he disappeared. Mokengeh was never again seen. Mokengeh mo Liwoh was a trado-culturalist, a true custodian of the Mokpwe customs and traditions, especially from the yowo or spiritual perspective. By virtue of his ranking position within the Malay, he was no ordinary member, and his life of poverty, isolationism, and mysticism were all pointers for the knowledgeable and critical eye. Mokengeh mo Liwoh had a Mo-nyio-ngeh Nyio-ngeh; that is, a disappearing formula or disappearing powers.

As we grew up as wana, we understood that Dr. Emmanuel Mbella Lifafa l'Endeley (a.k.a mopho-mo-low), a Prince of the Wakpwes, trained as medical doctor and eventually turned politician to become a statesman and a Prime Minister of West and Southern Cameroon, that his having a Mo-nyio-ngeh Nyio-ngeh saved him several times from assassination attempts by the Ewonda regime, while visiting in Ewonda for state matters after the "reunification." At the time when John

Livena Matute was the head coach for Prisons Buea, Mola Muambo mo Ligbwa was the yoworite of the team, taking care of the spiritual needs of the team. There was once an altercation between Coach and Yoworite which resulted in some physicality between the two wu-nya-na wa *Wakpwe* (Bakweri men). The younger coach who had done judo wrestling while training as a physical education instructor wasted no time in tackling the older yoworite to the ground.

In the scuffle, Mola Muambo mo Ligbwa's white shirt got torn. When they respectively returned to their villages, it took less than twenty-four hours for the whole town to know that Coach tore the yoworite's shirt in their fight. The yoworite Mola Muambo mo Ligbwa sent word back to Coach Livena Matute to replace his shirt with a new one within forty-eight hours. Mola Muambo mo Ligbwa was the only known Mokpwe with a Monyiongeh-Nyiongeh that was no secret. He was a tall, lanky, afroed man with very gentle mannerisms. How it became common knowledge that he had a Monyiongeh-Nyiongeh is not known, but he certainly used that to his advantage. Coach Livena quickly bought a new shirt for him after advice from several elder Wakpwes in the community.

Njohk'a Moto emerged from these events a "winner" or a "loser," depending on who you talked to. He was certainly a no-nonsense law enforcer and tax collector from whom you could apparently not hide, even if it meant he was unorthodox in the carrying out of his duties. He also emerged from these events of the evening to wear an eye patch for the rest of his biological life.

Njohk'a Moto retired or was retired shortly thereafter and settled down onto retirement life in Las Town. Like most Wakpwes in Vakoland, family clans lived in clusters, and Njohk'a Moto maintained living in this family clan where he was born and raised; all the while, he was a Buea City Council Worker or employee in the capacity of Tax Collector and eventually Chief Tax Collector.

Njohk'a Moto was a central and influential figure in his clan, not only because of his elephantine proportions. He was smart and a man of economic means with an air of authority all around him and just a little bit of arrogance. His social status in Las Town was higher than a comparable mate, age or otherwise. He spoke the English language all the time when the commonality was the Mokpwe language and Pidgin. He was commonly referred to as speaking "grammar," though he did not attend St. Joseph's College, Sasse, Buea (Sasse College). He also dressed smartly with his Khaki shorts, heavy boots, thick socks, a wristwatch, a stylistic haircut, etc.

By the time Njohk'a Moto retired, he did not seem to be a friend of his mates in Buea. He was viewed as a collaborator with the oppressors or occupiers, and he was also resented for using inside knowledge of his people to their disadvantage as compared to others. After the incident with Mola Mokengeh mo Liwoh, his fellow Wakpwes asked if he could dare go into "graffi or strangers' quarters" to pursue someone who allegedly owed taxes. Could he also do that in the Igbo or Yoruba quarters? *Traitor* and "misuse of power" were common terms thrown his way, though not so directly for fear of a physical confrontation. Thus, Njohk'a Moto's friends or fans in Buea were the wana and maylor-keh or Melokeh (children and youths), like myself, who did not know him outside that he was a brass band leader that entertained the Buea Town Community.

For most of Njohk'a Moto's mates, retirement was literally and practically a death sentence for many reasons. They never received their pensions, or if they did, it took forever after multiple layers of bribery. It was a sessile life of frustration in idleness and anger and oftentimes coupled with the consumption of what went by several names: a-fvo-fvo, vor-vor, kai-kai, ogo-go-ro, or sometimes just simply "Push me, I push you" (a fighting-induced alcoholic beverage) that sometimes ended up creating ulcer problems aside the daily or frequent intoxication. Kai-kai or vor-vor is called moonshine in North America. When locally brewed in Vakoland it has an estimated alcoholic content (ABV) of 90 percent making it 180 proof, U.S equivalent. It was a killer among alcoholics, and though outlawed, it was commonly available in local bars that served only locally brewed or produced alcoholic beverages. There were three brands: Kwa-tcha, also called corn beer, palm wine from certain species of some local palm trees, and the a-fvo-fvo distilled in underground bush distilleries.

Njohk'a Moto, however, started a brass band that was, in no time, the talk of the town. All of his bandmates were elderly, and instructions and communications were in the Mokpwe language. Njohk'a Moto was the main trumpeter of the band with a huge, twisted trumpet strung around his shoulders. His trumpet was bigger than an average one of us who followed him around town, and the windy air in the form of a sound that emanated from the expanded posterior vent could very well pass for a mini tornado capable of blowing to the ground an average one of us his little fans. Among ourselves, we pretended or lied that a child was once lifted off its feet and thrown several meters away because of its closeness to the exterior vent of the equally gigantic trumpet. For those that could, they hired Njohk'a Moto's brass band to play and entertain in social occasions. Hiring and contracting him to animate and or entertain on an occasion became the norm and a mark of social status.

Njohk'a Moto was also generous and served his local community as a whole at no price, or so we thought. His band also graced the atmosphere whenever there was a championship football game at the Buea Town Stadium. Other occasions where his entertainment was encountered were during national holidays, or rather, the eves of national holidays; for example, May 20, which was the day set aside to commemorate the day La Republique du Cameroun and Southern Cameroons united to form a two State Federation. On the nineteenth of May, there was always an evening ceremony that was usually addressed by the secretary general at the governor's office. Normally, we did not even understand what was said and what the event was all about, except for the fact that the next day would be May 20.

The evening event was normally entertained by the St. Joseph's College (Sasse College) band or the BTTC band (that is, the Baptist Teacher's Training College, now Baptist High School). BTTC was later on replaced by the Baptist Boys Secondary School, a.k.a. Bad Boys Secondary School and now Baptist High School). This evening and night event was originally hosted at the BTTC campus in Great Soppo, and later, the venue was changed to the governor's office at the Buea Town station.

Children liked these events only because of the music. You enjoyed the colleges playing the modern music, which was a taste and a foreshadowing of what was to be played the next morning during the march pass of all the schools and other adult groups, including the military if they did not have their own band playing for them. The official evening event of May 20 was a short one held on the eve of the celebration, that is May 19, and was normally and usually addressed by the secretary general at the Governor's Office in Buea. For many years, the secretary general was Mola Mbua Ndoko na Mi'a-na may-ni, a skin head very fair-skinned mu-nya-na Mokpwe, who was a very experienced and seasoned civil administrator. But it was also enjoyable after the official evening event of May 19th when we had to return to Buea Town with our own local brass band led by Njohk'a Moto. He and his men played all the way back to Buea Town as the Buea Town crowd trailed behind, oftentimes singing along to popular tunes.

Somehow, the Wajili and Igbos had all ganged up against the Wakpwes and composed what would be termed a minimizing song meant to annoy us, the Wakpwes, right in our land. The song went like this in Pidgin:

> Bakweri people dem fool
> Dem deny fogo soja
> Bicos dem too lazy
> Foseka kwakoko.

(The Wakpwes are fools, they have refused to join the colonial army [an army of occupation] because of ekwakoko.)

Okay, this was Mokpwe land (Bakweriland), and this was a Mokpwe band, and they thought it was funny that as we returned to Buea Town, they sang to the tune and melody of Mokpwe brass band by stating that the Wakpwes were foolish by refusing to join the national army, and they attributed this to laziness and Ekwakoko, the trado-cultural dish of Vakoland. But it was all due to their ignorance for they were ignoramuses.

The Wakpwes did not want to be collaborators with the occupiers, regardless of their origin and color of skin. The Wakpwes fought the Germans and defeated them the first time, and the Wakpwes viewed men-of-arms as an oppressive tool and an arm of the government and, therefore, wanted nothing of it because they had been victims.

It was again ignorance on their part because the Wakpwes were the only indigenous group in Africa from whose hands the strong German Army suffered defeat.

Under the heroic leadership of Kuv'a Likenye and Moudindi mo'Ekeka, a formidable world power suffered defeat from the resistance of local people without the sophistication and luxury of modern weaponry. The poisoned arrow that killed the occupation German governor was made in Wonya-Lyonga and yowonized in WonyaMongo, and the archer that dealt the deadly blow was Moudindi mo'Ekeka, a kinsman who was the Mokpwe Army General, and Kuff'a Likenyeh, the Mokpwe leader.

Moudindi mo'Ekeka was a warrior who was armed and used both poisoned arrows and also locally made guns commonly known as "chavu." The cartridges or bullets that are chavu used were called vindi. The vindi were poisoned variously, remaining the secret of the inventor. When the Germans were defeated during their first war with the Wakpwes, they went to Douala and trucked into Buea an armé Togolaise (Togolese Army; Togo is a West African nation, another colony of the Germans at the time Kamerun was a German colony). In their mundane tactics of divide and rule, they brought in the Togolese Africans to fight their war for them against another African people.

This Togolaise army was owed back pay while stationed in Douala, and therefore, their morale was very low. They looked ill-fed and lacking in the athletic stature characteristic of the Mokpwe Army which were in their turf. The German Togolaise army were in their thousands compared to the few hundreds of the Mokpwe army. The number difference and "modern" and deadly weaponry notwithstanding, the second round of fighting between the Wakpwes and the German-Togolaise was fierce.

Kuv'a Likenye l'Endeley, the leader of the Wakpwes, was a young man endowed with spiritual prowess and leadership skills. He had an E-vi-nj'a Moliki, a staff about his height that was made of Wotango *(Icroberlinia brazzavillensis)* and other tree wood combinations of unknown origins. The E-vi-nj'a Moliki was adorned with a skull at the superior end and had an assortment of colors and paintings and carvings along its length with symbols that communicated specific information, all of which was not decipherable by the ordinary man. When the Mokpwe army engaged the German-Togolaise army in the area that today constitutes the Governor's Office, Central Police Station, Prime Minister's Lodge, the Court Area, and the Buea Station as a whole, the German Governor was watching at a safe distance with some of the German military officers while other German military officers were embedded with the Togolaise army, commanding and controlling the fighting operations from the rear, middle, and forefront.

Kuv'a Likenye l'Endeley planted his Evinj'a Moliki into the ground to a depth of about thirty centimeters inside prearranged three stones like the three stones used in a fireplace for cooking or roasting. Three of these sites had been strategically selected for use for which one was used was dependent on many factors, and the Evinj'a Moliki could not just be planted anywhere. The leader mind had fore calculated that when the fighting began, and based on the Mokpwe army formation strategy when it was time to use the Evinj'a Moliki, the German-Togolaise army would sandwich the Mokpwe army. Thus, the Mokpwe army and the plantation point of the Evinji were sandwiched when the leader, Kuv'a Likenya, planted his Evinj'a Moliki staff into the Vako soil of Gbwea (Buea).

When the Evinj'a Moliki is being planted and after it has been planted, it and its planter are surrounded and guarded by an inner core of aide-de-camps and an outer circle of warriors who are among the best of their peers. Kuv'a Likenye did his incantations and danced around the Evinji with utterances that were indecipherable to the ordinary ear and brain. Shortly after he was done with the invocation of E-fva-szra Moto, the other Walimo wa Vako (the other Vako ancestral spirits) and the Liengu la Mua-nja (the goddess of the Atlantic Ocean) that constitutes the Szrawa (Coastline) of the Vakoland, the entire assemblage of the Mokpwe spirit world had been summoned and became activated. These spirits are to assist and be with their wat'o wa weh-na-ma protégées in this life-or-death war against a foreign and formidable power, alien to the Mokpwe, and therefore alien to them the ancestors and ancestral spirits.

The Evinj'a Moliki had two main effects on this battle. It started raining cats and dogs in the battle area, only in Buea, and it sowed confusion within the enemy Germano-Togolaise camp. When the Germano-Togolaise army encircled and sandwiched the Mokpwe army, that was a tactical victory for them, for it was a prelude to the eventual and inevitable decimation of the local warrior army. While the Germano-Togolaise army was mostly African-composed, its commanding officers where the Germans themselves embedded within their ranks. The heavy showers brought about by the Evinji also included some hailstones, but the rain and the hailstones were selective. The Wakpwes in this area of the downpour were passed over by the rain and hail.

In addition, the Mokpwe army, while being sandwiched by their enemy adversaries, transformed itself and relocated behind their enemy soldiers while their silhouettes were still stationed in the middle of the sandwich formation. There was agitation in the invader army camp and confusion and what amounted to a stampede. The enemy soldiers, at this point, started shooting at each other from the opposite sides as they thought they were seeing and shooting at the Mokpwe soldiers. It was chaotic scene with the Germano-Togolaise soldiers shooting at each other and sometimes coming so close to each other as to engage in hand-to-hand combat. In this confusion and chaos, the weapons of mass destruction used against the local warrior Mokpwe army jammed and became nonfunctional while the German-led army was self-decimating itself in a manner likened or akin to apoptosis.

The German governor, smelling defeat and humiliation for the second time in the hands of a local army, came out of safe hiding to fix the jammed cannons they used against their enemies. The unjamming of the cannons was not as easy and as fast as the governor and his close collaborators that flanked him had thought. After a few minutes of failure and frustrations, the governor lifted his head, and with his collaborators and aide-de-camp lateral to his body, he was a clean shot as he had exposed himself and made himself a target. Moudindi mo'Ekeka wasted no time to direct his chavu toward the target governor who was now issuing orders rapidly in what sounded simply as "Hien, hien, hien, hien."

The force of chavu on the governor's chest lifted and plastered him against a tree at some ten meters posterior to the cannons as Moudindi mo'Ekeka wasted no time to finish the job with a poisoned arrow that traversed the neck diameter, targeting specifically the carotid artery. The disoriented German-led army that was still alive retreated, leaving behind their dead governor. Moudindi mo'Ekeka, the triple-armed Mokpwe general, had on his person his chavu, archery assemblage, and a *vao* or *njambi* (machete) that he wore strapped to his waist with robes that served as a ngoli or belt. He wasted no time to decapitate the head of the dead German governor and retained to the village with this trophy. The whereabouts of these heads remain a mystery in Vakoland.

While its original destination was known to be the WonyaLyonga Village in Buea, thereafter, its whereabouts and custodians have remained a mystery of the occultic masters of Vakoland and Royal Endeley House of Buea. The Malay and the Nganya are the two most powerful and feared cults in Vakoland, followed by the Malowa, a cult of the walana. The Nganya is an offshoot of the Malay or rather begotten by the Malay and very closely associated with the Royal House of Buea. When the decapitated head was initially examined, a hole was found about its temporal bone area that was not related nor matched to Moudindi mo'Ekeka's chavu and poisoned archery arrow. Since the ballistics did not match any of Moudindi mo'Ekeka's weapons, it was concluded and thought that perhaps friendly fire might have also contributed to the demise of the German occupation governor.

When Motimbeli Kuv'a Likenye buried his Evinj'a Moliki thirty centimeters into the soil between the three stones, the hole between the three stones contained stones, water, and mud. The stones represented Efvaszra Moto, the Mokpwe deity of the Vako (Mountain); that is, half man and half stone, but it is not known whether this half and half are midsagittal plane divisions or transverse plane divisions, and likewise, it is known which part is *Mot'a weh-na-ma* (human) and which part or portion is *liyai* (stone); that is, it is the superior or inferior portion or it is the left or right side that is human or stone.

The water represented the Liengu la Mua-nja, the Mokpwe goddess of the Atlantic Ocean, and the mud represented other and lesser ancestral but essential spirits and powers gone ahead but are still in communion with the living. The bringing and summoning of these three powers together was understood by the Wakpwes to be summoning the Supreme Power, a monolithic power that surpasses all powers severally and individually. The Germano-Togolaise armed forces could be no match to this force and power. This monolithic power was variously known as O-va-szreh, Mai-keh, Lo-weh, I-wo-ndeh, Low'a la Moh-ngoh mo Nda-ndoh, I-wo-nd'a Lo-weh, Ta'a-t'I-wo-ndeh, etc., long before the arrival of the economic exploitative European colonial occupiers; the Portuguese, the Germans, the English, and then the French.

When the German Governor was nearing his end and was heard to be issuing orders that simply sounded like, "Hein, hein, hein hien," to the ordinary ear of the soldiers, that constituted the Mokpwe Resistance Army (MRA). Kuv'a Likenye and Moudindi mo'Ekeka, on the other hand, who had been schooled in the German language heard something else: "Töten die schwarzen Nyamfukas (Kill the black Nyamfukas). Töten diese schwarzen Jäger (Kill these black hunters). Töten diese schwarzen Bauern (Kill these black farmers). Töten diese schwarzen Matutu-Leute (Kill these black Matutu-People)."

Matutu was and is the palm wine that is tapped from the palm tree and was the highest caliber of an alcoholic beverage among the Wakpwe. A Mokpwe man made a name for himself, family, and clan by the quality of wine he tapped. Matutu is palm wine, an alcoholic beverage created from the sap of various species of palm trees. In Vakoland, the specific palm tree species is *Elaeis guineensis*. Matutu is mainly produced by cutting the stem and collecting the sap; the collecting process could take days. A Moi-nge-li is a palm wine tapper of repute.

"Töten diese Schweineliebhaber und Schweine fressende Menschen (Kill these *ngowa* [pig] loving and pig-eating people)."

The Governor knew the Mokpwe culture. The *ngowa* (Sus scrofa domesticus; pig) is the sacred animal of the Wakpwe wa Lelu (Upland or Mountain Bakweris) that is used for important ceremonies: marriages, deaths, coronations, honors, spirituals, etc.

"Diese Schwarzen zu töten (Kill these black people). 'Schießen diese singenden und tanzenden Bantu-Leute (Shoot these singing and dancing Bantu people)."

The "hein, hein, hein, hein" continued for the desperate governor who was evidently venting his last. It is not clear if the Germans wanted a war or not with the Wakpwes whose territory they occupied. It could well be that they were poised for a military victory and domination of the local population as well. A military victory would have ensured their total control and subjugation of the Wakpwes. When it was obvious to the Wakpwes that the Germans intended to stay for economic and other reasons at their expense, Kuv'a Likenya and Moudindi mo'Ekeka started putting together a small army discreetly, and when agreed upon by the two leaders, Moudindi mo'Ekeke orchestrated covert operations that were disguised as much as possible. Soft German targets were selected, and as their success grew, they became bolder but with a cushion. Only the inner core of the inner core knew of these covert operations—the leader, Kuv'a Likenye, and the MRA commander, Moudindi mo'Ekeka, and the few that he selected to accompany him in these missions.

May-szrango is Friday in the Mokpwe calendar. May-szrango is judgment day, a day cases are judged, a day set aside for the settling of disputes. The Mokpwe culture has an open justice system in which cases are judged in the open to the hearing of all present. May-szrango was set aside as judgment day. This day was for a specific activity, just as you had other days of the week set aside for specific activities; for example, market days, farming days, worship days, etc. Come May-szrango, the village square was packed depending on the nature of the cases that were to be judged. This open arena courthouses or houses of justice judged cases concerning all aspects of Mokpwe life, except issues deemed of a sensitive security nature that normally involved outsiders who are not part of the village or not part of the local community.

These open court arenas also judged cases that involved the death penalty. Such cases of a serious nature, though open, were limited to elders and took place late evening into the night. The highest profile cases ended up with being exiled from the community or, at the worst, being condemned to death by hanging. Mokala Mo'o-ngo was a "white man" and Wakala wa Mio-o-ngo were "white men" or just simply Mio'o-ngo or Wakala as the Germans were commonly known and referred to. They had outlawed hanging and the death penalty by the locals and arrogated those powers to themselves only. They had the death penalty in Germany, and they also exercised the death penalty by firing squad and also by hanging as the case may be in Vakoland, but this was not to be tolerated if carried out by the locals as they considered it "Barbarisch, unmenschlich, und unzivilisiert (Barbaric, inhumane, and uncivilized)."

These *wakala wa mio'o-ngo* (white albinos) decided to step up their authority and grip on the local Mokpwe population. This was not to be acceptable, though it was also realized and known that the wakala wa mio-o-ngo occupiers had the upper hand.

A high-profile case of murder was judged for three consecutive days. It started on a May-szra-ngo and ended on a Weh-yu Li-szra-mba (a.k.a. Szro-ndi)—that is, from Friday to Sunday—and these hearings were held late afternoons until late into the night and were only open to adults. The *Wa-kai-li* (judges) included notables and elders from neighboring and faraway villages. A *mbe-szra* (young man) killed his *e-wa-nda* (fiancée) in what seemed like a jealous love rage, and therefore, the Mbeszra and his family argued that it was an accidental death while the late *ngoh-ndoh's* (young woman's) family argued that it was premeditated because there were witnesses that testified that they had heard E-ko-ngol'a E-wou-nga (the mbeszra) vow, swear, and promise that he was going to kill Likowoh when stories spread in the village that Likow'a Ndima, his *ewandeh* (fiancée) was seeing some other person from a neighboring village. The night that Ekongolo attacked Likowoh and her Kiveh (lover), Likowoh was actually returning home late with a visiting ndomeh wa munyana from Bonavada (a visiting male cousin).

Likowoh died eventually of the attack after seven days, and Likowoh's cousin, Esru'a Nyameh, remained paralyzed waist down. While the defense contended and maintained that it was a passion crime and also that Esru'a Nyameh was not introduced and, therefore, not known by Ekongolo, he was not to blame. The bereaved and paralyzed family argued that besides the witnesses that had testified against Ekongolo, Esru'a Nyameh, their son (nephew), had just arrived at the village and had not even spent a night and that Ekongolo did not give them time to be introduced.

After three days, Ekongol'a Ewounga was found guilty of premeditated murder and attempted murder. He was, therefore, sentenced to death by hanging, and the hanging was to take place three days after the verdict. The hanging was to take place between the two great and feared trees in Gbwea, the wou-ma or baobab tree (*Adansonia digitata*) and the iroko tree (*Milicicea excels* is the iroko tree species that yields high quality timber because of its hardness and other physico-chemical properties trees that were situated in the hanging grounds that were seldom used). These trees were located at the south end of what became the Buea Town Stadium, a place that had previously served as a golf course for the Germans. The Germans converted sacred grounds to social grounds at the expense of the local population.

The Wakala—even if unofficially—knew and recognized Motimbeli Kuveh and Moudindi mo'Ekeka as the leaders of the people. When the Germans learned (through their foot on the ground spies; yes, they had many within the local population and when they had been discovered time and again, it was never well for them and their families) of the impeding planned hanging, they sent word through messengers to Kuv'a Likenya objecting to the hanging and insisted the Wakpwes had no powers, no authority, and no jurisdiction to carry out an execution by hanging or otherwise. They thus demanded that the condemned man be handed over to them, the German authorities, immediately and without delay.

The messenger was detained for two days, and when he was returned to his senders, he was a half dead man barely able to walk or talk with swollen facial features and a missing *liszroh* (eye). The execution by hanging was carried out as planned in the dead of the night, and the executioners were never known; very few in the village knew who they were. It was thought that it included the leadership of the Nganya and Malay, the *Watimbeli* (leaders), the executioners, and then the guards who held the condemned prisoners as instructed by the leaders and in prisons that were thought to be subterranean in caves or similar chambers situated beyond the Ule in the deep of the WonyaLyonga Village. The Ule is the mystic stream (stream is called Bayou in North America), that emanates or has its origins from a rock, associated with the spiritual features of WonyaLyonga. There is a connection between the Ule and the Li'a-nga-meh-leh, the other mo-szro (stream) that wreaks flooding havoc every so often in Gbwea (Buea). Flood havocs are often times attributed to the wrath or displeasure of the Paramount Chief of Buea as is also the case with the eruption of the Vako, when not attributed to E-Fva-szra-Moto, the half-human-half-rock deity of the Vako or Mount Fako. The most recent flood of 2020 of the Li'a-nga-meh-leh was attributed to the displeasure of the Nakuveh and Naliomo, Moti-mbay-li Moka mo Lifafa mo'Endeley. He was the physical paramount chief and ruler of Gbwea and the Wakpwes from 1990 to 2015 and remains the Nakuveh and Naliomo until his successor is enthroned, according to Mokpwe customs and traditions.

When the lifeless body of Eko-ngol'a Ewou-ngeh was found hanging between the two evil trees, as they were commonly called, the morning after the execution, there was mourning and wailing in the village by the bereaved families and quietness throughout the village.

German Cameroon (German: Kamerun) was an African colony of the German Empire from 1884 to 1916 in the region of today's Republic of Cameroon. German Cameroon also included northern parts of Gabon and the Congo with western parts of the Central African Republic, southwestern parts of Chad, and far eastern parts of Nigeria (from north to south). Buea and Vakoland was the capital of this African Empire for many reasons, including the climate, fertile soils, clean natural sparkling water, clean air, the abundance of game animals and fish species, the hospitality of the people, the walana, etc. Before the occupying Germans usurped and established large plantations in Vakoland, they loved Vakoland because their first and very profitable economic exploitation activity was ivory. The slopes of the Vako abounded with njoh-ku (Elephants; *Loxodonta cyclotis*). The Germans killed these animals en masse for their ivory, hide, and skin.

It was this hospitality they took for granted and it was this hospitality they abused. Chinua Achebe, the Nigerian author and novelist, wrote the novel *Things Fall Apart*, which was published in 1958, and its story chronicles precolonial life in the southeastern part of Nigeria and the arrival of the Europeans during the late nineteenth century. While Chinua Achebe might not have known the story of the Wakpwes in Vakoland, he wrote a story of the Igbos of Nigeria that would have made him a Mokpwe German historian. The Wakpwes had gone through a German ordeal long before Chinua Achebe chronicled British occupier rule in Igboland, Eastern Nigeria.

Kamerun was colonized in 1884 by the Germans who ruled Kamerun till 1916. When the Germans were defeated during the First World War, Cameroon was placed as a mandated territory of the League of Nations and given to France and Britain to rule it. They shared Cameroon in two parts with France, occupying three-quarters (the east portion), and Britain occupying one-quarter (the west portion). The entity known as British Cameroon lasted from 1916– 1961, while the entity known as French Cameroun lasted from 1916–1960.

During the British Cameroon era, there was an influx of numerous Nigerians into the territory. Buea was capital territory, and the British who had taken over the plantations on Mokpwe lands created by the Germans promised the Vakolanders that royalties would be paid to them and that their land on which the plantations were established were leased lands, remaining properties of the Wakpwes. It is not known whether this appeased the Wakpwes or not. The brutality of the colonial French Government in French Cameroun soon resulted in resistance, taking a cue from the Wakpwes who had successfully and initially fought and defeated a world power with little less than nothing.

The resistance fighters in French Cameroun, resisting occupation by the French. were termed *maquisards*—that is, guerrilla fighters— and later, their political party that gave them an umbrella cover, the Union des Populations Camerounaises (UPC), was banned. In December 1956, the UPC, which was banned from participating in the general elections set up an armed branch called the "Comité National d'Organisation" (Organization National Committee or CNO) and started an armed struggle, and then they became labeled as a terrorist group.

Felix-Roland Moumie and Reuben Um Nyobe were the initial and principal leaders of the UPC, and just like Kuv'a Likenye and Moudindi mo'Ekeka before them in Vakoland, the occupation forces sought their heads and would use all and any means to get these heads or leaders. The resistance to French rule in French Cameroun came mostly from the Bamilikis, the Bassas, and some from the Centre and

South portions of French Cameroun. To flee the French terror, leaders, fighters, men, women, and children from French Cameroun that opposed French rule fled to British Cameroons, especially Mokpweland in Vako as political refugees.

The Wakpwes are very hospitable and having resisted the Germans themselves earlier, they knew what it meant to be in exile; they knew what it meant to grant political asylum to a comrade that needed one. It is these political asylees (asylum-seekers) concentrated mostly in Vakoland of British Cameroons that became known eventually as the "la 11ème province" (the 11th Province). The "United Republic of Cameroon," for a long time, was subdivided into ten main political and administrative units now called regions and each had an appointed governor from Yaoundé and by the president. An eleventh province was thus more like a shadow province; it was Mokpwe hospitality and generosity."

There were always "official" and "backdoor" communication channels between the occupation German authorities and the local Mokpwe population led by Kuveh and Moudindi and also the Kuveh-Moudindi team had their informants inside German circles, just as the Germans had their own informants and spies inside the Mokpwe leadership and especially among the MRA leadership. Word from the Germans got to Kuv'a Likenya and Moudindi mo'Ekeka to abdicate their leadership positions and go to voluntary exile after the execution by hanging was carried out. Kuveh and Moundindi met in their E-wong'a Yowo Cave (Sacred Cave, which served as the leadership and war planning room) that was located somewhere between the Lia-nga-me-leh and Uleh (situated in the WonyaLyonga-Vako trait), freshwater catchment areas that provided crystal clear clean water to the wato wa Gbwea (Buea people) all year round. The exact location of their E-wong'a Yowo was a conjecture, and even after they had been long gone, the exact site had not been "located," at least officially. Oral tradition had it that when Kuv'a Likenye and Moudindi mo'Ekeka had decided that they would rather go to war, Moudindi mo'Ekeke had remarked that, "Nkweli Enay (This is suicidal, this is death)."

Buea became the capital of German Kamerun in 1901 after Governor Jesko von Puttkamer completed the construction of the building, which he subsequently named "Puttkamer Schloss" or Puttkamer Palace, today known as the Prime Minister's Lounge. Word was sent back to the Puttkamer Palace from the Ewong'a Yowo enclave by Kuv'a Likenye: "Das ist Mokpweland"

This is Mokpweland

"Das ist Vakoland"

This is Vakoland

"Land unserer Vorfahren und Vorfahren"

Land of our forefathers and ancestors

"Wir werden nicht von einem farblosen Albino Mokala wie Ihnen diktiert, eingeschüchtert oder gemobbt"

We will not be dictated to, intimidated, or bullied by a colorless albino mokala like you

"Vakoland ist kein Land für wakala wa mio-o-ngo"

Vakoland is not a land for wakala wa mio-o-ngo

"Wir werden für den Erhalt unseres Landes und unserer Kultur kämpfen"

We will fight to preserve our land and culture

"Sie und die anderen Mio-o-ngo may-wakala haben über-nachtet Ihr Willkommen"

You and the other Mio-o-ngo may-wakala have overstayed your welcome

"Du stehst uns, du behandelst uns wie Untermenschen, du sperrst uns ein, und jetzt willst du die Luft kontrollieren, die wir atmen, indem du unsere Kultur als Ausrede benutzt"

You steal from us, you treat us like sub-humans, you imprison us, and now you want to control the air we breathe, using our culture as an excuse

"Wir treffen uns auf dem Schlachtfeld und unsere Vorfahren, die Liengu la Mua-nja und Efvaszra-Moto, werden an der Seite unserer tapferen Krieger der Mokpwe-Armee kämpfen"

We will meet in the battlefield and our ancestors, the Liengu la Mua-nja and Efvaszra-Moto, will fight alongside our brave warriors of the Mokpwe army

Motimbeli Kuv'a Likenya concluded his message to the Puttkamer in the Mokpwe language

"Loweh l'azsru aweh-li ni szro"

Our God is with us

Puttkamer's response was short

"Sie und Ihr Volk sind in der Tat verrückt"

You and your people are indeed mad

The deliverer of Motimbeli Kuveh's message to the German occupier governor never returned home. His fate and whereabouts remained a mystery. The last German messenger to the Mokpwe leadership with the occupier Governor's brief and last words begged for his life when he delivered his message. It is thought that they got more from him as some sort of an "insider" as the Mokpwe leadership prepared for war.

The Evinj'a Moliki of Kinge and Motimbeli Kuv'a Likenya vanished immediately after Kuveh's death and has never been found thereafter. When the occupation German governor was killed and decapitated, the Germans became wounded lions and mad venomous reptiles and brought in more troops armed to the teeth with a significant number of German soldiers within their ranks. Kuv'a Likenya and Moudindi mo'Ekeka were wanted men, dead or alive, and so they escaped from Buea in the deep of the night with heavy rains and fog and the below zero temperatures cold that characterized Gbwea. They escaped from Gbwea through ravens that served as communications channels between the Liengu la Muanja and the Efvaszra Moto and without their bodyguards. These ravens were not meant for human travel except for the likes of the leaders of armed struggle against occupier forces. So, while they would have wanted assistance in their escape from their aide de camps, this was impossible.

Kuv'a Likenya was on exile in the forests of Mokunda mo Mbeng'a Mbowa, abandoning his palace in Mokunda mo Gbwea. Mbeng'a Mbowa is lower Mokpwe land, using the Atlantic Ocean and the Vako as references. It is nearer the ocean, than it is a Mbeng'a Mbowa; if it is nearer the mountain (Vako), then it is called Lel'a Mbowa. Moudindi mo'Ekeka left his WonyaLyonga and Woh-njoh-ngoh turfs headed also for Mbeng'a Mbowa and having in mind Woh-njoh-ngoh wo Mbeng'a Mbowa.

Kuv'a Likenye was on exile in the forests of Mbeng'a Mbowa, hidden, fed, and treated by the con-kinsmen of Mbeng'a Mbowa. Kuv'a was treated of gun pellets embedded in his abdominopelvic region. For fear of the Germans and their traitor spies and informants, Kuveh could not be housed. He thus had a prolonged stay hiding in the friendly forests of Mbeng'a and always on the move in an attempt to dislodge any trailers. A long stay or delay in the Mokpwe language is called "Endeya." Given that he could not and was not returning to Gbwea and considering that he was not living a normal life in Mbeng'a Mbowa, he soon became known and was referenced as a "mo'Endeli," meaning someone who has stayed for long, doing something or nothing. It was thus the "Endeya" that, with time, became "Endeli" and in its current form, "Endeley." The Mokpwe Royal House in Gbwea has thus preferred to use the name "Endeley" instead of Likenye for about the last hundred years or so.

While Moudidi mo'Ekeka self-exiled with Kuv'a Likenya headed for Mbeng'a Mbowa, his home of exile remains a mystery. Mo'Ekeka seemed to have simply varnished from the face of the earth. He might have settled in Woh-njoh-ngoh wo Mbeng'a Mbowa, he might not have reached Mbeng'a Mbowa and settled in one of the western Mokpwe villages in Western Vakoland just before Mbeng'a Mbowa. He might have assumed a new identity. There was no trace or word of him. Once in a while and time again, it was rumored that he was seen in WonyaLyonga and Woh-njoh-ngoh wo Lel'a Mbowa.

With the escape and varnishing of the leaders of the resistance, Kuv'a Likenya and Moudidi mo'Ekeka, came the effective and practical dissolution of the Mokpwe Army. The Germans, mortally wounded and humiliated with the death of their occupation governor and scores of officers and rank and file foot soldiers, returned yet again with a vengeance. They paid the back salaries of the hungry, malnourished, but well-trained and well-armed Togolaise mercenary fighters, thereby boosting their moral; they increased the number of Germans in the fighting ranks and also doubled the number of commanding German officers and quadrupled the number of mass destruction weaponry.

An estimated Germano-Togolaise army of three thousand men strong was trucked into Buea in plain daylight to the knowledge of all. It was a show of force; it was a statement of finality and superior military power. When the reconstituted Germano-Togolaise army arrived in Buea to combat with the Mokpwe Kuv'a-Ekeka led army that was only about 300 man strong, there was no army to fight. Wakpwes spies stationed from the Mongo River, Miselele, Tikowa, Likumba, Mutengene, lower Buea to Buea Town informed of the movement of the convoy at each stage, and the temptation to attack was real.

Because there was no resistance by the local Mokpwe population, the Germans started their occupation of Vakoland unchallenged. With a superior military hand, the Germans therefore intensified their efforts to locate the leaders of the resistance Mokpwe army and sought to blackmail the Mokpwe population of Buea, except if they produced Kuv'a Likenya and Moudindi mo'Ekeka. While the search of these Wakpwe leaders continued, the Germans plunged the hinterland of Vakoland with a savagery of economic exploitation. While the leaders of the resistance had vanished and were thought to be "in exile in Mbeng'a Mbowa," hiding in exile in Mokunda mo Mbengeh and Woh-njoh-ngoh wo Mbengeh, respectively, the "dissolved" or disbanded Mokpwe Occupation Resistance Army (MORA) resorted to a guerilla warfare tactic inflicting minor and moderate damages to the occupation forces now and again and avoiding large scale damage that would have enraged the Germans to the point of inflicting even harsher treatment on the local population.

Most able-bodied Mokpwe males ended up in jails for nothing. Kuv'a Likenye and Moudidi mo'Ekeka were reported seen time and again by some, especially of their immediate family members in the Buea area while they were still in "banishment." Their being seen or not was a matter of secret.

Bwua-szra (Bwassa) is a western village of Vakoland enroute to Mbeng'a Mbowa; its current Motimbeli was Mokuwa Moja Mokuwa Moja. He was a Motimbeli of exceptional powers as recognized by his peers in Vakoland, but they were equally worried that he had his hands in high places that were unusual for his rank and age as a traditional Motimbeli. He ran a branch of the Nganya that was feared near and far, and he had challenged traditional and conservative powers that had hitherto controlled Vakoland in the spiritual realm. Where is Kuv'a Likenya's Evinj'a Moliki? Where did Moudindi mo'Ekeka end up?

So, when the Wajili ignoramuses said or implied that the Wakpwes were weaklings, they did not know the Kamerun history and their African history. The Wakpwe wana, or precisely the may-lor-keh (melokeh), did not take this kindly. I experienced cases when these "fun" songs ended up with some exchanges of blows and punches and elbowing with spattering blood between the Wakpwes and the Wajili or the Wakpwes and the Igbos. I did not partake in this flexing of muscles because I was in no condition to. I was too young and too frail and only wished that these Wajili and Igbos would be taught a lesson, and yes, they received one.

I must say, though, that no matter the commotion that took place, the brass band continued to hum its way home, unabated until dispersal point. I normally disengaged before the dispersal point because of the location of our residence.

When I went home, however, the song that sang in my head and on my mind was "Wa Njani Toulou, Wa Ti-mba-na Toulou."

Toulou was known in Pidgin as "Gwashi." It is a minimalist design meant to cover the external male reproductive structures. It was thus a piece of cloth that covered only the scrotal sac and the associated intromittent organ. For this coverage to be sustainable, that piece of cloth was passed through the cleavage of the two gluteus maximus muscles that constituted the buttocks and then tied around the waist. So, when the Wakpwe May-lor-keh in the Njoh-k'a Moto band sang "Wa Nja-ni Tou-lou, Wa Ti-mba-na Tou-lou," it was their own way of hitting back at the Wajili by stating that they came to the coast primitive and poor, and they return eventually primitive and poor.

That was then, but now it is more like "Wa Nja-ni Tou-lou, Wa Ti-mba-na E-wa-mba-ni," literally meaning they came with a tou- lou and they return with a car, meaning they came poor, and they returned rich.

Another form of hitting back at the Wajili by the Wakpwe may-lor-keh (may-lor-keh, youths) was chanting, "Cam no go Cam no go. Cam no go" or singing it in mbo-lo-mbo-lo format: "Cam no go (leader) must go (others). Cam no go (leader) must go (others)."

A mbo-lo-mbo-lo dance was likened to a form of an electric slide dance favored by Mokpwe May-lor-keh (Melokeh; youths). Mbolombolo songs were instantaneous if the composer knew what to do and how to lead the crowd.

With the "cam no go must go" song, the maylorkeh (melokeh) moved or swayed backward and forward and then laterally to the left and then to the right, all in proper choreography.

At this dancing stage, the antagonizing youths forget their differences as Igbos, Wajili, and Wakpwes, occupied themselves with dancing and rather competing with each other to see who the better dancer is. At this stage, words like "No mash me eeh (Do not step on me)" was the usual common because those that were poorly choreographing usually would step on the toes or feet of others. But no one was about to be left out, so expert or not, you were sure to be part of the mbolombolo that seemed to animate them all.

CHAPTER 16

Mua-mba-la mo Wolowa

Njohk'a Moto's niece—that is, Nkwel'a Wana—was well-endowed with exceptionally big breasts and buttocks, a relatively small waistline, and very thin and bony lower limbs that obviously had difficulties supporting the superior weight that rained from above. Her niece was also known to be very fertile, more or less hatching kids as from a human factory. Another attribute of Njohk'a Moteh's niece was that of vulgarity. She was a "vulgarian or vulgarist" of epic proportions. In a society where men (wunyana) made it a point of duty not to reveal their inner thoughts, feelings, or emotions, her vulgar nature made even these wunyana cringe and shake their heads in pity, disapproval, and disappointment. This niece was, in addition, a *molana wa njuma* (a fighter) and a *mo'o-weh-li* or *mo'o-wa* (a loud-mouthed talker). Mention and/or reference to her in the midst of adults was always followed by an, "O'o-go?" meaning "That one?" In the Mokpwe culture, the word *o'o-go* is not only dismissive but could also be very belittling, one of no consequence, one of no substance, one from which no good should be expected, one that emanated something nefarious or negativity, etc.

Njoh-k'a Moto's niece's fame also included a high rate of infant mortality. She seems to have performed infanticide on her own born wana. Therefore, while her rate of conceiving and child production was high, she had no grown child for a molana aged thirty and above, taking into consideration norms and expectations of the local society.

Like was mentioned before, Njoh-k'a Moto's was a successful munyana by all means and standards and a local hero and champion in his own right—that is, a munyana wa Njor-keh, a true man of high social standing. He was thus scrutinized and attacked variously and pretty often. Njoh-k'a Moto, it was said, had "Nyo-ngo" and proof of what was his success. Considering that Nyongo involved the sacrifice of human life of a close biological relative, spouse, first degree in-laws, or persons with whom you have close proximity, constant contacts—e.g. workplace, social groups, neighbors, etc.—it was not hard or difficult to link the now common occurrence of the death of her niece's kids to him.

He had been attacked in public and in private for being a Mot'a Nyongo (Nyongo-man), albeit belonging to this sacred society that feasted on human life and blood. What was unusual about the accusations leveled against him was the fact that they came from without the family. This was odd because it was usually the reverse; the accusations started intra-family and then it was eventually picked up later by extra-family people in close proximity with the family. However, this is not suggesting that accusations may not start from outside the family and then ingress into the family. Accusations of Nyongo or Li-emba made from without seemed justified and with credence if they were seen or judged as corroborating an existing or prior accusations made by inside family members. In a society where age and any form of success is likely to be attributed to Li-emba or Nyongo, Njoh-k'a Moteh was emphatic and persistent in denying that he had Nyongo and attributed such unfounded accusations to his many detractors. However, while emphatically denying membership in this sacred cult, Njoh-k'a Moteh was very curious and very determined to know and get to the bottom of this infanticide stigma now in association with his family and, by extension, to Nyongo directly attributed to him.

The Nyongo society was a sacred cult known to have originated from the inner hinterland of Nyongoland also known as Jangiland, situated in the coal country regions of Cameroon. It was associated with businesspeople whose sole goal was making more money. Because they wanted to be very rich and very powerful, there was not enough physical time and enough physical space to churn out goods and services within a twenty-four-hour period. They thus operated agricultural crop farms for cocoa and coffee, for example, and industrial productions in the spiritual realm to meet the demands of their growing clientele at home and in neighboring countries.

The oldest and most known Nyongoland trader in Buea, Ni Szrimoni who could also speak the Mokpwe language, was an example par excellence. Due to political problems in Jangiland fighting the French, many Jangilites fled their natal homes to seek and take refuge in Vakoland because of the legendary and altruistic hospitality of the Mokpweli, a democratic and fearless people. The Nyongolite Szrimoni came to Buea as an infant in the company of his fleeing parents. He did not need schooling, neither did he need to work for the government or anyone. Because he never knew his natal village and never returned there, he grew up knowing only Buea.

He learned and knew the Mokpwe language and culture. He was a Buea Boy and, to a very large extent, a munyana Mokpwe (a Mokpwe man or Bakwerian). When for economic and other social reasons the Wakpwes decided that it was time for some of them to start working with the government, all of these men who got these government jobs were younger than Ni Szrimoni, and Buea Town being a village, a small town then, this Jangilite trader knew them all.

Ni Szrimoni came from a background that did not trust the government, and neither did the Nyongolanders trust any other institution, except that which they themselves set up and control. Ni Szrimoni was a trader businessman, and he was going to use his knowledge of the Mokpwe working class in Buea Town to his advantage. He always had a general provision store (groceries, house supplies, building supplies, etc.) that was always fully stocked. He seemed to have been restocking each night, but no one ever saw delivery trucks unloading merchandise anywhere near his business premise. Physically, he was seen occasionally making trips to Ngola (Douala) and small-time purchases of regular household items, like hygienic paper, body products, etc., all items that he carried with both hands and used the same public transportation that was used by all of us via minibus that plied the Gbwea-Douala route many times a day, seven days a week.

There was no way that these his handheld purchases were hardly enough to suffice a household of five persons and would be considered the supply of his well-known store, that was always stocked, year in year out and that had been sustained long before I was born and continues into my adult age. The continual stocking of his store with goods was, therefore, a mystery and often discussed only in hush-hush tones among *wambaki* (elders or adults). For those who had the capabilities of spiritual powers, they described what normally happened in front of this trader's store at night. The public road in front of his store became a waterway, and ships anchored there and off-loaded their goods, which were carried then up to his store by youths who had been given to Nyongo and were now working money for their "senders."

This store was more like a magnet and had as its top clientele, all the Mokpwes in town who were civil servants. These financially capable Wakpwes all had credit lines with this store. They and their families could therefore collect goods and then pay later. It seemed like the advent of credit cards hooked my people and made them permanently indebted to this Pa Szrimoni and economic entrapment linked to Nyongo. These Mokpwe civil servants were always in debt, they paid at the end of each month, then started taking and owing again to be paid at the end of the next month. They were no different from the Tole Tea Workers in Buea, near Sasse College, who were always indebted to the Estate Provision Store and who only got the balance of their pay each month after the management of the Tole Tea Estate that operated the store deducted what they owed and then gave them the balance. They left the pay office and straight back to the store to start obtaining provisions all over again in credit. These are the workers credited with the saying or mantra, "Kill you I pay."

It was common for these workers after payday, which was at the end of each month and after their provision store deductions, to treat themselves with some alcoholic beverages either at the club or bar run and managed by the tea plantation estate or other local beer parlors. After rounds of drinks and especially in the case of ogogoro, afvofvo, vor-vor, or kai-kai, the "push me I push you" begins, and these intoxicated men flex their muscles, ready to punch each other. Moreover, because they have some cash in their pockets, being payday, they are in the position of paying for a human life. Thus, they will dare to beat a colleague and pay the colleague's family money in the event that the beaten weaker colleague dies in the course of the fighting. "Kill you I pay."

While Ni Szrimoni was closely associated with Nyongo as a consequence of his origins, business, and the hooking or "telepathic" control of the Wakpwe working class in Buea Town, Nna Tio was not. Nna Tio was an Igbo man from Abba, a town in Nwangele Local Government Area (LGA) in Imo State, Nigeria. Abba is a great trading center in Southeast Nigeria, and folks from Abba, therefore, are "expected" to live up to expectations. Nna Tio ran a principally Breakfast Store with a few other aside household items and needs. Ni Szrimoni and Nna Tio all competed for the same population of clients, the working Mokpwe class, as their main business bases. While both traders and businessmen provided different services to their clientele, their modus operandi, was the same: They both provided their customers with "credit cards."

These clients and their family members, especially their wana, simply walked into these stores anytime and any day and took whatever they needed, signed the book, left, and paid at the end of the month. More often than not, all bills were not settled at the end of the month. There were carryovers, month after month, and additions to the carryovers, month after month. Nna Tio supplied his clients with bread, milk, sugar, other breakfast beverages, eggs, hygienic tissues, and a few other intimate household items.

Nna Tio was a facial-haired, mid-height, fair-skinned man and very young as compared to Ni Szrimoni. He was known to always go to Ngola (Douala) to replenish the supplies in his store, and his store was a small one. Many thought these frequent trips out of Buea Town for restocking sufficed or was sufficient, accounting for the reason his store was always fully stocked. Others thought that the "hand luggage" purchases made from these outside Buea trips did not suffice and could not suffice accounting for the permanently fully stocked provision store that he had with the high volume of customers that was known to visit his store.

Many also thought Nna Tio's Breakfast Store was a mere front for other more serious and lucrative business. Money laundry was thought to be a main business in addition to being a spy or an informant of the Nigerian government. Nna Tio was a successful businessman with lots of questions being asked, but he was never accused of being associated with nyongo.

Contributions to Nyongo productivity were in two categories: It was either by blood donation that was used strictly for spiritual purposes or as a manual workforce in farms and or factories. Older folks donated or contributed to Nyongo were only valuable as contributing to the blood bank. Younger folks donated/contributed to the economic workforce. The donor or sender was paid in full and only once for an agreed sum if the contributed headed toward the blood bank. For donations headed toward the workforce, you could be compensated in full once and for all or you could be given a specific sum after delivery and then a salary on a monthly basis as long as your "donation" continued to be productive economically. Either way, you had to die first before you could contribute to the Nyongo productivity; it was thus ghost work.

There were "records" of some who had been killed through Nyongo, contacting family members or close friends via dreams or visions or through a nga-nga medium, crying and complaining of the hardship they underwent working 24/7 in crop farms or factories. Death by Nyongo came variously and was dependent on the giver or contributor after clearance with the Nyong bosses—beheading with a machete, assorted forms of accidents, fights, "natural" causes, etc.

The donor of the Nyongoree was normally well-compensated for providing the course with a "tailless" cow. The amount received varied, depending on the social status, age, and gender of the donoree.

Birth control was not a norm in our society. Married and adult women used breastfeeding as a natural means of birth control. Most women breastfed for two years and were not pregnant during these years but immediately became pregnant thereafter. Most families, therefore, had a two-year gap between their children. This was well-known and could be used in predicting ages of siblings once you knew one of the ages. For younger women of reproductive age and that were sexually active, the story was different. They got pregnant and then resorted to very crude and lethal methods of abortions by themselves or through a second party. The drinking of bleach or some other poisonous herbal concoctions made and prescribed by a Mot'a Nga-nga was common, and so were related deaths. Sometimes these crude methods failed, and the pregnancy progressed to childbirth, or, in very unfortunate events, the young mothers lost their lives. Most cases where the pregnancy progressed to a childbirth were due to seemingly cunning, "crookish" abortionists who knew nothing about abortions and who simply prescribed and gave harmless leaf concoctions that were supposed to be used as a laxative, enema, or simply as a cocktail drink.

These women seeking abortions were also given certain rules to follow. Thus, when it did not work, they blamed it on the woman's failure to follow the proper instructions as given or directed. Death due to abortion caused lots of pain and anger, and this gave rise to antiabortion campaigns. Such campaigns were very much directed to the parents and the larger society. A child before marriage was a taboo and meant end of schooling, rejection, and more or less scorning by parents and other close relatives. However, some younger women who got pregnant had the funds and were informed about trained medical personnel who performed abortions and did follow this less risky route.

The abortion campaign in our town included contraception, safe sex, and abstinence. These were not very effective methods for several reasons—finances, ignorance, cultural (sex education was more or less a taboo subject), lack of will, youth defiance, and invincibility, failure of the churches, etc. Even the government ban on abortion by nontrained personnel did not have much of an effect but simply drove these quack doctors underground and made the situation even worse.

Due to the failure of the methods listed above, the campaign adjusted. Lots of attention and pressure was now put on the individual families to persuade their daughters to go ahead and have the baby in the event of a pregnancy. Mothers went on to assure and reassure their daughters that they would take care of their grandchildren if the mother did not want to and promised other forms of support as incentives. The thrust of these family campaigns was the saving of the life of the daughter and the unborn child and to protect the young woman from destroying her reproductive structures leading to future infertility and barrenness in the event of an attempted and botched abortion. This family-based approach that emphasized concern and care for the mother and child and which underplayed the villain tone and the assurance and promise of hell seemed to have greater success rate at preventing abortions and the death of the young mother than the previous methods.

In many instances, though, the young mother found out pretty soon that caring for their life and caring for their baby's life during pregnancy did not equal love after pregnancy when the baby was born safely. While they were still accommodated at home after their child was born, the young mother quickly felt overwhelmed with their own share of taking care of a new baby (finances, maintenance care, sleepless nights); they also had to deal with comments, insinuations, and sometimes straight up insults from close and not so close persons, were constrained to their social lives, the prospect of not having an education (for those who were students),and; very importantly, their inability to be able to attract a husband in the future. Was it worth it to keep the pregnancy? This was a frequent question on their lips.

Njoh-k'a Moto's niece was not one who would subscribe to an abortion. This was evident because of her previous pregnancies and her kids that she bore. Njoh-k'a Moto had heard *nko-ngo-sa* (gossip) around the family and outside the family that his niece may be pregnant again, and evidence of this was her continuous wearing of Kawa (a maternity-like gown) and corsets to conceal the pregnancy. He took note with no outward revealing of his inside thoughts. He increased his vigilance, and he could afford to do this now that he was retired and no longer the chief tax collector of the town of Buea.

Ngoh-ndoh ja walana (young women) evolved to developing different ways of "hiding" a pregnancy with the plans of doing away with the baby once it was born. It was a strategy that accomplished at least things in their favor. They could eat their "cake" and still have it. They did not risk their lives, they did not destroy their reproductive systems, they did not kill the developing babies, they continued with life normally, and it also ensured that they were eligible for marriage in the future. They chose to not to abort the muana but to kill the muana after it had been delivered. It was considered a lesser evil with a brighter future for the abortionist.

Our community was dominated by pit toilets, and these pit toilets were community utilized in certain instances. Some of the families in our community had tenants who rented and lived in parts of their homes or a separate building from the family house meant for commercial purposes only. These tenant families were usually Wajili with their own families, more often than not. Thus, a single pit toilet could be used by related families and tenant families. You could always know such toilets as you passed by a neighborhood that had one by the stench that emanated from it.

As kids, we normally would run past that segment of the road with our hands covering our nose, preventing breathing temporarily until we ran past the toxic zone. The strong smell that emanated from these toilets were smaller versions of the "condemned quarters" experience in Upper Farms in Buea.

There were three correctional facilities or centers in Buea. One south of Buea Town (Lower Farms), one west of Buea Town (West Farms that became the Boastal Institute—the correctional center for Juvenile Delinquents), and one north of Buea Town, slightly northwest of the Wonya-Lyonga Village (Upper Farms). If you took the western ascent to the Upper Farms and went past the Governor's office, the gendarmerie battalion, and the BICEC Bank to your left (now moved), you started ascending a steep hill in front of you. There was a first elevation and then a little respite, then a continuous elevation that increased in steepness as you advanced in your hiking.

"Condemned quarters" was called "Kondem Quata" in Pidgin. This was government housing for low-level government workers situated at the first elevation level. It must have housed ten or more families, some working with the Prisons Department as warders and others not. Detached from the main building that was partitioned to individual units for the respective families was the pit toilet. The units did not have their own toilet facilities, but there was rather a collective toilet, a public toilet to the right of the apartment building that was separated from the main building by the road that led up to the Upper Farms. The toilet complex, a pit hole complex, was a house that sat atop a humongous pit, a pit that received and stored all hygienic wastes from all members of the small Kondem Quata community year after year.

The stench that emanated from this toilet was legendary in about a 1,000-meter radius from the toilet complex, aided by its elevated position. Some nights, Buea was very cold and breezy, and the cold breeze swept the suffocating odor downhill, the downstream flow filling the air, but who cared about air pollution and what was air pollution? It was a foreign concept associated with the more industrialized nations with advanced economies and with industrial zones as we studied in Economic Geography; it did not apply to a nation like ours. The affected inhabitants grumbled in silence and aloud but to no avail because this was a government problem, and therefore, there could be no redress. In our Presbyterian School Buea Town, a.k.a. PSBT, we had some schoolmates and friends that were residents of Kondem Quata, and these poor kids bore the brunt of these pollution nuisances. Observations and phrases like, "a Kondem Quata Pikin (A kid from Condemned Quarters)" meant a lot and spoke volumes. Kondem Quata became associated with pollution, unhygienic conditions, and poverty.

Pit toilets were a favorite place for young mothers to dump their newborn babies, all wrapped up, sometimes alive and sometimes already dead. Some of such dumped babies were rescued if someone went to use the toilet and heard a cry from within the pit or perhaps just saw an unusual bundle in the toilet. In such cases, men would lower a ladder down into the pit and "rescue" the baby, dead or alive, and the police were normally called in to determine whose it was if the locals could not make a headway. Normally, the police would round up all the ngoh-ndoh ja walana in that vicinity and grill them with interrogations until they got their culprit. Rescued babies who survived and lived were named Wolowa, meaning toilet baby.

"E-Jay eeh (Come oh)! Neh-ni Mao-ngoh eeh (I have seen trouble oh). Neh-ni Mao-ngoh (I have seen trouble)!"

Njoh-k'a Moteh jumped out of bed immediately with his *e-szra-nja* (a seamless piece of cloth tied around in the semblance of a shirt, a traditional identity of the Wakpwes and the Bantus of Cameroon) that served as a pajama with the usual shorts underneath. It was about 4:00 a.m., and their compound was "dead," everyone in a deep sleep, and the first cocks had just begun to start crowing to signal the early dawn of another day. In such a still night, coupled with pitch darkness, any form of an alarm smelled of danger and something very serious. Besides, any mature and responsible adult could not afford to be an alarmist or not talk of a false one.

The alarm was certainly not from a child or a youth, for they normally would not leave their rooms or homes alone to traverse the yard in order to reach the toilet. They were always accompanied by an adult. Also, among the younger folks of our community, uttering a word in the pitch of darkness was considered as attracting attention and inviting the lurking devils and wa-i-emba to one's self. Dying in silence, therefore, seemed to have been the motto.

The small enclave that constituted Njoh-k'a Moto's turf was a semicircular formation that included three family homes and a common playground or front yard. Whilst these families had individual shower houses located immediately behind their houses, they all shared a common pit toilet located at the northwest corner at the fringes of their properties.

Njoh-k'a Moto and his two sisters had lived here all their lives. He was the last of the three, including the oldest sibling, E-lo-wa-lo-wa, and her husband and second sibling, I-wo-ta-mi. Iwotami had three grown daughters and was a widow. Her husband passed away five years ago due to a hunting incident in which he was attacked and mortally wounded by a troop of baboons. He was carried home from this hunting incident by his hunting partners, and all efforts to treat him and make him well again via the best Nga-nga in town failed after two months, and he transitioned to meet his ancestors gone before him. Another angle was that of zoomorphism in which he was said to have transformed himself into a baboon, but unfortunately, his transformation was not complete, so the other baboons in the troop could tell he was not one of them; thus, the attack.

On this same line, one of the hunters with him was thought to have blocked his total transformation, thereby exposing him to danger, and now that he was dead, the blocker now became the principal baboon hunter in the village. Iwotami had three daughters named Molo-ngeh, Etumba-tumba, and Ewoh-ngeh respectively. They were reproductively mature and active young women gone wild and out of control of their Iyaka's disciplinary powers. Their Mola, Njoh-k'a Moteh had to step in time and again to play the role of *ta'a-teh* (father), *mola* (uncle), and disciplinarian, even if just to keep her ndo-meh wa molana sane. He had to have been hovering over their shoulders to keep them behaviorally aright.

"Njoh-ku na way-li eh (Njoh-ku I am dead oh)! Njoh-ku na way-li eh (Njoh-ku I am dead oh)."

This was Elowalowa, Njohku's oldest sister, calling out for help in desperation. He was being summoned for desperate help at this ungodly hour of the day. Njohku ran out of his house, leaving the door open and a hunting rifle clutched with the right hand which he just loaded a few seconds ago and a lantern on the left hand. The cry for help was coming from the toilet direction, so he knew exactly where to head to, despite the darkness and the disorientation associated with waking up suddenly. As he rushed across the yard toward his ndomeh wa molana, he headed himself, saying "Ma-meh (What is it)? O-szro-ka Ngeh-ngeh (Do not be afraid). I-mba O-ngo Na'a-ja (I am on my way)."

Then Iwontami called out again, "Njohku, Nja'a-nu Ka-szri Ka-szri (Njohku, come quickly)," she beseeched her ndomeh wa munyana (brother). "Wanu Wa-i-emba Wa'a No'o-wa (These witches and wizards are about to kill me)."

At that, Njoh-k'a Moteh could feel the distress in his sister's voice, crying and pleading for help, and the Njohk'a Moteh had to not let his sister down and also not let down his reputation. Filled and rushing with adrenaline, he fired two warning shots into the air, illuminating the dark night, filling the air with gunpowder smoke at the same time tasting and swallowing the molecules of gunpowder. These warning shots were only meant to scare off Iwotami's attackers, but if need be, he would shoot to disable or to kill, depending on the situation. As he ran across the yard toward his sister, his eszranja fell from his waist, and luckily for the shorts inside, he did not have to worry about issues of nakedness.

As he continued running across the yard toward the action spot, and only for a split second, he thought he heard Iwontami say the attackers were Wa-i-emba. Did he hear her well or was he just imagining it? Either way, it did not matter now; those details would be sorted out later. For now, help was needed and requested for, and help it would be, and he would be the helper.

By this time, the whole neighborhood was awake, not just the Njohk'a Moto clan, and with torches and lanterns, a stream of adults talking excitingly amongst themselves were all headed toward the action spot. Breathless and already sweaty, Njohk'a Moteh reached the sister who ran out of the toilet and pointed hysterically to the middle door of the toilet building. The toilet building was partitioned, and each of the three matumba had their own segment. His oldest sister's family occupied the middle partition. Njohku shoved the sister behind him and approached the partially locked door and ordered whoever was there to come out with their hands raised above their heads in a surrendering gesture.

Njohku was in law enforcement, and as kids, it would seem the lingua franca for law enforcement was in the French language. Also, it was rumored that a series of recent robberies in Las Town was the handiwork of aliens or strangers from the Valley Mountains of the country because blatant day time robberies were a new thing in Las Town. In addition, it was claimed that they heard one of the members of the group suspected of committing these robberies speak in the Valley Mountain language, a language akin to the Njangilite language that was unmistakable. Valley Mountain people in the neighborhood protested, stating that other Cameroonians spoke just as much and as good Njangilese as the Njangilites. Njohk'a Moto's position in this community and public debate was made clear in the order he issued.

"Lève les mains et sort (Raise your hands above your heads and come out," Njohk'a Moto ordered. "Je suis armé d'un pistolet (I am armed with a gun)," he threatened and declared.

There was no compliance and only silence.

Njohku went on to remind them that "J'ai un pistolet chargé dans mes mains (I have a loaded gun in my hands). Je n'hésiterai pas à utiliser mon arme chargée si besoin est (I will not hesitate to use my loaded gun if need be). Vous venez d'entendre et d'assister à mon tir dans l'air sombre de la nuit et vous devez prendre cela pour votre premier et dernier avertissement et pour faire comme indiqué (You just heard and witnessed my firing into the night dark air, and you are to take that as your first and last warning and to do as instructed)."

Njohku went on to tell them this as he approached the pit toilet that served their small community.

All military and paramilitary training in Cameroon is done in French or so it seems. This is thought to be so because all Anglophones who return from such training become Francophonized automatically, and many of them forget completely how to communicate in English, Pidgin, or Mokpwe, and this forgetfulness is regardless of the duration of the training—three months, one year, three years, and so on. Njohku was trained as a paramilitary officer, and therefore, military-like orders and commands had to be effective in the French language. Until later on in life, as wana, we did not know that military communications or commands existed in other languages, only in French, we thought; though we also knew that the MORA (Mokpwe Occupier Resistance Army), or just simply the Mokwpe Resistance Army (MRA) of Kuveh and Moudindi, were commanded in the Mokpwe language. But because it was long ago, it seemed like a fairy tale, no different from the First and Second World Wars fought mostly in Europe.

The French speaking Las Townees in the crowd tried to persuade Njohku not to approach. "Les bandits kidnappeurs derrière la porte des toilettes (The kidnapping bandits are behind the toilet door). Pourrait être un piège (Could be a trap). Et ils pourraient être armés et dangereux s'ils sont des voleurs armés (And they could be armed and dangerous if they are armed robbers)," the Francophone brothers and comrades advised.

But Njohku was defiant and determined to knock down the door if they did not comply with his orders immediately. At the same time, the crowd was asking Iwotami how many men were there and if they were armed. They could not get an answer from her, for she just kept on repeating over and over, "Wa-i-emba wa-szra li no'o-wa. Wa-i-emba wa-szra li no'o-wa. (Witches and wizards are about to kill me. Witches and wizards are about to kill me)."

Among the assembling crowd and curious spectators were those who were asking what kind of attackers or thieves would make their base or operational quarters the toilet.

"Maybe dem go tif (Perhaps they went to steal) and then dem follow dem (and then they were pursued) and then dey run hide for toilet (and then ran and are now hiding themselves in the toilet)," someone in the assembling crowd offered in Pidgin.

In no time, the no-nonsense Njohk'a Moto reached the building, knocked down the toilet door with one kick, and exposed the elevated toilet seat in the interior made of concrete and a wooden cover. His kick was so hard that the toilet cover fell off, and the nearby spectators who followed closely behind Njohku with flashing lights could see adhering fresh and dry shit in the inside corners of the toilet. The crowd commented on that briefly and blamed it on the children or a careless adult and then once more returned to the issue at hand.

Njohku did not see anyone inside. Njohku quickly backed out and proceeded to forcefully open the other two doors of the adjacent partitions, and still, there was no one in sight. He ordered that the other men check behind the toilet building to see if there was anyone there. Their search was to no avail as he had expected. Njohku did not think anyone could escape from the toilet building from the back walls except if a back wall was broken down, and there was no evidence of that. But he also thought that if truly they were wa-i-emba, they had the capability of passing through walls without constraints, for they were spirits that defy physical laws.

The crowd went still and quiet after he fruitlessly searched the toilet building, returned empty handed, and walked toward his still trembling and hysterical sister, Elo-wa-lowa.

Njohku and the sisters tried speaking the Mokpwe language among themselves as much as possible, but for the most part, they spoke in pidgin. This was a Mokpwe litumba, but because their abode was in Las Town, the Mokpwe language was normally not the first language of choice, except during an initial shock of danger or when privacy was required.

"Did you see anybody inside there?" Njohku asked, and before Elowalowa could answer, he added, "Was there anyone in there with you?"

"Yes," Elowalowa replied, trembling due to fright or cold or both. And then she added, "I told you, they were Wa-i-emba."

"Did you see the Wa-i-emba?" her sister, Iwotami, asked her with an irritated and impatient voice.

"You do not see wa-i-emba, you moron, but you can sense or hear them," she retorted in defense and with an air of superiority over her sister when it came to the spiritual.

"So, what did you sense or hear?" Iwotami asked.

"They turned into muambala and are in the toilet, and as I sat down to clear my insides because of my running stomach, that is when I heard them," she concluded.

"You still have not told us what you heard!" Iwotami shot back angrily.

"I heard the muambala crying because they were going to kill me at last, just as I have been seeing in my dreams. This running stomach to bring me out here tonight was all part of their grand plan. The one crying was probably sympathetic to me, maybe someone I have been good to. You know, I give my kwacha to lots of people for free who cannot pay or are hungry and also give others for credit. Perhaps it is one of them who do not want me killed but is part of their group." Elowalowa was surprised with herself that she could speak so coherently and with such composure, considering what she had and was going through and amidst the poking by her sister who meant to discredit her.

"How did you know that it was a muambala that was crying?" someone in the crowd asked.

"I saw it in the toilet, opening its mouth to take in my moe-wa as it was passed out. When it takes in moe-wa that comes directly from the human body, then it is used in evil ways that results in the death of the person who passes out the moe-wa (feces or shit). I know of this because it has all appeared in my dreams." Elo-wa-lowa was in professorial gear and was going to use this moment to protect her credibility in their quarter.

"So did you shit?" a Mot'a munyana in the crowd asked, and in unison, all the walana present hushed him down and threatened to accuse or charge him of titikoli. Titikoli is a taboo in Mokpweland. Any reference to a woman's hygiene by a male is taboo. It is punishable by fines and or exclusion from the village or town. Cases of Titikoli are charged and judged by women's court. Such courts are operated solely by women. No titikoli case taken there ever returns a "No Guilty" verdict. If a case was referred to the court by a molana, it was a done deal. Normally, the accused man, his family, or friends opted to settle out of court. Settlements took the shape of a fine in monetary terms and buying stuff for all the women in the village e.g. salt, palm oil, bag of rice, etc.

The chief judge of the women's court who normally was the women's chief of the village or quarter and her fellow judges and jurors, in addition, got monetary compensations. The abused woman got the lion share of the cash penalty and some of the other products that come with the guilty fine. All wu-nya-na (men) accused of ti-ti-ko-li are almost certain to be judged in absentia. Attendance by a mot'a mu-nya-na in a ti-ti-ko-li court for trial meant being surrounded by hostile village walana (women), being ridiculed, being insulted, and being exposed possibly to naked bodies of the oldest walana in attendance. The mba'a-mbas, as they are called, may expose their nakedness waist up right up to the accused face, an accused trapped in a sea of angry and unsympathetic walana, who already know that you are guilty. An exposure to naked mba'a-mbas was considered an omen of bad luck. A guilty verdict is always certain. While there are select jurors and chief judge in a titikoli court, all village walana in attendance are jurors and judges, aggressive and loud ones for that matter. Wu-nya-na accused of titikoli thus normally opted for an out-of-court settlement. They negotiated to pay the fine from afar through intermediaries, but they never plead guilty. Their decision to instead settle out of court and trial, they argued, was because they were not guaranteed a fair trial.

More often than not, a respectable and elderly member from the family of the accused munyana, with status of a patriarch or near patriarch status, fronted for the accused and will quickly send word of settlement to the Chief Molana Judge of the Village Titikoli Court or the VTC. While the village titikoli court served as a bridle to wunyana with *Abelmoschus esculentus* (okro or okra) and diarrhea mouths, it was also seen and considered by the wunyana as a payback of some sort. Okro or okra (a.k.a. gumbo) are normally used in the village to make soups that are used for "swallowing-foods" that are generically called fufu or vuvu in West Africa and posho or matooke in East Africa. Swallowing foods are soft and need easy transportation without resistance down the i-go or esophagus. Soup made from or-kor-loh (gumbo) "draws" and is slippery, thus good for swallowing wak (food). If it was thus said that you had an okro mouth or diarrhea of the mouth, it meant that you needed a bridle like a horse to keep your vocalizations in check. For many centuries, walana and wana in Vakoland and of Mokpwe origins were not allowed to eat eggs. For the wana, it was argued, if they started to be fed eggs, they will start stealing. The walana were included in this ban because the wunyana had concluded that if the walana were allowed to eat eggs, then they, the walana, will surely give their wana. It was also culturally unacceptable for walana to eat gizzards and the sternum portion of any nyama (animal), especially the nyama ja wa-nga (bush meat). The titikoli courts were thus seen and perceived as ngi-nya ya molana (woman power), one that was used wisely and fairly, the walana will say and a ngi-ya ya molana that was mostly misused by the walana, the wunyana would say. It was common for a molana to make as a joke threat to a munyana to drag him to a titikoli court. It was ngi-nya (power) and ngi-nya has no gender, no color, no age, no social status, for ngi-nya was ngi-nya.

Matumba (families) of accused persons opted to settle out of court because not settling was not an option or rather, not a wise option. Failure to attend a titikoli court summon and/or failure to settle out of court could lead to very humiliating circumstances no respectable litumba (family) in the village will want to undergo, be associated with, or be known for. The worst-case scenario is if a titikoli caravan marched across the village to your family home or clan property. Immediate neighbors in villages are always close family members, siblings, and first cousins, and some others not too far removed, and therefore caravans visited clans and not a home. It was therefore in the interest of the clan to be quick and proactive in calling for a settlement and proposing an out-of-court settlement and fine.

"I think the muambala is still there, and perhaps if we keep quiet, we will hear it cry again. Or perhaps if you opt to go and *nya* (defecate), then you will experience what I experienced. And then you will become the insane or hallucinatory one. Do you want to try?" she asked the anonymous male crowd inquirer.

Njohk'a Moto went back into the toilet and looked into the pit and thought he saw something out of place. At his request, he was handed a lantern which he lowered as far as he could get a better view of the interior of the pit. Despite the heavy stench he encountered, he stayed calm and held his breath, concentrating instead on the job at hand. He thought he saw a bundle but was not very sure. He went on to use a rope and tied it to the lantern's handle and then lowered it as far down as the length of the rope would allow and specifically toward what he thought was amiss in the toilet.

The lamp touched the bundle and coupled with the brightness it produced, from the bundle emanated a cat's cry, loud enough for him to hear, even if not audible enough for the others around him to hear. Njohk'a Moto jerked backward, more in surprise as to being afraid. His worst fears may be realized or were being realized already.

"There is something down there," he declared, and at this same moment a prolonged, loud, and distinct cat's cry could be heard originating from the pit, and the crowd surged backward in fright and confusion.

"Na szro-wi (Didn't I say it)?" Elowalowa declared triumphantly and at the same time mockingly, mocking the *ngindi* (crowd) that had been making a mockery of her or at least just plain doubting her. While Elowalowa and her supporters were vindicated that there surely was a li-emba muambala in the toilet, others were talking of a very wicked Moto who would want to do such harm to a muambala. Others simply said the muambala must have fallen in the toilet pit in pursuit of the Chihuahua-sized rats associated with communal toilets.

Because of his size, a bigger opening was required if Njohku was to be able to enter the toilet. Using home axes for splitting firewood and other appropriate heavy-duty destroyers, the wunyana hammering furiously with anxiety and excitement flattened the elevated toilet seat and then proceeded equally quickly to widen its now flattened orifice or aperture to be able to accommodate and afford a passageway for Njohk'a Moteh. In their hammering away of hard and reinforced concrete materials in fury, Njohku kept on reminding them to be mindful of heavy debris falling inside and causing damage to the desired bundle, thus they proceeded with caution, though fast with hands carrying away structural material chopped away from the floor of the toilet.

While others thought that a muambala was not worth destroying a toilet, it was evident Njohku thought and seemed to know otherwise. Njohk'a Moto had ordered for a ladder, and one was ready for him by the time the hammering away of concrete was completed. He had to ask for a second ladder from his own backyard because the first one provided was not long enough for its intended purpose. He lowered the ladder and, with difficulty, was able to anchor it and stabilize it. He climbed down into the toilet while the head of the ladder was supported and held tight in place by other men who remained at the surface level of the toilet. Njohku was very cautious with his descent because he knew that any mistake or any accident would mean he would be struggling for his own life and drown, wading in a pool of moe-wa. Landing on the bundle could also as well mean unintended murder.

He quickly dismissed what he called negative and comical thoughts and instead concentrated on the job at hand. Njohk'a Moteh had hoped in vain that he would not have to leave the ladder, reasoning that by just stretching his hand, he would reach the bundle, grab it, and climb out of this hellish hole. But as it happened, the lowering of the ladder and Njohku's weight on the ladder as he descended produced some surface waves that caused the thick top layer of the shit mixture to move, and with it, the movement of the bundle further away from the ladder and now nearer the walls containing the pit. Thus, when Njohk'a Moteh reached the interface level of the ladder and shit mixture and stretched out his hand, it dawned on him that he would have to swim in thick smelly shit in order to reach the bundle. It also meant he would have to abandon the support of the ladder and take a walk from the bottom of the pit, i.e. its ground zero, so as to reach the bundle.

Earlier efforts to use some hooked stick to try and hook the bundle and pull it to himself had failed and instead resulted in pushing the bundle further away from him. He stopped at the interface of the ladder and shit mix and pondered for a while and made every effort to overcome the psychological aspects of it, which now seemed to be playing a huge part in his brain. The men hovering over him urged him on, "Eh-ndeh (Go or continue)," but he ignored them, instead concentrating to decide on the best course of action. While he was not responding to external communication, the surface assembly was divided in their thoughts, and various opinions were being floated and attempted to be sold.

Njohk'a Moto had been accused of Nyongo before and also of zoomorphism, and therefore, some in the crowd opined that he was the one trying to kill his nduh-meh wa molana, Elowalowa, while another school of thought was that the mua-mba-la (*Felis catus,* domestic cat) in the wolowa was actually Njohk'a Moto's—that is, his zoomorphic state. As a consequence, Njohku's hesitancy inside the wolowa seemed to be lending credence to the fact that he was communing and/or communicating in a zoomorphic way.

Njohk'a Moteh waded through the thick soup mix of shit with difficulty, barely being able to carry his own weight in addition to the resistance provided by his immediate milieu. He decided that if he was going to survive, he must start breathing again and therefore prepare himself for the stench and toxins he was going to inhale. He started pushing forward, stretching his hand ahead of him with the hope of touching and then grabbing it, but it seemed the nearer he got, the farther away the crying bundle moved, kind of backing away from him. The shit he was wading in was chest high, so he had to stretch the muscles of his neck so as to have his head as high above the shit as possible. Eventually, he thought he was going to come to an end, and the crying bundle was now backed up against the wall of the wolowa which he had now cornered.

He put in his last efforts against the thick soup, dragging his legs and entire body, which seemed like he was carrying loads of fifty-kilogram bags of cement. His fingers at last touched the bundle as he figured out how to get hold of it. His large hand enveloped the bundle about three-quarters its circumference, and he was convinced that he had a good grip for a return trip to the ladder. While he descended into the wolowa via the middle partition, he found himself under the right adjacent partition because of the "waves" that moved the bundle away from the center. He estimated that he had at least three meters to accomplish his return journey, and while this seemed like miles away, given the circumstances, his having the mystery bundle in his possession was motivation enough to forge ahead, mindless of the obstacles.

The shit or moe-wa (feces) he was wading in was chest high. He carried the bundle on his right shoulder and supported it with a firm hand grip. He used his left hand to chart his way back to the ladder. About halfway back to the ladder, two fighting Chihuahua-like rats landed just short of his face and splashed some thick shit all over his face, and he lost his balance temporarily.

"Weh-neh wio-meh weh weh-toe (These giant rats)!" he cursed under his breath and spat out that which entered his mouth and continued more or less furiously to the bottom of the ladder. He climbed the lower steps of the ladder under the shit, and while on the ladder and the shit only at knee level, he could stretch his hand out of the wolowa and hand the bundle to those at the floor-level of the wolowa above him. He thus called out for assistance as he projected the bundle above his head and onto the exterior.

"Eee Wo-nya Moe, Eh-no gwa-nay (My kinsmen, help me)," he cried out.

When those on the exterior saw the emerging bundle, they did not seem to know what to think, neither did they seem to know what to do. At this brief instant of frozen or limbo state of hesitation by those on the exterior nearest to Njohk'a Moto, a long and loud cry emanated from the bundle. At this point, the surface helper who was holding the oil lamp that illuminated Njohk'a Moto's subterranean travels exclaimed "Ta'a-ta eh!"

This was an exclamation of wonder, surprise, or fright, which simply meant "My father," i.e. calling on your father for an explanation or rescue as the case may be, but it could also mean calling on your ancestors at this instance of need.

And without hesitation, the surface lamp holder dropped the lamp as they all surged backwards and ran out of the wolowa building to become part of the crowd of onlookers gathered in the courtyard.

"May-gwe-gweh na woh-lor-kor (The fearful and weaklings)!" Njohk'a Moto said. Njohku struggled up the ladder with one hand, and when he was close enough to the floor of the wolowa, he gently placed the bundle on the surface and then climbed out himself. Chest downward, he was covered with shit, and above the chest level, he was splashed with shit. He was practically covered with shit, which was a combination of fresh and old shit with varying colorations and an accompanying intensity of scent and odor which also seemed varied.

"See dat Mu-nchi man (Behold the Munchi-man), A mua-na in the ngi-ndi," the assembled crowd said.

Munchi men drained pit toilets directly, and they also drained toilet reservoirs in the case of water or flushing toilet systems. It was a manual task normally accomplished at night, and everyone wondered where they hauled the cake-like or soup-like feces to. Thus, munchism was associated or related to shit carrying or shit work and at other times associated with any work related to hygiene disposal, including dumpsters.

Njohk'a Moto shook off what he could and then picked up his bundle with both hands and held it across his chest as you would a baby. He then stepped out of the toilet partition and started walking his way slowly and deliberately scanned the crowd assembled as he approached the courtyard. The assembled wato was equally silent and as Njohku moved slowly toward the center, the silent and expectant wato that he approached moved away from him simultaneously, keeping him in view and creating a passageway, which was eventually closed behind him as the ngindi enveloped him by the time he got to the center of the courtyard.

Besides creating a walking path for Njohku, there were those who were just plainly afraid of the Nyongo-man and the li-emba that was unfolding in front of their eyes. There were also those who had to make way because of what their eyes were beholding. A man of elephantine proportions covered with shit and smelling like stale shit was not a regular sight to behold. But instead of running away for good, they all stayed to witness the end of this witch saga, for it was going to be the talk of the town, and none present wanted to miss any details, talk less of the end, so they stayed. The "ekwakoko" question still remained. What was in the bundle?

Njohk'a Moto walked his way to the center of the courtyard and gently put his "precious" bundle down and proceeded to do some more primary cleaning of himself, sputtering shit (feces) all around him and attracting insults to himself from those whom he sprayed with some shit.

"E-neh yoma Nyama (This animal)!" they said. "A-ma-nja di Mot'a Moe-wa (He has become a shit man)," they added.

The ngindi around him had resumed being chatty in an excited and expectant mood, and there were calls for Njohk'a Moto to open his bundle grew.

"Li-fvo-wa lo'ow-ba (Open the parcel)! Li-fvo-wa lo'ow-ba (Open the parcel)!" the ngindi urged him on, becoming impatient as the climax of this saga neared.

He raised his hand for silence, and when this was attained, he declared and said in a loud voice, "Szre-ke-teh mua-mba-la (What is inside the bundle is not a cat)."

"O-ma ma-meh eh (What did you just say)?" the ngindi asked Njohku, wanting him to repeat himself or just making sure that they heard him well, loud, and clear.

"Szre-ke-teh muambala (It is not a muambala that is contained inside the bundle)," he repeated.

"Way-nga Mameh Szro (So what is it then)?" the ngindi demanded in an irritating manner, becoming more and more impatient with their Njohkeh.

Njohku held on to his captive audience and knowing perfectly well he was in control, and the attention he had meant power. He was used to power and attention, something he had missed ever since his retirement from the tax office. He was therefore not in a hurry.

"Li-emba la-ngoh (Is it your li-emba or witchcraft)?" an irritated and angry voice shot up from the ngindi, getting clearly tired with the suspense and waiting game and also taking this opportunity to make it clear what the community thought of him, Njohk'a Moto, of being a Li-emba.

Njohku ignored him, concentrating instead on the job at hand, thinking of a most proper way of breaking and unveiling the mystery contained in bundle that he also wanted to be theatrical about.

"Mua-na wa Mot'a Weh-na-ma (A human child)," Njohk'a Moto said.

"Mameh eh (What did you say)?" the ngindi asked again, not that they did not understand, but just for confirmation and to ensure that they were still conscious and therefore in control of their mental faculties.

"Muana wa Mot'a Weh-na-ma," Njohk'a Moto said again, swaying the wrapped parcel laterally in a gesture to show or expose the external to all present. Eyes, heads, and bodies swayed to the left and to right, like leaves and branches during a storm, avoiding not to miss glimpse of what was being exhibited before their own eyes.

There was dead silence, and then he asked the ngindi, "Na li-fvo-way lo'o-mba (Should I open the bundle)?"

"Eeh li-fvo-wa (Yes, open it)," the ngindi shouted back in unison, some clearly irritated with the delay tactics of Njoh-k'a Moteh.

Then the wana took it further from there. "Li-fvo-wa. Li-fvo-wa. Li-fvo-wa (Open. Open. Open)," the crowd cried in a chant.

A semicircle had formed in front of Njohk'a Moto. He moved closer and made the semicircle walk with his bundle still uncovered, but this time, the ngindi did not back away from him and his stinky situation, which should have been more intense by virtue of his proximity to the ngindi but did not seem to matter after all. And all of a sudden, he made his semicircular round, without opening his surprise, and then returned to his central point position, which served as his podium.

He started to peel back the external plastic wrapper but left the internal blanket intact. The external wrapper was coated with shit, and while the bundle was plastic-wrapped, the face portion seemed perforated, allowing for air diffusion but this also meant passage for liquid shit onto the below content. Njohku then lifted high the muana who, at this instance of exposure, started crying exactly like a muambala with fraying arms as is characteristics of newborns when they cry. The exposed content had shit on its face and hands so that the arms fraying and mouth opening during crying meant that shit got introduced into the gastrointestinal tract of the muana. There was a deep breath and an initial silence across the ngindi, and then, when the ngindi overcame its own shock and awe, the excited chatting started all over again, this time louder as in the Big-Mot-Market in Mutengene, Vakoland.

Iwotami rushed toward *mua-nyan-gwe-ni wa munyana* (her brother), that is, Njohk'a Moto, relieved him of the muana, and wrapped it immediately with the eszranja she had atop her kawa or sleeping gown and equally rushed it back into her *ndawo* (house) for cleaning and care. All this while, the muana cried just like a cat would do, apparently suffering from the "cri-du-chat" syndrome. Cri-du-chat (cat's cry) syndrome, also known as 5p (5p minus) syndrome, is a chromosomal condition that results when a piece of chromosome 5 is missing (deletion). Infants with this condition often have a high-pitched cry that sounds like that of a cat.

It was about 6:00 a.m., now almost two hours since this saga began, and the pitch darkness was giving way to the first rays of light and the saga was over and the mystery partially solved. The assembled ngindi had to return to their respective homes to prepare to start the new day—getting wana ready for school, readying for market, going to the farm, going to productive and legitimate employment, etc. The conclusion of the saga the ngindi now knew rested in the hands of the Njohk'a Moto's litumba and possibly the local police. But at 6:00 a.m., it was too early for any police officer to be found on duty. The dispersing ngindi was not, however, unanimous in their conclusion thus far. There were two main camps or schools of thought: Zoomorphism versus Murder. If it was zoomorphism, it seemed pointed directly at Njohk'a Moteh, and if it was murder or more correctly attempted murder, then the arrows were pointed at Iwotami's household and most especially to Molo-ngeh, Etumba-tumba, and Ewoh-ngeh, Iwotami's adult daughters. The school of thought, regardless, the dispersing ngindi knew and were expecting that on their return home later this day at the close of their irrespective businesses, they would get some sort of concluding information about the bizarre events of this morning. Their concern was that not being present during the conclusion meant they got secondhand or perhaps third-party information to complete their respective narrations. This had the potential for different conclusions and ultimately different stories.

For the walana who believed that the bundle was a muana wa Mot'a weh-na-ma, their primary worry seemed to have been if the muana was going to survive. Before they left Njohku's enclave, a group of five walana went into Iwotami, opting to assist in any way and manner and strongly suggesting that the muana be immediately taken to the nga-nga. While it was Iwotami's intention, she reminded them that at this hour, there was no nga-nga in the nga-nga to attend to a muana, so she would have to wait, clean the muana, and subject the muana to treatment based on her own trado-medical expertise. Then if it became necessary later that morning, she would take the muana to the nga-nga.

One of the last persons from the ngindi to leave for work was a manofarms already dressed in his paramilitary uniform and visible side gun attached to his waist band. Menofarms are rural police in the French law enforcement system, and this one lived down the road from Njohku and was attracted to the action spot like the rest of the ngindi by the gunshots earlier fired in the night starry sky by Njohk'a Moto, and since as he was on his way to work out of town, he stopped to find out what the matter was. He reached the saga spot before Njohku climbed out of the wolowa, and determined to see the end, he stayed and watched even at the expense of tardiness to work. When at last he had to leave, he simply said to the hearing of all around him, "Les Bakweris et leur sorcellerie (The Bakweris and their witchery). C'est comme dans mon village de WonyaLikaytie (It is like in my village of WonyaLikaytie)."

This negation or negative comparison between the Bakweris and the peoples of WonyaLikaytie was not to go unchallenged. The observer and commenter was some relatively young military personnel, probably in his early twenties, and he was "Un officier, sous-officier;" that is, a noncommissioned military personnel (NCO) commonly known as "sans galons." As their street name in Pidgin, that is "sans rang," without rank in French.

The sans galons and other higher ranks of noncommissioned military and paramilitary officers are the "low-streeter" law enforcers that worked for their "patrons," the "up-streeter" bosses. Street law enforcement bosses are apt to commonly being called or referred to as "patrons." Sans galons and their patrons were disliked, and this dislike, which sometimes verged onto hatred, was directed and targeted to these law enforcement officers but mostly the sans galons and other noncommissioned officers, for they were the ones in the community, and they were the ones in the streets and neighborhoods extorting a poor and powerless people for the benefits of their patrons and themselves. "Powerless" people terrorized and exploited in their own native land by their own scouts and menofarms.

This sans galon's comparison of the Bakweris and the "WonyaLikayties" of his village, vis-à-vis witchery, was not to go unchallenged and unchastised.

"Cenq Cents Manofarms, who are you (Five hundred francs officer, who are you)?"

These officers in uniforms that terrorized the citizens did it all for the sake of their bellies. Because at the end of the day, whether you were wrong or right, guilty or not, they still extorted the Cenq Cents from you or multiples of five hundred, depending on what they considered the gravity of the "offense." The Cenq Cents was the settler and answer at all times. Taxi drivers that had all their particulars (documentation) were in more trouble than their comrades without complete documentation. For if you had your complete documentation, it meant no cenq cents for the menofarms, and it also meant big Sasse Grammar on your part toward the menofarms.

This was a waste of time for the menofarms, the taxi driver, and the passenger in the car, waiting to be transported to their destination as they stayed by the roadside inside the car, while the taxi driver and the cenq cents manofarms or menofarms, as the case may be, haggled.

This was bad business for all concerned, and this was known by all. It was thus best to just settle the Cenq Cents and go about your business. For the passengers in the taxi would normally urge the driver to "settle," and a driver who resisted the "system" was sure to get bad publicity by the same main street population that was being exploited by the Cenq Cents Menofarms.

"Do you think this is WonyaLikaytie? We do not have li-emba and nyongo here as you have in WonyaLikaytie." The challenger went by the name Mor-nor-noh Gbwua, a well-known bricklayer in Las Town and a footballer when he was in Presbyterian School Buea Town. He was very muscular with unmistakable signs of skeletal muscles hypertrophy. He was reputed to be very powerful by virtue of his trade and his size. His peers at the Presbyterian School Buea Town were Eddy Malange, Bafia Nkangson, Tamfu Achidi, Nfor Achu. They were all big boys, being powerful, and therefore feared at the primary school level. We referred to them or answered them as "sah," because we were kids as compared to them.

All of these big boys were in the school football team, even if they did not a play a full match. Their fielding was much more of energy and fear occupants, rather than skills. There used to be lots of fighting among primary school pupils during competitive sporting activities, especially football (soccer). For example, Presbyterian School versus Government School Buea Town, Presbyterian School versus RCM (Roman Catholic School), Presbyterian School versus Ecole Francophone, etc. Thus, the Mor-nor-noh Gbwuas were essential and became handy. Mor-nor-noh Gbwua was a native of upper WonyaLyonga who moved to Las Town for business purposes.

"Take your Cenq Cents gun and khaki and leave this place." Then he added in conclusion, "You Nyam-fuka."

Before Mor-nor-noh Gbwua was done saying "Nyam-fuka," he was advancing toward the Cenq Cents Manofarms who was wise enough to extricate himself from the ngindi (the assembled crowd), running away in the opposite direction that was to have led him to work. At the Presbyterian School Buea Town (PSBT), during long break or interval as we called it (this was actually the lunch break), classes five, six, and seven (approximate equivalents of grades 4, 5, and

6) all played football (soccer) at the central field that bordered and was adjacent to the main public road that led to Buea Town. These classes five, six, and seven were called the senior primary classes unlike the junior primary classes that closed for the day at 1:00 p.m. or 1:30 p.m., depending on whether the class was low-lower level or high-lower level. The senior primary pupils closed for the day at 2:00 p.m. (It is noted that class seven no longer exists in the educational system that we knew; the primary level of education now ends at class six.) At the Presbyterian School Buea Town, each class or grade had two classes, usually designated—for example, as class 5-A and class 5-B. These classes were normally adjacent to each other, sharing a common wall as their border. The walls were not soundproof so often the happenings in one class were *recorded* by the pupils of the other class. Long break football (soccer) matches were normally class A versus class B, of the respective classes—that is, pupils of same level of education and about the same ages. In special situations, there were cross-class challenge football matches, which were not normally organized during long breaks but perhaps after class and/or the usage of a physical education (PE) period.

We all wore the same uniforms: white shirts and navy-blue khaki shorts. The *white shirts* for the most part were anything but white given the identicality of our wears, recognition of who was based on familiarity. In a normal football (soccer) field, the capacity is a total of twenty-two players combined from both teams, eleven players each. In our long break, soccer matches the whole class played if you were able to and you were interested, this meant that class A, for example, could have more players than class B or vice versa, and it also meant that one class—for example, class six—could have more than twenty-two players total on the field.

So, you had three games going on at the same time on a field with a maximum capacity of twenty-two players. If we assume an ideal situation of twenty-two players per class, then we had a total of sixty-six players on a field with a capacity of twenty-two pupil players. Because we all wore the same uniform, it would seem like confusion and chaos to an outsider onlooker. However, no, it was perfectly organized even if you prefer to call it organized chaos.

Each class had their own ball, and it was rare to have two classes having balls of the same color. The soccer balls we used were not provided by the school; it was individual students who were rich enough and very kindhearted and eager to share a game with classmates, who brought their footballs to school. It was not common for a class not to play a football match during a long break if none of the pupils came to school with a football. So, because balls came to school at random, the chances of the same color were very rare. When it rarely did, markers were used to deface or "grafitize" the ball from the junior class. Our balls were all plastic balls, but the class seven folks sometimes had a leather-ball-like one used by professional teams and the school team. Of course, we also used size and familiarity to recognize ourselves as a class and to further distinguish who was class A and who was class B.

The oldest pupils were in class seven and, to a lesser extent, class six. As the higher classes on the field, they ruled the football (soccer) field in its organized chaotic state. While the football pitch was for "all" to use during long breaks, there was a strict pecking order that had to be observed. This meant that class-seven pupils had priority. If the soccer ball of a lower and younger class happened to wander into the space of the class-seven pupils, or within ten to twenty meters of the class seven's current playing space, the ball of the junior class will be kicked at will by the senior pupils. The senior pupils kicked the junior class' ball anytime they saw fit, so long as they thought the ball was in their way, and therefore a disturbance, a nuisance, or a distraction. It should be noted that not all senior pupils had the audacity to kick the ball of a junior class. It depended very much on how powerful you were, which went with age, how accommodative you were, and your exhibited level or degree of bullying. A class-seven pupil who kicked the ball of a lower class must ensure that he was powerful enough not to be challenged by any member in that lower class right there in the field, or outside the field, after school. Nevertheless, the opposite could not be true. A younger pupil dared not touch the ball of a higher class, accidentally or not, except if you did not like yourself. You were dead meat. If a younger and junior student dared to touch and be touched by the ball of a senior class, you most likely went home crying at the end of the school day—crying that accompanied you all the way home.

When Mor-nor-noh Gbwua was in class seven, he was the school's half fullback defender. He was like a bulldozer, who clears the way for the fullback defender to clean after his mess or more correctly carnage in a fine finishing. Mor-nor-noh Gbwua was a like a freight train or a Nyama-Ku-ndu as he was referred to in Pidgin. A Nyama-Ku-ndu is a carterpillar roller used to level roads or used to smooth the surfaces of paved or ground (dirt) roads during road constructions or road repairs. Mor-nor-noh Gbwua had blood vessels that were and seemed extraordinarily large and very superficial. He looked like a stringed youth with a dominantly hypertrophied skeletal musculature.

Mor-nor-noh Gbwua decided one late morning (our long break period, which is at about 10:30 a.m.) to have fun with our class five ball that came his way—meaning that was a nuisance depriving him from concentrating on his senior class game. He met the ball and used his very powerful right leg and kicked the ball as hard as he could high into the air very effortlessly.

Like I said before, junior pupils cannot complain (for it was grumble in silence and stay), but just wait patiently for the ball to come back to the earth, or you junior pupils went into the nearby bushes to retrieve your ball (like bird-hunting retriever dogs) and then continue from there.

I was a defender for my class; and on this day, when Mor-nor-noh Gbwua, an adult youth pupil, decided to send our ball into the heavens, I was on the opposite side of the field. Mor-nor-noh Gbwua kicked hard at the ball this time into the air above and not deliberately into the nearby bushes. The ball *flew* from his defender goal post onto my own goal post on the opposite side of the field. The size of a football (soccer) field is about 100–110 meters long and 60–70 meters wide, so it had to take an adult youth pupil to catapult a ball for that distance or pole-to-pole, as we would say. Initially, as the ball hovered and staggered over all the pupils on the football pitch, it really did not seem it was my business. I was just waiting for it to land and for us to continue. Then as all the heads and the eyes lifted up to the sky and followed the leisurely motion of the plastic inflated balloon, it only took a couple of seconds for it to be evident that the ball may after all be my business.

"Moighai Bwanghai, Moighai Bwanghai…Head'am. Head'am!"

I was in a state of reverie, pleasantly lost in my thoughts, daydreaming and just fixated on the ball in the air above as it hovered and staggered oblivious of the fact that the ball's course was actually and practically directed at me coming to me and inviting me for action. As the main full defender for my team or more correctly my class section, my team and expectant pupil mates expected and needed their defender to head the approaching ball away from our goalmouth or what we called *clearance*. But for a defender who was lost in thought and not seemed ready for a defensive header away from his goal post (or eighteen, as we popularly called the *danger area*—the eighteen meters semicircle that constituted the inner space of the goalkeeper, where he can catch the ball with his/her hands. Any foul play here is an automatic penalty; the goalkeeper faces the kicker or striker alone. This is always considered a sure goal but not always, for there are those occasional misses that are very costly), his comrades had to wake him up or retrieve him from his reverie.

"Head'am. Head'am! Head it. Head it," they urged their defender comrade who was still nonresponsive.

"Moighai, I say head'am! Moighai, I say head it," the oldest boy in our class, who was our goalkeeper, finally commanded me to head the ball.

Still, in my trance, I jumped into a heading position and met the ball full force in midair, and then I returned to the earth on my buttocks with a loud thud on moist grass.

The whole field seemed to have gone quiet and silent. There were no verbal congratulations, and neither were there congratulatory well-done taps on the upper back shoulder areas—such gestures that normally come with a fine or difficulty safer.

Though I was still in my reverie, my eyes were still very functional, but I did not see the ball anywhere ahead of me in the distance for my header to qualify as a safer. While I was visually conscious of my immediate environment, my auditory faculties seemed to have taken leave of me, if only temporarily. I saw folks' lips moving, and they were pointing at my direction as I sat on my buttocks on the moist grass that covered the field with a thin underlayer of black mud that was characteristic of the mountainous volcanic soils of the Vako at whose feet Buea was located. For a second, I thought, I instead headed the ball into my own goal post—the one I was supposed to defend. It is a taboo for a player to score into your own goal in the name of defending, especially for a defender.

Our goalkeeper, the older boy in our class coming from behind, lifted me to my feet by his relatively large, hard, and rough palms; and as I turned and looked at him, his lips were moving with a combination of a smile grinning and a laugh on his visage. When I faced him, he was pointing at my ears, so I moved my hands onto my ears. They were not my ears I touched, but I touched what seemed like a military helmet covering my enclosed head. The goalie, whose name was Mu-szro-ngoh mo Wio-kwe-li, urged me to remove the "helmet" through sign language. I quickly complied and went ahead to delicately remove the encasement of my head. The helmet encasement was our class ball, the one Mor-nor-noh Gbwua had sent to the heavens. On its return to the surface of the earth, as it descended with great velocity, it collided forcefully with my bony head; the ball exploded, and somehow and perhaps mystically, it wore itself perfectly onto my head making me a perfect helmet that covered my ears. My cranial and facial skull bones were so pronounced that collision with an unreinforced plastic matter was certainly of no consequence, harm wise. My reverie continued.

The big news for that day and for future years was Mor-nor-noh Gbwua—the kicker of the football that exploded. It was not about the helmeted header, the junior defender of class 5-B.

In later years, folks narrated the story to me telling me how the ball exploded in the air like a gun or fireworks, not mentioning the collision with the defender. I was told my own story, and I heard my own story being retold with the addition of pepper and salt mystifying Mor-nor-noh Gbwua and erasing the part of the header defender. How many people knew that they were narrating my own story to me with all the convenient modifications? I never attempted to correct anyone, for I was a keen listener.

When the ngindi had all dispersed and Njohk'a Moto had cleaned himself, he immediately summoned a meeting in his house of his two *ndoh-meh ja walana* (sisters), Elowalowa and Iwotami, his three nieces, Molonga, Etumba-tumba, and Ewongeh, and the wolowa retrieved muana. He was sweaty, breathing heavily and abnormally, and generally fuming. His breath smelt of afvo-fvo (a.k.a. kai-kai, push me I push you, ogogoro, vor-vor), the illegally brewed concentrated gin drink. He sure did need this to try and calm his nerves, but with his fuming and pacing around the room, it could not be told if the vor-vor agitated him or calmed down his nerves. All were seated and in silence except for the cat-crying muana in Iwotami's care.

Njohk'a Moto proceeded dispensing of all mannerisms and courtesies or protocols. "Murder is a crime among Wakpwes and the government, punishable by *nkweli* (death). Attempted murder is not punishable by the Wakpwes but with the government it is accompanied by a long jail sentence. However, with the Bakweris, it is a source for a permanent family stigma, like suicide. Bringing dishonor, shame, and ridicule to our Njoh-leh Clan is not tolerated and therefore not acceptable."

Njohku only spoke in English to his nieces and nephews. While his Mokpwe was fluent, his nieces and nephews barely understood fragments of the Mokpwe language. Thus, effective communication had to be in English or in Pidgin. Communicating in Pidgin would have been beneath his level, so Sasse Grammar it had to be.

"Disturbing the peace of the quartier (*quartier* is quarter in French. As it is with a sizable number of Cameroonians of the northwest and southwest, French words creep into their sentences easily, and they seem to be totally oblivious of this mix and may even argue at times that words like *quartier* were actually English words) and disrupting their daily routine are bringing about public disorder. Subjecting me, Njoh-k'a Moto ma Njoh-leh, to occultism suspicion—that is, being in Nyongo or having li-emba—is not respectful and is not tolerated."

While Njoh-k'a Moto ma Njoh-leh laid out the stage for the purpose of the meeting he called, he was pacing all the time in his parlor while his invitees sat quietly, wondering what was coming. The "riot act" he laid out was not addressed to anyone in particular, and he made sure he was not making eye contact with anyone in the room. When he was done, he stopped backing them all and remained in this position for about three minutes. The tension in the room was palpable. Then he turned, suddenly all red-eyed and with evidence of perspiration.

"Nje-neh (Who)?" he asked. "Nje-neh a-gbwe-yi e-nay-ya ya mao-ngoh (Who did this terrible thing)?" he further asked.

From their faces and body language, Njoh-ku already knew who it was, and his suspicions all along were about to become true; he was about to vindicate himself.

Elowalowa started calling the young women by their names. "Are you the one?" Or as she said it "O-Wa'a?" Their auntie Iya Elowalowa spoke only Bakweri to them, and she expected them to respond or communicate with her only in the Mokpwe language. Living in Las Town was no excuse for Mokpwe wana not to know their ancestral language, and it was her position and was certainly no reason to adopt "Las Townian" mannerisms.

"Molo-ngeh OWa'a (Molo-ngeh talk. Are you the one)?" she asked her.

"Szre-ke-t'I-mba, na-szra li-ti (I am not the one. I am not pregnant)," she responded.

"E-woh-ngeh O-Wa'a (E-who-ngeh talk. Are you the one)?" she asked.

"Naliti, di na-szri-yai (I am pregnant, but I have not delivered a baby yet). Naweni lou-nga nor-meh-neh (I am still pregnant)," she concluded.

Elowalowa took her time, seeming to deliberately increase the level of tension that already existed in the room. The silence and all the eyes now turned and gazed at Etumba-Tumba.

Trembling with rage, Njoh-k'a Moto shouted out her name as an end to this saga and rather long and unusual morning, "Etumba-Tumba?"

She tried to bolt out of the room via the door, but her Iyaka, seated by the door, simply stretched her leg, and Etumba-tumba came tumbling over. That is what we call "kwacking." Njoh-ku was over her in no time and dragged her by her hair back to her seat and then asked again, "Ma-meh nde-nga-teh, ma-meh nde-nga-teh (Why, why)?"

"I did not kill the baby. It was dead when I threw it into the toilet," she explained.

"You did not intend to kill the muana, yet no one knew you had a newborn baby?" Iwotami asked. "Did any of your ndo-meh ja walana know?"

Taking turns, E-woh-ngeh and Molongeh denied any knowledge of her having a baby.

Asked whether they knew she was pregnant, they all responded to the affirmative.

"Let your consciences be your judge. We will treat this matter as in-house, and not a word of this conversation to anyone. I will go to the police and tell them the child was accidentally dropped into the wolowa by its mother when she was shitting with the muana in her arms and she fell asleep due to a medical condition, not disclosable. Etumba-tumba reported the muana falling in the wolowa immediately, and that resulted in its rescue. Any other story narrated by anyone else will be treated as matter of speculation." He would need to visit the menofarms office also to meet with the commandant. Njohku knew he had to visit both the scouts and menofarms offices because oftentimes, there seemed to be contradictions in their roles or rather competition for who had the authority and who did not have to be left out of the "makala parti" (bribery) polished and packaged as "lobbying" in some other societies to make it palatable and politically correct, and acceptable as an operational norm.

It was not uncommon for a citizen to go report someone to the scouts, and the scouts sent a summons or convocation to the accused, and then the accused turned around and reported his or her accuser to the menofarms and the menofarms too, sending a convocation to the original complainant. It was who you knew or, better still, which of the law enforcement agencies you did makala parti to. Normally it was expected such issues as the wolowa that one be handled by the scouts, and yes, it was the responsibility and duty of the scouts. But with the advent of the menofarms force, the "law" seemed to have deliberately made their roles and duties blurred to the advantage of the "law enforcing agencies" and to the disadvantage of the citizenry. Njohk'a Moto knew this just too well, just like all adults knew. Njohku also knew that the "sans gallon" manofarms from WonyaLaytie who had witnessed this early morning saga and by virtue of his proximity to the residence of the Njoh-leh clan was sure to report or bring to the attention of his commandant back at the office for several reasons, including being a "good subordinate" who reported lucrative situations to his boss, putting him, a sans gallon, in the good books of his patron and also the real possibility of him being remembered for a small cut when the Makala parti was eventually made and realized.

What we called "sans galon" was actually meant to describe military or paramilitary officers without epaulets or without an externally visible rank on their person. They were either new recruits or older law enforcement officials who had not satisfied their "masters or patrons;" that is, superior high-ranking desk scouts who expected "returns" from them, extracted directly or indirectly from the local population. To meet their financial quotas to their heavily "epauleted patrons"—that is, the desk scouts and desk menofarms—they terrorized their people, the very ones they were meant to protect and serve in order to extort them.

Njohku therefore knew that "settling" with the Scouts and not also with the menofarms very much meant that his niece would end up in a cell until he was able to make Makala parti accordingly. Makala parti was a street norm by law enforcement agents who dealt with the local populations. Makala parti was identical and no different from the court of law in which "justice" meant the best lawyer or best defense. Yes, the best defense meant justice. Justice and rights thus remained elusive. But as the menofarms would ask, "Qu'est-ce que la justice, quels sont les droits (What is justice and what is rights)?"

"Nous définissons et représentons les deux (We define and represent the two," the menofarms would say. "Vous devez vous conformer et suivre (Yours is to comply and follow)," they would finalize with an air of "authority" and rather brute power only associated with the possession of a gun. They had the gun, the power, and the "law" on their side.

Once I had confronted a scout about makala parti choku business while we were in a taxi from Molyko to Buea Town, rather naively, and he "educated" me. Why was I picking on them? Then he proceeded to enumerate; entrances to professional schools through concours (competitive exams), treasury workers, tax collectors, ministries, etc.; he had pointed out and then he seemed to have concluded, "Pourquoi nous seulement, petit frère (Little brother, why us only?"

I had no answer. I was a high school pupil. This man could deal with me any way he wanted, and there would be no recourse. After all, who was I? Just another "no-nothing," a "nating man" as far as the law was concerned.

We were in a taxi, and in my silence, he added, as if talking to himself more or less, "Les chefs traditionnels créés par le gouvernement (Traditional rulers were created by the government)."

And then as I left the taxis, having reached my destination, he concluded, "Les terres de Fako volé par des bandits supérieurs et desbandits de rang inférieur en collusion avec des chefs créés (Fakoland was stolen by high-ranking and low-ranking bandits in collusion with created chiefs)." And then the taxi driver summed it all up like this: "you just have to be a party carrying card member, be loyal to the party, be an advocate for the party overtly and loudly, challenge no one in the upper ranks of the party, and be in the good books of the party bosses. Then anything law does not apply to you." In other words, you become a lawmaker, an operative of the justice business, a law enforcer, or a person of high social status, for they are the law.

It is, however, noted that law enforcement officers were extracted from the same population with the same values and same expectations. They were, thus, a reflection of their community.

The child survived and was named Wolowa. E-tumba-tumba was nicknamed correctly or incorrectly Nkwel'a Mua-na, or in pluralistic form, Nkwel'a Wana; that is, someone who causes the death of a child or just simply a "child killer." There were other instances before now that lent credence to this naming. While Wolowa was the official name of the saved muana, as he grew up and other wana got to learn of his story, they instead called him Mua-mba-la. We somehow thought that there was muambala in him or he was a muambala in Moto (human) form. My ndohmeh wa munyana mombaki had tried to explain to me that Wolowa's condition was the "Cri-du-chat syndrome."

Whatever that meant, I had no clue, and then instead argued that he was a human cat. Wolowa remained a mystery child, and as kids, we were all kind of afraid of him and sometimes encouraged by older family members to stay away as much as possible from him, for there were still those who thought of him as a li-emba associated mystery of Njohk'a Moto. Staying away from Wolowa was not really a problem with us kids in the part of the village.

Wolowa lived in Las Town and only visited our village as an in-law time and again. His auntie was married to the ace footballer, Tiya Efvumeh, who was our neighbor. Children played freely and commonly together in our village, and we especially wanted to show visiting kids how good we were at whatever we engaged in with them. Mua-mba-la, with time, had kind of gravitated toward me and therefore was sure to have a playmate whenever he visited.

The other kids took practical steps to avoid him. It was predicted that I was soon to start crying like a cat by virtue of my association with Mua-mba-la, and also, the mysticism that was associated with him was thus going to be part of my own loaded and growing portfolio in the yowo realm. Wolowa is today called Wolason instead.

CHAPTER 17

Walana wa Njuma

As earlier mentioned, the Eszrong'a Maykomba clan was one easily, and often, associated with public fighting and insults. It was either one of the wu-nya-na in the clan was beating his molana or it was the walana-in-laws fighting, specifically Efvumeh's sisters-in-law and molana on the one side and Efvumeh's *ndoh-meh ja walana* (sisters) on the other. Efvumeh, the football star, found himself always caught between these groups of walana who were an integral part of his life and whom he evidently loved very dearly. That the Efvumeh clan landed property was an open amphitheater for public dramas, that all of the characters were played by members of the Efvumeh clan, and that the directors and executive directors of all performances were members of the Efvumeh family was well-known. There was to be one last drama as a final farewell to Tiya Efvumeh, and this time, it was Efvumeh's wife and sisters-in-law versus the Efvumeh family.

This has always been the pitching setup, but this time, it was different. The moral pressure on the Efvumeh clan was enormous, and some members of the Efvumeh clan were sympathetic and silently sided with the crazy in-laws or just were plain neutral.

Fourteen days after Efvumeh was buried and the other after burial rites accomplished (the Szra-Szras) according to Mokpwe traditions, customs, and culture, a team of four walana left Las Town to ascend the hills of our village, WonyaLyonga (a.k.a. Pa Ecor Village, but sometimes also called Wo-nya-Libiyeah if the emphasis or reference was based on our immediate clan, which was considered not part of the village because we were situated at the very start of the village with characteristics that were not akin to the rest of the village that subsequently followed), our village, to make a public statement. It was an intended public statement of tradition—that is, comme d'habitude and perhaps also one of mourning and grief from a sincere position.

A trio of the four molana team made the advance trip, Efvumeh's widow and two of her grown up adult nieces. Efvumeh's widow Mokuszra had exiled herself from Wonya-Lyonga immediately after the burial. She was incensed by the Efvumeh family. Later on, I learned from Gbwido Matoe that she claimed it was Gbwido Matoe's ta'a-teh, King'a Walana, who killed Tiya E-fvu-meh through Nyongo, a form of witchery understood and thought to have originated from Jangiland, also known simply as Jangi. So, throughout the funeral preparations and activities and before, there was an obvious strained relationship between them, and this tension was extended to the larger Efvumeh family.

Nyango Mo-ku-szra and two of her sisters, Molo-ngeh and Ewoh-ngeh, ascended the hill that constituted our village and went to her house to pick and pack some things that they were to return with to Las Town after the spectacle they had planned.

Nkwel'a Wana, the third sister of Nyango Mokuszra, was to follow later and as usual, accompanied by kids; one strapped behind, another strapped in front directly facing her, and one on either side of her—these ones she pulled as she moved along, oftentimes insulting them with her usual vulgarity when she thought that they were slowing her down. For reasons already stated, Nkwel'a Wana's ascent of the Pa Ecor Village hill was particularly slow as she took it upon herself to engage anyone on her way that provoked her or anyone she perceived not to be friendly. She was sure exhausted by the time she ascended the hill and reunited with the other team members, and they were sure late to start the show based on their plans.

The most important thing was that she was there and that their plan was to proceed. They needed this show to relieve themselves of the venom that was accumulating inside them. But Etumba-tumba's—also known as Nkwel'a Wana—ascent was not as quiet and uneventful as they had planned, for she still managed to pick up a few "fights," trading insults with kids who dared call her kids names associated with poop-eating.

I must have mentioned earlier that Tiya Efvumeh, the village and regional football hero, was another wife-beater like his older ndomeh wa munyana. His molana was from a portion of Buea called Las Town, meaning "Last Town." This was the city limits on the south-side of town. It was inhabited by *wajili* (strangers), it was stony, dirty, cramped with lots of bars, crimes, and other vices and next to the market. Children who emanated from Las Town were stereotyped in school and other social gatherings. It did not seem that anything good could come out of Las Town.

Efvumeh's molana, Nyango Mokuszra, was from Las Town, was very well-endowed at the *nge-ngeh* level (chest level) and she was not short either. She was tall but kind of stout with a very much protruding nge-ngeh portion. She was Mokpwe (a Bakwerian) but could not speak the Mokpwe language, so we only talked to her when one had to, and occasionally, when our paths crossed in the narrow village roads, in Pidgin English. Nyango Mokuszra came from a litumba of loudmouthed walana and who also did not seem to know the meaning of shame. Whenever her ndo-meh ja walana visited our village from Las Town, it was like a market with vulgarities being exchanged as they updated their ndo-meh wa molana of the latest in their home and Las Town as a whole. I did not get the feeling that they were very welcomed in the village, for they were a subject of much conversation and gossip by both the adult wunyana and walana.

Tiya Efvumeh hardly spoke, but we knew from the football pitch and in the administration of his household that he was certainly a no-nonsense man. I do not know who beat the molana more frequently, he or his *ndoh-meh wa munyana wa mombaki* (older brother). What surprised us as kids was that Efvumeh was a lanky man and his molana was heavyset, which we equated with physical strength. Nyango Mokuszra's strength, however, seemed to have begun and ended with the talking and the blowing of hot air. She was smart, though;

oftentimes, she started her verbal assault of Tiya Efvumeh from outside their house and was ready to run to the downer or any neighboring compound for shelter once as Joe came out charging. If she managed to get to another yard, Efvumeh did not pursue because she had "sought protection," and it would have been against the Mokpwe culture to still seek to punish someone who had sought protection from you, especially *wa-mba-ki wa walana* (older women).

If a molana or a mua-na took "shelter" behind a *mo-mba-ki* (an elderly person), it was considered automatic protection; they had placed themselves under the protection of that person. If in the pursuers' anger the "protection trust" was violated, it resulted in a fine that must be paid and quickly too. You were also thought of as having no respect for your elders and the traditions and culture of your people. This was not good because you could become hunted one day, even if not physically, needing the protection of wa-mba-ki and also claiming protection as guaranteed by native customs and traditions.

Sometimes Nyango Mokuszra did not run fast enough to claim protection, and the athletic Tiya Efvumeh caught up with her before she reached her intended destination and dragged her back to their house by the collar of her neck for admonishment and discipline. However, if any of Efvumeh's *ndoh-meh ja wunyana ja wambaki* (older brothers) were around, she would scream and curse to the top of her voice to the unavoidable hearing of one of them. Any of the ndohmeh's that was around would come out and put an immediate stop to it. They knew how to handle or rather discipline their *ndoh-meh wa munyana mo-szra-li* (younger brother), and he evidently respected them.

Efvumeh's children were also very sympathetic with their Iyaka. Unlike Nyango A-szra-toh Maijeh's wana, when King'a Walana was beating or fighting with her, Nyango Mokuszra's wana did less of the crying and instead would rush to alert one of Efvumeh's ndomeh ja wunyana to come to their Iyaka's rescue. Why Efvumeh's *ndoh-meh ja walana* (sisters) did not seem interested or supportive was not apparent. However, they also came to their *monya's* (sister-in-law's) rescue but perhaps not with rapid results as their ndomeh ja wunyana.

They, unlike their *ndomeh ja wunyana* (brothers), would be critical of their *monya wa molana* (sister-in-law) in the open and publicly make it clear that her behavior was unbecoming of a molana of our village standard.

To our amusement, such exchanges between the monyas or sisters-in-law sometimes ended in a munyana-molana confrontation as a new molana-molana conflict came to life. At which point, Efvumeh would simply shake his head and return to his home. The war of words among the walana would continue. Sometimes we were ordered to leave the drama scene, partly because of the vulgarity that was exchanged. When we were not ordered to leave, it usually ended with Efvumeh standing in front of his house and commanding Nyango Mokuszra to return home with alacrity. I thought Mokuszra always waited for this moment because facing two monyas ja walana at a time was no easy job, especially in their turf when they would spare no opportunity to let you know that you did not belong and remind you always of your Las Town origins or heritage and, therefore, lowly estate or inferior social status.

As children, we remembered vividly what we called Tiya Efvumeh's "Las Fight" (the last fight). This was a phrase we all learned from watching Chinese action movies that normally, expectedly, and predictably ended with a sometime poorly orchestrated last fight. It normally took the pattern of the actor (main character) having a bloody mortal combat in the martial arts (which we commonly called karate) with the "Chef Bandit" or "Patron" (the last, the most powerful, and the leader of the bad dudes). After the patron's associates were all killed, then it was time for the one-on-one between the actor (principal/lead character) and the chef bandit.

What made us laugh was the nature and portrayal of some of the patron's associates who normally numbered in their tens. When the actor was beating the hell out of one of them, the others did not attack but rather would be dangling around the actor in circles with funny expressions on their faces, just waiting for when it would be their turn to be beaten or "killed." They dressed funny and also looked funny, with chicken-like, long, dry and bony necks with a dominance of the Adam's apple. Sometimes these she-she characters had a long tuft of hair on some out-of-place spot on their visage that increased their funnier and comic looks. We did not think that these tufts of hair, like the one found on the chest of the *Meleagris gallopavo* (wild turkey), was natural but rather a creative costume design plant. Their roles seemed to have been clownish, and we called them "she-she." Eventually, we used the word *she-she* to either refer to a weakling or a funny looking fellow.

When all the she-she were killed or mortally wounded, then it was the turn of the principal character and the chief bandit. Many a time, though, the "she-shes" were not "mortally" wounded and neither were they "killed;" it was just simply such that when they received an initial thrashing from the main character goodfella, they all ran and abandoned their "patron" or "chief bandit" when the principal character attempted to come their way for a second or third round of whooping. They normally ran, tripping over each other, and sometimes with busted pants that exposed their under buttocks. The last fight or combat between the principal characters we called the actor and the chief bandit usually ended with the chief bandit being killed or rarely arrested.

The combat normally started on an even footing, and then an "unavoidable" mistake was made by the patron, which then gave an upper hand to the actor for the rest of the fight. Sometimes the director of the movie made it so sloppy or so one-sided that we left the cinema hall in disappointment, thinking that the chief bandit was not treated fairly and actually concluding that the chief bandit was more powerful than the actor (lead or principal character). We only made such conclusions if the actor was a lesser-known one. We could say no such thing or make such conclusions if the actor involved Bruce Lee or Jackie Chan.

Nyango Mokuszra was for all intents and purposes not a fan of her sisters-in-law, and they too were very obviously not a fan of hers. Nyango Mokuszra got comfort and sympathy only from her brothers-in-law, especially the most elderly, King'a Walana. King'a Walana's down house, which was his own residence, shared by his second and elderly wife, was also home to Kinge's wana from the Wokwai molana, and very importantly home to the aged patriarch, Eszrong'a Maykomba. Tiya Efvumeh, the last child of Szrango Mola Eszrong'a Maykomba, was the patriarch's jewel, his "Joseph" of the Holy Bible.

In our culture, the oldest child, and particularly the son, takes primary responsibilities for aging parents, the rest of the siblings playing associate roles, more or less. This was understandable considering that there were normally decades in age difference between the first child or first children and the ones bringing up the rear. In fact, it was not uncommon for the oldest muana's own first and sometimes second muana to be older than his or her younger siblings were. Thus, a niece or nephew could have aunties and uncles that were younger than him or her, making the use of words or appellations of "uncle" or "auntie" awkward.

This led to further complexities in which an older cousin had kids of her own, older than a much younger cousin. Our society is very respectful, so the use of prefixes is very important and must be precise. Thus, a much younger cousin may find himself or herself referring to her much older cousin as "auntie," for example, just so that the younger ones are not seen to be disrespectful.

Tiya Efvumeh was such a sibling and such an uncle. King'a Walana was a defacto ta'a-teh to him, and his aged ta'a-teh was housed and taking care of Mola King'a Walana. The King'a Walana household number one was, therefore, the power center and center of all authority and commanded all the respect due it in all corners of the clan. Thus, Nyango Mokuszra knew that if she could just manage to get to King'a Walana's house, she was safe from the brutal punishment that came from her munyana's hands.

King'a Walana's own residence was southwest of that of Efvumeh's. You descended a hill to a plateau topography a distance of about seventy-five meters on sometimes stony terrain. This was the southern limits of the Eszrong'a Maykomba clan property and the path from the northern territory to the south was wide for a village pathway and could have easily accommodated a vehicle. This meant that it was a good running track for speed but also a track that it very possible and easy for one being pursued to be caught or stopped. Whenever Nyango Mokuszra had to run for her dear life, she left an in-law house opposite theirs and ran down the path to her intended destination, going past two other in-law homes to the right and hut-like in-law abodes to the left, adjacent to what served as the graveyard for Patriarch Mola

Eszrong'a Maykomba clan. The hut was owned by one of Efvumeh's nephews who was older than Efvumeh and who was popularly known as Molali. Molali left his molana and muana there to work in Muyuka and only returned occasionally as a visitor.

This day was a Friday, and Tiya Efvumeh had returned from an overnight duty shift as a warden. This overnight shift was not planned for, so Tiya Efvumeh worked grudgingly all night. Their normal schedule was two weeks nights and two weeks day shifts. Tiya Efvumeh had finished a two-week rotation and returned home a very tired and exhausted man on a Tuesday. He therefore slept in all of Tuesday and the better half of Wednesday and was well-rested. With a boost of energy, he decided to go hunting early Thursday.

Tiya Efvumeh was a hunter who specialized in small game animals that abounded the slopes and hills at the foot of the Mount Vako. His favorite game to hunt was the Kor-ti or the grass cutter, and while he used hunting as a relaxing sport, he also looked forward eagerly to the pepper soup that was made out of the catch and the remainder that would provide some nyama or meat to his family of five in the next couple of days.

Thryonomys swinderianus goes by the common names grass cutter, cane rat, or cane cutter. It is a wild hystricomorphic rodent (the porcupine larger group) widely distributed in West-Central Africa and exploited in most areas as a source of animal protein. This micro-live-stock species is a favorite of pepper soup kitchens and goes under the holistic and collective name of bush meat. Kor-ti, as *Thryonomys swinderianus* is known in the Mokpwe language by Wakpwes, is a delicacy and a cherished catch of a hunting trip. A normal hunting day saw Tiya Efvumeh return home with two animals as we always wondered how he did it. Sometimes he went hunting with his footballer (soccer) teammates of Prisons Buea Social Football Club.

While Efvumeh specialized in the Kor-tis, our own junior league hunting club specialized on the Kwai (*Francolinus camerunensis*; the partridge or bush fowl), the bush fowls. Late afternoon, Thursday, Tiya Efvumeh returned from his hunting trip that started about midmorning, tired but happy with his catch. When he reached home, there was a message waiting for him that the chief warder had requested that he report for duty that evening for a night shift because of a shortage and that he, Efvumeh, was to treat this request as urgent and very important. Chief Warder Eto'a Lila, who was of dual origin from Wo-nya-Likao and Wo-nya-Ndaa all of Vakoland, was not liked by his subordinate junior workers because it was open knowledge that he was using the Prisons department for his own personal gain and could care less for the prisoners and workers that were put under his care and control. He was known to be an untouchable because his powers were rooted in Ewonda, and he hailed from the Lila-Lila Villages of WonyaLikao and WonyaNdaa.

Tiya Efvumeh barely had enough time to get ready and be present at his workplace by the 6:00 p.m. mark when shifts changed. We commonly say in Pidgin that "order pass power." This means that it is not how physically strong or powerful you are that matters, but rather that "orders" supersede "physical power or physical strength" at all times. Tiya Efvumeh was more powerful and could crush Eto'a Lila with his bare hands, so he had the power or rather the physical strength and the athletic physique that accompanied it. Eto'a Lila was the smallish one but wrapped in the power from Ewonda. Thus, Eto'a Lila had the upper hand, without him speaking English nor Pidgin, nor the Mokpwe language.

Because "order pass power," Efvumeh obliged and was a grumpy fellow all night. He could not wait to return to the comfort of home and settle down eventually to his Kor-ti kill. While Nyango Mokuszra was said to be a good cook, Tiya Efvumeh made it a point of duty to prepare in any form all of his catch and controlled portions consumed by each member of his household. Tiya Efvumeh had three wana—one *ngoh-ndoh* (female youth) in the middle, and two *wana wa wunyana* (boys). The wana wa wunyana longed and looked forward to their ta'a-teh's hunting trips and his eventual cuisine that followed and accompanied them.

Normally, Efvumeh effected the preparation and preservation process of his *nyama wa-nga* (bush meat) only hours after returning from the hunting trip, but this time, he had to abandon his kill and head to work as ordered by his superior officer. Because he had to leave in a hurry, he left everything in the li-kwe-nji, the Mokwpe traditional male carrier backpack with straps made of cane and used for the back storage and transport of bush cargo back to the home. These included his kor-ti, water bottle, and other things required for a bush-hunting trip. He returned home Friday to a welcoming stench of decaying flesh, the putrid odor of decaying organic matter, and evidence of spoilage of his kor-ti that had been left unattended in his absence.

Microorganisms such as fungi and bacteria abound in the wet and humid tropics and are common causes of meat spoilage. These microbes present in meat cause proteins and fats to break down, spoiling the meat, and their populations could reach levels that are unsafe or unsavory for human consumption.

When Tiya Efvumeh entered his house, he was greeted by the smell of decaying and rotten meat; that is, composed largely of cadaverine (pentane-1,5, diamine) which is formed by the decarboxylation of protein amino acids known as lysine. Efvumeh was home before 7:00 a.m. because the morning shift begins at 6:00 a.m. He had enough time walking on foot to get home before 7:00 a.m., a time when most of those who were sleeping in would still be snoring and wrapping up dreams, good or bad.

Nyango Mokuszra was still sleeping, and so was the entire Tiya Efvumeh household when he returned. It was the norm. Fuming with anger, he rushed to where he had left his li-kwe-nji in the *ki-sz-ray-ni* (kitchen) and opened it up, quickly hoping that he was just suffering from some kind of olfactory hallucination, but it was for real—the decomposition of his nyama had begun. "Li-nye-ngeh, Li-nye-ngeh, Li-nye-ngeh (Flower, Flower, Flower)!" Efvumeh yelled to the top of his voice, angrily.

Efvumeh called his wife, Li-nye-ngeh, and he seemed to have been the only munyana in our village of WonyaLyonga to have had a pet name or romantic name for his molana. The other wunyana of the village simply called their walana by their first names or last names as the preference seemed to be. Those of the yesteryears generations simply called their wives "Molana" or "Woman."

These three calls that were more like shouts woke Nyango Mokuszra suddenly, and as if she was experiencing some nightmarish situation, she jumped out of bed, ran out of the house shouting, "House di burn!

House di burn! House di burn (The house is on fire! The house is on fire! The house is on fire)!" she repeated herself over and over.

"Shot-top, di house no dey for fire (Shut up, the house is not on fire)!" Efvumeh said rather harshly and impatiently. "No start brin people dem for here dis sharp, sharp morning (Do not start assembling a crowd here so early in the morning)," Efvumeh added. "Na me i-bidi call you (I am the one who called you)," Efvumeh continued.

Nyango Mokuszra "petized" as Li-nye-ngeh was a Mokpwe molana, but growing up in Las Town in an immediate family that did not make the speaking of the Mokpwe language a priority and a must and by virtue of growing in an environment out of the family confines where the Mokpwe language was only occasionally heard, she grew up like her other siblings, understanding rudimentary Mokpwe but unable to speak in a manner that could sustain a meaningful conversation, especially one that required details and with lots of expressive words in order to convey comprehensively, and in totality, what needed to be conveyed and said.

Considering that Efvumeh did not go to Saint Joseph's College, Sasse, in Buea and also that Li-nye-ngeh did not go to Saker Baptist College in Limbe, Pidgin, the lingua franca of West Africa, was the means of communication in the Tiya Efvumeh home. Pidgin was used among the parents and children. This was frowned upon by many a parent in the village who felt scandalized that children being brought up in the village were not given the opportunity and were not being taught the language of the ancestors. Their identities were therefore being robbed from them by their own parents. Nyango Mokuszra was to blame and only a small blame to Szrango Tiya Efvumeh.

"Cam back inside house (Come back inside the house)," Efvumeh commanded Li-nye-ngeh. "Cam for kitchen ya (Come into the kitchen)."

When she reentered the house, Efvumeh invited her to the *ki-szray-ni* (kitchen) and then proceeded to ask her, "You nobi see dis kor-ti dem way I-bi killa'm yesterday (Did not you see these kor-tis that I killed yesterday)?"

"And so waiti (And what about it)?" Li-nye-ngeh replied in a challenging manner.

"You say waiti (What did you say)?" Efvumeh asked her.

"I beg Efvumeh no brin me bad luck this sharp sharp morning (I beg of you, Efvumeh, do not bring me bad luck so early in the morning)," Nyango Mokuszra continued. "You be tell me make I touch'am (Did you tell me to touch it)?" Li-nye-ngeh asked him. "You di ever, ever leave me, make I touch your hunting kor-ti nyama dem (Have you ever allowed me to touch your kor-tis you bring home from your hunting trips)?"

Nyango Mokuszra continued to interrogate Efvumeh who was now quiet and boiling inside him the more Nyango Mokuszra spoke, being on the offensive and putting him, Tiya Efvumeh, on the defensive.

Efvumeh, who had been mostly quiet, cut in and in rapid succession kind of rested his case. "So, you be sabi say di nyama be dedey (So you knew that the bush meat was there), but you just decide say you no go do anything (but decided you will do nothing about it)? You decide say you no go touch'am so dat make e spoil (You decided not to touch it so that it will get bad)? Na so (Is that it)?" Efvumeh concluded and wanted an answer.

"Efvumeh, Efvumeh, na palava you want'am dis sharp-sharp morning so (You are looking for trouble and problems so early in the morning)," Li-nye-ngeh said to Tiya Efvumeh, her munyana, but this time, her tone was not challenging because she realized that her munyana was boiling and this was not going on well for her in any way. Was her earlier adversarial approach now already working against her?

"Just leave me make I do my morning work (Just leave me alone so that I can do my morning chores)," Nyango Mokuszra pleaded.

"Which kind woman you dey sef (What manner of a wife are you even?" Efvumeh shot back.

"Na woman whey i-nodi fear you (It is a woman that is not afraid of you)?" Nyango Mokusrza also shot back. Evidently, she could not hold back or perhaps she did not just want to show Efvumeh that she was scared.

"You say waiti (What did you say)?" Efvumeh asked, approaching her with dilated veins all over his face and upper limbs.

Nyango Mokuszra knew what was coming, so she bolted out of the house as fast as she could, knowing that Tiya Efvumeh would be just a step behind her.

Adults of Tiya Efvumeh's immediate neighbors, who were for the most part family members, were already out in their verandahs, just waiting to see how this exchange was going to end and somehow predicting the next move because such exchanges between Efvumeh and Linyengeh had a predictable pattern, like a protocol or manual that was adhered to religiously. It did not seem that it was in their interest or thoughts to intervene at this stage so that it did not proceed or escalate to the next stage. The next stage being physicality.

Before Joe could leave the house in pursuit, Nyango Mokuszra was already approximately fifty meters down the road, headed for her father-in-law and most elderly brother-in-law's house, for there was her refuge, awaiting to shelter her. But Nyango Mukuzra's *may-nya may walana* (sisters-in-law)—that is, Nyango Likoweh and Nyango Litakay who knew the routine too well—also knew that if they stopped their sister-in-law from reaching her safe harbor, then their *ndomeh wa munyana,* Efvumeh, would have the opportunity to teach this rude and mal élevé las town molana who had no place in their village and who only brought disrespect and shame to the Eszrong'a Maykomba clan.

Though heavyset, Nyango Mokuszra was running, and being that it was downhill, it helped with the speed and the relatively limited amount of energy required. The second family clan house to her right down the hill was the residence of her sister-in-law, Nyango Litakay, and the rock hill behind it was the residence of Nyango Mo-tor-wu mo Wana; that is, King'a Walana's second and younger resident molana, the lanky molana from Wokwaongo who seemed to have gotten more than her own fair share of beatings from her munyana.

Mor-tor-wu's three wana were Bwido, Maliya, and Wio-leh, in decreasing order of their ages, and the last two were *wana wa walana* (female children). Between Nyango Moh-tor-wu mo Wana and her three wana, their library of Mokpwe insults and the use of vulgarity seemed to have surpassed the equivalent collective of all other homes in our western part of the village. As the Tiya Efvumeh saga was unfolding, Maliya was awake and stood on their hilly vantage position, looking down at what could have been properly described as a "valley" that contained a large view of their clan's landed properties. She could thus see above and over Nyango Litakay house with a total and good view of the road that now served as emergency passage for Nyango Mokuszra.

"Iya Mokuszra Ta'a-teh Efvumeh mo'o-ngo aja'a! Iya Mokuszra Ta'a-teh Efvumeh mo'o-ngo aja'a!"

In Mokpwe culture, there are no paternal uncles. Paternal uncles are fathers, but maternal uncles are the uncles they are and, therefore, referred to as Mola; therefore, the word Mola, if used properly, means maternal uncle. In our culture, when a ndomeh wa munyana passes on, his *Mokuszra* (widow) will be redeemed by one of his *ndoh-meh ja wunyana* (brothers). If there was none in the immediate family, then the *szra-ngo-wa* (redeeming offer) would be extended to other family members. If you were szra-ngo-wa a Mokuszra, then you inherit all of her wana of the previous *li-Wa'a* (marriage)

Thus, Maliya was warning and urging her auntie-in-law to increase her speed to safety, reminding her that Ta'a-teh Efvumeh was just a step behind her. Because in Mokpwe culture, we do not have "aunties," for they are mothers, so auntie was equally a mother, be it a blood auntie or an in-law auntie. Maliya thus called her Nyango Mokuszra "Iya," short form for "Iyaka," which means mother in the Mokpwe language and culture.

"Iya, wa'a-nga! Iya, wa'a-nga (Iya, run! Iya, run)!" Maliya continued to urge Nyango Mokuszra on. "Naweleh Ta'a-teh wami King'a Walana (I will call my father King'a Walana and alert him)," she reassured her, if only she could make it to safety.

The Eszrongo Maykomba Clan property was bisected horizontally and vertically by roads, making almost four equal quadrants. Of these four quadrants, they owned three with the exception of the lower right quadrant. About 70 percent of the family lived on the upper right and left quadrants while the remainder of the clan lived on the lower left quadrant. Mola King'a Walana and her ndomeh wa walana Nyango Likoweh lived on the lower quadrant. Nyango Mokuszra's destination was the lower left quadrant, which meant she had to go past the residences of two of her sisters-in-law, Nyango Litakay who lived at the lower portions of the upper left quadrant, and then Mokuszra would have to cross the road, go past Nyango Likoweh's property before reaching her father-in-law, Mola Patriarch Eszrong'a Maykomba, for protection.

This day and early in the morning, Nyango Litakay had an errand to take care of very early in the day, and she left home when it was still dark. She was thus returning to her home only to meet the unfolding drama that now seemed characteristic with their family; that is, a "comme d'habitude." As young Maliya's voice pierced the morning air with sharpness and clarity, the urgency in her voice and the desperation could not have been missed by anyone within range of hearing her. Litakay knew where the target was headed to, and considering that she was headed that way also, only that she was coming from the south and headed north, she quickened her pace and steps and then found herself running up the hill with the sole aim and goal of cutting Nyango Mokuszra, ensuring that she did not get to her intended destination. Perspiring and out of breath, she was now at the lower limits of Mola Walana's property while Mokuszra was at the upper limits of Likoweh's property, so she decided to call out Litakay to come out and be part of the efforts meant and designed to stop Mokuszra from reaching their ta'a-teh. In other words, to cut off her protection bid by preventing her from reaching her intedend destination.

"Likowo, wu-szra eh! Likowo, wu-szra eh (Likowo [same as Likoweh], come out oh! Likowo, come out oh)!" Nyango Litakay urged her sister as Nyango Mokuszra had just now started traversing her property, heading south. By the time Nyango Likowo came out, Nyango Mokuszra was about halfway down her property, and Nyango Litakay, surprising herself, was now almost at the northern limits of Mola King'a Walana's property.

"O-mo le-mbeh (Catch her, stop her)! O-szri mo-weh-meh ar-ka'a (Do not let her pass)!"

Nyango Litakay urged the sister. At this point, the two *ndoh-meh ja walana* (sisters) were closing in on Nyango Mokuszra while Szrango Tiya Efvumeh was about fifty meters away in hot pursuit. Nyango Litakay traversed Mola King'a Walana's property and was now crossing the road that took her to the upper left quadrant, now a focal point in which was found her ndomeh Likoweh in close proximity to

Mokuszra, and she was only about twenty meters away from Mokuszra. Nyango Mokuszra now had no doubt what was happening and what the plan was, but being younger and stouter than either of the women meant that she would attempt to bulldoze her way through these human obstacles and defenses like a Razorback football player from the University of Arkansas as quickly as she could so as to reach her intended destination. The alternative was not an alternative because a retreat meant she would be delivering herself in a golden platter onto the hands of the waiting enraged munyana of hers.

"Wona dis witch woman dem (You, these witches), make wona no try touch me (make no attempt to try and touch me)," Nyango Mokuszra had said as her two *may-nya may walana* (sisters-in-law) closed in, just meters away from her and clearly with the intent of stopping and restraining her with the ultimate aim of delivering her to her munyana for discipline and punishment.

Nyango Likoweh tackled Nyango Mokuszra from behind, and as Nyango Mokuszra lost her balance, Nyango Litakay was pulling on her loose *kawa* (an almost seamless gown commonly worn by szra-wa or coastal walana) that served as her nightie on the front end, with the intention of adding to the force and pressure synergistically that was expected to make her fall to the ground. They wanted her to fall to the ground and then pin or hold her there if only for as little as two to three minutes or actually less time than that. They just needed to temporarily and momentarily halt her descent, at which time their brother would have reached them to claim and take over their catch.

Nyango Mokuszra lashed out with both hands at Nyango Litakay, trying to dislodge her hold of her kawa and free herself, but it would look more like leeches that were glued onto her skin with the added force and pressure that pinned her to the ground. Mokuszra was surprised at their strength, considering they were older walana and also comparing their strength levels based on previous encounters, for this was not their first physical encounter, even if the circumstances were not the same.

"Wona leave me ooh (Leave me alone)!" Nyango Mokuszra demanded and employed her may-nya may walana. "Wona wan kill me (Do you want to kill me)?" Mokuszra had asked her captors mockingly.

"Buea wona, came oh (The people of Buea, come to my assistance)!" She employed a larger audience to be sympathetic to her cause and her plight; she needed to be protected from her in-laws.

"Ta'a-t'Eszrongo, ja eh, (Father Eszrongo, come to my assistance)," she called out to her *szra-ng'a liwa* (father-in-law). "Mola King'a Walana, ja eh!"

Mola King'a Walana was her oldest *mo-nya wa munyana* (brother-in-law) who was also like a father figure to Efvumeh. Nyango Mokuszra was thus calling out for help from him also. Mola King'a Walana was the "Chop-Chair," meaning when their ta'a-teh passed on to join the ancestors, he King'a Walana would assume the position of patriarch in the litumba with all its responsibilities. As chop-chair, he would also oversee the equitable distribution of wealth and properties left behind as inheritance by their ta'a-teh Mola Eszrongo Maykomba among his other *ndoh-meh* (siblings)

Mola King'a Walana housed Ta'a-t'Eszrong'a Maykomba, and while this was Mokuszra's intended and final destination, she finally did not make it, even though this destination was practically less than thus reasoned that she could be heard and rescued by her protectors or more correctly her potential liberators as this situation was.

The athletic Tiya Efvumeh football star of Gbwea was upon the scene almost immediately, a scene of walana piled atop each other, one of his molana struggling to free herself, and the other two, her ndomeh ja walana determined to hold their captive down to be delivered to him, Efvumeh, the star of Gbwea.

When Nyango Mokuszra beheld her munyana, looking at him straight in the face, she pleaded with him to free her from his *ndoh-meh ja walana* (sisters-in-law).

"Mof dis ya craze sista dem for ma skin (Remove these crazy sisters of yours from my body)," Mokuszra said in an instructive tone to her husband and then added, "Tell dem make dem go fine man (Tell them to go look for husbands)."

"Eh mo-weh-meh (Leave her alone)," Tiya Efvumeh ordered his older ndomeh ja walana, and gradually, they did without uttering a word. And then, pointing to Nyango Mokuszra Efvumeh, she said

said, "Pass go back for house (Return home)," pointing to the uphill direction of their home.

As Nyango Mokuszra returned uphill, somewhat subdued. Efvumeh was right behind her, about two meters behind her, and while Efvumeh was silent, a torrent of words full of vulgarity and directed to the two sisters-in-law ceaselessly emanated from the mouth of Mokuszra all the way as they marched northbound to their house. Words like *Ashawo*, *Akwara* (Home breaker; Man-woman dem), etc.— all derogatory social stigmas meant to hurt as much as possible and whether true or not was not important.

There was no response from the sisters-in-law as Nyango Mokuszra remained the sole speaker during this period of ascent back to their home and putting an end to this early morning saga by, yet again, the Eszrong'a Maykomba clan.

Whereas Mola King'a Walana had been a protector of Nyango Mokuszra and whereas Mola King'a Walana's house had served as a safe haven for Nyango Mokuszra many a time, Mola King'a Walana, a.k.a. Chop Chair became to Nyango Mokuzra the villain immediately following Tiya Efvumeh's death. Nyango Mokuzra knew some-how and therefore concluded that Efvumeh was killed by his own brother King'a Walana. Mola King'a Walana killed Tiya Efvumeh, his *ndo-meh wa mu-nya-na wa mo-szra-li* (younger brother), through Nyongo. That made King'a Walana a nyongo-man. Nyongo persons killed others as business. It is not known if Nyango Mokuszra had known before her husband's death that King'a Walana was a nyon-go-man or if she only came to that conclusion after her husband's death.

These conclusions or accusations were not acceptable to the Mola Eszrongo Maykomba clan, and while nyango Mokuszra immediately ceased all communications with King'a Walana, there was barely much of any communication between the Eszrongo Maykomba clan and the Nyango Mokuszra Las Town family as arrangements for Tiya Efvumeh's funeral were made. The Eszrongo Maykomba Clan took over all arrangements, hardly acknowledging their in-laws in the form of consultations expected between both families in matters like this. What also made it hard was that if Nyango Mokuszra had to mourn her munyana in the Mokpwe tradition, then she had to be prepared as a *Mokuszra* (widow) in the Mokpwe tradition for this very important aspect of a molana mourning her munyana. Failure to mourn a munyana properly in the manner prescribed by culture could be interpreted variously, including you, the molana, having killed your munyana through nyongo or li-emba.

For example, she had to sleep on the floor in the kitchen next to the fireplace, and the sleeping had to be on wood ash. She was not to bathe for nine days, and in these nine days, she could not leave the house nor be seen. The Mokuszra was also required within this first nine days to wake up every morning at 5:00 a.m. and cry loudly; that is, mourn loudly to the hearing of all in the village and neighboring villages. This was a trado-cultural sign for the molana to prove to the world that she sincerely missed her husband, a profession of love, and also an expression of pain and deep loss. After this initial nine days, the mokuszra would graduate from sleeping on the floor and the morning cries to phase two.

In phase two, the mokuszra was given a skinhead cut and wore only black mourning clothes for twelve months. During these times, she made no social appearances. After the black clothes phase, the mokuszra entered the last and third phase in which she wore blue mourning clothes only and maintained a low haircut, not necessarily skin cut.

During phase three, the mokuszra started venturing in some social activities in a limited manner. Phase three lasted for at least two years but sometimes beyond even five years. It was mostly the choice of the mokuszra. After phase three, the blue clothes were abandoned, and the mokuszra "returned" to society fully with no hindrance of what she could do or what she could not do. This reintroduction into the society was normally followed by a thanksgiving church service and an elaborate party with plenty to drink and eat for all those invited, including the church officials. This party was also a bonding activity between both families and a show of strength and unity to the larger community.

A grieving wife had to be briefed on the traditional norms by elderly walana of the family or from outside the family if there was no one considered well-versed with these traditional norms. Nyango

Mokuszra's Las Town background meant that no one from her family would be considered versed enough to go through the briefings and coaching with her, for they could barely speak the Mokpwe language and only understood to an extent. The responsibility, therefore, of this cultural protocol rested in the quarters of the walana in the Eszrongo Maykomba clan and/or anyone they chose to bring in to accomplish the task according to native laws and customs. The non-communication or barely any communication between these two families therefore made the attainment of this task not so tenable.

Three walana, in particular, from the Eszrongo Maykomba clan, were front liners in denouncing Nyango Mokuszra and her family for daring to bring such allegations and accusations of yowo and nyongo on their family, especially targeting the second-in-command of the whole Eszrongo Maykomba clan. They were her Tiya Efvumeh's two ndoh-meh ja walana, Nyango Likoweh Maykomba, and Nyango Litakay Maykomba and their adult niece Nyango Namondeh Ewondeh nee Likokeh; that is, the widowed daughter of their ndomeh wa munyana, Mola Likokeh Maykomba.

You will recall that Nyango Namondeh Ewondeh was married to Szrango Ligbwea Ewondeh, and Ligbwea died as a sick man after a fight with his molana Nyango Namondeh mo Likokeh. Nyango Namondeh was accused of nyongo for killing her husband. She was dispossessed of all inheritance by her in-laws and was not allowed to officially sit as a Mokuszra as the native laws and customs would demand. The only thing her in-laws left with her was the children for her to take along with her. Though Nyango Namondeh mourned the passing of her husband from her parents' home, it is not known whether she followed the real and prescribed protocols, because this was normally supervised by walana who were the in-laws and rather hawkishly. We saw her mourn, though, for she wore blue for many years, and I remember we used to pity her whenever she passed by, referring to her as a husband-killer.

I-wo-ntam'a Szri'awu, Mola Njoh-k'a Moto's sister, had four daughters—Mokuszra, Etumba-tumba, a.k.a Nkwel'a Wana, Ewongeh, and Molonga listed chronologically age-wise. Oftentimes, Mokuszra was left out of this lineup because she no longer lived in their family house and was married, unlike her other younger adult sisters who were still living at home, even as single parents starting their own family while still depending on the original family. So, while Nyango Mokuszra had three in-law walana that detested her, she also had three walana of her own gene pool that were on her side and that were equal to any confrontation that may come her way or ward off any hostility directed at her.

When Etumba-tumba made the long trip from Las Town to Wonya-Lyonga in which it was full of drama all the way—her wana wating or playing with feces, her being confrontational all the way, Nkwel'a Wana being mocked or provoked to anger and reaction, etc.—this was a day that was planned by the Las Town walana to meet in WonyaLyonga (a.k.a. Pa Ecor Land) at their sister's house and then carry out their plan. Their entrance into the village was supposed to be uneventful and quiet, so while this was the case with Molonga and Ewongeh, it was not so for Nkwel'a Wana. The planned confrontation still had to be staged and accomplished, Etumba-tumba's loudness notwithstanding, though the Las Townies were afraid that their element of surprise may have been compromised by themselves.

I was trying to do some homework from school when my *ndomeh wa munyana wa mombaki* (older brother) dashed in. In-between panting, he said, "If you wan see cilima go for Tiya Efvumeh i-house (Should you need to be entertained, the Eszrongo Maykomba family is setting the stage for drama, and if you want to be a witness, then this is your time to head out there)."

Maykomba was their family or clan name, but considering Tiya Efvumeh's star status or stardom, the family name became him and his identity, so why other family members were directly referred to Maykomba, their family name, for Efvumeh, was simply Efvumeh, and some non-villagers actually thought the family or clan name was Efvumeh.

My brother was right, though. By the time we got there, there was already a sizable crowd gathered not on Efvumeh's yard precisely but approximately on the southern portion of the greater Eszrongo Maykomba clan property. Between our house and this location took less than a minute's walk if you were in a hurry, the obstacle or barrier being a big high-rise rock that we sometimes sat on to oversee Las Town that was situated southeast, the football stadium that was situated south, and other distant locations situated at lower elevations. Some of the gathering spectators stationed themselves on this higher elevation, overlooking the would-be outdoor stage unfolding beneath them.

The joint Eszrongo Maykomba Clan property was road-divided into four approximate quadrants. The latitudinal divide was a public road or, better still, a footpath while the longitudinal divide was also a road or footpath that ended up with the Eszrongo Maykomba property north and continued southbound to merge with the main public paved road that separated the stadium and our village. Therefore, if you were headed northbound after the intersection between the road-divides, you were bound for Eszrongo Maykomba country. My clan, the WonyaLibiyeah, were the only non-Eszrongo Maykomba's who also frequented this northbound path that ended at the forest edge, which was technically and practically the start of the journey to our family farms. These farms were called *mboli* (meaning goat) because due to their proximity to the village, these voracious range herbivores easily made their way to these farms and fed in abundance on the succulent leaves that characterized crop plants to their pleasure but to the detriment of the owners.

The "Pygmy Goat" *(Capra aegagrus hircus)* is a variety of small domestic goats that are a native to the Cameroon basin of West Africa. They are Bovidae bred for their meat, hair, and skin, but also, they are milk producers and rarely working animals and pets.

It always baffled me why the Maykombas did not have crop farms in Mboli. They were not known to be the farming type and also learned that they were relatively new settlers in the village; hence, their clan location and the fact that all nearby farm plots to the village had been occupied before their arrival. They were a people that depended on their government or other paid jobs for their survival. This was uncharacteristic of villagers. The only other titular villager we knew in our portion of the village whose family did not engage in any form of farming was Mola Ewang'a Moto who was a mid-level civil servant with the government and who was labeled Mot'a Nyongo. He had electricity, a car, and a phone in his house, which made him a rich man, and because of this and perhaps other reasons, he was known as a nyongo man.

The Eszrongo Maykombas were not rich civil servants, so how were they surviving on their government salary? Now even if it was enough, which evidently it was in the Eszrongo Maykomba clan, not farming while permanently resident in the village was considered *mo-ngwe-ngwe* (that is, laziness). But if you were a high government official or a businessman, making lots of money, then you're not having a farm was considered high social status and, at worst, yowo or nyongo.

The latitudinal divide, therefore, was a natural recruit of onlookers who could do with a little drama before heading home and making good dinnertime stories about the Eszrongo Maykombas or the Wakpwes, as the case may be, and depending on their preferences, which one they had to put down. Outside the villages, this road was traversed mostly by subsistence farmers who came from neighboring quarters in Gbwea (Buea). For example, Las Town, Bonaberi, Stranger Quarters, Babuti, Kondem quata, etc. Most of these folks were not Wakpwes (not of Bakweri origin) and not of the WonyaLyonga Village and, therefore, were collectively called Wajili, which just meant strangers or aliens. They lived in quarters or subdivisions in Gbwea with residential houses and businesses practically against each other with no room for play and no room for anything, much less farming space.

In addition, somehow these quarters seemed to have been located on a continuous solid and naked rock. It was an "Arizona" onto which "houses" were hewed. Normally, Wakpwe indigenes did not live in these quarters, though a few did. For those who did, they had access to "good" farmland just outside the limits of the Wakpwe residences and the start of the thick equatorial forest at the foot of the Vako, also known as Mount Fako. Mokpwe villagers did not need to go far into the forest to farm except if they chose to. Far meant approaching the Vako. While Wajili did not have access to near farmland, they equally could not be allowed to have farmland approaching the Fvako, for this would have been displeasing and disrespectful to the Mokpwe god or deity, E-fva-szra-moteh.

Efva-szra-Moto was the god of the Vako and was half-man and half-rock, but it was not clear which part was which. But it was known that this division was cross-sectional or transverse, making two portions, one superior and the other inferior. It was generally assumed that the superior portion was the human portion, but that did not seem to have ever been confirmed.

Wajili were, however, allowed to have farms far removed from Mokpwe villages and nowhere near the Vako. It was common for the government dominated by Wajili to create farmlands to be distributed to the needy Wajili but they had to pass through the Mokpwe villages, and the latitudinal divide road was one such footpath to crop farms. Aside from the villagers, this road was populated around the seventeenth and eighteenth hours by returning farmers often laden with loads that made them look like beasts of burden—sweaty, tired, raggedy clothes, hangry (hungry and angry), and gladly would do with some rest, especially a rest that promised to be relaxing and entertaining. This junction had an added feature for crowding. It had a public tap for fetching water for household use and thus was a natural spot for rest, but today, there was an added impetus or reason for wanting to get this rest and prolonging the rest if possible.

These farmers, mostly women and some children congregated in a pack, and it would seem some of them originated from Las Town and therefore knew Nyango Mokuszra and Efvumeh's *may-nya may walana* (sisters-in-law). They spoke mostly in their language, leaving me wondering what they were saying. I was not happy to see them because this was a village and Mokpwe matter and not for Wajili. It was interference into our private affairs, and they were being made privy into internal Mokpwe and upper WonyaLyonga Village matters. Another thing was that they could complicate things. They were likely going back or to the side with Las Town sisters because they were of the same quarters and off-course. Nyango Mokuszra would be on their side if the situation was reversed. These Wajili were sure to return to their homes, bad-mouthing the people of my village and the Wakpwes as a whole.

How I really wish they were not present, for whatever happened here would spread like California wildfires within hours of its occurrence and would continue in the near future. Then there was the other side constituted of the Eszrongo Maykomba clan. Then there was the village, and most importantly, there was Tiya Efvumeh, a man of very little words. Would he be on a side of his own or would he align himself with one of the many potential camps?

When the stage was being set for the last fight, Tiya Efvumeh was not around, and I sincerely wished he came home now and put an end to this drama show even before it started, but I also realized that the momentum and the force already gathered may make it perhaps impossible to stop. A manager was therefore needed to perhaps try and calm down the tempers, but who would that be?

Bwido Matoe was a young adult of the Eszrongo Maykomba clan, named after the patriarch of the family; that is, his *Mba-mba wa evaru ya szrango* (paternal grandfather), and therefore, his first and last names were Maykomba. We called him in the Mokpwe language *Gbwido*, meaning dark in skin tone or complexion, which was the exact opposite of what he was. He was very fair-skinned, with conspicuous jug ears (*Matoe*), and sometimes we simply called him "born Blanc" which was the street French name for fair-skinned, properly referred to as "peau claire" or "teint claire" in the French language. We also used born blanc to refer to Caucasians erroneously called "white men."

Gbwid'a Matoe was in my age group and was one of four sons of King'a Walana. Their house was situated on the plateau of the rocky hill situated in the western mid-portion of the landed Eszrongo Maykomba property and, therefore, the nearest Maykomba household to our Libiyeah clan. Thus, within the intimacy of our secluded part of the village, Bwido was called Maykombeh and Tiya Efvumeh was simply called Efvumeh by his peers and older folks and Pa Efvumeh by us, the wana in his litumba, and by other wana who were close to the Eszrongo Maykomba clan due to property proximity and more importantly due to the fact that an outside Eszrongo Maykomba muana had an equivalent or equal playmate or playmates within the Eszrongo Maykomba clan. I had three football (soccer) playing mates within the Eszrongo Maykomba clan.

Bwido Matoe was the son of Nyango Moh-tor-wu mo Wana, the younger molana of the two King'a Walana housed in the village. She was a tall, well-trimmed molana from Wokwaongo who was comfortable trading vulgarities and insane insults between her and her wana (children) to the amazement and embarrassment of all in the village, wambaki, and wana alike. As a consequence, even their last born could trade insults of insane proportions, even verging at taboo subjects in the village and culture. These uncultured mannerisms were attributes normally associated or characteristic of another neighboring village, but certainly not characteristic to us and, therefore, alien.

Oftentimes, the Eszrong'a Maykomba clan had been said to have brought disgrace and disrepute to the village by virtue of the walana they married and brought to be part of our village. No one in our part of the village dared challenge the Nyango Motowu mo Wana immediate family to an insult bout, and their household was pretty fluent in the Mokpwe language. How I wished the insane insults vocabulary they knew could just be made to dissolve or be erased from their memory.

Once, as my brother gave the 411 or information of the pending active drama, I immediately set out, not wanting to miss any bit of it. The homework would be taken care of afterward. The Gbwido Matoe's were just about twenty meters away from ours in a northeastern direction, and their house, which was on a rocky hill, was about fifteen meters away downhill, slightly southeast to the congregating crowd. As I approached Gbwido's house, I called out to him, not knowing if he was in or not.

"Bwido Matoe. Maykombeh, Maykombeh. Bwido Maykomba."

There was no answer, and I thought he either was not in or perhaps he had already taken up position at the open field theater down the hill. As I gave up and hurried along, the answer came through a cracked window.

"Comarade Yoma Yoma," He called out to me. It was his shorthand for Yamamoto, one of my names.

"You nova go (Not gone yet)?" I inquired of him, assuming correctly that he knew what was happening or was about to happen. Bwido Matoe was an ear to the ground in the village. He was a source of information, accurate or inaccurate, and also in a timely manner. And therefore, yes, I assumed he knew what was happening or about to happen, for it concerned his family. It was taking place or about to take place in their clan property, and the stage being set was practically next-door to him.

"Massa I-bi di try finish some small wak here (I was trying to finish eating up some food here), he said in Pidgin. "I-bi dey faim (I was hungry; *faim* in French)."

In a mixture of Pidgin and French, and using the prefix *comarade* (comrade in French) as a sign of an intimate bond of friendship, Matoe explained why he was still at home, not intentionally but as a matter of necessity. Among wana of my age group, Pidgin was the lingua franca, as it is in most of West Africa, with some variations from colony to colony ("country to country"). Cameroon is situated in West-Central Africa, the minority population of English extraction occupying the western territory, which is technically and with all practical purposes in West Africa, while the rest of the national terrain and majority population is in Central Africa. The Cameroon Pidgin is harder than other Pidgins in the sub region. Cameroonians can understand the other Pidgins quite comfortably, but other West Africans will find it hard to understand the Cameroon Pidgin.

This is not to say that Cameroonians understand 100 percent the Pidgin of other sub-regional nations but rather that Cameroonians can understand up to, say, 80 percent when others speak with the 20 percent exception being specific local slang or street-specific or culture-specific words. The Cameroon Pidgin, in addition, is sometimes mixed with some French words inadvertently or sometimes deliberately inserting French words to create what has been termed *Francanglaise*. It is thus common to use the word *Camarade* as opposed to *Comrade* and would seem that most folks who use the word *Camarade* may not know that the English word is *Comrade*; but if you used the word *comrade* in a conversation, you would be politely corrected that it was *camarade*.

The first president of Cameroon, Ahmadou Ahidjo, was commonly referred to as "Grand Camarade;" thus, the Grand Camarade title could not be used for any other, for it was to be considered treason. In primary school, we sometimes prefixed the camarade. Older pupils may, for example, call a younger pupil that had attained some kind of status among them—such as academic excellence, sports, etc.—a "Petit Camarade." That was an honored title among us, for you were distinguished among the other camarades. Grand camarade became synonymous with the word *President*, for all the years that he reigned as president from 1960 to 1982 under a one political party system, even though the "constitution" said multi-parties were allowed. If you really wanted to be respectful or placatory, you could use the "grand" to address someone without the camarade.

"Wait me (Wait for me)," he requested of me.

I obliged and waited by slowing down my pace while still heading toward the scene, and in doing so, I had climbed the overhead rock and could see the valley below and in front of me that was the planned outdoor stage for the last fight.

"I say eh, na waiti di happen for ya (What is happening here)?" I had asked him in Pidgin when he joined me shortly.

"I kno kno, I no sabi (I have no idea)," Matoe replied. "Me too I-di just kukuma see people dem di gada for ya (I also do not know. Just like others, I am wondering why people are assembling here)," he continued.

"Ee look like say na wona compound go be cilima hall today (It looks as if your Eszrong'a Maykomba family compound will be the cinema theater today)," I said when he caught up with me and we stood side by side, taking a panoramic view of the scene developing beneath us.

Then he said, "Na da craze woman dat (There goes the mad woman)," actually referring to Nkwel'a Wana.

It happens or turns out that when Nkwel'a Wana made her dramatic ascent in which she aroused the whole village with her and her wana attracting so much attention, the Las Town walana had decided to put off their surprise plan into action. They decided it was not going to have the element of surprise needed, given that just about all who lived in their portion of their village were in their houses and looking through house outlets, like doors and windows or cracks through walls, to catch every and any moment of the pending and unfolding saga. Precisely one week after the postponement, their plan was to be actualized and realized, and like the past week, Etumba-tumba, a.k.a. Nkwel'a Wana, must have a dramatic entrance into the village. She seemed a quiet woman of some sort but easily provoked to action or reaction. This was well-known and exploited by teenagers and sometimes wambaki. You just had to ask her a question that touched any aspect of her family or her social life, and it turned automatically to be provocative.

She also had the habit of talking to herself aloud and, therefore, you could be behind or coming from the opposite direction and you would find yourself wondering where the other communicant was. She had the ability of running scenarios in her head aloud and then verbally attacking the imaginable opponents as we thought. Etumba-tumba could hurl vulgaristic insults onto her imaginary opponents or adversaries while talking and responding to herself. If you did not know her, you would think that she was hurling insults at you, just because you were passing by her.

Because she was known to be that way, she was considered to be a "craze woman." When a villager passed her on the way when she was in one of those heated and self-combative moods, and especially the younger folks who did not have any respect for their elders, they would ask her, "I say eh, you di craze (Are you crazy)?" they would ask.

In our village, talking to one's self was considered a mental condition or mental illness, especially when you talked and then responded to yourself.

"Who you di tok for (Who are you talking to)?" they would press.

At this point, Etumba-tumba would go wild, and if she knew your parents and house, she marched straight there to address your parents after using all the vulgarities she could on you.

So, when Bwido Matoe said, "Na da craze woman," it was not only understood, but it spoke volumes and it needed no elaboration. It smelled of a long-drawn drama and action, and perhaps one that exceeded what was already known in the past. After Tiya Efvumeh's death, the village was aware of the tension that existed between the Las Town family and their village in-laws, and knowing the nature of the walana on both camps, it was said that it was only a matter of time before the pent-up anger and inside pressure exploded to the surface, but perhaps no one was expecting it so soon after Tiya Efvumeh's death, barely four weeks ago.

Fights in Gbwea were predictable, depending on the category. A woman-to-woman or girl-to-girl fight was aimed at pulling at each other's hair and to making every effort to tear the clothing of the adversary. This was followed by the insult "Akwara Ting," "Ashawo Ting," "Bogdeur;" meaning a "harlot" or a "slut" repeated over and over with other "disclosures of "indiscretions." If one of the women succeeded in exposing the nakedness of the other, it was big news in the community, and it seemed she who succeeded in tearing the clothes and exposing the nakedness of the other "won" the fight.

The exposure of nakedness was not common with older women's fights, for it was clearly not a target. They simply tore at each other's hair, talking and or insulting more than any physical action and emphasizing over and ove, that the other was a witch, citing many "instances." The winner in such fights seemed to be the accuser because being accused of li-emba or nyongo was a social and otherwise stain that was penned "forever" in the books of the villagers; it was easy retainable material on the minds of the villagers. Occasionally, there were boys and girl fights, but these were rare. Boys seemed to want to inflict maximum pain by punching hard and as many times as possible onto the girl's breasts while verbally assaulting her with the words "Akwara" or "Ashawo" or "Bogdeur" as often as possible.

The girls, on the other hand, being less muscular and relatively petite, had only mostly their mouths to inflict their own maximum pain.

"Dirty ting;" "Tif ting;" "Because I deny for follow you (A dirty boy, a thief, and because I refused your advances and passes) were words the boys found very painful, and these words seemed to touch on their nerves that made them "mad."

However, girls who wanted to inflict bodily harm also on their male aggressors made use of their long nails to scratch and to leave marks on their assailants' faces or necks and used these marks as a reminder to their assailants not to attempt a next attack them. Such marks that lasted for a while were also used by other males to mock or make fun of the males with the marks. Words like "yab man" and "babelac" were used on them to indicate that they were weaklings, essentially saying you were beaten by a woman. This was used in the future by your male peers. For example, if a male peer wanted to let you know that you were inferior to him from a fighting perspective, they would say they would bring the "girl" that gave you those scratch marks to deal with you instead. This was considered a low blow and aggravated the tension between adversaries and usually ended with punches and some bleeding noses and swollen eyes or other inflamed body parts in the head and neck regions in the days to come.

So, when Bwido Matoe said "Na da craze woman," the mad woman was known to be Etumba-tumba and was also known as "actor." Etumba-tumba and her sisters were well-endowed with mammary glands, genes evidently inherited in totality from their iyaka. Otherwise, Etumba-tumba was smallish, characterized by gazelle-like feet and a very pointed and protruding backside that was not on the heavy side. Very importantly, she had what could be described as large axe-like incisors befitting a large game predator. And yes, she had used those teeth for defense and offense several times, as the story goes, and during her most recent fight in the market with another molana, she was helped from the ground and emerged with a piece of skin tissue attached to her teeth after drilling her incisors into the back of the neck of her opponent. When the piece of dark skin dropped from her grip as she attempted to spit out blood she was avoiding not to swallow, the incisors were all bloody as the gathered crowd in unison said in a chant, "Dracula, Dracula, Dracula!"

Nkwel'a Wana was an extremely loud molana and a deoxyribonucleic acid (DNA) type repository of vulgar literature in Pidgin and in the Mokpwe language. While she could not engage in a substantive Mokpwe discussion, she could understand about 80 percent of a conversation and then respond in Pidgin. However, she could be placed at an advanced Mokpwe language level when it came to Mokpwe insults, especially in the taboo subject areas. She was one that was mostly avoided and/or people strove to be on her good side. Her most notorious attribute, however, was infanticide.

Nkwel'a Wana was not married, but she had a couple of kids. I never really quite knew them. The number of live kids she had was estimated at conservatively half the number she would have had if not that she was an Nkwel'a Wana (child killer). She seems to have been one who got pregnant in rapid succession and just as the deliveries came, so also came in rapid succession the deaths of these kids. She was pitied by many a molana in her family and local community, and this was actually attributed to be one of the reasons why no Munyana would want to marry her because she seemed to have had an infanticide gene.

Immediately following Tiya Efvumeh's funeral, his widow, Nyango Mokuszra, exiled herself from the village, taking her children with her to her Las Town family home. However, she left all of the property behind, and many in the village knew that her self-exile being accommodated in their family home would only last past the honeymoon period before she would voluntarily return to the village.

Her quick exit was in protest, accusing the Eszrongo Maykomba clan of giving or taking her husband in Nyongo. Her not staying in the village and in their house to mourn Tiya Efvumeh, according to the customs and traditions of our people, was frowned upon by all. However, she returned two days just before it was fourteen days after Efvumeh was buried. Her return was quiet and ignored by her in-laws who knew it was a matter of time before she returned.

Two days after her return, at about noonish, her two younger sisters visited her with small, packed handbags; this was Molonga and Ewongeh. At about 4:00 p.m., Etumba-tumba arrived not quietly like the others, but she arrived and always arrived with a big bang. The Molombine clan had earlier postponed this event for some days because they thought Etumba-tumba had compromised their element of surprise, but even with the postponement, she did not seem to be helping the situation.

Etumba-tumba ascended the hill that led to the Tat'Eszrongo Maykomba clan landed property, all dressed up for the event. She had her kawa on and the underneath shorts, tied the kawa at the waist level, and wore Kayja shoes (rubber-made sandals normally for male wear and not commonly worn by women, except the elderly women who used them as bush [farm] wear). She was lucky she did not have to worry about long hair because the pulling of long hair was inevitable in walana fights. For a molana, Etumba-tumba had short hair, so she tied the base of the hair with a piece of black cloth and inserted on the right side a brown rooster feather and a green leaf on the other side of her hair, tucked into the bun that held her short hair together. Etumba-tumba, a.k.a. Nkwel'a Wana, had what was called "meh-szroh" in the Mokpwe language. This was a form of alopecia that made two wide roads of about ten centimeters wide on either side of the frontal bone, stretching backward onto the parietal bones and onto the center of the skull, so despite her short hair length of about twenty centimeters high, her may-szro were very visible and gave her a unique visage, one that sometimes, scared wana.

Normally, it was men who tucked feathers into their hats, and it was mostly the elderly men. As Etumba-tumba passed the houses of her sisters-in-law downhill to further ascend to her sister's house, she could not help throwing insults or alerting her adversaries that it was just a matter of time now.

"Wona dis Eszrong'a Maykomba witch ting dem, wona go see-am today (You, these Eszrong'a Maykomba witches, you will see it today)," she said as loud as she could to their hearing. She was walking up the hill as fast as she could with a company of four young wana—one on her back, one in her arms, and the two older ones trailing behind her. She wanted to get to her sister's house so quickly that she thought the wana were slowing her down. In an effort to hasten them, she said, "Dis witch pikin dem way dem no get papa, wona no go waka quick quick (These bastard evil-possessed children, would not you walk faster)?" she yelled at them.

Then someone on her way responded through a cracked wall hole from wooden wall, "Nobi na you di decide who di papa go bi, na di pikin dem (Is it not you who decides who the father is to be, is it the children that are to know)?"

Without turning to see who was challenging her, she had simply said, "Ya mami pim ya. Gbwe-mi toh-roh. You dor-ty ting. Um-gbwa ma'a-teh-teh"

A series of vulgarities spat out in rapid successions.

"When dis tif-tif massa dem cam waiti dat their sweet mot, you fit deny (When these bandits who call themselves men come with their sweet and placatory words and talk, can you resist them)?"

"You bi small pikin way dis massa dem di fool you (Are you a child that these men just fool you with their placatory and sweet tongues)? How many time dem go fool you before you get sense? How many times will you be fooled before you get wise?" the anonymous voice pushed on.

Nkwel'a Wana had bigger fish to fry, and she was late, so she was not going to waste her time.

"Ya mami pim three times, make tunda kill you (A vulgarity followed by 'Let you be struck by thunder lighting and killed'). You no sabi di mba-mbeh tifting dem (You do not know these ba-mbeh 'thieves')."

"Ba-mbeh boys," as they were popularly and commonly known were not thieves. They were "carrier boys," and though they were called Mba-mbeh boys, their ranks included adults who had this as a profession that put garri (food) on the table. Ba-mbeh boys were normally located in the market, and other commercial properties where "carriers" were required. They were normally hired to carry people' loads to their homes. These included market goods, building materials, and anything that needed carrying. The high-ranking ba-mbeh boys also known as "Boulow Boys" had a small two-wheeled barrow with one central control bar (commonly known as "trucks" or push-push). The uppermost echelon of the ba-mbeh profession had open-back small truck vehicles as compared to the lowest or entry level of the profession, where the ba-mbeh lifter-carriers carried their loads on their heads. Having a push-push was the most common phenotype of a Ba-mbeh boy. They loaded their cargo and pushed it to its destination. The younger and low-ranking mba-mbeh boys carried the load on their heads and made as many trips as were required to finish their tasks.

The high of the highest Boulow Boys had very old small open trunk trucks. Such trucks had doors that were tied with ropes, made weird polluting sounds, were bent to the left or right, and always could do with a wash. The trucks had Boulow Boy written all over them just by its appearance. And as wana, we were sure to shout out the owner's name as he cruised by or if he happened to do some mba-mbeh deliveries for our families.

The most famous and perhaps the only one who ascended into the rank of owning a truck when we were wana was Mola J.K. He was Mola J.K. to all of Buea.

"When dem don come waiti dat their small monie (When they come with that, their small money), dem go tell you how they love you from Buea to Bokwaongo then to Muea and then back to Buea (when they come, they will profess their love for you and tell you the length and breadth of their love for you from Buea, to Bokwaongo, to Muea, and then back to Buea). Dem go tell you say ya kata na ma bor-ta. Dem go tell you say ya snoring na Sasse Band melodie (They use these flattery words on you)."

"Me too na, I kno kno book, I kno get work, nobi I go believ'am (I am not educated, I do not have a job, so I believe them). Which kind life be dis (What manner of a life is this)?" she concluded with a question.

Then as an afterthought, she added, "All dis mba-mbeh tif-tif dem get their line for me (All of these mba-mbeh thieves have their line for me). Mami, you fine eh (Woman, you are so pretty). Their mami dem all (Their mothers, all of them insulting all of their mothers)."

When she eventually reached Nyango Mokuszra's house, she met the other three sisters who were already ready and just waiting for her. In kawas over their shorts, kawas tied to the waist level, and their long hair properly tied to protect against it being a target of a pulling attack. The four of them stepped out of the house barefooted and headed immediately to Nyango Likoweh's yard which was downhill and close to the public tap and road.

As they descended, they called out to their targets, "Likoweh witch woman, na di ting way you no get man (Likoweh, you are a witch, and that is why you do not have a husband). Litakay witch woman, na yi make'am all man dem di run you (Litakay, you are a witch, and that is why men run away from you). Namondeh witch woman way you kill ya massa for property (Namondeh, you are a witch that killed your husband because of property). And wona broda or abi na uncle way na nyongo man (And your brother or it is an uncle that is a nyongo man [wizard]). Na wona all don join kill Tiya Efvumeh we sista e massa, wona go kill we all too, today (It is all of you that colluded to kill Tiya Efvumeh, our brother-in-law. You will kill all of us also today)."

The houses of Nyango Likoweh and Nyango Litakay were adjacent to each other and faced east, located respectively in the mid-portion and the lower portion of the upper left quadrant that constituted the Eszrongo Maykomba clan property. The attacking and verbally assaulting women remained on the road, not entering the yards of their target, protecting themselves somehow from trespassing. The verbally assaulting women faced west so as to be facing the front of the houses of their victims, or more correctly, their two main victims. The other two targets, Nyango Namondeh and Mola King'a Walana, were north and south respectively of what looked like the main targets.

The Eszrongo Maykomba clan graveyard was located at the lower limits of their upper right quadrant of their landed property, making it opposite the houses of Likowo and Litakay, being separated only by the longitudinally situated road.

Ngal'a Molomba was an older classmate of mine at one time at the Presbyterian School Buea Town at the lower primary level. His school attendance was very erratic, and after two or three years, he dropped out of school completely. He started doing odd jobs around in town and in the village as a handyman. But as he worked as handyman, he simultaneously was developing his expertise as talented drummer. He soon teamed with another talented guitarist in the village, called Ikom'a Loko, a much older Mola wa Mbowa (an elder of the village) than himself.

This duo became sought for entertainers in the village and beyond, for they matched their instrument talents with voices to match that took their cha-cha brand of music to a new level, creating awareness and preserved it for posterity. The main fault of this duo was the rapidity with which they got annoyed. As they became more and more popular, the higher the rate of their annoyance soared. When they got annoyed, they stopped playing, even if they had just been playing for a minute or less. Everything and anything annoyed them, from their host not treating them well (meaning low pay and without surplus food and drinks) to the audience not treating them well (meaning criticizing then for their tempers or simply not applauded); or it could simply be an argument between the two of them related to the way the singing should go, the drumming being out of rhythm with the guitar, the guitar being out of rhythm with the drumming, Ngal'a Molomba being disrespectful to the older guitarist, Ikom'a Loko, or Ikom'a Loko not recognizing that Ngal'a Molomba needed respect also, though younger, and so on. There was no shortage of reasons for there to be a disruption to their playing. Therefore, demand and respect for their once most sought-after music started to decline, and then Ngal'a Molomba decided to go back to school after about seven years of dropping out.

Ngal'a Molomba returned to school to be classmates with kids who were by far younger than he was. He was a Pa'a in elementary school. But he knew he had to go back to school in order for him to obtain his First School Leaving Certificate, which was the only way for him to be assured of getting a job with the government or any other employer. When Ngal'a Molomba returned to school, he was a "Pa" in his class and his level as a whole. He was made head boy of his class and proved to be a very strict disciplinarian, treating his classmates as he would his own kid at home. He could not speak English, so he administered his class prefect role in Pidgin, though Pidgin was generally forbidden in school. It would seem an exception was made for him.

Ngal'a Molomba had this exceptional talent and ability to make music out of nothing and to use the present situation to compose a song with the accompanying drum rhythm. Somehow, Ngal'a Molomba was passing by when the Molombine walana had just started the first phase of their verbal assault on the Eszrongo Maykomba family.

When the Las Town Molombine walana hard exhausted their "witch/wizard" accusation mantra, they now turned to a mockery of song and dance, daring the Wonya Eszrongo Maykomba for a physical confrontation.

"Wuwu-wuwu witch ting dem di fear. Wuwu-wuwu witch ting dem di hide. Wuwu-wuwu we go show wona today."

Ngal'a Molomba, the master drummer, quickly approached the Molombine walana and immediately made a makeshift or improvised drum with sticks and then started drumming and singing with the women, urging them on. As the women beat the orifice of their mouths while exhaling, it produced a sound that was matched with Ngal'a Molomba's drumming and his own words that he had inserted to bring about a patterned rhythm, harmoniously choreographed as the Molombine women now seemed to be pacing up and down and sometimes in circles and semi circles. This was a setup to attract a crowd, and a crowd was attracting all right.

Bwido Matoe caught up with me, and by the time we got to the outside stage, there was a full crowd, a mixture of people, young and old. We pushed our way to the front of the crowd from the west end,and while I stayed put in my vantage front position with a clear view, Matoe proceeded to bring about some order and also tried to determine who should and who should not be a spectator. Holding a small whip in his hand, he moved back and forth the semicircle, ordering and/or pushing spectators to move backward so as to create a larger staging area. He said repeatedly, "Wona mof for back, wona gibwa for back," and then in cases where he met with some resistance, he would say, "Wona dis graffi dem, waiti wona di do for ya (You, these strangers, what are you doing here? Wona di see waitin di happen for we village then wona go, go tok, for Las Town say, Bakweri people dem na bad people (You are witnessing what is happening here only for you to go to Las Town and badmouth the Bakweris)."

The folks he addressed mostly ignored him. These were mature men and women; that is, adults with their children returning from their farms. Matoe was just another rude and irrespective kid that needed to be ignored and tolerated, just as some other adult would ignore and tolerate their own kids when they got naughty. When Bwido Matoe was done with his policing, he returned to his spot beside me and declared, "I really wan see waiti dis Las Town woman dem, wan do today (I really want to see what these Las Town women have up their sleeves today)."

The three Molombine sisters formed a semicircle behind Etu-mba-tu-mba as she had clearly taken the role of lead antagonist and spokeswoman of the quartet, and she was approximately fifteen to twenty meters ahead of the semicircle behind her and already in the yard of Nyango Likoweh, daring her with insults and her entire family to come out so that woman-to-woman—or perhaps more correctly, women-to-women—they would solve and put to rest once and for overall this problem that existed between them now made complicated and compounded with the li-emba of the Eszrong'a Maykomba family and these women that she, Etu-mba-tu-mba, and her sisters were now targeting because these walana were the mouth-pieces of this family that hated them up to the point of killing their own son and brother because they hated the Molombines. As she spoke her immediate support cast sisters concurred with her all the time and urged her on. We could hear words like:

"Tell dem witch ting dem (Tell these witches)," they urged, "We nodi fear dem (We are not afraid of them). If dem be woman make dem komot kam fight we." And then daring the womanhood of the Eszrongo Maykomba women by provoking them to come out for a fight.

Nyango Namondeh Ewondeh nee Likokeh was niece to Nyango Likoweh Maykomba and Nyango Litakay Maykomba, and having returned home from what seemed like a failed marriage that ended with the death of her husband Nyango Li-gbwe-ya l'E-wo-ndeh, she now lived with her parents in the same room she occupied when she was a spinster. Allegations that she killed her husband for property inheritance and making her a li-emba molana had not made life back in the village welcoming at all. It was only the Moloumbines who were aliens in the village and aliens to their clan that took it upon themselves to make her life miserable.

Namondeh's residence faced south, and Efvumeh's house was lateral to theirs on the left side. She thus had to descend to the assembled crowd against her initial instincts and decision. She wore a kawa atop trousers and the Tchang shoes or kay-nja shoes she used for yard work and other rough and tough terrains. These footwears were made from reinforced plastic materials and were painful when applied with force and enough pressure onto human flesh while they were airy and in sandals format or design. They had, in addition, studs for traction but also a handy weapon to inflict pain when fighting. Namondeh used a piece of cloth to tie her kawa around the waist level and then tucked her fairly long hair securely with a head-tie that was just tight enough to not make the hair loose but also ensuring that she allowed for blood circulation in her head region.

Namondeh was prepared for a fight, and she was now under the control of her autonomic nervous system and specifically the sympathetic division that controlled the adrenaline "fight or flight" mode. Namondeh felt the rush of adrenaline in her blood as she heard herself say, "Na-mo-ndeh ma-meh na-szre-ni (What has Namondeh not seen)?"

Nyango Namondeh nee Likokeh reached the outer spectator ring of humans and did not bother to say, "Excuse me" as she plowed and pushed her way through this first barrier and as some women in the crowd cursed after her for almost pushing them to the ground rudely. She ignored them and went straight to the inner trio semicircle ring of humans and specifically the Molombine women and shoved her way through, elbowing them as they staggered on their feet, having been taken by surprise. She quickly proceeded and charged E-tumba-tumba from behind and, like a veritable Mokpwe Wrestler, gathered her around the waist region with both hands, clasping her on her left shoulder viced by her neck and head, and partially lifting her off her feet, she pushed or rather bulldozed her like a *nyama kundu* (a caterpillar roller usually used for road construction particularly for leveling and compaction) straight into the swine pit mud pool that was located on the left hand side of Nyango Likoweh's yard just next to the fence that demarcated her boundaries with neighboring properties. The swine pool was more of a marsh with lots more mud and less water, and the shores of the pool were littered and adorned by swine feces, dried and fresh and from the old and the young.

In our village, we had a range of domestic *ngo-wa* (*Sus scrofa domesticus* or pigs). These ngo-wa loved muddy pools to "swim" or rather wade in and or use the more watery portions of the ponds to drink water. It was an assemblage place for all the ngo-wa in our portion of village, and whenever you passed by, you could tell which ngo-wa belonged to which family and which ones did not. This mud pool attracted the boars, gilts, and/or the sows and the shoats and/or piglets. During mating season, this was a fighting spot for the *ngo-wa ja mo-meh* (the boars) as they fought with each other for access to the *ngo-wa ja mua-li* (the female swines) that were estrous (estrus).

We used to visit this mud pool and stay away at a reasonable distance so as to watch and see how these conflicts originated and eventually culminated in fights as these animals competed for access to the females. Based on these observations, we knew which boar or boars were the dominants and those that were secondary. This pool was very territorial, and any stray boar from somewhere else that did not belong was jointly and fiercely attacked by the resident boars. During fights, intra-clan or inter-clan, we saw protruding canines we called "fangs" lateral to the mouth on both sides used for the weapons. They were to inflict mortal injuries on opponents and antagonists. The dominant boars were those with extra-long canines that were curved and, for the most part, discolored because these were the weapons used to uproot underground stems or roots of cocoyam plants for food and also as a weapon of defense and offense in which case they were quoted with blood. Darker and longer canines meant seniority and dominance status.

On this day, when the walana wa njuma were on public display, the ngo-wa mud pool was not very populated, but it had a prominent occupant. There was a *ngo-wa ma-nyio-ngeh* there (a nursing sow) with ten *weh-koh-szre-leh weh ngo-wa* (piglets). While the weh-koh-szre-leh wae ngo-wa played with each other, the ngo-wa ma-ny-io-ngeh circled the mud pond with menacing grunting sounds as it warned all to stay clear of its *weh-koh-szreh-leh* (piglets). We knew in our village as wana that you do not joke or play or go near a ngo-wa ma-nyio-ngeh, and it would seem even the dominant boars knew this. Ngo-wa ja ma-nyio-ngeh were known to attack boars and or anything living that ventured to come near the weh-koh-szre-leh weh ngo-wa. They normally charged as the ngo-wa do, generally by first hitting their target with their head with the force their body weight can muster and then later make use of the incisors and canines to pierce and tear out flesh from their adversary.

When the crowd was assembling and eventually concentrated itself around Nyango Likoweh's front yard, this crowd was essentially encircling the ngo-wa pool and its occupants. The ngo-wa ya ma-nyio-ngeh felt trapped and threatened, and its rate of agitation increased by the moment as the walana wa njuma saga unfolded. Thus, when Nyango Namondeh mo Likokeh bulldozed E-tumba-tumba into the ngo-wa mud pool, she was careful enough not to enter the pool, but she had to at least advance to the shore where she had to step on a mixture of *moe-wa ma ngo-wa* (ngo-wa feces). Her open Kay-nja shoes or Tchang shoes (sandal shoes that seemed to have originated from Dschang in Cameroon also meant that there would be moe-wa ma ngo-wa all over her feet and between her toes.

With all her force, she pushed E-tumba-tumba into the ngo-wa mud pool, and E-tumba-tumba fell into it face down, having been taken by complete surprise. But Namondeh had miscalculated, because though E-tumba-tumbeh had been taken by surprise, she was not a light weight molana, so if Namondeh was to accomplish her goal of dumping her into the ngo-wa shit-pool, it meant that she too Namondeh had to enter the shit-pool. So Namondeh "towed" E-tumba-tumbeh past the shores of the shit-pool, onto the peripheral interior of the mud pond, and then pushed with all her might to untangle herself from her.

Namondeh succeeded, and once as she had E-tumba-tumbeh face down in the pool, she quickly proceeded to leave the pool, but E-tumba-tumbeh was not to be taken advantage of a second time. With a mixture of mud and feces all over her, including in her mouth, she immediately arose from the bottom of the pond, just in time to see her assailant attempt to flee from the muddy scene.

"O sa you wan go, you dis witch woman (Where do you think you are going to, you witch)?" she demanded of Namondeh as she pulled her back into the mud-feces pool with both hands grabbing and holding her by her legs. Namondeh lashed back with both trapped legs with all her force in an attempt to dislodge herself from her captor. As she did, the force threw back Etumba-tumbeh, this time in very close proximity of the ngo-wa ma-nyio-ngeh and its wae-koh-szre-leh, and at this, the ngo-wa ya ma-nyio-ngeh attacked E-tumba-tumbeh without hesitation, hitting her first on her head as she fell backwards, this time face up and back into the muddy pool, which covered her entire body except her toes and protruding breasts. As E-tumba-tumbeh lay in the pool still for a few minutes and her head and that of the ngo-wa ma-nyio-ngeh met, the ngo-waa ya ma-nyio-ngeh wasted no time to plant its incisors and canines into the protruding breasts of E-tumba-tumbeh. With the inflicted pain, E-tumba-tumbeh came back alive, screaming, "Mami I die oh, Mami I die oh (Mother, I am dead, Mother, I am dead)!" She called for help. "Dis witch shu-wine di cam kill me oh (I am about to be killed by this li-emba ngo-wa)!" she continued.

The ngo-wa ya ma-nyio-ngeh dug into her breasts and emerged with some fleshy tissues, and despite the thick mixture of feces, mud, and water, one could still see the redness of the blood in the mouth of the ngo-wa and the red teeth that had tasted blood and human flesh.

When E-tumba-tumbeh zoomorphisied the ngo-wa as having li-emba, a grassland (graffi) molana spectator who all the time had been sympathetic to the course of the Molombine sisters, based on her utterances and side comments which were all challenged and or contradicted by villagers and who evidently knew and perhaps came from Las Town herself, said at the top of her voice. "Chei wona Bakweri, wona witch go so-teh reach shu-wine dem (It is indeed fascinating that the Bakweri Li-emba now includes even swine)! Na so so wona wan kill wona own sista using shu-wine. The anonymous molana in the ngi-ndi (crowd), who apparently was sympathetic to Nyango E-tu-mba-tu-mba and attacking the Wakpwes of the village, went on to continue her Mokpwe affront." She was bold to say that E-tu-mba-tu-mba was a Bakweri woman with Bakweri blood and a sister to the village but now the same Wakpwe-li want to o'o-wa (kill) her, passing through a sow. She was being zoomorphic and drawing "zoomorphological" conclusions. "Na really daytime Bakweri witch be dis (This is broad daylight Bakweri witchery)," she had concluded.

My friend, Bwido Matoe, who had held himself thus far and who was a family member and who, as it happens was on his own turf, had taken and stomached enough, therefore had to respond. "I must tok for di graffi bush woman dem (I must respond [address] to these alien farmwomen," he declared to me and then stepped out of our portion of the ring and across to where the molana was to stand face-to-face as he addressed her.

"I say eh mami, wona dis Las Town people dem wona really dull."

Mami is a terminology in Pidgin which could mean mother or "lady;" that is, a word used for respecting an elderly woman, especially one judged to be capable of being your mother or older. So, while Matoe had an angry point to make, he started out by being polite and respectful. He thus said, "Mami, you folks from Las Town must be very dumb and certainly a dumb bunch. You no kno say shu-wine way e-get pikin di wild (Don't you know that a sow with piglets is aggressive toward protecting its piglets)? Wona get shu-wine dem for Abakwa?"

Abakwa or Bam'da were terminologies used generally to refer to grasslanders from the Northwestern portions of the national territory. So, my *mbou-nda's* (friend's) question was, "Do you folks have ngowa in Abakwa? Because if you did, you should know the behavioral attributes of a ngo-wa ya ma-nyio-ngeh. See how wona Las Town di cam disgrace wona sef for we village, wona di make we village like Las Town market (You Las Townies come to our village and disgrace yourselves, making our village look like the market that is associated with Las Town)." He walked back to his position next to me to continue watching the unfolding drama.

All the while E-tumba-tumbeh was struggling in the swine mud pool, her siblings were only engaged in urging her on, "Show dem di witch ting dem (Teach these li-emba folks a lesson)." "Show dem say we komot na for Las Town (Show them that we are Las Townies)! Show dem say that their witch no fit do we no noting (We are untouched by the li-emba of the Maykomba family)!"

Evidently, Nkwel'a Wana wanted more than just verbal support from her sisters-in-arms and sisters-in-combat, so in pain and all muddied in mud and poop—and frustrated, it seems—she lashed out at her sisters.

"I say eh wona di akwara dem, wona no go cam helep me (When will you sluts think of helping me practically and not just with words)?" She shot back at her *ndo-meh ja walana* (sisters) who were part of the walana wa njuma team, but thus far only verbally and no action. "Na so so tok tok for wona (It is only the talking with you folks)."

Meanwhile, Namondeh, on the other hand, urged her aunties not to worry, for she was capable of taking care of these filthy rags from Las Town without them soiling their names and their reputations. So, she said to her aunties, "Wa iyaka wami e-szru-nda nghey-nghey (My iyakas [mothers], do not be worried). I-mba mbi-ti na ta-neh (I alone am capable) li-wo-wa may-nay may-ti-ti may walana (to take on these filthy walana)."

So, the aunties left her alone to deal with the Molombine sisters by herself while they kept watch at a close distance, prepared to assist in teaching these Las Town a final lesson. They also knew it was to their advantage if the final results and the news was that it was their niece who solely defeated these bunch of *mal* élevés *walana* (badly brought up women).

Provoked by their muddy and wounded sister, the Molombine sisters, Molonga and Ewongeh, joined their sister E-tumba-tumba in the marsh to help constrain Namondeh who was at this point trapped by Etumba-tumba who held her against her bosom and chest as she lay face up and back down in the marsh, her hands from the sides and over Namondeh's midsection glued to her. Namondeh, desperate to free herself, bit Etumba-tumba's ear, parting with some piece of tissue and blood in her mouth and bloodstained teeth. It was this ear biting that finally brought the other two Molombine sisters to their sister's aid. Nyango Mokuszra, while cursing her in-laws, coached and encouraged her sisters but did not by herself take part in the fighting.

"Mami I don die oh, Mami I don die oh, dis witch woman don chop ma ear (Mother, Mother, I am dead, my ear has been bitten by this witch)!" she cried out in pain and also cried out for help.

"I go shot-up dis ya big dortie mot today, way you di so so take cush people dem (I will finally shut this big dirty mouth of yours that you constantly use to insult others)," Namondeh said as she remained entangled with E-tumba-tumba.

When Namondeh opened her mouth to talk, her mouth and teeth were bloody, and thus a small kid in the crowd pointed out, shouting, "Dracula, Dracula!"

And the other kids in the crown picked it up, chanting, "Dracula, Dracula, Dracula!"

By this time, the two Molombine sisters had reached the entangled duo. Molonga laid atop her, while Ewongeh was making every effort to pin her feet into the mud. They did not seem very keen on liberating their mud-trapped sister with bleeding breasts and ears. These four women rolled around, taking different turns to be at the bottom of the muddy pool, while the crowd cheered and sometimes members of the crowd, pushing at each other, tried to start their fights because they supported opposite camps. While E-tumba-tumbeh was initially only interested in trapping Namondeh, she—besides using her teeth as a weapon—also had hands free, which she used to scoop up mud mixed with feces that she fed into E-tumba-tumba's mouth but making sure she did not choke her.

E-tumba-tumba had calculated that her sisters would come to her rescue while she endured the pain, and it was their failure to join in the fight that led her to call them spineless sluts.

"Elimo, Molimo, Elimo, Molimo (Devil, Zombie, Devil, Zombie)!" This was the alarm sounded by Maliya. Maliya was Bwido Matoe's younger sister, and their house was on the high-rise rock that was situated behind the houses of Nyangos Likoweh and Litakay. Maliya was a sympathizer to walana who were beating victims of men and more specifically their *wunyana* (husbands). As was seen earlier, Maliya was also particular and very sympathetic to Nyango Mokuszra, like when she alerts her that Efvumeh was in hot pursuit and just a step behind, and she opted to alert her father, King'a Walana, to come out and protect her from the wrath of Ta'a-teh Efvumeh. She did not go to the open theater stage that was unfolding below her, despite the proximity. By virtue of her elevated position, she could see over the two houses whose courtyards or frontages were the scene for the unfolding drama.

Being young and a girl, if she went to the actual action spot, she would not have been able to see much, except if she was able to push or force her way to the forefront of the lines or crowd assembled. Older boys did this readily, and besides, girls were readily discouraged from action places because they were considered un-lady like and because they were also apt to being transformed into an all-fight arena catching up to the present. This was an unusual fight, pitching her aunties and her aunties-in-law. It was usually easy for her to pick sides and support the walana no matter what, but today, this was a molana-molana aggression, a molana-molana confrontation.

"Why do walana have to go physical like their male counterparts?" she had asked herself over and over. There were lots of things going on in her heart and head. In addition, in this particular case, her mother, Nyango Moh-tor-wu mo Wana, had specifically told Maliya and her sister, Wvioleh, not to go the developing action scene, describing it as "I-szro-ni ja wat wa walana (A disgrace and shame to women folks)."

When the sisters asked their iyaka why they should not go, given that Bwido Matoe, their brother, was going to the action scene, she said, "A-we-li di mua-na wa munyana, de-nga-veh aweli matoe (He is a boy, and besides, he is stubborn)."

The crowd that was watching the women's saga was in an approximate J-shaped formation facing westward. Thus, those located in the long arm of the "J" were backing the Eszrongo Maykomba clan graveyard. Maliya was situated west, and therefore, the open amphitheater was east, making her face their clan's graveyard while having a bird's-eye view below of the scene.

Maliya did not see Tiya Efvumeh rise from his grave, but she saw Efvumeh walking to and headed toward straight into the midpart of the "J-Section" of the crowd, evidently headed for the center of the scene where the walana were piled on each other, through the human ring. Efvumeh, now the walker, was walking toward the action spot with his white and brown khaki clothes as buried. He had on white hand gloves and white socks and then the brown clothes worn by warders; that is, he was buried in his professional uniform, except for the military-type black boots. The brown cap and brown belt were put in the coffin with the rest of his remains, but now as a walker or an elimo, he "arose" only as his person or remains were dressed.

When Maliya first shouted "Elimo, molimo!" Either she was not heard, or she was just simply ignored, and all eyes and thoughts were fixated on the fighting walana.

"Wona run oh, Ta'a-teh Efvumeh di cam, Ta'a-t' elimo di cam (Run, all of you, for Ta'a-teh E-fvu-meh is coming, the spirit Ta'a-teh E-fvu-meh is coming!)" This time, she pleaded with a louder and crying voice with the hope she would draw some attention. She wondered why she was not attracting any attention, given the seriousness and oddity of her alarm. She was not just an alarmist. Couldn't they see what she was seeing?

Normally, Maliya and her sister, Wvioleh, only spoke in Bakweri, except if they encountered someone who was not Mokpwe. But Maliya, even at her young age, knew that this crowd assembled was a mixture and probably more non-Wakpwes than Wakpwes, and accordingly, her alarm was in Pidgin, the lingua franca of Buea and indeed most of West Africa, taking local variations into consideration. Pidgin, however, is not a lingua franca in West African nations that were occupied and economically exploited by the French but rather a commonality of West African nations that were occupied and economically exploited by the British.

By Maliya's second plea, warning folks and trying to steer their attention to the Efvumeh elimo that she was seeing, Ngal'a Molomba's drumming has taking a strange and mysterious tune, and while Ngal'a Molomba was not singing and while she was not seeing anyone singing, Ngal'a Molomba's drumming rhymed perfectly from the singing that was emanating from the environment somewhere.

E-szro-szru'a maija Wonya walana wa szra-mbo
E-szro-szru'a maija Wonya walana eh szra-mbo
E-szro-szru'a maija Matanga ma njinga
E-szro-szru'a maija Weh-szro weh nyama
E-szro-szru'a maija Walana wa njuma
E-szro-szru'a maija Walana wa Wakpwe
E-szro-szru'a maija Jeh Jeh Jeh

Arisen Elimo Molimo Efvumeh, now a walker or a zombie, was now inside the human ring, and by this time, about half of the crowd had fled while the antagonist walana and those onlookers or spectators that were so deeply concentrated on the ongoing fight that they shot out all other aspects of their senses were still oblivious of the unfolding event of an elimo molimo presence.

"Ta'a-ta eh, elimo e-nay (My father, my ancestors, this is an Elimo)."

When Ngal'a Molomba sounded the alarm of the presence of a walker or a ghost, he dropped his drum and drumsticks and ran in the opposite direction for his dear life. At this point, the remainder of the crowd, including the fighting women, had Ngal'a Molomba's attention and saw the walker approaching the pile of the fighting women.

By the time the walana wa njuma saw the elimo molimo approaching, the walker was at the center of the stage, now visible to all, even those who were so engrossed in the fighting that while others were running, they were oblivious of what was happening because they did not want to miss any part of the action. The crowd fled in all directions, some in silence and others in shock and awe that they uttered unintelligible words as they fled.

"Ta'a-ta ko-ko eh, elimo enay (My father, my ancestors, this is really a devil [ghost]," some said.

"Jor-keh-jor-keh ono mua-na Efvumeh a-szra-wayli (Truly, truly, this child Efvumeh has not really died)," others said.

"Na really Bakweri witch be dis (This is really Bakweri witchery). Bakweri wona own witch don too much Witchery among the Bakweris is beyond comprehension)," yet others said.

As the Elimo Molimo approached the walana wa njuma, it was Molonga and Ewongeh who first saw it and immediately abandoned the fighting and, without a word or warning, fled the scene as they mingled with the other spectators that were fleeing in all directions, except toward the Elimo Molimo "apparition," for their dear lives. Namondeh knew there was something amiss when the pressure from the two Molombine girls that held her down was eased abruptly and when she lifted her head briefly to see spectators fleeing. She did not think this was normal. Why were the spectators fleeing when the show they came to see was still on and just getting even more interesting? And then E-tumba-tumba let go off her as she said, "Chei, na witch die, dis (This is witchery death)."

At this point, Namondeh raised her head and looked over her shoulder to the left and then caught a glimpse of the approaching Elimo Molimo. Namondeh immediately fled and hurriedly climbed the short stone staircase that ascended to Nyango Likoweh's house. Nyango Likoweh and Nyango Litakay had been watching the saga from

Nyango Likoweh's verandah or porch, but when Namondeh reached the verandah, there was no woman there, and the door was locked. However, before she could knock or say a word, the door cracked open, and she was pulled in hurriedly by Nyango Litakay. Meanwhile, and not to be left alone, E-tumba-tumba was at the heels of Namondeh, so when Namondeh was pulled in and without a word, the door was closed behind her immediately, preventing entry by E-tumba-tumba.

"Sista Likoweh, I beg open door for me oh, no leave me for outside here me one (Do not leave me alone out here)!" She pleaded with Nyango Likoweh and even addressed her as sister. "Please open the door for me to enter! Wona really get witch (You people are really witches and wizards)!" were E-tumba-tumba's, a.k.a. Nkwel'a Wana's last words.

"Very strange things have been happening in this village lately," Limungeh began after properly welcoming her wi'a-nyi (visitors) in the village way. Welcoming in the village way meant taking care of a mue-ni's (visitor's) gastronomic needs first before any other thing.

"What strange things?" Naloweh Ngoweh asked her host.

Naloweh Ngoweh was a respected and sometimes feared mua'na in the family because of her naming origins. She was named after her living mba'a-mbeh and her living ti-mba-li-mba'a-mbeh, respectively. She was a first mo-mba'a-mbeh (grandchild) and a first ti-mba mo mba'a-mbeh (great-grandchild). She was therefore named after her living grandmother and great-grandmother, respectively. As a growing child, she was a "report card," "reporting," or snitching on any and every one, with powers to ask (which was more of instructing her namesakes), to reprimand and/or punish anyone who did not show her the expected respect or any one that did not conform according to her whims and caprices. Because her mba'a-mbeh and ti-mba li mba'a-mbeh also inherited or got their names from some ancestor gone ahead, and ancestors who were respected, they felt obligated sometimes to grant her request even if not considered fair to the other wana (children). Naloweh Ngoweh had become so spoiled with her "power" that she sometimes played mind-games with or even attempted to blackmail her namesakes, if her namesakes did not grant her wishes or did not act accordingly. For example, she will ask her namesake mba'a-mbeh or ti-mba li mba'a-mbeh, who was not willing to or who was reluctant to grant her wish of reprimanding or punishing another sibling or who denied her a personal request, for example a new pair of shoes, if not granting her this request, will please the mba'a-mbeh's or ti-mba li mba'a-mbeh's own namesake ancestor gone ahead. She seemed to consider herself as a reincarnation of the ancestors gone ahead that she was named after. Nevertheless, it was the same children in the clan whom she "dealt" with, who ended up orchestrating her exile from our village to another village in Buea. She was exiled to Mo'o-li to a distant relative, where she was safe from her nagging immediate family. The Mo'o-li family had wana her age who were more accepting of her. When she was dropped off in Mo'o-li, it was said that

"Wa mua-nya-gwe-ni w'amo ta-ki-szrey szrai-szrai"

Her other siblings trouble her a lot was the reason given for her relocation to Mo'o-li. For they had stepped up their antagonism of her, one and all, with the sole intent and purpose of making the home environment hostile, especially when there were no adults at home.

Limungeh briefly described the events that recently took place in the village that culminated in the "vumuwarization" or jirop ("resurrection") of Tiya Efvumeh. When Limungeh finished her brief narration,

"Is this true? Were you there?" Naloweh Ngoweh asked her skeptically.

"Ndiv'a Elimo was there," Limungeh, the host narrator, answered her.

"Ndiv'a Elimo?" This was Nyango E-fo-szr'a Szrae, Limungeh's second visitor asking Limungeh with an even higher degree of doubt than Naloweh Ngoweh. Nyango E-fo-szr'a Szrae unlike Naloweh Mgoweh, who was a local visitor, was visiting from the land of the mio-go may wakala, a land across the seas and far away from Vakoland.

Nyango E-fo-szri then proceeded to educate them. "Ndiv'a Elimo, or Ndiv'a Molimo as he is called, is already known to be a human ghost or a human spirit, and you are thinking this human ghost is a good source for getting ghost stories that are related to wat'o wa weh-na-ma (human beings)?"

"Villagers in this village need to make up their minds. They cannot be going to church and doing yowo left and right. It is either they trust and believe in Lo-weh or Ta'a-t'I-wo-ndeh (the Lord God) or they are not. Their misinterpretation of '…give to God what belongs to God and to Caesar what is Caesar's…' could not be more wrong and could only be a spiritual foolery at their detriment," Nyango E-fo-szri concluded.

ABOUT THE AUTHOR

The author Martin Moluwa Matute was born in Buea, Cameroon. He is currently a Professor of Biology and an academic administrator with the University of Arkansas System. He lives in Arkansas with his wife, the Princess Mariana Mojoko (nee Endeley), and their children Mavita, Malingo, and Moname. Though not trained in the creative arts, Martin Moluwa Matute has always been attracted to novel reading. His contribution to the literary world brings story telling packaged in drama, action, and humor, a combination that makes for captive and pleasurable reading. The author takes natural events and glues them intricately into a seamless entertaining story time with a subtle message all the way.